Keeper of my Heart

A MORGAN'S GROVE NOVEL

TRACI BORUM

Keeper of My Heart
Red Adept Publishing, LLC
104 Bugenfield Court
Garner, NC 27529
https://RedAdeptPublishing.com/
Copyright © 2025 by Traci Borum. All rights reserved.

---

1.   http://StreetlightGraphics.com

To Brandon and Kailey Anne, two beautiful souls, and their precious families

Chapter One

Lexi Price jiggled her key inside the stubborn lock and opened the door to the heady scent of dark-roasted coffee. It comforted her to know that Ruby always entered the store a half hour early each morning. The coffee was already brewing, the window shades were already lifted, and the front-desk candy bowl was already refilled, all waiting on Lexi to begin her day.

"C'mon, boy." She ushered Bailey through the entrance, waiting until his wagging tail made it all the way inside, then closed the door behind them. As he did every morning, Bailey pointed his beagle nose skyward, inhaled the strong blast of coffee, then gave a blustery sneeze.

"You're so silly," Lexi told him as she unhooked his leash and watched his tan-and-white frame jog toward the enormous pillow disc behind the counter. He would stay there most of the day, blissfully napping, until a customer—usually a child—spotted him sleeping and rushed over to disturb him with a few gentle strokes across his fur.

"Good morning, Ruby!" Lexi called out, hearing some quiet commotion coming from the back room. She imagined Ruby filling a second cup of coffee then going over the inventory or perhaps counting out the petty cash.

"Mornin'." Ruby's faint response floated to her while Lexi moved toward the store's interior.

Lexi knew that many people dreaded entering their workplaces each morning, loaded down with quiet sighs and internal wincing at the thought of facing yet another boring, tedious, or stressful day. But entering her antiques store energized Lexi. Over the years, it had become a second home to her, comforting and familiar. She strolled down the main aisle of the horseshoe-shaped venue, roaming her eyes over the pieces—some newly acquired, some not—and occasionally clicked on a lamp or switched on some fairy lights. This was her favorite part of the day, waking up the store.

She remembered her great-grandmother doing the very same. As a child, Lexi would hide under one of the antique dining tables and watch Gigi open the store, walking leisurely down its aisles, bringing it to life. Occasionally, Gigi would slow to a halt as she adjusted a piece or removed a bit of dust then carry on. It was her morning ritual, making certain everything was in its place as she prepared for customers who would soon walk those same aisles. And all these years later, it had become Lexi's ritual too.

Once, when Lexi was eight years old, she had watched Gigi pause longer than usual as she picked up a Limoges porcelain figurine then turned it delicately over in her hands. As Lexi peered out from beneath the table, she watched Gigi linger and gaze into the lovely young maiden's face.

Lexi emerged from her hiding spot and stood next to her great-grandmother. "What are you doing?"

Gigi's lips curled into a mischievous smile, her eyes still firmly on the statue, and replied in a whisper. "I'm listening."

"Listening? But statues don't talk."

"This one might." Gigi leaned in, holding the figurine between her own ear and Lexi's. "Sometimes, these old antiques will give up their secrets. If you're willing to listen real close."

Intrigued, Lexi drew closer to the figurine. After a few quiet seconds, she frowned. "I don't hear anything."

"That's because it's not an actual voice. It's more of a feeling, an impression you get from an object." Gigi sat down with a small grunt on a nearby antique chair then placed the figurine gingerly back on the table. She clasped her hands to explain further as her eyes roamed around the room. "A first-edition book trimmed with gold-leaf pages or a hundred-year-old trunk that sat at the end of someone's bed all those years or maybe a vintage toy adored by children from another age or even a hand-painted plate used at parties and family gatherings—each item is infused with memories of long-ago days and long-ago people. These aren't just 'things.' They represent people's lives—their passions, their interests, what was precious to them, what made them happy once upon a time. All the items in this store are slivers of someone's past. And it's my job to take care of them and pass them on, hopefully to someone who will appreciate their worth as much as I do."

The vivid memory left an unexpected ache of grief that pinched Lexi as she pictured her great-grandmother's warm expression and hearty embrace. She wished her great-grandmother could be beside her, drifting along the aisle to make sure everything was in its proper place. She sometimes wondered if Gigi would've approved of the changes made since Lexi had taken over the store. She had kept the wooden floors but hired a contractor to restore them and also to add a fresh coat of paint to the walls. She'd reorganized the merchandise into cleaner, more accessible rows, so that every item could be easily seen and approached. Lexi had entered too many antiques stores that *felt* antique—buildings with dusty floors, cluttered items, musty odors, and dark, shadowy spaces impossible to access. But when Lexi had inherited the store, she'd envisioned an even brighter, more cheerful space than it already was. A warm, inviting place where people would want to stroll, have a coffee or two, flip through a book, and—ultimately—browse and lollygag as long as they wished. She wanted them to forget what time it was, to abandon their troubles, and to enter a world full of lovely old things in a clean, comforting atmosphere. To step back in time.

To that end, last year, Lexi had purchased a rather enormous soda counter from Doosey's, a classic Austin soda shop that had closed down after eight decades. Lexi had moved the entire counter—along with its vintage stools and the back mirror still intact—into her antiques store and turned it into a candy bar, lined with ample jars of sweet delights that always attracted the customers' children.

During all the changes and upgrades, Lexi had told herself that the store's name, Antiquated, was merely a play on words, allowing room for her newer ideas. But more importantly, she had received the ultimate stamp of approval from the one person who mattered. Shortly before Gigi had passed away six years ago, she'd clutched Lexi's hand and said, "The store is yours now. Do whatever you wish with it. I trust your instincts."

Lexi paused at the end of the aisle to admire her newest "find" in a coveted corner of the store. She reached out to touch the honey-colored wood of the hundred-year-old grandfather clock that Darius had delivered from an estate sale yesterday.

"Beautiful," she whispered.

"Isn't it?"

Somewhere during Lexi's daydreamy morning browse, Ruby had sneaked up to join her.

Ruby handed her a steaming cup of coffee. "The guys will be here before nine to put up the banner. I told 'em to go ahead and get started since we'll be in our meeting."

"I thought they were coming tomorrow."

"We got moved up on their schedule." Ruby's eyes wandered toward the clock. "This might be my favorite piece in the shop."

"They're all my favorites." Lexi grasped the cup's handle and shrugged. "It sometimes feels like all of these treasures are mine—just for a short while. I'm their temporary custodian. I'm almost sad when someone scoops them up and takes them home. Part of me wants to keep them all for myself."

"Well, that wouldn't be very practical for our bottom line, would it?" Ruby gave a sly smirk then drank from her cup. Her silver hair glistened in the light of the morning sun sifting through a nearby window.

Ruby Harper was a seventy-eight-year-old widow who'd recently reduced her status at the store from full to part-time. She had first been employed by Gigi over fifty years ago and was considered the backbone of Antiquated. She and Lexi had become fast friends when Lexi was a little girl and had scraped her knee on a rock while playing outside the store. After Gigi had patched her up with a Strawberry Shortcake bandage and offered her a beanbag chair in the back room, Ruby had wordlessly sidled up beside Lexi and handed her a cherry lollipop as a distraction, twisting it between two fingers. "I've been told it contains magical healing properties," she'd said with a reassuring wink. Lexi dreaded the day when Ruby would officially retire. It was unthinkable, the notion of running the store without Ruby's perfect balance of kindness and sass.

"I realize I'm weird, not wanting to let the pieces go. But I want them to find the right owners." Lexi chuckled. "Listen to me. I sound like I run an animal shelter, not an antiques store—hoping they go to a 'good home with nice people.'"

"It's not weird. It's sweet. And it's your great-grandmother all over again." Ruby tapped her painted fingernails against her own mug. "In fact, she said something similar to me once... about feeling a responsibility to the original owners of the pieces. It was hard for her to see them walk out the door."

"I still miss her, Ruby. I wish she could see all this."

"I miss her, too, hon." With her free hand, Ruby gently squeezed Lexi's shoulder and touched heads with her.

Lexi's phone buzzed in her pocket with a call just as the new grandfather clock issued its beautiful, sonorous chimes for the eight o'clock hour.

Ruby shuffled off. "See you at the meeting."

Lexi moved swiftly away from the clock's gongs to the other corner of the store as she answered her phone. She was expecting a call from Mike, the glassblowing professor at UT, regarding one of her newest brainstorms—to turn an old warehouse on the property into a glassblowing workshop and store. Tourists and townspeople could watch the glassblowers at work then could buy handmade products on site. A percentage of the proceeds would go toward a scholarship benefitting art students at the university.

This would only be her second call with Mike, since the idea was still in its early infancy. But when she looked at her phone, Lexi saw another name instead.

"Hey, Daddy."

"Hi, sweetheart. How's Bailey this morning?"

"Oh, I forgot to text you back last night. He's much better—a broken acorn shell got stuck in his paw. You know those squirrels leave them all over the yard. Anyway, he's back to his old self this morning."

"Great to hear. Listen, I'm making your favorite tonight. Spinach ravioli. Are you free?"

"For your cooking? Always."

Lexi's father was a trained chef and owned three critically acclaimed Italian restaurants in nearby Austin. He had been trying to retire for the past two years but could never completely pull away from the lure of the busy restaurant life.

"It'll be ready at six, but come anytime."

"Okay. Love you."

"Love you too."

They rang off as Ariel walked in from the store's east entrance.

"Sorry I'm late," she said to Lexi as she closed and locked the door.

"You're not. I've still got a couple of things to do before the meeting." Lexi noticed the dark circles under Ariel's eyes and wondered if her new antianxiety meds had taken effect yet. Though she was twenty-three, Ariel had experienced the harshness of life early on, through a series of encounters with bullies in school, the untimely death of her father, her mother's subsequent alcoholism, and a traumatic breakup with her boyfriend last year. Over the holidays, she had admitted to Lexi that she'd been seeing a therapist and had agreed to try a medication regimen.

Ariel brushed the messy bangs away from her eyelashes—Lexi envied her naturally raven hair and dark eyes that needed no enhancement from makeup—and said, "I brought some treats for Bailey." She raised her right shoulder to reveal the bag tucked beneath her arm.

"His favorite. He'll love them, thanks."

Lexi saw the wisp of a smile as Ariel moved toward the front counter. A minute later, she heard Ruby offer Ariel a jovial "Good morning."

When Lexi had first hired Ariel two years ago, she wasn't quite sure Ariel would fit in at the store—she was introverted and withdrawn. *How will customers react to her? Can she be the type of sales assistant the store needs? And how will she and Ruby get along?* But in the end, Ariel proved to be a warm, genuine personality. She might not have displayed the brightness or over-the-top fawning over customers that some shops' assistants possessed. But she turned out to be an old soul who appreciated the antiques almost as much as Lexi did, which made her the perfect fit for the store. Even Ruby sensed it early on and welcomed her on board, knowing instinctively when to tone down her usual sarcasm in favor of a gentler demeanor with Ariel. The two of them had built a sweet, respectful working relationship over the years.

THE STAFF MEETING—WHICH Darius had also joined—contained a swift agenda regarding the week ahead, including scheduled deliveries and estate sale possibilities. But Lexi spent most of the meeting detailing plans for the Let's Get Crafty grand opening. The ambitious venture had been in the works for the past year and a half—turning an enormous warehouse that Gigi had used for storage into a special arts-and-crafts destination for the entire community and, hopefully, beyond. The idea had sparked after Lexi had viewed a local Austin news segment about a growing phenomenon—that people who were bored with restaurants and movies as their main source of entertainment were gravitating toward quirky social activities instead. Family members, friends, dates, business colleagues, all learning together how to paint a landscape or to create a vase or to craft a quilt. Lexi's thought, after clicking off the segment, was *Why not Morgan's Grove?* And the idea took root. Early on, she hired a contractor to help her map out her vision of the warehouse split up into three separate stations: painting, pottery, and needlework. Shortly after that, she secured a small business loan, and the idea became a working reality.

Over the months, Lexi hadn't had time to process the whirlwind of it all. But as she wrapped up the morning's meeting and announced the hiring of a new Let's Get Crafty manager over the weekend, she felt the satisfied surge that meant all the pieces were fitting neatly into place. They were no longer ideas caught up in her head or scribbled haphazardly on paper. They would become a tangible certainty in a matter of days.

As she adjourned the meeting, Lexi swallowed the last of her coffee, patted Bailey's sleepy head, then opened the front door of her shop, ready to welcome customers.

A middle-aged couple waited patiently for Lexi to swing the door wide and let them enter. Beyond them, Lexi saw a balding man in jeans and a plaid shirt. He dusted off his hands and gestured toward the entrance.

"All finished," he said as Lexi stepped underneath the green-striped awning to meet him outside.

"That was quick. Let me pay you."

"Ruby already did. We're all squared away. Have a good one." The man climbed into his truck and drove away as Lexi backed farther into the parking lot to get a good look.

When she pivoted toward the shop, she saw the banner, bolted high above the front door in bold colors: 75 Proud Years of Serving Morgan's Grove.

She heard the store's door open and close but couldn't take her eyes off the banner. In her peripheral vision, she noticed Ruby coming to stand beside her.

"Seventy-five years," Lexi whispered. "What a legacy."

"Yes."

"And a lot to live up to."

Ruby nudged Lexi's shoulder. "You're more than capable. You've got your great-grandmother's genes. And her stubbornness."

"Is that supposed to be a compliment?"

"You know it is."

DURING MOST SEASONS, central Texas was well-known for its wildly fluctuating temperatures, unexpected pop-up thunderstorms, and thick humidity. So Lexi always tried to savor the rare peerless days that occurred in between—the ones that carried a mild breeze, a bright-blue sky, and seventy-degree temperatures. Springtime produced front yards dotted with multicolored azaleas and vivid green leaves that rustled gently on every tree, creating a soothing *swish* that Lexi wished she could bottle and save. April was Lexi's favorite month of all, and she was glad to have an excuse to be out, enjoying the season in all its splendor.

As she approached the Morgan's Grove founder's mansion, a block away from the town square, she craned her neck so she could see the canopy above the tree-lined path. Since there was no traffic, she sauntered in the middle of the road and kept her gaze high, raising her arms out to her sides and letting the sun cast dappled shadows through lacy branches onto her face—something she remembered doing as a little girl.

She moved her focus to the grand three-story façade and realized that the imposing structure always made her feel underdressed—no matter that most of the tourists who visited the mansion wore tank tops and jean shorts to view the property. The elegant gables and Tudor architecture invoked images of another era, when ladies dressed in petticoats and dresses and gloves.

Lexi climbed the mansion's steps then set down her bag and took a quick minute to shake loose her chestnut hair from its ponytail. Using the window's reflection as a guide, she combed her thick strands with gentle fingers and tousled it, letting her hair fall below her shoulders, then buttoned her jacket and smoothed out her black jeans. *Presentable enough.*

She retrieved her bag and opened the door to see Colleen manning the front desk, collecting fees for the daily tours.

"I'm early," Lexi whispered.

"She's upstairs," Colleen said. "Almost finished with a tour. You can go up if you want."

Lexi stuffed a couple of dollars into the donation box then headed up the familiar imposing staircase for the thousandth time, never taking for granted the luxurious details of the mansion: rich wooden floors, comforting beige-colored walls, thick Oriental rugs, sunlight streaming in from a second-floor stained-glass window. The house had been a historical museum since the 1970s, when it became an enticing tourist attraction with its fifteen bedrooms, sixteen fireplaces, four bathrooms, enormous kitchen, cozy parlor, two drawing rooms, spacious dining room, and extensive library. The mansion had even been featured, years ago, on the TV show *America's Castles*.

As Lexi climbed higher, her fingernails tapping against the smooth wood banister, she could hear Jolene's voice floating down from one of the upper bedrooms: "And this was Morgan's bedroom as a little girl. You can see her favorite doll on the bed, a vintage Simon & Halbig..."

Lexi paused outside the bedroom and listened, mouthing the words, having practically memorized Jolene's speech over the years.

As her cousin came to the end of it—"I hope you've enjoyed your tour of this legendary mansion..."—Lexi slipped inside the room, caught Jolene's eye, and continued to mouth the remaining words along with her, using her free hand like a puppet, in a fruitless attempt to break Jolene's unflappable concentration.

Without missing a beat, Jolene lifted her mouth in a half smile as she diverted her eyes and finished the lecture. When the cluster of tourists filtered out of the bedroom, Lexi met Jolene in the center.

"Hungry? I brought lunch!" Lexi raised the bag in her hand.

"Starved! But I wasn't expecting you."

"I know. You mentioned a videoconference at two, but I figured you could squeeze in a quick meal."

"You're a lifesaver. I wasn't going to eat today. I completely forgot my salad—still sitting in the fridge at home."

"Salad, shmalad. I brought chicken piccata with veggies and bread. For both of us."

"My favorite!"

Lexi and Jolene had always been more like sisters than cousins. Both were only children, and Jolene had been raised by a single mother a few blocks down the street from Lexi and her parents. As kids, they spent practically every waking hour together, including at school, where they were often placed in the same classrooms.

"Let's move to the office," Jolene said. "I have time to eat before the conference call starts." She wore her usual uniform of a navy blazer and skirt with matching low heels, and her dark hair was swept into a pristine bun. She'd been the manager of the founder's mansion the past three years and wanted to look the part—polished, knowledgeable, and professional.

Lexi followed Jolene to the end of the hallway, though Lexi already knew the way. She and her cousin had spent hundreds of hours in the mansion throughout their childhood. Back then, Jolene was as obsessed with the mansion as Lexi had been with her great-grandmother's antiques store, and she often badgered Lexi to visit the mansion whenever they could. Kids could enter for free, so cost was never an issue.

Jolene's office stood discreetly behind a locked door. It had become her haven where she could take a break, kick off her heels, and let the modern world seep in again. The room echoed the rest of the house's warm décor—luxurious paneled walls and sumptuous wooden floors—but it was up-to-date tech-wise, holding a flat-screen TV in the corner, chargers for Jolene's cell and tablet and laptop, a full-sized "smart" refrigerator, and a La-Z-Boy sofa for the occasional nap.

Lexi removed her bag's contents onto the round center table. The rich, tart scents wafted up as she opened the first container of food.

Jo nodded toward the glossy white box on the table's edge. "And how about some donuts for dessert? They're left over from this morning's staff meeting. I saved 'em just for you."

Steeling herself, Lexi reached for the box and, without even opening it, shifted it deftly to a side table near the sofa. "Thanks, but no! I've kept off my five-pound weight loss for a whole month, and these little devils will put it right back on."

Most people had a strong weakness for chocolate. Or for cookies or cakes. But Lexi's only weakness had always been donuts. Glazed were her favorite, but any donut would do. She'd been fighting that particular comfort-food craving all her life.

"Tell me how last night went." Lexi returned to her lunch at the table and took a seat. "You never texted."

Jolene had been internet dating for the past five months, and the night before, she'd had a first date with a media consultant from Austin. They had been texting for two weeks.

Jo puffed out a sigh as she shut the refrigerator door then placed two bottles of water on the table. "There wasn't anything worth texting you about." She leaned her hip against the table before cracking open her Styrofoam container and gestured with her plastic fork. "He ended up talking about his ex the entire time. *Debra.* She's a single mom, works at a café in Pflugerville, has a dog named Randy, and is addicted to some Korean Netflix series I don't remember the name of. I learned more about Debra last night than I did about him."

"Why are men who aren't ready to date... dating? It's such a waste of time." Lexi was eager to eat but waited patiently for Jolene to join her before diving in.

"Exactly. *My* time." Jolene plonked into her chair, kicked off her heels, and spread the paper napkin across her lap. "At least the scampi was good. And—he paid."

"I would hope so!" Lexi took her first bite of chicken, which melted in her mouth. "Well, I envy your tenacity to keep trying. You're braver than I am."

"Or dumber. Part of me wants to delete all four dating apps—"

"Four?"

"Hey... don't judge." Jolene took a bite and gave a soft "mmm."

"Sorry. This is me totally not judging. Continue."

"Anyway, *why* am I having this much trouble walking away from these apps? Part of me still believes he's out there. And I realize how clichéd that sounds—fate, destiny, kismet. It's completely unrealistic, the idea of some perfect guy, sitting by his phone, waiting to meet me at the right moment. But I can't help myself. These apps are all about the what-ifs. *What if* I walk away from them, and then Mr. Amazing appears, and I would've missed him?" Jolene tilted her head. "Hey, I think I've answered my original question."

Jolene had a habit of doing that. She would talk everything to death, and by the time she was finished, she had come back around to her original point, full circle. Lexi had learned over the years to let her finish out her circular thinking, however long it might take her.

"I've had the same thoughts," Lexi said. "The what-ifs. It's human nature, wondering what's around the corner and being afraid of missing something amazing. Or, as it happens, *Mister* Amazing."

Jolene tore off a corner of her roll. "Or even worse, what if he's not out there at all? What if every single date ends up being a complete waste of time and nothing *ever* materializes? And then I've spent my prime years searching for a man who never existed in the first place!"

"That's my biggest fear too. Not that I'll miss him but that he's not even real to begin with. Maybe meeting the right one is a Hallmark movie that we've built up inside our heads."

Jolene's stare extended past Lexi. "Could be. But I do know a few happy couples in real life—or at least, they appear happy on social media or walking hand-in-hand in the town square. Your parents are one example. I want that for myself. That comfortable, great-big, life-long love. Who gets to decide why some people have *that* and others never do?"

"That's the eternal question, and I have no answer for it." Lexi let her eyes wander toward the window displaying lime-green leaves that shivered in the breeze. "Aside from my parents, what do I know about healthy relationships? My own marriage was a complete failure." She said it with a half smile, though she recognized the wince inside. It felt strange to mention the union aloud, since she rarely did anymore, even to her cousin. Lexi was five years past it and hadn't spoken to her ex even once since the divorce papers were signed. He was remarried with a new baby, last she heard.

"Oh, Lex. The marriage didn't fail. Neil did. He was the one who cheated. He broke those vows, not you."

Lexi wished she had never brought it up. Even hearing his name aloud brought some old—and sad—memories to the forefront that she'd worked hard to forget. "Anyway, you're brave to keep putting yourself out there. And I hate admitting this, but I sort of enjoy living vicariously through you and your dating apps. I mean, you're older than me—"

"Only by a month."

"And you're supposed to have it all figured out. I plan on watching and learning."

"You'll learn nothing from me. I mean, I was with Brady for six years, and it ended so abruptly. I never saw it coming. I guess in hindsight, it made some sense, though. We were never working toward building a future together. We were marking time, spinning our wheels in different directions."

"Six years is a long time. You still need time to heal."

"But maybe the healing is in moving on? I mean, all these dating apps, keeping my heart open—maybe it makes the healing go faster, speeds up the process."

Lexi had a choice here: make her cousin feel good by validating her with an emphatic yes, or tell her the awful truth, from Lexi's own experience. She chose the latter, but softened it. "I'm not sure it works that way. You really can't force the healing. You have to push through the pain and face it head-on, not ignore that it's there."

"Okay, Dr. Phil. But even so, there's no real harm in putting myself out there at the same time. I mean, while I'm doing all this 'fun' healing, can't I still keep an open heart, an open mind?" Her pensive expression shifted into that familiar, radiant, megawatt smile.

Lexi stared at her eternal-optimist cousin and felt a tangible stab of envy. After all the pain Jolene had endured, she wasn't willing to give up on love. Lexi didn't know if she could ever be that hopeful. A part of her even secretly wondered if she would ever marry again. Instead of confiding any of this to Jolene, Lexi said, "Yes. You can do anything you want."

Jolene shook her head. "How did this conversation get so serious? Okay, I'm turning the tables on you. Could I ever talk you into signing up for a dating app? I'm an expert with all the ins and outs. I could totally tutor you! Or if you want a more 'in person' venue, there's speed dating at this quirky new bookstore in Austin. And I've even heard of—"

Lexi put her hand up and waved it between them. "Turn those tables right back around, cousin. I've got my hands way too full. Let's Get Crafty is taking all my time these days. Not to mention the glass-blowing venture on the horizon. There's no way I have time for dating. I'm happy with it just being me and my business."

"And that's enough?" Jolene raised an eyebrow.

"It's enough for now."

WHEN LEXI'S PHONE ALARM beeped, she let out a small groan of frustration, still elbow-deep in paperwork she couldn't afford to leave till tomorrow. Everyone at the store had gone home an hour before, leaving Lexi to lock up and continue working. Some might call her a workaholic—a trait she had proudly received from both her parents as well as from Gigi. But sometimes, it left her feeling scattered or neglectful of other areas in her life.

She tapped off the alarm then remembered why it was beeping in the first place.

"The bakery!"

Bailey blinked up at her.

"We're late!" She shuffled the papers neatly back into their folder, deciding she suddenly had higher priorities. "C'mon, boy. Maybe we can still make it."

Mentally kicking herself, Lexi latched Bailey's leash on, clicked off the desk light, then led him out the door so she could lock it.

As she moved toward the town square, her phone rang—a call from the professor.

"Hi, Mike."

"Lexi. Sorry I'm late returning your call. Things were crazy today—student projects, midterm grades. That time of year."

"I understand. We could postpone, if you need to—"

"Nope. I'm curious to hear your ideas. I think a glassblowing space for the students is an amazing idea. I'd love to get it off the ground as soon as we're able."

Elated, Lexi continued her walk, with Bailey guiding her toward the town square, a stone's throw from her antiques store. After agreeing to meet with Mike tomorrow to answer some of her basic questions—*What type of furnace is needed? What about ventilation and safety concerns? And how much will everything cost?*—she ended the call, marveling that Bailey seemed to know exactly where they were headed... and why.

The dusky evening still held a chill, and Lexi wished she'd worn her jacket. Too late to rush by her house and pick it up. She would have to put up with the cold.

She noticed the energy of the entire square winding down—shops closing, streetlights glowing, traffic thinning. The space was beautiful at any time, day or night, but it held a particular charm during the near-twilight hour, as tiny white lights that decorated all the square's trees created a comforting glow year-round.

Even as they approached Lucille's brand-new bakery at the edge of the square, Lexi knew they were too late—the Closed sign was up in the window.

"Oh well, we tried," she said to Bailey. But as she guided him in the opposite direction, Lexi heard the door clicking open.

"There you are! I was about to come find you." Lucille Wright, the silver-haired seventy-something bakery owner, held two boxes high in one hand while navigating leashes with the other. Lucille often brought her corgis—George and Gracie—to her store. The minute Bailey saw the dogs, he bounded toward them, jerking his leash straight out of Lexi's hand. Lucille stepped deftly around the dogs and met Lexi at the sidewalk. The canine reunion continued with play bites and slobbery kisses.

"I thought we were too late. I lost all track of time."

"It happens to the best of us." Lucille's kind eyes squinted in the setting sun. "I've got your cookies. And also the dog biscuits you ordered. We sold out again today—I had no idea how popular they'd be when we started baking them last week. But no worries. I set yours aside this morning, when you called in the order."

"You're the best." Lexi fished inside her purse for cash then exchanged it for Lucille's boxes. "He will love these. Bailey, look—your favorite!"

With her free hand, Lexi grabbed the leash again and tugged, showing Bailey the box. He tore his attention away from the corgis long enough to sniff the box and let out a happy yelp.

"We're late. Thank Lucille for the cookies."

He yelped again as Lucille chuckled and waved goodbye. "Let's have a doggie playdate soon!" she called out. "Bailey's welcome at my house anytime."

Lexi moved Bailey along through the rest of the town square. As she always did, she made a mental note to carve out a half day off from work and do some window shopping... to slow down and browse the candle shop, the bookshop, maybe even eat at The Pit (best barbecue in Texas) or take in a movie at the century-old theater. *Wishful thinking.*

At the end of the square, Lexi and Bailey made their way to the first residential block and made a right turn. Lucille actually lived on that corner, and Lexi's parents owned the house at the other end of the block. It had been Gigi's house for decades, until she passed away and Lexi's mother inherited the home.

Bailey knew the way and pulled Lexi eagerly toward the house. Although Lexi hadn't grown up here, she held a special affection for this place—a white two-story Colonial house with forest-green shutters. She'd spent most of her childhood Sundays there with Gigi after church, only the two of them—baking chocolate chip cookies or building pillow forts or dancing around the living room to catchy disco music.

Lexi climbed the two shallow brick steps and tapped on the door. Within seconds, her dad appeared in the doorway and leaned down for a warm hug. His six-foot-three frame nearly swallowed her whole as his graying beard scratched her cheek.

"Sorry I'm late," she said as he backed away and closed the door. "I was swamped today."

"It's fine, sweetheart. You're right on time." It was a lie, but Lexi appreciated it anyway.

As she stooped over to release Bailey from the leash, he sniffed the air then saw Winston, the cat, and playfully lunged toward him.

"Bailey, be good. Leave poor Winston alone."

"Aww, they'll be fine. They always are," her dad said, reassuring her. A timer in the kitchen buzzed, and he clapped his hands. "I'd better go check on that."

"Can I help?"

"Nope, it's all under control. We'll eat soon."

As he rounded the corner toward the kitchen, Lexi's mother descended the staircase, looking elegant as always—pressed beige slacks, low heels, a patchwork blouse. Her newly colored brunette hair rested on her shoulders and gave a light bounce as she reached the last step. Her mother had impeccable taste. Her appearance, along with her house, was always pristine. Never a hair or a cushion out of place.

"You're here. I tried calling you a couple of times." She waved her phone between them.

"Oh. Sorry. It was turned off."

Her mother leaned in for a brisk cheek-kiss then folded her arms. "What's this?" She looked down at the two boxes that Lexi had forgotten she held.

"Italian wedding cookies. I thought they'd go well with the meal. And I snuck in two gingerbreads for Dad. I know how much he loves them."

Her mom crinkled her nose. "I'm not sure why Lucille bakes them year-round. Gingerbread is a *Christmas* cookie."

"Well, they must be popular, or else she wouldn't be selling them." Lexi could feel the makings of a subtle headache creeping toward the top of her forehead.

"What's in the other box?"

"Biscuits for Bailey. In fact, I meant to give him one earlier. Bailey, where are you? C'mere, boy!"

Winston appeared from another room, clearly petrified, and jumped straight into Lexi's mother's arms.

"Sorry. I should've warned you that I was bringing Bailey tonight."

"I'll put Winston in our bedroom," her mother said, unsuccessfully attempting to hide her annoyance. "Safer there..." She trailed off as she moved toward the stairs once again.

"Here, boy." Lexi bent forward to offer Bailey one of Lucille's biscuits, and he devoured it greedily. "Be extra good tonight, 'kay?" she whispered. "Don't make me regret bringing you."

IN THE KITCHEN, AFTER a quick wash of her hands, Lexi helped her dad with the garlic bread then ladled his simmering homemade marinara into a ceramic bowl.

"Everything smells delicious," she said as they moved the food into the dining room, where her mother was setting out the cloth napkins.

Bailey had curled up in the corner with a deep sigh, happily settled on a doggie bed that Lexi's dad had bought for him last year.

They sat down to eat, and the ravioli was as scrumptious as Lexi had anticipated—soft pasta pillows filled with spinach and delicate cheese and slathered with zesty marinara. It had been Lexi's favorite meal since she was a child.

"Is everything coming along with the new arts-and-crafts center?" her dad asked halfway through the meal. "What's it called again?"

"Let's Get Crafty. So far, it is. I expect some glitches and issues to pop up, but right now, everything is on schedule."

"I'm proud of you, honey." Her dad reached across to give her hand a squeeze. "Let us know if your mother and I can help with anything."

"How is that other venture of yours, the glassblowing center?" her mother asked between bites.

Lexi had casually mentioned it to her parents a couple of weeks before as a faraway idea—which it was. But hearing the shadows of skepticism in her mother's tone made Lexi regret ever mentioning it. She shifted in her seat, preparing her sales pitch. "Great. As a matter of fact, on my way here, I got a call from the UT professor. We're meeting tomorrow. Early stages, of course. But he sounds enthusiastic."

"I think it's a genius idea." Her dad gave an approving nod. "A partnership with the university, an education for the whole community. Plus, the tourists will love it, too, and you could even bring in classrooms of students for tours."

"That's exactly what I was thinking. When the ball gets rolling, I'll speak with the school principals in Morgan's Grove and then probably some Austin schools after that."

"Genius," her dad said again.

"But I need to get the new arts-and-crafts center up and running first," Lexi said, circling back around, knowing what her mother would say next. She practically mouthed it along with her, inside her mind, as she took a sip of water. She'd heard it all before.

"I think you might be taking on too much. You're so busy as it is. Not to mention the financial risks of another new venture. Don't you think you're stretching yourself—and the store—too thin?"

Lexi gathered courage, though she couldn't manage to look her mother in the eye. She fiddled with her fork. "I've always wanted to do something with those two warehouses on Gigi's property since she gave it to me. In fact, we talked about it once—she said she hated the idea of them sitting there, mostly useless." She met her mother's gaze. "I think she would be proud of me."

"She would, honey," her dad said. Then he turned toward his wife, and his voice softened nearly to a shy whisper. "I think Lexi knows her own limitations. She can handle it." He removed a white pill from the edge of his plate then placed it in his mouth.

"New medication?" Lexi asked, hoping for a diversion.

"Just a pill for cholesterol. Doc says it's a bit high."

On Lexi's final bite of garlic bread, her mother pressed the napkin to her lips then folded it onto the table. "Ben, will you get the box from the living room? I want to show Lexi what we found."

"Will do." He gave a hint of a grin, leaving Lexi to wonder what on earth her parents were up to.

Her mother explained as Ben left the room. "We've been tidying the attic. Well, more like a giant spring cleaning. We might move your dad's study up there. Anyway, we found a box that belonged to Gigi. It was tucked away in a back corner. I've never seen it before. We thought you might appreciate it."

Lexi's father carried a medium-sized cardboard box to the end of the dining table. Her mother opened it while Ben returned to his seat. She was clearly in charge of this show.

"A beautiful scarf." Her mother narrated as she gently drew out each item and passed it over to Lexi, who had risen from her chair to gain closer access. "Some very old photos—this one is dated 1947—that's your great-grandfather." She tapped his face with her index finger. "And here's a movie ticket stub for *Goodbye, Mr. Chips* and a baby's bonnet."

"Incredible," Lexi whispered, handling the items with great care as her mother continued to share them.

"And this." Her mother raised a flat, velvety, palm-sized box. "Do you think you could have this analyzed, find out the date or the origins?" She cracked it open to reveal the most beautiful necklace Lexi had ever seen: a silver teardrop with a pear-shaped diamond sparkling from its center.

"Gigi's birthstone," Lexi mused. "And a filigree setting." She ran a light fingertip over the decorative border surrounding the gem.

"I'm sure that your great-grandfather gave her this. But I want to know more. It also has an inscription."

Her mother removed the necklace and dangled it in front of Lexi, who leaned in closer, catching the teardrop with eager fingers. She swiveled it to reveal the back side and read the tiny inscription. "Keeper of My Heart." Her pulse raced faster, the same way it did when an unexpected new treasure came into her antiques store. "I can have Max take a look at it."

Maxwell Lewis was Gigi's primary antiques appraiser, located in Austin. Lexi consulted him whenever she wanted a deep dive into a piece that had questionable value. He had decades of experience as well as online contacts with unique research capabilities.

"Why didn't she ever wear it?" Lexi rotated the teardrop to study the filigree work again.

"You know Gigi. She rarely wore jewelry, always thinking it was too grand for her. She was probably afraid to lose it. I'm not surprised one bit that she kept this hidden away in a dusty attic all these years."

Lexi could verify this. Her great-grandmother never wore any jewelry—not even a watch or earrings. "I'll need some good lighting so I can snap a pic. I can forward it to Max tonight."

"The living room is probably best lit," her dad said, reentering from the kitchen and carrying Lucille's powdered-sugar cookies on a plate.

Lexi's mother followed her into the living room. "I wonder if it's possibly World War II era or thereabouts? That's when your great-grandparents met, shortly after the war ended."

Lexi placed the teardrop on the bare surface of an end table, with the lamp providing a strong light. She zoomed in with her camera phone, avoiding any glares, and snapped multiple photos of each side of the necklace. "That should do it."

Her mother held the box open, and Lexi spiraled the chain down inside, setting the necklace back where it had been hiding for who-knew-how-many decades.

"You keep it." Her mother offered Lexi the box.

"Are you sure?"

"Positive. Max might need to see it in person."

"It'll be in good hands."

Lexi slipped the treasure into her purse near the front door then joined her mother again at the dining table. After sitting down to text Max and attach the photos, Lexi started to reach for a wedding cookie, but the moment her finger touched the plate, she watched a text message appear on her phone. "Already?" But it was merely an autoreply, and her hopes sank. She read the message aloud to her parents. "'I'm currently unavailable due to a family emergency. Thank you for understanding.'"

Lexi pouted as she clicked off her phone then selected a cookie. "Guess we'll have to wait. Poor Max. An emergency doesn't sound good. I can research some other appraisers tomorrow."

"You don't have any backups?" her mother asked then drank from her coffee.

"Actually, no. Max is always so... available. I've never had to depend on anyone else."

"Mm," her mother said, lifting her eyebrows.

Lexi shrugged off the urge to continue on, to explain further *why* there were no backups. Gigi hadn't needed one, either. *What was good enough for Gigi...*

But it was pointless. Pushing back against her mother's constant disapproval rarely resulted in anything but frustration. And it would only invite further disapproval. Best to stay quiet, finish her cookie, gather Bailey, and be on her way back home. It had been a long, long day.

TOSSING HER KEYS ONTO the entry table and releasing Bailey from his halter, Lexi flicked on lights as she entered her small-but-cozy rental house and headed toward the kitchen. Her dad had given her a take-home portion of ravioli, insisting that she "remember to eat—even on your busiest days. *Especially* on your busiest days."

Shutting the fridge door, Lexi leaned backward against it and tried not to think about tomorrow. Another full day with an equally busy agenda. She couldn't remember the last free day she'd had, when she wasn't worried about payroll or bills or inventory or estate sales or arts-and-crafts centers. But this was her life, and it was the one she had chosen.

The phone rang in her hand, and she tilted the screen to see the caller. She answered quickly. "Max! I didn't expect a call from you tonight."

"Sorry, hon. I didn't realize the hour. I'm in a different time zone."

"How are things? Your message mentioned a family emergency?"

Lexi moved a few feet to sit at the kitchen table and heard Bailey lapping up water from his bowl in the corner.

"It's my brother. He was moved to hospice two days ago. Colon cancer. I'm here taking care of things."

"I'm so sorry, Max."

A deep sigh came from his end of the call, and she thought he could be fighting tears. Max was never one to show his emotions. In fact, she had known Max most all her life, through her great-grandmother's store, but knew almost nothing about his personal life. *Did he have children? A wife? A cat or a dog?*

"Thanks. Anyway, I wanted to give you the name of a colleague who could help with your necklace. He's fairly new at antiques appraisal, but he's got all the right credentials. And great instincts to boot. I've been mentoring him for the better part of a year."

"I had no idea."

"I've actually been phasing myself out. It's time to retire. And with my brother in this state... Well, in any case, this new guy will take good care of you. Ready for the info?"

Lexi scrambled to find a pen and paper in a nearby drawer as Max rattled off the name—Graham Faulkner, history professor at the University of Texas.

"I'm actually headed to UT tomorrow," Lexi said. "To see a glass-blowing professor. I'll swing by Mr. Faulkner's department while I'm there." She paused. "Is it mister? Or doctor?"

"Doctor. But 'professor' probably works as well."

Lexi set down the pen. "Max, I'm really sorry to hear about your brother. Can I do anything for you? Swing by your house, water plants or feed a pet?"

"I've got a neighbor picking up the mail. No plants or pets. Everything's already done."

"Okay. Well... take extra-good care of yourself during these next few days."

"Will do."

As they rang off, Lexi heard Bailey lightly snoring at her feet. She hated to wake him up, so she remained at the table.

She slipped a hand inside her bag for the velvet box then opened it to see the teardrop again. She imagined her great-grandmother's vibrant, youthful expression when it was first presented to her, decades ago—the tiny gasp in her throat, the widening smile as she read the same inscription that Lexi touched now.

"What secrets are you holding?" she asked the necklace then tipped the lid closed again.

Chapter Two

Stepping onto UT Austin's immaculate college campus, Lexi saw students lounging on sun-drenched lawns, heard classical guitar floating out from the fine arts building, and watched a young couple holding hands as they walked to class—all of which offered vivid flashbacks of her own time spent on that campus as a student a decade before. The lengthy study sessions in the library, the late-night dorm gossip about who was dating whom, and the hush of spacious lecture halls where she scribbled down notes and filled her mind with new information—she had loved all of it. So much that once upon a time, she'd considered becoming a professor just to spend the rest of her working life on a college campus with its enlightening, studious energy that couldn't be matched elsewhere.

This morning, though, Lexi was on a specific, purely nonacademic mission. She was scheduled to meet with Mike at eleven, but beforehand, she had some free time after leaving an estate auction in Austin earlier than planned. So she ventured to the other side of campus first, with Gigi's necklace tucked safely inside her leather satchel, to pop in on the history professor.

On the way, her phone jingled, and she saw Ruby's name on the screen.

"How did the auction go?" Ruby asked.

Lexi recounted the sad truth. "I had my eye on this gorgeous armoire, but it was way out of our price range. It went for three thousand."

"Whoa. Well, I have some more bad news for you."

Lexi stopped in her tracks on the sidewalk. "Tell me."

"The pottery wheels are stuck in Memphis."

Lexi shut her eyes tight. "You're kidding."

She visualized both of the kickwheels—three thousand dollars and three hundred pounds each—sitting on the truck bed, *not* making their careful way to Texas in time for next week's grand opening. Lexi had purchased the wheels two months ago, but there had been a delay on the manufacturer's end that prevented delivery. And now, this.

"I wish I were kidding. The truck broke down on 79 and had to be towed. They might have to order parts."

"Can't they get another truck?"

"That's my next call. No worries, I'm on it."

"You're the best, Ruby." Lexi felt a fat, unexpected drop of rain plonk onto her head then slide down her scalp. "I've gotta go. I'm sensing a downpour coming, and I forgot my umbrella. When it rains..."

Ruby chuckled. "Yep. Stay dry. We'll talk later."

Lexi clicked off then moved swiftly toward Garrison Hall as the drops multiplied, splashing onto sidewalks and rooftops all around. She somehow managed not to become completely drenched by the time she reached the safety of the covered entryway. She huddled with a couple of dampened students before opening the door and combing out her hair with her fingers, hoping she was presentable enough to speak with the professor.

A quick glance at a mounted board containing the list of offices led Lexi around two corners and down a hallway before she approached Dr. Graham S. Faulkner's office, dark and locked. She scanned the schedule on his door, which told her that he was currently teaching a class upstairs, followed by another class, then a break for lunch, then office hours and a later class. She looked at her phone for the current time and did some quick math. She couldn't stay in Austin and wait around until late afternoon to speak with him. *But perhaps he wouldn't mind a spur-of-the-moment visit in between classes?*

Taking a chance, she spotted the nearest staircase and headed up to his classroom. She could hear the muffled drone of several teachers wrapping up their lectures from behind closed doors as she located the correct room. Lexi leaned against the wall and drew out her phone to check texts and emails while she waited patiently for students to zip up book bags, gather water bottles, and shuffle out the door. As dozens of students poured out, Lexi recognized that particular room as one of the enormous lecture halls she'd taken classes in long ago.

She paused as the final students trickled out then peeked through the open doorway. She wasn't sure why, but she had assumed Dr. Faulkner would look like every other history professor she'd had or known—in his sixties, with thinning gray hair, wearing thick-rimmed glasses and a threadbare herringbone jacket he'd owned for two decades.

But Graham Faulkner looked nothing like those other professors. In his early thirties, he had a full head of thick caramel hair and wore a crisp navy blazer over a pair of faded jeans. He didn't need any glasses to read the text that captured his interest on his phone. He frowned, scrolling the screen with his thumb. A soft guttural sound of disapproval came from his throat.

Lexi hated to interrupt him, but she'd already stepped awkwardly into the room. She cleared her throat lightly, and when that didn't work, she added a soft "Dr. Faulkner?"

His eyes remained on the phone.

"Professor?"

He seemed to hear but couldn't pull his focus away from the screen. "Just a moment..."

Lexi laced her fingers together while she waited. When he finally crooked his neck to peer at Lexi, the frown he'd worn while staring at his phone deepened slightly. It was clear she had intruded.

She took a sheepish step forward to explain who she was. "I'm Lexi Price. I emailed you this morning?"

His face relaxed slightly as he fixed his light-blue eyes on her. "Which of my classes are you in?"

"Oh. No, I'm not a student. I'm a friend of Max's. Max Lewis, the appraiser." When his expression still didn't change, she continued. "I own an antiques shop in Morgan's Grove—small town outside of Austin—and I have a necklace that needs appraising." She reached around her waist to open the flap on her bag, realizing she was regurgitating everything she'd already said in her email to him. "Max is my usual appraiser, but he's had a family emergency and gave me your name. I should've called first, but I was already on campus, and—"

Just as her hand had grasped the velvet box, the professor's phone gave a *ding*, drawing his attention back to his screen. The frown returned, and the professor shook his head. "Just give me another second..." he mumbled.

Lexi paused, immediately regretting having interrupted him in the first place. She decided to postpone their chat for another day. She removed her hand from the box then readjusted the bag's shoulder strap. "This isn't a good time. I should have called. I'll try again later."

"What's that?" he asked, glancing up.

"I think another time would be best. I'll make an appointment with you."

"Oh." He looked down again. "That would be fine," he muttered then began thumb-typing quickly.

Lexi shook her head as she pivoted to leave, wondering if Professor Faulkner treated his students that way—distracted and utterly preoccupied. *Rude.* As she walked back downstairs to the low rumble of thunder, she decided to find another appraiser altogether. This wasn't only about her necklace—it was about many future research assignments for her store, for years to come. She needed someone capable she could rely on, someone as steadfast and attentive and available as Max had been.

IT TOOK EVERYTHING in Lexi not to sneak a bite of a French fry or even a dollop of Mississippi Mud as she transported her Pit order to the antiques store. On the way back from Austin, she wanted to surprise Ruby and Ariel with a barbecue lunch, with enough left over for her delivery guys as well. The tangy smell was heavenly, and Lexi's stomach responded with an impatient growl.

When Lexi walked into her store with the sturdy box of food, Ruby gave a small, happy gasp—The Pit was her favorite restaurant in town—and met Lexi around the edge of the counter with widespread arms.

"What did you *do*?" she asked, peeking into the bags as she took the box from Lexi.

"Lunch for everyone!" Lexi announced it loudly enough so Ariel could hear her too.

"I'll put this in the back room," Ruby said. "What a treat. Thank you!"

Lexi moved a few steps to find Bailey stretching in his pillow, with the tip of his tail thumping against the floor when she approached. "Did you have a good morning?" she whispered, scratching the top of his head as he yawned. "We'll go for a walk soon."

As she stood up, she noticed an enormous clear bag filled to the brim with glossy colored eggs leaning against the corner behind the counter. Each April, Morgan's Grove held a citywide Easter egg hunt, and the businesses who chose to participate were given two hundred plastic eggs to fill—and more if they requested them. The eggs were donated by the city council, but the businesses provided their own treats and candies, and they also went to the trouble of hand-stuffing the eggs. Gigi's store had been part of this tradition since its inception, and the employees always looked forward to it. During slow moments in the store, they would each spend their time filling the eggs. Lexi made a mental note to send Ariel to the dollar store tomorrow for the miniature candy and prizes.

Ruby reappeared from the back as Darius entered the shop carrying a Victorian-style chair with intricate wood carvings and sumptuous needlepoint cushions.

"This is the piece I got last week," Ruby said, reminding Lexi. "At the Johnson estate sale."

They moved out of the way as Ruby pointed to an empty spot nearby where Darius could set down the chair.

"There's barbecue from The Pit," Lexi told him. "It's in the back. Help yourself."

Darius grinned then disappeared toward the food. He had been with the shop for at least eight years, when Gigi had hired him on the spot. From the start, she'd called him her "gentle giant with the strength of Sampson." His frame was massive—six foot six and well over three hundred pounds. He'd played professional football for three years after college but then made his way back to Morgan's Grove when an injury sidelined him permanently. He'd spent the last few years doing a variety of odd jobs around town to raise a family, and he even coached little league football on the weekends.

Lexi ran her fingers over the chair's carvings—as beautiful as Ruby had first described—and had a strong feeling the piece would be snatched up within the week.

"Something *else* came into the store this morning." Ruby's raised eyebrows told Lexi it must be intriguing. "Follow me."

Ruby crooked her finger and walked toward the other corner of the store, where she paused and folded her arms. When Lexi's eyes roamed to find the new treasure that had been added to her store, they stopped dead on ten new pieces, each one about eight inches high.

"Gnomes," Lexi said with a shiver.

She'd always had an aversion to the harmless garden statues. Not a phobia, exactly, not how some people feared clowns or spiders—but the aversion was strong enough to make her cringe inside every time she saw a gnome. It had been that way for Lexi ever since she was a girl, thanks to a children's book she'd once read, with illustrated gnomes who came alive at night and created all sorts of mischief around the garden. One year, unaware of her great-granddaughter's fears, Gigi had purchased two gnomes, placing them in two separate corners of the shop. Lexi, seven years old at the time, was terrified when she believed that the gnomes had moved an inch or two each morning, all on their own. She was convinced that at night, after her great-grandmother closed the shop and turned off the lights, the gnomes had wandered around the store and terrorized the other figurines then hurried back into place for the morning.

Of course, Lexi realized as an adult that whoever had dusted the night before had been responsible for moving the gnomes a few inches. But the impact of Lexi's childish wild imagination had been traumatic enough to linger for all these years.

"Who brought them in?" Lexi asked, keeping a steady eye on the little guys.

"I didn't recognize him. Some man who said he was moving. His deceased wife kept a collection of them. He didn't want to throw them out and thought our shop might want to have them. So he donated."

"How kind of him," Lexi quipped. "Well, as long as they're not dispersed all throughout the shop where I have to see them everywhere, I'm good. Let's keep them in this cluster. Maybe some gnome-loving gardener will grace our shop this week and take them all off our hands."

"Let's hope."

"Do me a favor—choose two of them and stick them in the back. Preferably covered up and hidden away."

"For you?"

"Bite your tongue! They're for Jolene. Her birthday is in a couple of months. She has a collection of gnomes in her yard. Which is why I never go back there."

Ruby snickered. "Will do."

"I nearly forgot—what happened with the pottery wheels? Any updates?"

"Well, good news and bad." Ruby put one hand on her hip and gestured with the other. "The truck's part can be brought in from a nearby city, but the repair will take another day, at least. Earliest ETA is Friday. The latest is Monday."

Lexi calculated the dates. "Doesn't give us much room for error before next Friday's opening. Assuming that there's not a third delay around the corner."

"How did your glassblowing meeting go?"

"Great. I think Mike is more excited than I am. He answered my questions and gave me some good ideas for the financing. It might become a reality sooner than I thought."

"Fantastic. And the history professor?"

Earlier in the morning, Lexi had shown Ruby the necklace, including the inscription, and had told her all about Max's phone call along with her plan to visit the possible new appraiser on campus.

Lexi smirked. "Not so fantastic. To be fair, I caught him off guard, right after his class. I should've made an appointment. But let's say I wasn't high on his list of priorities. He was... preoccupied, cold. Borderline rude."

"Well, that doesn't sound good."

"It was enough to make me think that we need to find another appraiser."

"No worries. I can get on that."

"Great. Find me someone reliable. And knowledgeable. Max indicated the professor was new at appraising, so maybe it wasn't meant to be. I want someone we can trust." Lexi's eyes found the gnomes again. "Now, if we can only get rid of these guys that easily." She lowered her voice. "Let's put them on clearance."

"Done."

GRAHAM FAULKNER NUDGED his office door shut with his elbow then plonked down in his chair, making room on the desk for the bag of Panda Express he'd bought on campus. A working lunch would surely distract him from the texts he'd received a couple of hours ago, immediately after his World War II class let out.

But against his better judgment, Graham ignored his lunch and tilted the screen to reread the two curt texts for the umpteenth time, trying to read between the lines, analyzing each word to death.

I've been giving it a lot of thought, and it's time for a break. I'm sorry.

I think we should see other people.

There wasn't much room for interpretation. Clearly, it was over.

Graham wondered if Theresa had already been "seeing other people" before she even composed the texts.

He had tried three times to craft a response that didn't reek of either groveling desperation or seething anger. Or both. Silence was best at the moment. Maybe she would change her mind. Or maybe he would change his and start to agree with her, that it *was* time for a break.

He set the phone face down on his desk and ran a hand through his hair. If he was honest, things had been off between him and Theresa for a while. The past two months, they'd grown more distant, often "too busy" for their usual date nights out or their binge-watching nights in. As a hotel manager, Theresa's job was incredibly demanding—she sometimes took night shifts or had to leave Graham abruptly to go put out a fire that her assistant manager couldn't handle. He'd known this about her when they began dating ten months ago, that she was practically married to her job. But he didn't know if her job was an actual factor in the breakup or a good excuse to let him go.

Graham opened the bag and brought out the orange chicken and crab rangoons, usually his favorite, but today, nothing sounded appetizing. He forced a bite of chicken then slid his laptop in front of him. Surely, work could be a healthy diversion. There was plenty of it—a dozen new student emails to respond to, next week's D-Day test to finish writing, some professional development to catch up on, and freshman essays to grade. He had been employed as a full-time professor at UT for the past seven years and was well aware that the workload was intense every semester, though it could wax and wane day to day. For some reason, this semester, the organic enthusiasm he usually had while standing in front of students and talking about his favorite subjects had begun to dampen. He could feel it with every hesitation to grade another paper, every extra snooze button he pushed in the morning, every new competing technology that the students held in their hands. Each semester, it grew harder and harder to capture students' attention and to make history interesting—they cared more about last month's latest social media trend than the Nazi plundering of Jewish art and treasure. Graham also used to enjoy socializing with other colleagues during faculty meetings, but lately, he found them tedious. Both the meetings and the colleagues. He couldn't pinpoint why, but he hoped it was nothing more than the typical weariness that began to show on most teachers around this time—a seven-year itch of sorts.

He scanned the emails to see which could wait and which couldn't, and his eyes landed on an email from a Lexi Price. The subject: Necklace Appraisal.

Lexi. The woman who'd approached him after class, the one he'd mistaken for a nontraditional student. She had mentioned sending an email—he just hadn't read it yet. The breakup texts, which he'd received seconds before Lexi entered the room, had been an incredible distraction in the moment, and he'd barely registered her visit, unable to focus on anything except his phone. *Had he been ungracious with her? Even gruff?* He couldn't remember, but their conversation hadn't lasted long. When he had looked up from his phone again, she was gone.

Clearing his head of everything else, he clicked open Lexi's email, determined to give it the consideration it deserved.

Chapter Three

Lexi spritzed glass cleaner onto the countertop and gave a satisfied wipe of her rag, watching the moisture evaporate and create a clear, glistening shine. Moments before, the eagerly awaited pottery wheels had arrived, and Lexi had watched the men install them at the back of the venue, inside the pottery station of Let's Get Crafty. An art student from UT would ultimately be the one conducting the pottery classes, but Lexi still wanted a basic idea about the wheels' usage and asked the men for a tutorial. Afterward, she'd kept busy with unnecessary tasks: checking inventory at the coffee bar installed a few days before and then cleaning the front countertop that held the register.

There was another, sneakier purpose to Lexi's sudden need to check and clean: It gave her the opportunity to eavesdrop on her new manager, Pam, currently conducting a training meeting for the four new staff members hired last week. Pam's voice held both kindness and authority, which was what Lexi had been looking for during all those job interviews. Previously, Pam had been the assistant manager at Painting with a Twist, in Austin, so she had solid experience in this particular area. Pam came into her interview with creative ideas for girls' nights, date nights, student nights, holidays, and more. Lexi knew, overhearing Pam's confident lecture to the new hires where she advised them "always keep your cool, even with unhappy children or their unhappy parents," that the venture was in excellent hands.

Lexi left the register and tiptoed discreetly behind Pam and her employees to walk through the rest of the space at a leisurely pace. Throughout the weeks, everything had been such a flurry of important decisions regarding color, lighting, and furniture choices that

Lexi hadn't yet had an opportunity to see the nearly completed picture. There was still more to do—stocking the shelves and drawers with materials that were back-ordered as well as doing a final deep cleaning of every inch and corner to create a gleaming first impression. But for the most part, the job was done.

She walked slowly, hands behind her back, letting her eyes absorb the colorful painting station with its empty easels and canvases, the ample shelving soon to be stocked with necessary supplies, and the example paintings covering the walls. Then, she moved on to the quilting and knitting station, with its wall of cubbyholes, which would end up displaying thread and yarn in every color of the rainbow, and its chairs set in a semicircle and two plush beanbag chairs arranged in the corners. And finally, the ceramics station toward the back, with its pottery wheels, two hefty tables, a sink, and a large bureau of shelving for all the pottery supplies that would hopefully be arriving tomorrow.

Over the last several months, the hundreds of hours of work—most of it spent during late nights or early mornings—had all come down to this. Lexi's gaze swept the entire space as a smile curled her lips. At the same time, a hint of unexpected tears welled up as she recognized the bittersweetness in the moment. Gigi wasn't there to share it with her. Lexi envisioned her great-grandmother's tight hand wrapped around Lexi's waist in a hug as they stood side-by-side and scanned the space together. Her great-grandmother would have been completely amazed at the warehouse's transformation from dusty, cobwebbed, and dark. And yes, she would have been proud.

Exiting the open double doors of the warehouse, aiming her focus forward, onto the rest of the day's agenda, Lexi saw someone approaching. She wasn't expecting anyone, and it was too early to have customers. She stopped and raised a hand to shield her eyes from the bright sun. The man seemed familiar, but he wore sunglasses, so she couldn't be sure. He was dressed in a plaid blue shirt with jeans and carried keys in one hand.

He came to a pause in front of her then removed his glasses. The history professor. *What's he doing here, in Morgan's Grove?*

He offered a grin and a slight tilt of his head. "Lexi. Right?"

"That's right." She folded her hands together near her waist. "Professor Faulkner." He didn't seem as tall as she remembered him from the other day.

"Just Graham. 'Professor' is for my students."

"Which you thought I was."

"Yes." He dipped his head, and his smile turned slightly lopsided, which made him seem self-effacing. "Rather embarrassing, that assumption."

Another thing she hadn't noticed the other day was his accent. He wasn't a native Texan. *A transplant, perhaps? But from what part of the country?* His *r*'s disappeared sometimes.

"I took it as a compliment," she said to reassure him. "I haven't stepped on that campus as a student in nearly ten years."

"So you went to UT as well?"

"Majored in business, minored in history."

"We might've had some classes together."

Under these casual circumstances, with both of them in jeans and standing on a dusty road outside of a warehouse, Lexi could feel her defenses evaporating.

"What brings you to Morgan's Grove?" she asked.

"I'm actually scouting some properties in the area..." He used his free hand to gesture toward a nearby pasture. "And I remembered your email. The signature had your store's address. I was nearby, so I thought I'd come and take a look. And to apologize in person. I'm afraid you got a not-wonderful first impression of me."

This unexpected admission softened Lexi even further, and any remaining traces of leftover frustration from their first meeting disappeared. He could've merely responded to her email, but instead, he had sought her out in person to apologize face-to-face. She hadn't known many men to be that humble—to admit a wrongdoing so freely and easily. Perhaps she had misjudged him.

"When you came into my classroom that day, I had just received an alarming text. One I hadn't expected. I was distracted and couldn't think straight. It's a poor excuse, but I don't think I even registered who you were until I read your email later in the day."

"It's okay. I've gotten a few alarming texts before." And she also understood what it was like to get off on the wrong foot with someone then hope desperately for a second chance. *Why not give him one?* "Did everything work out? With the text?"

His hesitation told her everything. "To be determined. I guess time will tell."

Suddenly, the pieces fit together, and she could pinpoint his accent after all. She wiggled her index finger between them as the lightbulb came on. "You're British, aren't you?"

"Good catch. The accent has faded over time."

"What part of the UK are you from?" Lexi was genuinely interested. England was a place she'd always wanted to see but had never gotten around to visiting.

"I grew up in a small Cotswold village then moved to the States when I was ten. Been here ever since. My mother was from Cornwall, and my father was born in Austin."

"So you've got a foot on both continents."

"More or less. But England will always feel like home. How about you? Native Texan?"

"Born and bred. Can't you tell by my twang?"

"Yours isn't nearly as strong as some I've heard. It's charming. Brits are as fascinated with Southern accents as most people are with British accents."

"I never knew that."

Graham shifted his weight and slipped his hand inside his jeans pocket. "Something else has actually brought me to your doorstep. Curiosity. Do you still have the necklace? The one you mentioned?"

"I do, and you're in luck. I actually brought it to work with me this morning." And thankfully, Ruby had been uncharacteristically slow in researching other appraisers and hadn't yet given Lexi the name of a single one. Perhaps it could work out with Graham after all. "In fact, I was headed into the shop when you walked up."

"Good timing, then. How long has the shop been yours?"

"It belonged to my great-grandmother, and then she willed it to me a few years ago. And this"—Lexi pointed behind her to the warehouse—"is my newest venture."

"Let's Get Crafty." Graham read the sign that had been delivered and mounted yesterday morning.

"There were two huge warehouses on the property when I inherited. I always wanted to do something with them but wasn't sure what." Feeling at ease, Lexi mentioned her future glassblowing plans for the second warehouse. "That's why I was on campus the other day, to visit the art department and do some research."

As she offered a few details, Graham listened intently—a complete turnaround from the man she'd originally met—no longer distracted by his phone or by anything else.

"Sounds impressive. And both your new ventures would pair very well with antiques."

"I hope so. Our grand opening is next week, so we'll see if the public agrees."

Graham walked beside her as they pivoted and made their way to Antiquated, twenty yards away. After he opened the door for her, they headed toward the front counter, where Ariel sat on a stool, filling plastic eggs with treats. She paused when she saw Lexi approach.

"Ariel, this is—"

"Professor Faulkner!" Before he could respond, Ariel went on. "I was one of your students. About four years ago. You won't remember me—it was one of those huge lecture classes with, like, a thousand students. I really enjoyed your class."

"Thanks."

Ruby approached from behind them, having finished answering a customer's question. After a quick side glance toward Lexi, she said, "Hello there. I'm Ruby Harper."

"Graham Faulkner."

"The history professor. Welcome."

Two customers carrying various items came near the front desk, and Ruby dutifully attended to them while Ariel returned to her plastic eggs.

"The necklace is through here," Lexi told Graham, stepping behind the counter.

When he spotted Bailey asleep on the cushion, Graham paused and squatted to scratch his head. "Beagle?"

"Yes. Bailey. He's our shop dog."

"Store mascot?"

"More or less."

"I had a beagle mix when I was a boy." He gently coaxed Bailey's chin higher. "He had the same sweet face. Soulful eyes." After a final pat, Graham stood up to follow Lexi into the break room.

"Can I get you a coffee or water?" she asked.

"No, thanks. I'm good."

As Lexi moved toward the cupboard that held her leather satchel, she heard the click of nails on the floor and craned her neck to see Bailey, coming to get a second look at their new guest.

"He never does this." Fascinated, she watched Bailey, his metronome tail waving, sit directly in front of Graham, craving more attention.

"Can you shake?" Graham asked. Bailey obliged, plopping his paw into Graham's open palm, and got a vigorous chest rub in return. "Good boy!"

Watching Graham with her dog—"One more? C'mon, boy, you can do it..."—Lexi realized she wasn't used to much male energy in the store. Sure, Darius and his brother would come and go with spotty deliveries, and the occasional husband or brother would reluctantly tag along with a female shopper, or perhaps her own father would stop by for a brief visit. But overall, the population of the store was mostly female-centric.

Bailey quickly tired of the tricks and made a circle on the floor then plopped onto Graham's shoe.

"You've made a friend."

"This is a great dog." Graham sat carefully on the couch, his shoe remaining respectfully underneath Bailey's chest.

"Thanks. The customers love him. Sometimes, people will stop by just to see him and then leave!"

"Local celebrity."

Lexi resumed her task and found the necklace's box deep inside her satchel. She held the velvety case between her palms and faced Graham. "The necklace actually belonged to my great-grandmother. Gigi, the one who owned this shop. I can't remember if I mentioned that."

"You didn't. I assumed it was a piece you'd acquired for the store."

Since Graham was forced to stay right where he was—Bailey's deep, contented sigh made it clear he wouldn't be removing himself from Graham's shoe anytime soon—Lexi joined him on the sofa.

"My mother owns Gigi's house and discovered this tucked away in the attic, inside a cardboard box that hadn't been opened for decades. We'd never seen it before." She cracked open the case and handed it over to Graham, who accepted it with respectful, delicate fingers.

"Teardrop style. And look at this filigree work. Beautiful. It's at least how many years old?"

"Possibly as many as eighty. Maybe fewer. We're not sure. No one remembers her ever wearing it. There's an inscription on the back."

Graham lifted the chain while Lexi lowered the case to her lap.

He gingerly twisted the teardrop around and laid it in his palm. "'Keeper of My Heart.' Romantic. Do you know who gave it to her?"

"My great-grandfather, we assume. He was her first love. Her only love. They were married forty-one years."

"Incredible." Graham brought the necklace closer and flipped it over to see the front once more. Lexi could see his "appraiser" wheels already spinning—likely thinking ahead to places he could seek some information, which online forums he could try, or the many possible jewelry stores he could research. As he uttered "Magnificent" with a barely discernable shake of his head, Lexi recognized his expression. It was the same one she always developed whenever she studied a new treasure that came into the store. A twinkle in the eye, a lift in the spirit. An excitement and acknowledgment that something special was in her presence, something old and beloved from generations past.

"May I take some photos?" Graham was already reaching for his phone.

"Of course. Do you need to take the necklace with you for research?"

"No need yet. The photos should be enough."

Graham nodded toward the table a few feet away. "That manila folder. Would you mind... I'm sort of stuck." He grinned at Bailey, who had readjusted himself on Graham's other shoe with his front paw.

She snickered as she stood and fetched the folder then returned to the seat beside him.

"Could you hold it here, like this?" He gently circled his fingers around her wrist and moved the folder into position.

"A backdrop?"

"Right. I'll get a cleaner photo that way."

She worked with him to drape the necklace in front of the folder so that the teardrop was the primary focus.

"Perfect." His British accent came through strong on that word, Lexi noticed. He took a couple of snaps with his phone then turned the necklace over to the inscription's side.

When he'd gotten the photos he wanted, Lexi lowered the folder and necklace to her lap.

"Look at this," Graham said, scrolling through his photos. He leaned closer toward Lexi and held the phone between them, zooming in with his thumb and finger.

"What is it?"

"'M. S.' It's stamped below the inscription."

"I didn't even notice that." She squinted, trying to see M. S. on the necklace itself, but it was barely visible. She ran her fingertip over the slight indentation. "What do you think it means?"

He studied the photo again. "Could be a manufacturer's stamp? Or maybe the initials of the jewelry store itself. It'll give me a starting point to go on. But try not to get your hopes too high. I'll do my best to date the piece, at least within a few years."

"That's all I can hope for. Honestly, no pressure if you hit a dead end. We plan to keep this piece in the family no matter what. I don't really care about the monetary value, but I'm eager to know the story behind it."

"If it's near eighty years old, that puts it into World War II territory, which is my specialty. I'm fascinated by that whole era. I've written a few articles about Holocaust survivors and Allied soldiers' experiences."

"Well, you're the perfect one to investigate. So, how will this work?"

"I'll start with some online research and probably contact a few jewelry stores in the area. Was your great-grandfather from Morgan's Grove?"

"Yes, born and raised. But the last jewelry store in our town closed a decade ago."

"Yeah, that's been happening with the popularity of online sales. We could try some Austin stores, and then—"

A tap at the door drew Graham's attention away and startled Bailey as well. Ruby stood in the doorway. "Sorry to bother y'all. Pam has a question for Lexi. About some inventory."

"I'd better let you go," Graham told Lexi. After they exchanged contact information, he said, "I'll let you know what I find out."

Ruby coaxed Bailey out the door while Lexi rose from the couch along with Graham. "That would be great." She returned the necklace to its case then slipped it back inside her satchel. "I'm glad you came by."

"You had given up on me, hadn't you? About the appraisal?"

Lexi shrugged.

"I can't blame you. I would've given up on me too."

"Well, I won't give up on you now. I have a hunch you're going to solve this mystery."

"I'll give it my best shot." He stepped aside to let Lexi out of the room first. "I think I'll take a look 'round your shop before I leave."

"Sure. Let Ruby know if you have any questions."

After Graham walked out from behind the counter and made his way toward the far corner, Ruby tugged at Lexi's sleeve. "Hey, he's a cutie!"

They watched together as Graham paused at an aisle to examine a stack of old books, pick one up, and carefully thumb through it. Lexi always cringed when certain customers—especially children—got ahold of antique books and rifled through them careless-ly, sometimes tearing pages. But Graham knew how to properly appreciate and handle them.

"Ruby! I don't think of employees that way," Lexi whispered, trying to sound as horrified as possible.

"He's not an employee, though, is he?"

They watched Graham set down the book and make his way into the heart of the store, near the candy display.

Lexi moved her focus to Ruby. "But he's going to appraise the necklace. He's working for me. Sort of."

"True, but this is a personal request. For you and your family, not for the store."

"Semantics. I ask him to do a job, he'll do it, then I'll pay him. It's still a business transaction."

"Did you ever think of Max as your employee?" Ruby asked.

That one stumped Lexi. She never saw him that way, not the way she did Ruby or Ariel or even Darius—all physically inside the store, working with her every day, nose to the grindstone. "Not really. More of an outside consultant."

"Precisely."

Lexi hated when Ruby was right. She let out a playful grunt then walked toward the exit in search of Pam.

"LIGHTLY SALTED AND heavily buttered. As requested." Lexi handed her cousin an oversized bowl filled with hot, fresh popcorn.

Lexi settled on the opposite side of the couch with her own popcorn bowl and searched for the remote, which she found sandwiched between the cushions. Bailey lay between Lexi and Jolene, snoring deeply.

Every Friday night, with the exception of a date or an emergency or an "I'm too tired" excuse, Jolene and Lexi hosted a movie night in each other's homes. Each week, one of them would select the movie (rom-coms for Jolene, suspense or documentary for Lexi), and the host would also provide the meal, usually an easy takeout. Tonight was Lexi's turn, and they'd just finished their gourmet pizza from Sam's, a new place on the outskirts of Austin.

"Tell me more about the professor." Jolene popped three pieces of popcorn into her mouth at once.

"I already told you everything." Lexi tucked the plush blanket around her bare ankles and stared at the hypnotic flames in the fireplace—chilly spring nights still warranted a cozy fire—knowing she would fall asleep before the first plot twist of the movie. It had been such a hectic, nonstop week.

"Well, sure. You showed me Gigi's beautiful necklace then told me about going to see him—Grant?"

"Graham."

"And then how he surprised you at the store today. But I want more details. I'm living vicariously through you." Three more pieces then a swig of Mr. Pibb. "The most exciting thing that happened at the mansion this week was that a bird flew in, causing panic and squeals from every female in the room."

"Seriously? How did you get it out?"

"I somehow remained calm while a nervous tourist crouched behind me. She wouldn't stop screeching in my ear! Then I told Colleen and Macy to open up all the doors, and we flipped the lights off and waited. I was about to call animal control for help, but the poor bird shot out through the front door. Big drama at the mansion."

"Sounds like." Lexi tried her popcorn and enjoyed the strong butter flavor.

"Anyway, back to the professor."

"So, I told you about our first meeting."

"Where he was a jerk, yep."

"Not really a jerk. Just... distracted. He barely knew I was in the room. Anyway, when he came to the store today, he apologized. And seemed sincere. He said that he'd gotten some sort of upsetting text that day—hence the distraction."

"I love the word 'hence.' I need to use it more. Okay, so that seems legit enough. A reasonable explanation. And he drove to your store to tell you this, when he could've just returned your email. So get to the good stuff. You said Ruby said he was cute. What did *you* think?"

Lexi rolled her eyes. "I admit—he *is* cute. But shorter than I'm used to, about five-eight or so."

"But you're only five-three!"

"Five-four."

"That's perfect. I hate it when guys are too tall and it becomes awkward fast. Remember John, in high school, our senior prom? He was like six-four, and you two tried dancing together—"

Lexi giggled into her open hand, picturing it. She had been highly embarrassed that night—for herself and for John. Her arms stretched up to try and clasp around his neck, but her forehead made it as high as his armpit. They'd laughed it off, quit the dance in the middle, and spent the rest of the prom at a table, talking.

"That was pretty awful," Lexi said.

"But five-eight is perfect for you."

"Jo, there's no 'for me' here. I barely know this guy."

"Time will tell. Continue. What was he wearing?" She grabbed another fistful of popcorn and waited impatiently.

Lexi wouldn't be able to start the movie until her cousin had had her complete fill of today's minutiae, so she indulged her. "Today, he was casual, dressed in a plaid shirt. With jeans." She pictured him again in her mind's eye, his mannerisms, his overall appearance, and tried to capture it in words. "He's got this boyish quality, even though I think we're close to the same age. He's at least early thirties. And his hair is sort of thick and rumpled. Oh, and he squints when he smiles."

"What color eyes?"

"Blue. I think. Anyway, he's... nice. I misjudged him at first. But I think he's got a good heart, good intentions. He seems to love old things the way I do. His eyes lit up when I showed him the necklace. And Ruby told me he browsed the store for quite a while after I left. He took his time. Ended up buying a couple of pieces."

"He sounds very compatible."

"Jo..."

"Hey, it's an observation. I'm allowed that, aren't I?" She lowered her popcorn bowl into her lap. "On a serious note—it makes perfect sense that you would hesitate when a possibility enters your sphere. That you'd keep your guard up. You've got trust issues. But don't let them keep you from something great."

"But what's weird is, it's not the guys. It's myself I don't trust... my own judgment to choose the right person. Neil had me fooled the whole time we were dating and even deep into the marriage. Three and a half years. I never thought he would be the type to cheat. Never. So how can I ever rely on my own instincts again?"

Jo didn't have a response—just nodded thoughtfully as she took a sip of her Pibb—so Lexi continued on, feeling a certain sweet release from saying things aloud she'd kept locked inside for too long. "And anyway, what's wrong with being single? Everyone seems to be in a rush to pair up. I'm tired of society shaming people who haven't found their 'person.' Honestly, there are some nice things about being alone. Room to think, room to be on your own and figure out what *you* want in life, without someone else looking over your shoulder or making judgments. Some people want so badly to have a partner, but they never ask themselves why. Is it to stop that uneasy feeling of being lonely? Or to erase the stigma of being partnerless? I don't think those are very good reasons to look for a man."

Jolene twisted the corner of her mouth as she looked past Lexi and toward the crackling fire. "I think people are scared—and maybe I'm scared too—to face things alone. Tough times or empty nights or even an empty house. Who knows. I wish I *could* be happier on my own, be in the moment and enjoy my own company. I like your advice. I'm just not that sure I can follow it."

Jo smirked and tossed a piece of popcorn into Lexi's lap, lightening the mood. Lexi reciprocated, which led to a gentle popcorn fight that woke Bailey briefly.

"Okay, cease fire. Let's start this movie, or we'll never finish." Lexi pushed play then plucked up the pieces of popcorn from her lap and placed them back in her bowl.

GRAHAM CROSSED OUT "1939" and scribbled "1941" above a student's response with his red pen. Marking essay tests on a Saturday afternoon wasn't his idea of fun, but he'd promised to pass them back to the students on Monday, and he prided himself on fulfilling commitments. Even to students who were probably slacking off this very minute, pushing aside their essays—due Monday, in fact—and getting ready for a night of indulging in Austin's infamous Sixth Street college-age activities, which included live music, clubbing, drinking, and general shenanigans.

He remembered those days as a student, so he couldn't exactly judge them for the same irresponsible youthful behavior. Abandoning his red pen, Graham stretched his arms over his head then reached for his phone, which he'd kept on silent to focus on grading. Still nothing from Theresa, but today was the first day he'd been okay with that. In fact, this morning, he had deleted her photo from the home page of his laptop, tablet, and phone, replacing it with a generic Hawaiian sunset.

Intending to return to the stack of tests within the hour, Graham moved them aside and shifted to his laptop. He'd already done some sparse research on Lexi's necklace yesterday, after his visit to Morgan's Grove. He was eager to get started and already had a few ideas in mind—contacting appraiser forums, researching the filigree pattern online, and doing a quick search for "M. S. Jewelers," or anything close to that. But nothing came up. He could always have any jeweler give him a general appraisal of the necklace, but Graham wanted to go deeper, even this soon. His current goal was to locate the original shop where the piece was purchased, in order to glean information about the necklace that he couldn't possibly find anywhere else. A tall order but worth trying.

He clicked on the local Austin forum he had scoured yesterday and saw five new replies to his inquiry, each listing possible "M. S." responses. He hadn't expected answers so quickly. This sort of research sometimes took weeks or even months—or longer—and with no guarantee of getting to the bottom of anything. Still, his hopes were unreasonably high. He could see the anticipation in Lexi's eyes when she opened the necklace's case. Perhaps one of these suggestions would at least put him on the right path.

A new text popped up from his dad, asking if he'd be free for lunch tomorrow with Beth, his father's newish girlfriend. Graham had met her once before and frankly didn't have an opinion about her one way or the other. She seemed cordial enough and was at least in his father's age range, unlike the last girlfriend. Graham could sense that his dad craved his approval of Beth, but he couldn't muster it. Plus Graham never enjoyed these kinds of meals—family obligations filled with empty chitchat and social banter. But his father was relentless and would surely ask him again next week if he said no. Why put off the inevitable?

Sure, sounds great, he typed in before returning to his research.

Chapter Four

"Lexi, come and see your surprise! It finally arrived!" Ruby called. She'd asked Ariel to help her open the mystery package that had been delivered to the store a moment before. The box was flat and at least three feet long.

Lexi stood near the front counter, watching the two of them struggle with the endless bubble wrap that emerged from the box. There was a brief lull with customers at the moment, so the three of them could pay full attention to the unveiling.

As Ariel unraveled the last of the bubble wrap, a flash of silver emerged. Ruby held the object upright with a bright "ta-dah!" motion.

"Scissors?" Lexi's face scrunched up as she struggled to understand. "Giant scissors."

"For the grand opening, your big day!" Ruby said. "Ariel bought the ribbon, and I ordered the oversized scissors. We can practice first, to make sure it'll cut the ribbon clean through."

Lexi beamed as she put both hands over her heart. "This is amazing. I can't believe y'all did this without me knowing."

"Maybe it's corny, but this is a special day," Ariel said. "It should *feel* special enough to match."

"Not corny at all. I love it. Thank you both." Lexi rounded the counter so she could give them individual hugs.

"I'll store it back here until the big day." Ruby carried off the scissors and box while Lexi helped Ariel discard the bubble wrap.

The bell above the front door jangled, and Lexi prepared her welcome-the-customer face, bright and relaxed. But instead of a customer, she saw her dad walk in with a basket on his arm.

"I wasn't expecting you!" She let Ariel finish the job and joined him around the counter, leaning up on her tiptoes to kiss his bearded cheek.

"I made some fresh paninis for lunch. With how busy you've been lately, I assumed you had a wilted salad sitting in the fridge that you'd forget to eat."

"You know me too well."

"I brought enough for Ruby and Ariel too."

"Do I smell food?" Ruby emerged from the back with a grin.

"Your radar is always impeccable." Lexi chuckled then asked her father, "Can you join us?"

"I need to go check on the restaurants, so I can't stay. And I've already eaten." He handed over the basket to Lexi, who could smell the delectable mixture of smoked meats, melted cheeses, and yeasty toasted bread.

"You're the best, Daddy. Thanks for looking out for me."

"This is an important week, with the grand opening. Your mother and I will be there with bells on. Can't wait." He squeezed Lexi in a side hug and kissed the top of her head before turning to leave. "Bye, honey."

"Thanks, Mr. Price," Ariel and Ruby said in unison.

Lexi reached inside the basket for a warm sandwich and a paper plate. "Y'all go ahead and take your break," she told Ruby and Ariel. "I'll mind the store."

"Okay, but holler if you need us," Ruby said, accepting the basket.

Even the commotion of the scissors and her dad's delivery couldn't rouse more than a disinterested grunt from Bailey, who shifted in his pillow and went back to sleep.

With no customers around, Lexi felt safe enough to dive in and take her first bite of the panini. But the moment she did, her phone rang on the counter. "Perfect," she muttered through her mouthful. Chewing quickly, she glanced at the screen.

She swallowed hard then answered. "Hey, Graham."

"Have I caught you at a bad time?"

"Not at all," Lexi lied, sliding her plate aside for the moment. "Thanks for the updates you sent me yesterday." Graham had texted screenshots of the responses he'd received about the necklace from some online forums.

"Sure. I've got class in a few minutes, but after that, I'm free for the day. I was planning to visit three jewelry stores that might be connected to 'M. S.,' and I was wondering... Do you want to come along? Maybe even bring the necklace? The photos don't do it justice."

"Today?"

That was the last thing Lexi had expected from Graham—an invitation to help him in his quest. Max was always a lone worker, offering her major updates and insights *after* his research was mostly complete. And he would certainly never have asked her to join him on site.

Still, it made sense to have the jewelry stores see the necklace for themselves. It might make all the difference.

"I know it's short notice," Graham said.

Lexi thought ahead to the rest of her afternoon. She didn't have time to spare—the grand opening was days away, and there was still much to do. But she did have a couple of errands to run in the Austin area. Ruby and Ariel could easily watch the store, and Lexi could always field calls or answer texts and emails on the go. No reason to stop working entirely.

"Sure, I'd like to come."

"The stores are a few miles apart, near campus. It shouldn't take us long. How about meeting me here, at my office? We could drive together rather than you following me from store to store."

His suggestions all sounded reasonable, so Lexi agreed to meet him at two o'clock, remembering that she would need to pop by her house to retrieve the necklace. When they clicked off the call, Lexi returned to her panini, which was still warm and gooey-delicious.

LEXI'S VISIT TO THE campus was decidedly less hurried—and less sopping wet—than last week's. Every flower was in full bloom, and Lexi took her time walking to Graham's building as she inhaled the generous mixture of floral scents. She didn't know much about gardening or the names of flowers, but her senses could appreciate their beauty—bright yellows, dark purples, soft blues. A mocking-bird sang nearby, and two squirrels chased each other around the trunk of a tree, chattering as they circled higher and higher. Lexi's teal skirt fluttered against her bare legs as a warm breeze approached. During rare quiet moments, she wished she could slow down her life without listening to her inner "work" voice, the one that was always glancing two steps ahead, always planning, always making lists to en-sure that everything was accomplished. A juggler with balls in the air, she had to be certain none of them could possibly fall.

The squirrels had ceased their bickering and cautiously ambled down the trunk to search for acorns in the grass. One of them, a few feet away, sat upright and peered straight at Lexi. She slowed to a stop and took out her phone to capture the moment—the squir-rel posed long enough for her to grab the shot then scurried up the tree once more. She looked at the photo and made it her new home screen, a reminder that taking a break was equally as important as working hard.

Inside Graham's building, she found his office from memory and heard voices drifting from it. She paused outside his cracked-open door and pressed her back against the wall, scrolling through her messages to see if any were important enough to read. She couldn't help but listen to what Graham was telling his student.

His voice lifted with enthusiasm. "Yeah, Nancy Wake is a great choice. She had this depth of courage most people don't have. She felt a strong duty to take on the Nazis, at huge risk to her own life, time and time again. It's an incredible story that hasn't been noticed until recently." After a pause, Lexi could hear him say, "Here's her biography. I read it last year. You're welcome to borrow it for your essay."

"Thanks!" the student said.

Lexi doubted many other professors would lend books from their personal library to their students—knowing good and well that the books would probably never be returned.

The student exited the office, paused to find a place for the book inside her bag, then went on her way. Lexi tapped on the doorframe before peeking around at Graham, who had just closed his laptop and scooped up his keys.

"I was about to text you. Sorry I'm running a bit late. A student dropped by..."

"It's fine. I was enjoying my walk, taking a bit of a break. It's so beautiful on campus this time of year." Lexi stepped inside the office.

"It is. I forget sometimes to look up from my grading long enough to enjoy the scenery."

"I know the feeling." She scanned the small space—a desk with a laptop and a smattering of papers, an empty coffeepot in the corner of the room, and one narrow window flanked by two enormous floor-to-ceiling sets of shelves packed with books of all sizes and bindings. She wondered if the shelves were the university's or if Graham had added them himself. She suspected the latter. "I was eavesdropping a bit," she said. "Your door was open. Sounds like a fascinating assignment."

"I'm hoping so." He leaned against the edge of the desk. "It's hard to keep the students interested in the details of a war that happened decades ago. Most of them know so little about it, and no textbook could ever do it justice. I'm always trying to find new ways to reach the students—media, documentaries, interviews—to make the stories come alive for them. This is a new paper, my first time assigning it. The students have to explore a little-known hero and write a paper about that person—anyone who displayed bravery against the Nazis or risked their life to help save someone else."

"My eighteen-year-old self would have loved this assignment. I've never heard of Nancy Wake until today."

"There are thousands of stories like hers that have disappeared over time. She was this incredible heroine who was trained in the UK as a female spy then formed a ragtag army of French Resistance fighters in the forests of—" He bowed his head. "Sorry, I'm in teacher mode, giving you a lecture."

"I didn't take it that way. You've made me want to read about her too. Your enthusiasm is infectious."

"Well, I hope the students feel that way." Graham shifted his keys to his other hand. "Ready for our own historical exploration?"

"I've got the necklace with me. Lead the way."

She watched him lock the office door, then they walked together out of the building and into the glorious sunshine.

"Faculty parking," he said as they walked past another building. "It's closer than some of the other lots, but it's still a bit of a trek."

"I don't mind." To fill the time, she asked, "How long have you been teaching?"

"I'm at the end of my seventh year."

"Did you always know you wanted to teach?" These were safe, commonplace questions to lob at someone she didn't know very well, but Lexi was genuinely interested. She always liked knowing how someone had discovered their passion in life.

"Not until university. I had to answer that age-old question, 'What can you do with a fine arts degree?' Teaching was the most logical choice. But I've always been curious about the subject of history." Graham's arm brushed lightly against her elbow as they slowed to an easy stroll, passing a couple of giggling students, caught up in their own youthful world. "I think it started with my mum. She was fascinated by history and human nature—why things happened, why people made the decisions they made, and how it affected future generations. She was always asking questions. And she would watch documentaries, read books. I guess I absorbed it by osmosis."

"She must be proud of you, becoming a professor."

Graham nodded. "She was. She passed away several years ago."

"Oh, I'm sorry."

To fill the brief gap in conversation that followed, and also to move outside the realm of conjuring sad memories for Graham, Lexi asked another, less personal question. "You mentioned World War II as your specialty. Why that war above all the others?"

He pondered before responding then half turned toward her as he walked. "The easiest answer is that my great uncle and great-grandfathers all fought in the war, which makes me personally interested. But beyond that, I guess the paradoxes fascinate me. On one hand, there's this unthinkable brutality going on—the SS, the concentration camps, the millions of innocent lives lost. And on the other hand, there's this amazing heroism happening at the very same time. Ordinary people doing extraordinary things. I read these stories and wonder, 'Would *I* be able to do that, under those circumstances? Risk my life for strangers and hide them in my attic? Or drop everything to become a spy in an occupied territory? Or lie about my age to join the military at sixteen and jump out of a plane?'"

By now, they had reached the faculty parking lot.

Graham stopped at what Lexi assumed was his car, a white Honda, and swiveled toward her. "I think most historians love the battles—the strategies and military operations and casualty numbers. But I'm more interested in the deeper human aspects of the war. There are thousands of stories that will likely never be told. The Greatest Generation has practically died out."

"You should write your own book about the war. From the human angle. It would open up history for people who thought it was boring. Because nothing you've just said was boring at all."

He opened the Honda's passenger side for Lexi and propped his elbow on top of the door. "It's weird that you say that... I've actually been tossing that idea around lately. For a new book—a historical fiction of some kind. I've even scratched out some notes for topics." He gave a one-sided grin. "I haven't told anyone that. Not even my dad or my colleagues."

"I promise to keep your secret." Lexi matched his grin and started to slip into the passenger seat but stopped short when she saw a thick, well-worn copy of *Band of Brothers*, a book Lexi had always meant to read but never had. She leaned inside then handed him the book.

He gripped it tight. "Guess I'm a walking cliché. A history teacher obsessed with history. Even in my spare time."

"Well, then I'm a cliché too. I browse antiques stores for the fun of it. And I've always got my eye out for new treasures for the store." Lexi paused before slipping into the seat, holding the top of the car door, her fingers accidentally grazing his. "But I guess that means we love our work. What's wrong with that?"

Graham gave a nod. "Nothing at all."

"I'M SORRY I COULDN'T be more help." The store owner winced as he slid Lexi's necklace case across the countertop. It had been the second jewelry store on Graham's list—and the second strikeout.

Minutes ago, the man had peered through his handheld magnifier to examine the teardrop, commenting on the "exquisite" engraving and the "intricate" filigree. He admitted he wasn't a qualified appraiser so refused even to guess at the age or current value of the diamond. But he did confirm one important thing—the necklace wasn't a piece that originally came from that store. They didn't stamp their jewelry and never had.

"Thanks for your time," Graham told him.

Lexi couldn't let Graham see her disappointment, especially since on the way to visit the second shop, he'd told her about the enormous amount of research he'd done in the past few days, calling up dozens of jewelry stores with possible ties to "M. S." to see if any of them were eighty-plus years old. There were three—the ones they were visiting today—including Miller & Sons, the last on their short list.

As Graham started the ignition, his stomach growled loudly enough for Lexi to hear. She found her seat belt and laughed while Graham gave a sheepish "Sorry. I didn't have time to eat today."

"You should've told me! I would've brought you one of my father's scrumptious paninis. We had some left over." Seeing his confusion, she explained. "My dad is a chef—well, semiretired. He runs three restaurants in Austin."

"Impressive."

"Yeah, I've been pretty spoiled my whole life. Today, he dropped by the store, a total surprise, and handed me these homemade paninis—Italian sandwiches."

Graham placed his hand behind Lexi's seat as he eased out of his parking space.

Lexi saw the time on the clock's dashboard. "Listen, I'm in no hurry. Why don't you grab something to eat? You can't go exploring on an empty stomach."

"You sure? I know how busy this week must be for you, with your grand opening."

"I have time. Really. We could even go inside, sit somewhere." She assumed that, like herself, Graham spent most of his meals working—hunched over his laptop or grading papers, grabbing a quick bite here and there of whatever would cost him the least amount of time. "In fact, it's on me. I insist. You've spent a lot of time on this necklace. I want to thank you for it."

Graham contemplated this then finally said, "Only if you're sure."

"Totally sure."

"There's a bistro a couple of blocks away. It's got soups and sandwiches, with this amazing gourmet grilled cheese. But you've already eaten..."

"That's okay. I'll have some dessert."

"Well, this place is best known for its Krispy Kreme bread pudding. Melts in your mouth."

"Now you're making *my* stomach growl. Let's go!"

LEXI LIFTED A FORKFUL of salad to her lips and took a bite—crisp, cold iceberg lettuce, with the perfect proportion of cheese to dressing. She had ordered a side salad so that Graham wouldn't be eating alone.

"This place reminds me of Christine's," she said.

He had already made his way through half of his grilled cheese sandwich and was reaching for a thick-cut, homemade steak fry.

"In Morgan's Grove?"

"Yep. Same type of menu items, same European vibe." She examined the wood beams on the ceiling, the exposed-brick wall behind Graham, and the flames crackling in the corner fireplace.

"I come here and grade sometimes. It's quiet." Graham dabbed his mouth with a napkin. "I wonder if all small towns have the same qualities. The English village where I grew up feels similar to Morgan's Grove. Gentle, charming, even a bit quirky."

"It sounds like you miss it... living in a small town."

"I do. I miss the sense of community. Some days, living in the heart of Austin is a struggle—the traffic, the busyness of it, the noise. I prefer a slower pace."

Graham's phone buzzed on the table, and he seemed to ponder whether it was rude to check it.

"Please, go ahead," Lexi said, taking another bite of salad.

He flipped the phone over to view the screen. "Hmm. Wow." He paused then texted a brief reply.

"Wow-good or wow-bad?"

"Well, it's good for someone. It's from my dad. He's apparently gotten engaged. This is the first I've heard of it." Graham angled the screen so Lexi could see the zoomed-in photo of a woman's hand displaying a sparkling diamond. *She said yes!* was the text beneath.

"Pretty ring," Lexi said.

Graham set the phone back down beside his plate and carried on with his sandwich. After swallowing a bite, he said, "Beth's nice enough, I guess. My father's been dating her for about two months. They met online."

Unsure of how to respond based on Graham's mixed reaction, Lexi took the safest way out and acknowledged him with a hum as she took another bite of salad.

"So I guess that's the second alarming text I've had in your presence." Graham chuckled.

"I hope I'm not bad luck," Lexi said with a lilt in her voice, trying to lighten the mood.

"Naw, it's a coincidence. And this one's not really alarming. More like... surprising. The other text was harder to take." He made eye contact and said, "My girlfriend had just broken things off. Theresa. That was the text I was reading when you came into the classroom that day. I had opened it up right after class."

"She texted you to break up?" Lexi cringed. "That's heartless."

"Yeah. I was trying to process everything when you were walking in. She texted me a couple days later to make sure I got the message—that she wanted to see other people. We haven't spoken since."

The server appeared at the table, sparing Lexi an awkward reply to Graham—how could she respond without sounding too patronizing or poor-you?—and took up their empty plates before setting a bowl of bread pudding down in front of her and then another in front of Graham.

"Anyway, it's all good, as they say. I've had a bit of time to reflect, and I realize now that Theresa had been pulling away for a while, but I hadn't recognized the signs. I've decided to lick my wounds and move on."

"How long were y'all together?"

"Less than a year. We both have busy careers, so maybe that's what contributed to things ending. Who knows."

Lexi could relate to having odd, unsatisfactory breakups—she'd dated a couple of guys since her divorce, but neither of them had worked out for very long, ending awkwardly. Even if Graham could've gotten a straight answer from Theresa about the reasons, would it have made the impact of the cruel breakup text any softer? Likely not.

"So, let's talk about something else over dessert," Graham said. "I want to hear more about your shop, your love for antiques. Did it begin with your great-grandmother?"

"It did." Lexi took her first bite of Krispy Kreme bread pudding then put a hand up to her mouth, still chewing. "Oh... this is insane!"

"Told you."

After swallowing her bite, she said, "No, you don't understand. I have a real weak spot for donuts. My favorite dessert in the world." She attempted to steer her focus back to the conversation. "Anyway, yeah, I was super close to Gigi, especially as a little girl. Since both my parents worked, I would spend whole days with her in the summer months at the store. I helped her with inventory, dusted the furniture, greeted customers." She stole another quick bite of bread pudding as she pondered the rest of her response. "I definitely inherited her love of antiques. They have this quality... this living history. Here and now. They're tangible, right in front of you, not hidden away in some dusty old textbook. No offense."

"Zero taken." Graham was nearly finished with his bread pudding.

"I can see the history, touch it for myself—silverware used by a family for a hundred years or vintage clothing someone wore in the 1920s."

"Or a teardrop necklace, given during wartime."

"Speaking of..." Lexi took her final bite and dabbed her mouth with her napkin, knowing she would have to walk Bailey an extra time or two around the block this evening to counteract her naughty indulgence. "I'm ready to try this final jewelry store. I have a good feeling about it."

MILLER & SONS WAS LOCATED in an unassuming pocket of downtown Austin, "a real hole in the wall," Lexi thought. Graham had found accessible parking a half block over, then he and Lexi walked into the jewelry store to find it empty of customers. Lexi scanned the space and noticed the usual enclosed glass cases filled with rings and bracelets, watches and necklaces. Biding her time, she moved to one of the cases and saw a collection of brooches and mused over whether the pieces were original to the store. Some older jewelers surely handcrafted their pieces in-house.

Soon, a man around Ruby's age emerged through the back room's curtain. He seemed surprised to see any customers.

"Oh. Hello there." He wore a thick gray moustache and had squinty blue eyes behind thick glasses, which he adjusted higher on his nose. "How may I help you?"

Graham stepped forward, closer to the glass case that stood between them. "I'm Graham Faulkner. I spoke with you on the phone yesterday, about a necklace."

On cue, and for the third time that afternoon, Lexi pulled the velvet case from her bag.

"Oh yes, I remember," the man said. "We spoke about a teardrop? I'm Henry Miller."

"I'm Lexi, the owner of the teardrop." She stepped forward beside Graham. "So, this is your family's business?"

"It is, indeed. Three generations, first opened in 1932. We handcraft many of our pieces, here on site. Each generation trained by the one before."

"How wonderful. I run a family business too—my great-grandmother's antiques store in Morgan's Grove. In fact, the teardrop belonged to her." Lexi opened the lid and slid the case across the countertop. "We're hoping to get it appraised. I'm sure my great-grandfather gave Gigi the necklace, and they first met after the war, so I'm assuming it was the mid to late 1940s. But I would love to have it confirmed."

Henry leaned forward and examined the piece. He lifted the necklace from its case with experienced fingers then turned the teardrop over and grinned through his thick moustache. "This is one of ours."

"'Ours,' as in, your store crafted it?" Lexi felt a hopeful excitement thrum through her body.

Henry tapped his index finger on the inscription's side. "That's right. 'M. S.' Miller & Sons. We stamp it on every original piece."

Thrilled, Lexi shared an eager look with Graham.

"We need any information you can give us about this one," Graham said.

"Anything at all would be helpful." Lexi tried to temper her expectations. "I'd like an appraisal. I'll pay."

"Surely," Henry said. "But I won't take your money. I offer free appraisals. I can also access the ledgers. My grandfather kept meticulous records. It might take some time."

"We can wait." Lexi confirmed this with a nod from Graham.

She hoped he felt as she did—that any possible plans for the day could easily be suspended for this remarkable new development. *Ledgers? The original jewelry shop? With a third-generation store owner offering research?* They had struck gold.

"All right then, I'll get started," Henry said. "I'll take the necklace along with me."

Lexi stared up at Graham with wide eyes as Henry disappeared once more. "I can't believe our luck," she whispered, nearly breathless. She realized she had grasped his sleeve when she said it and quickly let go.

Graham replied with an amused smile. "Me either. It's the best possible outcome."

"I wonder what 'a while' means."

"Hopefully not too long. Let's stay busy. I've got some emails to respond to."

"Good idea. And I'll check my messages."

Graham gestured toward the two-seater table near the front window, and Lexi joined him there as they brought out their phones.

It took Lexi four minutes to return a couple of unimportant texts before the anxiety of waiting bubbled up again. "I'm antsy. I'll go look around," she told Graham, who kept his eyes on his screen but nodded.

As she browsed the jewelry store, she marveled at the wide-ranging selection. She imagined decades' worth of customers going to the trouble and expense of designing an original piece for a loved one—adding inscriptions, choosing stones and settings and precious metals, hoping to get it just right. Lexi pictured a nervous man praying his girlfriend would say "yes" to his designer engagement ring or a mother anticipating the expression on her sixteen-year-old daughter's face for the one-of-a-kind tennis bracelet she would receive or an older man commissioning a diamond-encrusted watch for his bride's fiftieth wedding anniversary—all heirlooms now, handed down generation to generation. She hoped Henry fully appreciated the enormous legacy of his grandfather's store and his own part in it.

Nearly an hour after he'd left, Henry emerged from the back holding five dark-green leather-bound books. "I have good news and bad news."

Graham swiftly joined Lexi at the glass counter to hear more.

"Good news first, please," Lexi said.

Henry set down the ledgers and rubbed his wrists. The necklace was laced around the fingers of his right hand. He handed the teardrop over to Lexi. "I can place the necklace's origins, based on the diamond and setting, within the 1940s. It's a European-cut diamond, which was popular up to the early forties, and I suspect the use of sterling silver was due to the shortage of minerals during the war. And that filigree setting would've been uncommon—quite expensive in light of rationing. I'd say the piece's current value is around six thousand dollars. Also, I found the ledgers that should hold details about the necklace's commission and design."

"That's fantastic news," Graham said. "And the bad?"

"Well, it could take quite a bit of time to *find* those records, since we're dealing with a decade's worth of potential orders. Here are the first five ledgers, 1940 to 1944." He stopped and scratched his head. "Oh—but you'd said your great-grandparents didn't even meet until after the war?"

"That's right. And married a couple of years later."

"Well, I'll go dig out the other years, then."

He started to scoop up the ledgers he'd already laid down, but Graham set his hand on top of them. "Actually, I'd like to browse through these if you don't mind? I'm a history professor and would love to scan these records."

"Sure, have at it. I'll go get the other ledgers. It would go faster if the two of you helped out, looking through them. If you're up for it."

"Are you kidding?" Lexi couldn't contain her excitement. She was about to lay eyes on an eighty-year-old ledger that held details about a loving gift commissioned by her great-grandfather, whom she never knew. "We're up for it." As though proving her point, Graham was already cracking open the 1940 ledger and seemed not to hear her.

"You're welcome to stay where you are or have a seat, whatever's more comfortable. Would you like a coffee? Or soda?" Henry asked.

At the risk of spilling a beverage on these precious documents, Lexi politely refused. Graham was too preoccupied to respond—he'd already made it through the first few pages of the 1940 ledger. "Amazing," he whispered, running his index finger down the length of a page.

"We don't want to take up too much of your time." Lexi didn't intend for their investigation to upend someone else's whole afternoon.

"No possibility of that," Henry said. "As you can see, we don't get much business at this hour. Fact is, I'll probably be retiring next year. Closing her up for good."

"Oh, I hate to hear it," Lexi said and meant it. Any family business's closing became a personal loss to her. "Nobody can carry on the shop for you?"

"Nope. I'm a widower, ten years. My son and daughter are both married, living in different states. No interest in running this place." He gave a casual shrug that Lexi didn't buy. "It's time to let it go."

As Henry disappeared again to locate the other ledgers, Lexi leaned in closer to Graham and watched him flip to another page. "Look." He pointed. "Every entry has the same details: date, method of payment, name of the commissioner..."

"And this one is illustrated," Lexi said.

"The notes about each design are scrawled here, probably told to the jeweler on the initial visit."

"'Cross pendant,'" Lexi read from the page Graham held open. "'With three rubies down the length of the cross.'"

"And a rendering of it." Graham pointed to the pencil sketch, faded with age, at the bottom of the page.

Lexi could hardly wait to view the other ledgers. To pass the time, she took up the 1941 book and sifted through entries of pearl rings, diamond necklaces, gold watches, and silver bracelets.

She had been moving rather casually through the ledger when her eyes stopped dead on the next page. She recognized the drawing instantly—a clear sketch of the teardrop shape, with a diamond in the center.

"Graham!" she whispered. "Look!"

Her gaze moved to the bottom of the page, where she saw a second drawing—the back side of the teardrop and, below it, the inscription.

"'Keeper of My Heart,'" Graham whispered near her ear.

Lexi moved her index finger up to the top again. "October 4, 1941." Her eyes met Graham's, inches away. "I don't understand."

"Here we go!" Henry pushed through the back door's curtain with another stack of ledgers. As he placed them down on the glass counter, he paused. "What's wrong?"

"This can't be right." Lexi swiveled the ledger around so that Henry could see. "There must be some mistake."

Henry looked through his glasses then beamed. "That's your necklace!"

"Yes, but look at the date. 1941. My great-grandparents hadn't even met yet." She slid the ledger back around to her side and read the details aloud: "October 4th, 1941. Paid by check." Lexi paused on the next line and stared at the name. "James C. Fisher. Who is that? My great-grandfather's name was Peter Monroe."

"Well, that's odd." Henry scratched his cheek then walked around the counter to stand beside Lexi. He peered down at the ledger, ran his finger down the side to the sketch of the necklace, then studied the inscription once more. "Same necklace," he said. "No doubt about that."

Lexi frowned at the name again. *James.* "Could there be some mix-up?"

Henry examined the front of the ledger again. "This date is accurate. 1941."

"What about copies?" Lexi asked. "Like, maybe my great-grandfather came along a few years later and browsed through these sketches and wanted this exact same piece for my great-grandmother. He could've commissioned one identical to it, right?"

"With the exact same inscription?" Graham asked.

Unlikely, Lexi knew. But the only other alternative was to believe that someone else, *other* than her great-grandfather, had given Gigi the necklace. A necklace she never wore and never told anyone about. One that was found tucked away in a box in a dark attic decades later...

"That's always possible. But my grandfather kept meticulous track of the one-of-a-kind pieces, knowing their value would be higher. They were always marked as such, with a checkmark at the bottom corner. See?"

Lexi followed his fingertip down to the page's corner and saw it there. The checkmark.

"And if someone else had come along later and asked for an exact duplicate, he would've marked through the checkmark to show that it was no longer unique. This piece is one of a kind."

"It doesn't make any sense," Lexi whispered.

"Are you sure about those dates? When your great-grandparents met each other?" Graham asked.

"Well, I thought I was sure. But maybe I've gotten them wrong. My mother would know." She turned to Henry. "May I take a photo of this page?"

"Of course. In fact, I'll do better than that. I'll make a photocopy for you. I've got a machine in the back. And if it'll help out, I'll be glad to pore over those other ledgers for ya tonight—the '45 through '49 pages—to set your mind at ease about that copy theory of yours. Got nothing better to do."

Somehow, through her daze, Lexi responded. "Thank you so much. I'd be grateful."

Henry moved to the other side of the counter and gathered up the ledgers once more.

"I don't get it," Lexi muttered, the wheels in her mind turning fast. "I've always been told that my great-grandfather was Gigi's first love. Her only love." She studied Graham's face. "But maybe that wasn't true."

Sometimes, these old antiques will give up their secrets if you're willing to listen...

What if Gigi had been talking about her own secrets?

Chapter Five

"Daddy? Mother? Anyone here?"

Lexi breezed through her parents' house after using her key to let herself in. She could try the second story, but on a beautiful spring day, she would most likely find her mother in the garden. Lexi peered out the French doors' windows into the backyard, where her mother knelt, busy at work with her pruning scissors.

Lexi opened the door to a gentle breeze then walked onto the lush grass. The entire garden resembled a painting—pristine and welcoming, just like her mother's style inside the home, with every cushion in place, carpets vacuumed twice weekly, piano tuned every six months. At any moment, a photographer from *House Beautiful* could've entered the home and taken immaculate shots from any angle.

The same could rarely be said of Lexi's house, which at this very moment was the torrential result of her hasty activities from this morning when she'd struggled to get to work on time: the contents of her purse that spilled onto the sofa when she'd tried to locate her missing keys, the two pairs of shoes she'd tested then discarded in favor of the ones she currently wore, and the pile of dishes in the sink from the past three days of neglecting them. Her mother would've been equally horrified to see Lexi's unkempt backyard, filled with growing weeds and patches of dry grass—which was why she never let her mother see the backyard. When her parents came for visits, Lexi always made an excuse to keep them indoors.

Whenever Lexi chided herself about her own minor domestic transgressions, she remembered her legitimate excuse: a dizzying work schedule that meant she rarely spent any time inside her own home—as opposed to her mother, who had been retired from interior design for the past five years.

"Oh, hello." Her mother looked up as she pushed away a lock of hair with the back of her glove. "I didn't hear you."

"Those are pretty." Lexi pointed to the pink-and-white cluster of flowers her mother had been pruning. "Rhododendrons?" She took a wild guess.

"Camellias," her mother said. "They're thriving in this mild weather." She peeled off her gloves one at a time then stood to face Lexi. "You look a bit frazzled."

Lexi assumed that was a gentler word for "haggard" or "disheveled," but either of those terms would probably be accurate as well.

"It's been a long day."

"Well, I made some tea earlier. Want to join me?"

"Sure." Lexi followed her mother back through the French doors, noting what a particularly good mood she was in. But then, her mother was always in a good mood after gardening, her favorite activity in the world.

The truth was, Lexi didn't have time for tea. She had come straight from her Austin outing at the jewelry store, which had taken more time than she'd planned, leaving her with an even lengthier to-do list ahead for the evening. But the necklace had moved to the forefront of her mind, and she couldn't work—or rest—until she obtained answers to some pressing questions.

All the way to Morgan's Grove, Lexi had sorted through any possible scenario where her great-grandfather hadn't actually given that beautiful love token to her great-grandmother. And none of them fit. She had to go directly to the source.

"Sweet or unsweet?" her mother asked as Lexi settled into a chair at the table. "I made both." The breakfast nook was a sunny, airy room where hundreds of family meals had taken place over the decades. Lexi's favorite room of the house.

"Sweet, please." She accepted the glass from her mother then clinked the ice cubes together with a swirl of her wrist.

"Is something wrong?" Her mother sat across from her with her own glass. "I wasn't expecting to see you today."

"It's Gigi's necklace. The teardrop. I've come from the jeweler's where it was designed and purchased."

Her mother's eyes grew wider. "I didn't know your research had gotten that far. What did you find out?"

Lexi told her all about Henry, the necklace's appraisal, and the carefully detailed ledgers he'd produced. Then, she pulled Henry's folded photocopy from her bag and pushed it toward her mother. "Do you recognize the name at the bottom?"

Her mother focused on the paper then pursed her lips. "James Fisher. Not a clue. Who is it?"

"The man who bought the necklace. For Gigi."

Lexi met her mother's gaze across the table, knowing it was the very same expression she'd had on her own face when she had connected the dots for the first time.

"But this can't be right." Her mother stared at the paper again. "October the fourth..."

"1941. The date the necklace was first commissioned. I thought you'd said that Gigi first met Paw-Paw after the war ended. Did I get it wrong?"

Her mother frowned in memory. "No, you're correct. They were married in 1947. They met during one of the last USO parties given in Morgan's Grove—which would've been in 1945 or '46. That's what Gigi always told me. You might verify it with your cousin. Jolene should have access to all the history about the USO functions, since they took place in the founder's mansion."

"That's a good idea. I'll text her. Maybe she can look to see if this James Fisher person attended them too."

"What if there's another explanation? Perhaps your great-grandfather did commission this necklace, but a few years after 1941?"

"That was my first thought. But Henry said that his grandfather kept meticulous records back then. He swore by their accuracy, said that this was the only piece issued. It was one of a kind. He promised to look through the other ledgers tonight—I'm anticipating a text from him. But truthfully, it's looking more and more like someone else gave Gigi the necklace. Did she love another man before Paw-Paw?"

Her mother folded the photocopy and slid it back toward Lexi. "Not that I'm aware of. Certainly no one she ever mentioned. I suppose it's possible."

Lexi smoothed out a folded corner of the paper with her thumbnail. "It's so confusing. I had to come here and ask you first. Were there any other clues in the attic? Other boxes you and Daddy didn't sort through?"

Her mother shook her head firmly. "No, we went through absolutely everything. I was tired of the mess up there and wanted to be done with it."

Lexi had hoped, on the way to her parents' house, that her mother could produce *one more box* to sort through, the magic one that would hand her all the answers to this growing mystery and would satisfy Lexi's blossoming curiosity.

"Oh well. It was worth asking." Lexi's phone buzzed, a text from Ruby. "I'd better get going. I want to help Ruby close up the store tonight." She rose from her seat and slipped the photocopy back inside her bag.

Her mother stood to reach out for an unexpected hug then gently brushed a wisp of hair from Lexi's forehead. "I'm sorry I couldn't be more help."

"That's okay. It was worth asking. I might do some more online research, but I'm not hopeful it'll lead me anywhere. James Fisher is a pretty common name. And it was eighty-something years ago."

"True." Her mother gave a sympathetic wince then walked her toward the front door. "Let me know what you find out."

"I will."

BEFORE ENTERING THE store, Lexi took a detour toward the warehouse to see if the backordered supplies had finally been delivered. She spotted someone approaching in her peripheral vision and turned to see her cousin. "Hey, I was about to text you again."

Jolene reached out for a tight hug. "I'm on a break and needed some fresh air. Plus I wanted an update. I got all your texts. Crazy stuff! So, Gigi was having an *affair*?"

"No! Not an affair. You read too fast, didn't you?" Jo had a terrible habit of skimming her texts and then jumping to all the wrong conclusions. "Gigi was in love *before* Paw-Paw. Or so we think."

Lexi walked a few feet over to the bench that sat under a shaded tree near the warehouse. Jolene followed her and sat down, crossing her slender legs toward her cousin. "I just came from seeing my mother about everything. She's clueless who James Fisher was. I haven't had a chance yet to investigate. I need to see the warehouse, close the store, get some dinner, then answer a thousand messages first." Lexi yawned at the thought of a nice comfortable bed waiting for her at the end of the day.

"Stop it. That's contagious," Jolene mumbled through her own yawn.

"Oh, and I wanted to ask you about the USO parties at the mansion. Can you look up some old dates for me? That might help us figure out what's going on with the necklace."

"Sure. Happy to."

"I'll text you more of the details. It might be a day or so. Honestly, my brain can't handle any more dates or new information. It's been an exhausting afternoon."

"So, back to the professor. You spent the whole day with him?" Jo arched one eyebrow.

Lexi smoothed out a crease in her jeans and hid a smirk, knowing exactly where this was going. "Not the whole day. A few hours. But it was business. He was really helpful with things... the necklace, I mean. And all the research he did with the jewelry stores. He's the reason we found the ledgers."

"*Only* business? Did y'all talk about anything else?"

Lexi reflected that, actually yes, much of their time had been spent talking about things other than Gigi or the necklace. They chatted off and on about their own lives, their dreams, their goals... conversations she hadn't expected to hold with him.

"Sure. I mean, we had some time to kill, stopped for a quick lunch."

Another raised eyebrow.

Lexi play-slapped Jo's arm. "Quit it. He's not even on the market. Well, technically he is. But not for me."

"What does that mean? How can he be on *and* off the market?"

"He's got this ex, Theresa. She's the one who was texting him, that first day we met."

"When he was rude to you."

"Standoffish. Well, he explained today that the minute I walked in, Theresa had just broken up with him."

"By text? That's brutal. So, what do you mean, he's not on the market? Are they already back together?"

"No. But they broke up less than a week ago. And you know how I feel about rebounds. I run away fast. Those relationships are never permanent. I'm not going to be somebody's replacement."

Jolene tsked. "You and your rules. Can't you break one of them now and then? Admit it. You had a lovely time today with him. Isn't there even a chance for romance?"

"In another time or place, maybe. But I'm up to my neck here with work." She gestured with both hands, one toward the store, the other toward the warehouse. "And he's busy, too, with classes. And still heartbroken."

"Did he say that?"

"No. But I can tell he's processing the breakup. Trust me, he's a total rebound. There's no getting around it. Do you remember Craig? First guy I dated after Neil? How I thought, 'Hey, he's free—just broke up with his girlfriend three weeks ago.' So I took a chance on him, and we dated."

"I remember."

"And after several weeks, when I thought it was safe to get attached, Craig admitted he was still in love with his ex and broke it off with me. I was completely blindsided. What a waste of my time. And a waste of my heart. I swore then—I am never doing that again."

"Fair enough." Jolene flicked a piece of lint off her skirt. "Did I ever tell you about Evan?"

"The name doesn't ring a bell."

"I met him when I was heartbroken over Brady... I think it had been two weeks since we broke up... and I couldn't stand the pain anymore. So I accepted a blind date, Evan. He was perfectly nice—in fact, looking back, I can't think of a single thing that was wrong with him. We had about three dates. And on the third date, in the car outside my house, he leaned over and kissed me. It was sweet and gentle, but I was comparing Evan's kiss to Brady's. I couldn't help myself. It's like Brady was a ghost, right there in the car with us. And it took all I had not to burst into tears right after the kiss. I ended it quickly, made some lame excuse about having to get up for work the next day, then rushed to my front door. When I got into the house, I dropped to my knees and started bawling."

"Jo, why didn't you tell me?"

"I think I was ashamed. I felt stupid, like I didn't have the courage to wait, to try and heal without a man on the horizon."

"You weren't stupid. Your timing was off. Under different circumstances, maybe you would've had a shot with Evan. Did you ever think about reaching back out to him? Later on?"

Jolene shrugged. "He's already taken. But my bigger point is that... I understand about being cautious with rebounds. Because I *was* one. You have to protect your own heart, follow your instincts. It's all about the right timing."

Lexi paused and thought of Graham, the easy banter with him, even being virtual strangers. "I'm actually not sure what my gut is telling me after today. I'm comfortable around him. We do have a lot in common, and—"

"What are you saying? Graham might be an exception to the rule?"

"No, not that. But there's no harm in being friends with a rebound guy, spending time with him and not expecting a romance. Is there?"

"*If* you can keep it that way—purely platonic."

"I think there could be freedom in being only friends. I'm not trying to impress him or get him to date me. We're work colleagues at the least and potential friends at the most. I could be okay with that."

"NO WAY THEY DON'T CALL a penalty. That was high sticking!"

"Totally!"

Brad and Matthew, two of Graham's teacher friends, pointed at the hockey game on the screen then took another swig of beer. Graham didn't enjoy hockey as much as they did and preferred to stream rugby or Wimbledon tournaments instead. But Brad and Matthew had wanted to see "the big game" on his TV since he had the newest, high-def brand.

His friends taught in different departments at UT—computer and communication—and didn't have half the workload Graham did, which made these school-night games quite taxing for him. They had ordered pizza an hour ago, and Graham sat in his recliner, trying *not* to think of all the papers and emails waiting for him in the other room. He would tackle them as soon as his friends left.

His phone jingled nearby, a call from his dad. He scooped up the phone and darted past the TV toward his bedroom as his friends commented on another play. There was no way he could hear anything above their enthusiastic shouts.

Graham shut the door behind him as he answered.

"Hey, Dad."

"Busy?"

"Nope. Everything okay?"

"Sure, fine. I'm going to see your sister this weekend, thought you might join us. I wanted to tell her the news about my engagement. Thought it might be easier on her with you there too. Sort of lighten the mood, ease the tension."

His father was right—Shelley's reaction would be unpredictable. It would be best to have Graham's support as she learned the news. He still hadn't processed it himself.

"Sure, count me in."

"Good. Also, something else to tell you. Beth and I have set the date. First Saturday in May."

The long pause told Graham his dad was waiting for a response.

"Wow, that's... less than a month away."

His father cleared his throat. "Well, we figured... I mean, neither of us is getting any younger. And we've both been married before, so this won't take much planning. Beth has a church in mind, and I think she's already booked it. I'm letting her handle all the details."

"Right." Graham knew his lawyer father well enough to presume that his next question wouldn't be a sensitive, *How does that make you feel, son?* He wasn't the care-about-your-feelings type, never had been. So Graham cut through another awkward silence to offer up the expected "I'm happy for you, Dad. Let me know if I can do anything to help."

They ended the call with a plan to see Shelley on Saturday. Graham heard his friends in the next room celebrating another goal. Knowing he should join them, instead, he sat on the edge of his bed and scrolled through his phone mindlessly, still thinking about his father's call. Graham had meant what he'd said, in theory—he did want happiness for his father. And after his mum died, Graham assumed that, eventually, his dad would find someone else and marry her.

Beth—stepmother. The word was foreign in his mind as he rolled it around, tried it on for size.

For a new distraction, Graham clicked through his texts to see if there were any he'd neglected to respond to and paused at Lexi's name. He hadn't heard from her since a couple of days before, right after their jewelry-shop quest. That night, Lexi had forwarded Henry's text, verifying that there were no other teardrop necklaces commissioned in those later 1940s ledgers, essentially solidifying the theory that another man had given Gigi the necklace. Graham wondered if Lexi had already researched James Fisher and whether she would even need Graham's assistance anymore, since the necklace's origins had been discovered. He remembered that her big grand opening was coming up tomorrow, so there was every chance she hadn't had time for anything but that event.

He reflected on their lengthy chat over bread pudding at the bistro—the conversation had flowed effortlessly. He hadn't expected to click with someone again that quickly. Or to tell a practical stranger about close-to-his-heart topics, like his mother's death, his recent breakup, or details of the new book he hoped to write.

He remembered Lexi being silent on the drive back from Henry's store to her car on campus, and Graham hadn't interfered. He had let the radio play soft music in the background, knowing she would talk if she wanted to. Occasionally, she would bring out her phone and type in a text, and he couldn't help but wonder who they were being sent to. *Mother? Best friend? Boyfriend?* In those spaces of silence in between texts, where she stared out his car window, Graham assumed she was trying to wrap her head around the news about the necklace, attempting to make sense of it. When Lexi got out of his car, he'd hoped she might open up, tell him what she'd been thinking. But she had merely given a preoccupied wave along with another "thank you" then climbed into her Toyota to drive away. He hoped it wouldn't be the last time he ever saw her.

Graham's thumb hovered above Lexi's name as he considered reaching out. He could always use the excuse of wanting an update on the necklace, simply being an interested party. But he wanted more from her—to see her again, to hear her airy laugh, to watch the wind filter through her golden-brown hair. After Theresa, he had fully intended to be smart about everything—to nurse his bruised ego and take a break from all potential relationships so he could heal properly before trying again. But he found himself thinking about Lexi, wishing she would text him, hoping she wanted to see him about something other than the necklace.

The guys erupted in another boisterous shout from the other room. With a sigh, Graham clicked off his phone, heaved himself off the bed, and braced for the energetic second half of a game he cared nothing about.

Chapter Six

It had all come down to this. After a final walk-through of the warehouse to make sure every single element of the new arts-and-crafts center was perfectly in place, and after checking in with Pam and her staff for some last-minute preparations, Lexi was ready, and so was her new venture. Or at least, she hoped it was. There was always the potential for disaster when your expectations were this high.

As Lexi hovered outside the warehouse while people gathered, she was glad that the morning had brought beautiful cool weather without a single cloud in the sky. For weeks, she'd debated about when to hold a grand opening—nighttime or daytime?—and then decided that a morning opening would give new customers the chance to browse and use the facilities throughout the rest of the day. She checked the time again—a few minutes away from the big moment—then combed through her new side-swept bangs with nervous fingers. She'd made the time to visit Trudy's Beauty Shop for a trim early this morning, before her own store opened. It was a special day, and Lexi wanted to look the part. She wore a floral-printed sundress and sandals that showed off her new pedicure.

She was running on nervous energy, having slept a combined ten hours for the past two nights. She had stayed late every night during the week leading up to the grand opening to finalize each detail, making sure nothing had been overlooked. Ariel, Ruby, and Pam had joined her when they were able, and one night, Lexi turned their joint efforts into a midnight pizza party, with perky eighties music blasting from the new sound system as they vacuumed, swept, and spot-cleaned nearly every square inch of the space until it shined.

"Lex, this is so exciting!" Jolene approached her from behind. "What an awesome businesswoman you've become."

As they hugged, Lexi whispered, "Thanks." Over her cousin's shoulder, Lexi noticed her parents walking up the path to join them. Her father presented her with a petite bouquet of flowers, tightly bundled.

"Thank you, Dad." She accepted the fragrant bouquet and took a deep whiff. "These must be from the garden."

"They are," her mother said. "I chose them this morning."

"We're incredibly proud of you, honey." Her dad blinked away what seemed to be the start of tears.

Lexi reached out for his hand. "I'm glad y'all came. It means a lot." She was barely able to get the words out before her own tears formed.

"The countdown is about to begin!" Ruby made the announcement as she breezed past the group with her enormous scissors, saying a quick "hi" to Lexi's parents and then making her way toward Ariel, who was securing the ribbon across the warehouse's wide-open doors.

"I guess this is it!" Lexi sucked in a breath and wiped the corner of her eye. "I wonder what Gigi would think if she were here. I miss her."

"I do too," her mother said. "She would be beaming with pride, no doubt. And standing right by your side."

Ruby took charge and ushered Lexi toward the ribbon, which was ready to be sliced down its center.

As the eager crowd gathered in front of her, Lexi recognized multiple townspeople among them: Lucille with her corgis; Chaynie Mayfield with her boyfriend, Greg; Mrs. Haversham, the B&B owner; Jill McCallister, the famous novelist; Bicycle Bob, the town crier; and so many more.

Lexi's heart warmed at the thought that they took time out of their own busy schedules to support her newest endeavor. Before she could shift her attention back toward Ruby, Lexi saw another familiar face at the far edge of the crowd. Graham had come. He gave a small wave when their eyes locked.

"Ready?" Ruby asked, exchanging the scissors for the flowers Lexi held.

Lexi handled the scissors awkwardly, and the crowd chuckled as she tried not to drop them. She wished she'd rehearsed this part earlier, but there hadn't been time. *How often in life does one get the chance to fumble with a giant pair of scissors in front of interested onlookers on a momentous occasion?*

She grasped the scissors firmly and angled them toward the crimson ribbon. Amy, the Morgan's Grove newspaper photographer, was poised and waiting for the big moment.

"Five, four, three..." Ruby began the countdown, and the crowd followed along, increasing their volume with each number.

On the "one" count, Lexi gave the scissors' handles a decisive push and slashed the ribbon in half, watching the ends twirl down.

The crowd erupted with cheers and applause, which for some reason startled Lexi, and she tried once more to hold back tears as Ruby took the scissors from her and gave back the flowers.

"Thank you, everyone!" she said as the clapping died down. Lexi hadn't planned a speech, but a thick pause in the air told her the crowd was expecting one. The moment needed to be acknowledged. "My family has been wonderful through all of this, so supportive. And thanks to my amazing team—Ruby and Ariel. And of course, to all the contractors and workmen, and to Pam and her fabulous team." She gestured toward them, standing to her side. "None of this would've been possible without them. May this facility be used as a place of education, of wonder, of fellowship, and of creativity and inspiration for many generations to come."

Lexi clapped along with the crowd this time then stepped aside for Pam to enter the warehouse with her staff so they could move into place. The townspeople filtered through the warehouse, craning their necks to take in all that the center had to offer. Lexi heard audible gasps and "Look!" as the crowd chattered and gravitated from one station to another.

Stepping out of the way to savor the moment, Lexi nearly ran right into another familiar face. "Henry! I'm glad you could make it!" A few evenings ago, when he'd texted to let Lexi know that the other ledgers did not contain any teardrop commissions, she had thanked him in reply and mentioned her new store's grand opening—including the delicious gourmet treats catered by Lucille's bakery, as well as door prizes donated by local businesses—and invited him to attend.

"Glad to be here," he said through his bushy moustache. He wore a forest-green fedora that matched his trousers. "I might even get brave and try my hand at the pottery wheel. Make a bowl or maybe a vase..."

"Hey, Lexi, do you have any more copies of our signs?" Ruby was suddenly at Lexi's side, squeezing her arm. "Silly me, I forgot to add one to the front of the antiques store."

Ruby stopped short and looked over at Henry then curled a gray lock of hair around her ear. Lexi had never, in three decades, seen Ruby in a shy or flirtatious state.

Lexi suppressed a knowing smile and said, "Ruby, this is Henry. He owns Miller & Sons' jewelry store in downtown Austin."

"Pleased to meet ya." Henry gave a courteous nod of his cap.

"You too," Ruby said, holding his gaze.

Lexi swore she could feel the atmosphere shift right then and there, only returning to normal when Ariel joined them, out of breath. "Did you find the tape, Ruby? I don't see it anywhere."

"What? Oh." Ruby still hadn't removed her attention from Henry. "It's... Oh, yes. Here it is. Right here in my hand. Silly me."

"Okay, well, c'mon! I found the extra signs. And we'll also need to..." Ariel's voice drifted away as she tugged on Ruby's sleeve, pulling her along.

Lexi turned back to Henry. "We have refreshments inside, and there's also a coffee bar."

"Thanks. I might stay a while." Henry pushed his hands inside his pants pockets and wandered toward the warehouse.

Lexi heard another voice behind her say, "Congratulations." She pivoted to see Graham, dressed in khaki slacks and a forest-green sweater—the kind of attire Lexi always imagined history professors wearing during their days off.

"You're here," she said. "I didn't think you'd have time. I mean, it's quite a drive from Austin. And I assumed you'd be up to your elbows in tests or essays to grade."

"I usually have faculty meetings on Fridays, but this morning was a rare exception." He squinted. "Your hair looks different."

So far, he was the only one who had noticed. "Oh. Yeah, I got it trimmed. With bangs."

"I like it." Graham produced a box the size of his palm and handed it to her. "I brought you a present. I figured you'd probably be getting a lot of flowers today." He nodded toward the crook of her arm, where she had tucked her parents' bouquet after the ribbon-cutting. "I wanted to give you something... permanent. To commemorate your achievement."

Intrigued, Lexi lifted the top of the box to reveal a colorful bouquet of three glass red roses attached together by a green stem lying atop a velvety pillow. She touched the smooth surface of the roses. "Beautiful," she whispered. "Where did you find it?"

"An antiques store in north Austin. I wasn't sure what I was looking for, but when I saw it... I knew."

"Thank you. For this and for coming to my opening."

"It's a great turnout." Graham scanned the still-large crowd milling around, laughing, chatting, and pointing to various sights inside the warehouse.

"I wasn't expecting this many people. I hoped friends and family would attend, but not the whole of Morgan's Grove. My heart feels so full, seeing them all. Even Henry came."

"I saw him in the crowd! Nice of him to stop by."

She took another look at the flowers then pushed the lid safely back in place. "Can you stay, have some refreshments?"

Graham checked his watch. "Maybe. I have a couple of properties to swing by and see before I leave."

"You mentioned properties the first time you came to Morgan's Grove. Are you looking to buy a house?"

"No, just land, several acres. With a barn. Or at least, room for one. My father and I are going into a partnership together, of sorts. We've had this brainstorm for a couple of years, to establish a horse therapy ranch for kids."

"That sounds amazing."

"I've promised Dad I would scout out some locations, and there are quite a few around these parts, on Austin's outskirts."

"We have a lot of open acreage outside Morgan's Grove, with several ranches. In fact..." She attempted to reach for the phone in her bag, but between clutching her dad's flowers under one arm and holding Graham's glass flowers with her other, she struggled not to drop anything.

"Here, let me." Graham took both sets of flowers gingerly from her, freeing her up to find her phone.

"I know a Realtor—her name is Savannah. Her day job is as a teacher at the local high school, but on weekends and in the summers, she sells and buys properties. She knows this area like the back of her hand. I can send you her contact info."

"Brilliant."

Hearing Graham's British-tinged response, Lexi lifted her mouth in a half smile. Every now and again, he would let his UK roots come through.

"Okay, there. It should be in your phone." She took back the flowers from Graham. "No pressure, though. Only trying to help."

"It does. It'll save me some time for sure."

"It's the least I can do for all your efforts with the necklace—finding Henry's store, helping me get some answers..."

"Which only led to more questions. Did you find out anything new? About James Fisher?"

"No, unfortunately. I didn't have time for more than a couple of hasty internet searches this week, and there are way too many James Fishers in Texas alone. And the ones I tried to track down amounted to nothing. Realistically, it would take dozens of hours to eliminate them all and find the right man. And even then, who's to say his family members would have a clue what I'm talking about with the necklace? Gigi was so secretive about it—I'll bet that James was too. His family might not even know Gigi existed. But still... it's hard to let go. There's this secret waiting to be uncovered. I want to know more."

"There's definitely a story there."

"I asked my cousin to try and find any record of a James Fisher at the USO parties." Lexi explained Jolene's position as manager of the mansion and its role with the USO parties during wartime. "Anyway, she told me yesterday that she didn't see any evidence of him attending but she'd keep digging through some other records. So, quite a few dead ends this week."

"Lexi! Come and take a selfie with us!" Ariel was posing with Ruby near the Let's Get Crafty sign. "I want to put it up on Instagram!"

"Duty calls," Lexi told Graham. "Thanks again for the roses. Really sweet of you."

He gave her one last nod then drifted off toward a cluster of peo-ple waiting in line at the refreshment table.

"Coming!" Lexi told Ariel, grabbing one more quick look back at Graham then heading toward her crew, ready to continue the cel-ebration.

LEXI HUMMED ALONG TO James Taylor's "Fire and Rain," one of the dozens of songs in her Folk Singers playlist, as she finished her third attempt at threading her hair into a loose braid to drape over her left shoulder. At almost thirty-two years old, she didn't know if a braid was too youthful or not, but she didn't care. The serene playlist, as well as yesterday's successful grand opening and the supportive turnout, had her waking up in a happy, breezy mood the next morn-ing, and the braid was a product of it. She wanted something differ-ent.

As Lexi applied a thin layer of lip gloss, Bailey woofed at a squir-rel he saw outside the bedroom window. She flicked off the bath-room light, grabbed the leash, then urged him out of the house.

Lexi wasn't supposed to darken the door of the antiques store this morning—Ruby had insisted she take an *entire* Saturday off, for once—but Lexi couldn't help herself and headed in that direction with Bailey. The store was on her way to the square anyway, where she had some errands to run, so why not pop in for a minute?

She felt the breeze on her bare legs—she'd settled on shorts and a navy T-shirt—as she and Bailey turned the corner at the end of the block. She savored the fresh air of the late morning while Bailey searched high and low for more squirrels.

Lexi tugged on his leash again. "C'mon, let's go see Auntie Ruby. I'm sure she's got some bacon treats for you."

Hearing the word "bacon," Bailey halted in his tracks and looked straight up at her with hopeful, unblinking eyes.

"Not *with* me. We have to go to the store to get them." She nudged him along and let him lead the way.

Lexi entered the store to the fully expected "What are you *doing here?*" from Ruby, which included a firm hands-on-hips pose and pursed lips.

"It was on our way. Bailey and I have errands to run. In the square."

"A likely story." Ruby tsked.

"Lots of customers," Lexi said. "More than we usually get on Saturdays."

"I think it's extra traffic from Let's Get Crafty. People are curious about it. Pam says she's already booked out for the painting tutorials for the next two weeks! I think word of mouth has spread. The quilting lessons are filling up too. Hopefully, the antiques store will continue to get their spillover."

"Fantastic!" Lexi wanted, more than anything, to pop into Let's Get Crafty to check on the new staff, but she didn't want to undermine Pam's authority—and she needed Pam to trust that Lexi had faith in her, especially during the early days. *I'll visit on Monday,* she thought, dropping Bailey's leash and letting him wander over to Ariel, behind the desk.

"Hey, where are the gnomes?" Lexi saw that they were missing from their usual spot. Maybe Ruby had moved them elsewhere.

Ruby's eyes darted toward Ariel before saying, "Someone bought them up yesterday."

"All of them?"

"Well, except the two you saved for Jo's birthday. They're still in the back."

"That's weird. Most people want maybe one or two for their garden. But eight gnomes at once? Must be a pretty spacious garden."

Ruby gave another fast glance toward Ariel, who then busied herself giving Bailey a treat.

"Okay, spill. What's the big mystery?" Lexi crossed her arms, knowing Ruby was incapable of keeping secrets.

Ruby took two steps forward and gestured with her hands. She whispered, "I promised him I wouldn't say anything. I mean, I've been positively *sworn* to secrecy."

"Him who?"

"Your professor friend. The handsome one."

"Graham? Why on earth would he buy eight gnomes?"

"Well, he was here yesterday, browsing after the grand opening. And he pointed out the gnomes, made a comment about them. And I... let it slip that you were... well, petrified of them—"

"You actually used that word? Petrified? I mean, you're overstating a bit, don't you think?"

Ruby clucked. "Please. You whisk right past them every time you enter the store. You don't think I notice?"

Lexi hadn't thought she did. "Okay, fine. I have a weird, irrational fear of gnomes. But you actually told him that?"

"Sorry. I made it pretty clear you weren't a fan."

"I'm still confused. Why did he buy them?"

"To get them out of your store, out of your sight. So that you wouldn't have to look at them anymore. I made Darius help carry them to his car. The least I could do."

Ariel piped in from a few feet away. "The professor said he has 'plans' for them."

"For gnomes?" Lexi asked. "He doesn't even have a backyard or a garden. He lives in an apartment."

"Have you been there?"

"Ruby! No. I haven't. He mentioned it when we were doing research for the necklace."

Lexi pictured Graham scooping up armfuls of gnomes and carrying them to the front desk to pay for them, all because he wanted to help save Lexi from having to look at the nasty little creatures on a daily basis. On top of the thoughtfulness of bringing her glass flowers—which she had placed on her nightstand this morning—Graham was proving to be quite the opposite of the man she'd first thought he was.

Rebound, rebound, rebound, she scolded herself.

"Well, I thought it was a very sweet gesture," Ruby said definitively.

"In any case, I'm glad they're gone," Lexi said. "I don't have to avoid them anymore. Hey, no judgment from y'all!" She pointed from Ruby to Ariel and back again. "We all have quirky hang-ups."

Ruby held up her right hand as if she were swearing an oath. "I have no defense. You know my strong aversion to Christmas tinsel." She shuddered.

Ariel screwed up her face. "And I hate those charcoaled lines on hamburgers and steaks. Gross! I have to fleck them off with my knife."

Lexi rolled her eyes. "Y'all. Those aren't exactly the same as 'fear of gnomes,' but thanks for trying to make me feel better." She saw three customers heading toward the front register, so she bent over to reach for Bailey's leash. "C'mon, boy. Let's leave these ladies to their day. We've got a whole afternoon ahead of us!"

Chapter Seven

On any given Saturday, especially during springtime, the town square was bustling with tourists and townspeople who shopped and chatted and ate and enjoyed the weather. Kids played and shouted while their mothers looked harried, old friends met on the sidewalk with warm hugs, and strangers exchanged friendly hellos. It was Lexi's favorite place in the world, this town. She had traveled a bit in her youth on summer vacations with her parents, then later, during brief trips to major cities across the U.S. in her twenties—Denver, Vegas, L.A., Boston. But none of those locations held the comfortable fit of Morgan's Grove. She wanted to live here for the rest of her days, as Gigi had, happy and satisfied and unapologetic.

Today, Lexi had a couple of errands to run for office supplies and groceries. She also considered stopping at the bookstore to buy a book she would never have time to finish. Otherwise, her day was empty, and she had no real idea how to fill the rest of it.

As she stood on the corner of the library's lawn, trying to make up her mind where to go first, Bailey let out a classic beagle "ba-*roo*!" and took off. The leash whipped out of Lexi's hand, and she gasped—realizing he was headed straight for the street.

"Bailey!"

This wasn't like him. He never ran off without her. She sprinted after him, glad there was no traffic at the moment. At the other side, Bailey stopped short on the sidewalk to jump up high on a startled man who nearly dropped his coffee.

Lexi caught up with them, out of breath, and bent over to grab Bailey's leash while telling him to "Sit!"

"I am *so* sorry," she told the man, embarrassed by her dog's outrageous behavior.

When she rose up, she came face-to-face with Graham. Bailey's unexpected detour finally became clear. He had seen his newest friend and merely wanted to greet him.

"Oh. Hi!" Lexi brushed out her bangs.

"Hey, you two." Graham had righted himself, and his coffee cup was fully intact—no evidence of stains on his camel blazer.

"Sorry about Bailey. He was eager to see you."

"That's flattering." Graham stooped over to rub Bailey's head.

As he rose, Lexi said, "I meant to text you last night about the glass flowers. I couldn't remember if I thanked you yesterday or not... Everything got crazy-busy." She shifted her weight, *also* wishing she could thank him for removing the gnomes from her store but knowing that she would be betraying Ruby's confidence by doing so.

"You did thank me. I'm glad you liked them."

"You're back in Morgan's Grove?"

"It was a last-minute thing. I called the Realtor last night, the one you suggested, and she had time to squeeze me in this morning before her other appointments. I had some time to kill afterward, so now I'm browsing the square."

Lexi had been right about Graham's eyes—light blue—and when they focused on her, she lost her concentration.

During a quiet beat between them, she refocused her energy. "Was it successful, your meeting?"

"She thinks there might be a few ideal properties in this area. I'll tell my dad this afternoon, and maybe we can move forward soon, look at them together."

Beyond Graham's shoulder, Lexi could see someone approaching. She recognized Greg Peterson, who had an office a couple of doors down. He had attended school with Lexi years ago, though he was such a quiet student back then, she hadn't known him well.

When he fell in love with Chaynie, the librarian, a few months ago, he broke out of his shell and became quite a regular in Morgan's Grove, participating in the local activities.

Greg stopped on the sidewalk as they greeted each other, and Lexi started the introductions.

"Greg, this is Graham Faulkner. A history professor at UT."

"Nice meeting ya. I'm an architect here in town," Greg said.

"He recently renovated our library," Lexi told Graham. "It's gorgeous inside. In fact, it's a historical building—over a hundred years old."

"I'd love to see it." Graham's eyes lit up at the prospect.

"I could take you on a tour sometime," Greg said.

Lexi remembered a tidbit that Savannah had recently shared with her and asked Greg, "I've heard that the sale of your parents' ranch is on pause?"

"Yeah, the buyers can't move in for another six weeks. But it gives my mom and dad more time to pack up. Speaking of—Chaynie and I are throwing a dance at their barn, sort of a last hurrah for the ranch. Maybe an end-of-spring event. Y'all should come."

"Let me know if you need help with things. Tell Chaynie to text me."

"Will do."

Lexi turned to Graham. "Greg's parents also have horses. Or *had* horses." She looked back to Greg. "Have they been sold too?"

"Actually, no. That sale fell through completely. We're still looking for buyers."

"You might've found one," Graham said. "It's probably too soon for this conversation, but my dad and I are looking to start up a horse therapy ranch. It's early in the game—we're scouting out properties around town."

"Jem and Cinder would probably make perfect therapy horses. Very gentle, well trained. Great temperaments for beginners or kids.

I can show them to you anytime you like." Greg paused and checked his watch. "Except right now. I'm late to meet Chaynie. Next week would work, though."

Graham and Greg exchanged contact information, then Greg sprinted off in the direction of the library.

"Nice chap." Graham took a final sip of his coffee then moved two steps forward to toss the cup into a nearby receptacle.

Bailey must have assumed it was a cue for adventure, because he stood up, tail wagging, and strolled forward at a leisurely pace.

Graham snickered. "Guess he's ready for a walk."

Lexi and Graham fell in line behind Bailey and matched his easy stride as they strolled together along the row of shops, each one topped with matching green-striped awnings. "I don't have anywhere important to be," Lexi said, waving at Mrs. Haversham as she passed by them. "It's a weird feeling. A rare day off."

"My meeting with Dad isn't until three, so I have some time to kill."

"Oh, I forgot to tell you something—I went to see my mother after we visited Henry's shop that day. I even showed her the copy of the ledger."

"Did she have any insights about James Fisher?"

"None. Except to confirm that my great-grandparents met *after* the war, in 1945, then married a couple years later."

"So the mystery deepens."

"I asked my mother if there were any other boxes in the attic, and she told me there weren't."

"You sound unsure." He gave her a side glance.

"It's just... I don't know whether my parents went through every single nook and cranny." She paused on the sidewalk to face Graham. Bailey paused too. "They were probably in a hurry when they brought the boxes down. I think they did a surface-level scan of the space. Plus, they weren't hunting for treasures at the time. If Gigi was so intent on keeping this secret, couldn't there possibly be something else my parents overlooked that she'd tucked away? I'm not ready to give up on this yet."

"Why don't you search the attic for yourself? What would it hurt?"

Graham had confirmed the same thought that had flittered through Lexi's own mind that very morning—with time on her hands and a mystery nagging at her, why *not* explore the attic, put her doubts firmly to rest?

"I think you're right. In fact—" Lexi eyed the old-fashioned metal street clock that stood on the corner. Plenty of time until Graham's three o'clock meeting. "Why don't you come with me?"

"To the attic?"

"Sure, to my parents' house, a block away. I could use a pair of fresh eyes."

"Count me in."

LEXI'S SHOES SCUDDED across the wood floor of her parents' attic, swept clean. She hadn't been inside the space since she was a child. Gigi had let her use it as a play area—as long as she always had help getting up and down the precarious ladder below. As a little girl, Lexi had spent countless hours playing dress-up with her dolls or reading books in the enormous purple beanbag chair Gigi had purchased. Lexi could see it in her mind's eye, could feel the encased pellets beneath her elbows as she shifted positions and turned another page.

"It's pristine for a house this age." Graham whistled, climbing into the attic. "And check out those windows. Nice light in here."

Lexi was grateful not to have the huge job in front of her of sweeping away cobwebs and dust or sorting through old boxes. "This shouldn't take us long," Lexi mused, "now that everything's gone." Still, she lowered her hopes once again as she realized the truth—surely, her parents would've already discovered a new treasure peeking from behind a box or rolling out from a dark corner. They had covered every square inch of the space. What more could she or Graham possibly discover?

"Why don't you take that end." Graham nodded toward the north wall. "I'll start over here."

"What are we even looking for? Evidence of a love affair, but in what form? Photographs, letters, trinkets? I'm not even sure. If *I* were a secret document or treasure, where would I be hidden away?"

"The walls have possibilities. See the slats?" He pointed to one of the nearby panels. "They hold pockets of space, areas your parents likely didn't investigate."

"True." Lexi moved toward her designated side. "And maybe even here, around these beams that go from ceiling to floor—lots of open crevices and nooks."

Always one to fill silence with music, especially when a tedious task was at hand, Lexi clicked on a favorite Sinatra playlist then placed her phone near the back wall and returned to her corner, deciding to tackle the beams first then the slats. Running her hand behind the first raised beam, she was rewarded with sticky cobwebs. "Ick," she muttered, brushing them off on her shorts, wishing she'd brought along some paper towels. The second beam produced the same result.

Moving on, she leaned up toward the wall's slats on her tiptoes, figuring it would be pointless to go higher, since her great-grandmother had been even shorter than Lexi and couldn't have reached any higher either.

It took her half an hour to cover her end. "Anything yet?" Lexi asked.

"Nope." Graham had removed his jacket and placed it on top of the staircase banister then rolled up his sleeves. His technique had been to slide his fingertips along each slat since his hand was too large to squeeze down between them.

Lexi tackled the panels that ran along the middle wall next, while Graham moved to the opposite side. *Nothing.* Reaching as high up as she could on her last panels, she brought her hand down, knocking her wrist against her thigh in defeat.

"Oh well," she said to Graham, crossing the room to meet him as Sinatra sang about pennies from heaven. Graham had finished his last section too.

"Sorry," he said. "I know it's frustrating."

"It feels like such a personal blow. I mean, it's different with the store. Whenever we're getting jewelry assessed, we hardly ever know the exact history of a piece or the players involved. I don't mind the mystery of not knowing—I'm okay with it being lost to time. Occasionally, we might get a possible date or a story told by the owner as it's transferred to us. But this is different. It's *my* history, part of my story. And it makes me wish Gigi could be here to fill in the gaps in her own words. Why was James so important to her? Who was he? And why did she keep him hidden?" She shook her head and looked around the space again.

Graham dusted off his palms then lifted his hand to cradle Lexi's arm near her shoulder. It was a tender gesture, appropriate for the moment. He gave her arm a gentle squeeze then released it.

Puffing out a sigh, Lexi moved toward her phone to click off Sinatra mid-note. Pocketing the phone, she took a step toward Graham and paused. "Did you hear that?"

Graham stared at her feet. "No, what?"

Lexi lifted her left foot then pushed her weight down again. "It's a weak board. Feels loose."

"Let's take a look."

They squatted down with the board in between them. Together, they pressed on the wide slat to confirm it—definitely loose.

"I'll try this end." Lexi placed her fingernails under the plank, expecting resistance. But the board slipped out of place easily, and Graham helped her remove it. As he set it aside, Lexi gasped. Inside the hole, she spotted three bundles of papers, tightly packed and secured with lavender ribbons.

"Letters?" she whispered, reaching for the first dense bundle with both hands. It was the thickness of a football. She dusted it off gently before handing it over to Graham then lifted out the second and third bundles, clasping them both to her chest. "I can't believe we found these." *How long had they been there, waiting to be discovered?*

"We almost didn't. If you hadn't noticed that weak board—"

"Lex, I'm home!" her mother called out from below. When Lexi and Graham had first arrived at the house, her mother had been out shopping while her dad was in the kitchen, deciding what to make for lunch.

"I've got to show my parents," Lexi said, breathless, unable to contain her smile, which stretched wider with every syllable.

"Let's go."

Lexi handed one of her bundles of letters over to Graham and let him climb back down the precarious attic stairs first, one-handed. Then, she followed him down, with the third bundle tucked securely under her arm. As she took the final step, she felt the light touch of Graham's hand near her waist, guiding her down.

Lexi led the way toward the main staircase like a kid on Christmas morning. The excitement surged inside her with every step as Graham followed behind.

"Mother? Dad?"

"We're in the kitchen."

Lexi bounded around the corner of the dining room and into the kitchen, where her dad stood chopping onions near a steaming pot of soup, while her mother emptied the contents of a grocery bag onto the spacious granite island.

"You'll never believe this," Lexi said, grasping the letters with both hands.

But her mother's gaze wasn't on Lexi or the letters. It was on Graham.

"Hello," she said in her politest tone.

"Oh, sorry," Lexi said. "This is Graham Faulkner. Professor at UT. He's the one who helped me with Gigi's necklace, getting it assessed."

"Very nice to meet you." Her mother nodded.

"You as well."

Graham had already met Lexi's father when they first arrived, so Lexi continued with her original mission, bursting to share her news.

"We went back for one more look at the attic—anything we could find related to Gigi's necklace. And we discovered something under one of the floorboards. It was loose, and Graham helped me wedge it open." She could read her interior-designer mother's thoughts and held up a hand before she could protest. "Nothing was damaged, I promise. The floorboard popped right out, and we've already replaced it. Anyway, look what was underneath!"

They each placed their bundles on the empty section of the island to let everyone have a good look. Then, Lexi did what she'd been wanting to do ever since she'd laid eyes on them—she reached over to her stack and unlaced the bow.

Her mother had abandoned the groceries and inched closer to Lexi, while her dad had halted his onion chopping and stood behind his wife, hand on her shoulder, for a peek.

Lexi lifted the first envelope, yellowed with age. She read the front of it and frowned. "It's airmail from Italy. Addressed to a

'Blanche Saunders.' With no return address." Lexi looked at her mother. "Who is Blanche? That wasn't Gigi's first name."

"No, it wasn't." Her mother's frown matched her own. "I've never heard that name before."

Lexi shuffled carefully through the first few envelopes. "They all say Blanche."

"I wonder if the letters were hidden there before Gigi moved in," her mother said. "Her parents weren't the house's original owners."

"I didn't know that. I thought our family built the house."

"No, but they bought it quite new, in the 1930s."

Her father chimed in. "Well, that could explain Blanche's name."

Lexi returned to the first envelope to examine it again. "I see a postmark, but the ink is faded. 1943? I think?" She slipped her fingertips into the already sliced-open top of the envelope then slowly pulled out the letter and unfolded it. "Dated February 2nd, 1943. It starts, 'To Louise, my love.'"

"Louise. That's Gigi," her mother said.

Lexi shook her head. "Then why was it addressed to someone named Blanche?" On a hunch, Lexi flipped to the letter's final page to see the sender's name. "It's signed 'James.' And it closes with, 'You're the keeper of my heart. Forever yours.'"

The silence in the kitchen grew as they all took in the strong and undeniable implications the letters held. Gigi had indeed had a first love. But it wasn't Lexi's great-grandfather. It was James Fisher.

"I can't believe this," Lexi whispered, wanting to devour all the letters in one sitting. But this discovery was worthy of their time, so she pushed away the desire to rush through them all at once. "Let's read them together," she said and didn't receive a single objection from the group.

"We can move into the living room," her mother said, "and get comfortable. I need to find my reading glasses." She began to open drawers in search of them.

"I'll finish up the vegetables for the minestrone so it can simmer," her father said. "I'll join you in a bit. Start without me."

Graham and Lexi gathered up the letters and walked into the living room, where Bailey was sprawled out and snoring in the middle of the carpet. He jolted awake when he heard them enter.

Graham approached Lexi with a whisper, making her pause at the sofa. "Maybe I shouldn't be here."

"What do you mean?"

"Well, this is... It's a family matter. Private. Personal."

She waited until he made eye contact then said, "You're the reason we found these letters in the first place—the necklace, taking me to see Henry, then urging me to do a search in the attic today..." She grabbed his free hand, squeezing it reassuringly. "It wouldn't have happened without you. You're part of this now. I want you here."

His nod told her that he wanted to be there too.

"Lexi, why don't you and Graham take the sofa?" Her mother had walked in then settled into the straight-back chair near the window and crossed her legs. She adjusted her glasses securely over her nose.

Lexi sifted through her stack of letters as Graham unlaced the ribbons on the bundles he still carried. He handed one batch over to Lexi's mother.

"Let's try to keep them in order. I'm sure they're all dated." Lexi sat on the other end of the sofa, leaving a whole cushion between herself and Graham, so they could have room to keep the letters organized.

Bailey had awakened and stretched then moved a few feet forward to plant himself on Graham's shoe again.

The room became hushed as all three of them opened letter after letter, reading at their own pace—smiling at certain moments, nodding, or even blinking back tears. A few minutes in, Lexi's father quietly appeared and walked behind his wife's chair to read silently over her shoulder.

Every so often, in no particular order, one of them would read a passage aloud to the group while the others would pause and listen. It quickly became clear that all the letters were written from James to Gigi/Louise, with each envelope addressed to "Blanche." The first batch of letters had been posted from Texas and Oklahoma while James attended military training sessions. But the rest were postmarked from Italy, during various combat missions he experienced as a medic.

"Listen to this one." Lexi's eyes zoomed in on James's narrow, slanted script, some of which was difficult to read. "'I carry you with me, every hour of every day. You are my safe place, my harbor. The memory of your raven hair, your bright-blue eyes, your rosy lips. They stay with me everywhere I go. And I know that I will see them again someday.'"

"Romantic," said her mother then turned back to the letter she held. "Here, he says, 'How is your sister? My prayers are with her. She is strong and will pull through this illness. Stay brave, my love. She will need you.'"

"What illness? Is he talking about Great-Aunt Maggie?" Lexi asked.

"Gigi's only sister." Her mother removed her glasses and gestured with them. "I remember Gigi telling me that Maggie had life-threatening pneumonia when Gigi was about eighteen or nineteen. She did pull through but then was involved in a car accident several years later and passed away."

"Oh, that's sad." Lexi sifted through the remaining letters she held. "You know, I wish we had Gigi's responses to James, but none of them seem to be included here. We only have half the story." She looked at both her parents and winced. "Does it feel a bit icky, reading these?"

"What do you mean?" her mother asked.

"Well, they're personal letters... romantic letters, written to Gigi, for her eyes alone. She buried them away for a reason, under a floorboard. It's weird, reading them aloud. Reading them at all. It's intrusive almost."

"Honey, I don't think she would mind our reading them. So many years have passed," her dad said. "And frankly, she didn't destroy the letters, just hid them away. Maybe for her family to find someday, after she was gone?"

This notion satisfied Lexi, and she felt better about continuing on.

After another few minutes of silence as they read their letters, Graham ran his finger down the edge of the letter then stopped to read aloud. "He says here, 'I'm torn. On one hand, I want to protect you, my love, from the horrors of this war. But on the other, I need to tell my confidant about my experiences. I lost a friend today, a brother. Mac O'Reilly III died in my arms this morning. I can still sense the impression of his head against the crook of my elbow. I did everything I could to save him but to no avail. His last breath held his mother's name, and tonight, I will write and tell her that he died a hero's death.'" Graham's voice faded away, and Lexi assumed he was trying to choke back some emotion.

"I didn't think they were that honest, the soldiers," Lexi mused. "I always assumed they hid the gritty details from their loved ones in letters home."

"They usually did. But he felt comfortable enough with your great-grandmother to give some honest detail. Maybe it was a catharsis for him." As Graham flipped to the next page of the letter, a four-by-six black-and-white photo fell into his lap. He picked it up and held it between his thumb and index finger. "It's a man—James, I assume—with a dog."

He handed the photo over to Lexi, who saw a young soldier kneeling down, wrapping one arm around a panting dog. The soldier, who had dark hair and deep-set eyes, smiled for the camera. "So this is James. Mother, look."

She passed the photo across as Graham read the last paragraph: "'Meet Max. He's the stray who's been hanging around camp the past week or so. He doesn't seem spooked by all the shellfire. Guess he's used to it. The boys and I slip him scraps of food when our commander isn't looking.'"

Next, Lexi offered a paragraph from the letter she held. "'My dear, your description of your ideal wedding dress was so vivid. I can see it in my mind's eye, and you wearing it. As I soothe myself to sleep tonight, I will picture you walking down the aisle toward me, beaming through your veil. When I enter that moment for real someday, I will have to hold back the tears. I see a long life in front of us, filled with children and grandchildren and great happiness. Well, that's what I'm hoping for. I'm a dreamer, but I'm a realist too. Your father might not ever come around. Or worse, I might not make it out of this war, and if I don't, you must open yourself up to happiness again. I want you to live a full and joyful life. You must. Promise me.'"

Lexi looked across at her mother. "So they were engaged? And Gigi's father was against the wedding. I wonder if he ever came around."

Her mother shook her head. "I'm not sure. But knowing your Gigi, she wouldn't have let a little parental disapproval stop her from loving someone."

Lexi's dad chuckled. "That's for sure."

"You know, now that I think about it..." Her mom pursed her lips. "The family folklore always mentioned some kind of rift between Gigi and her father, years long. But it improved after Gigi married your great-grandfather and had children. Then again, I have no idea if any of those details are true. My aunts and sisters were the ones who told me—Gigi never spoke of it herself. But you know how family legacy turns into myth somewhere along the way. The truth becomes a fictional account that changes with every generation."

"I'm curious..." Lexi stared down at one of the envelopes. "Whether Blanche might've been a friend of James's. Or even Gigi's. Maybe someone she trusted, who could protect the letters between them."

"Like a go-between?" Graham asked. "Maybe James addressed his letters to Blanche, who hand delivered them to your great-grandmother in secret?"

"Right, to prevent her father from knowing they were in touch," Lexi said. "Gigi wouldn't have wanted letters from James coming into the house. They could've been confiscated."

As they all came to the end of their stacks, Lexi held the final two letters chronologically. One was dated August of 1943. She read the most interesting portion aloud: "'Lulu, I've made a decision. We've talked about eloping after the war is over. But I want your father's approval and a big family wedding. We'll talk him into it, the two of us. Nothing can stop us. I'm tired of hiding our love or feeling the least bit ashamed of it. Surely he can understand how in love we are. Please consider it. If I were with you this evening, I would stroke your beautiful hair, look you deeply in your eyes, and ask you, once again, to be my bride. I want to be yours for the rest of my life.' And then he closes with 'You keep my heart. Always.'"

The last letter was dated September of 1943. Before Lexi moved her eyes to the first sentence, a black-and-white photo dropped out from the last page. She held it up to see a young couple—the man in a suit and tie, with his arm wrapped around a beautiful petite girl wearing a long-sleeved cocktail dress and a neatly bobbed hairstyle. Both were smiling their brightest smiles, evidence of happier days.

Lexi brought the photo closer. "I think I see the teardrop. She's wearing it."

Lexi passed the photo to her mother, who brought it close to her glasses. "I can't quite make it out."

"Here." Lexi's father took a few steps backward to the desk against the wall then pulled out a drawer to find a magnifying glass, which he passed to his wife.

She gazed through the glass—"That's it, the necklace"—then flipped the photo over and read the inscription: "'James and Lulu, November 1941.'"

"Lulu. He used that in a couple of letters. It must've been his pet name for her," Lexi said.

Her mother passed the photo, along with the magnifying glass, over to Graham, who confirmed the necklace's presence. "November. James had commissioned the necklace a month earlier."

Curious to finish the final one, Lexi went back to the letter. But she noticed the handwriting was different from all the rest.

"Oh no," Lexi said. She let the letter speak for itself as she cleared her throat. "'Dear Louise, I hate, more than anything, having to write you this letter. But James made me promise. If the day that we all dreaded occurred, and tragedy struck, my strict instruction from him was to write to this address and let you know. I regret to say that your beloved James is gone. Early this morning, in an unexpected dawn raid, our unit came under intense fire. We lost half the unit, including my friend who I considered a brother, James Cunningham Fisher." Lexi looked up from the letter to see everyone listening with rapt attention. She continued on, realizing how invested they had all become in James's journey. "'He passed from this earth at 8:27 a.m. He was clutching this photo when he took his last breath.'"

Lexi read the rest of the soldier's letter aloud, about how he would inform James's family of his passing and how he wished her all the best in her future. "Signed, 'Timothy Barbosa, Second Lieutenant.' Gigi must've been devastated, reading this. All her future plans, evaporated in one letter." Lexi lowered the letter to her lap. "I wish I could reach back through time and give her a great big hug. I hate the idea of her feeling alone. No family to support her..."

Graham handed Lexi the photo with a sympathetic tilt of his head as she wiped a tear away and attempted a chuckle. "I can't believe I'm getting this emotional about events that happened decades ago. To a man I've never even met."

"War letters are powerful," Graham assured her. "I've read some during my research. Those young people were facing life and death every day. The soldiers—many of them just teenagers—realized how fleeting life could be, and the loved ones waiting behind on the home front dreaded a letter like that one, prayed it would never come. I'm sure, every day, they were holding their breath."

Lexi nodded. "Those scenes in war movies, when the telegraph comes to the front door. It always meant bad news."

"And it could come at any time," Graham said. "So each day became precious to them."

"Gigi must've been devastated." Still deep in thought over the final letter, Lexi whispered, "Amazing, what that whole generation lived through. But Gigi never talked about those war years. At least, not to me."

"Me either," her mother said. "If anyone brought up the war, she would evade the issue entirely and move on to another topic."

"Keep calm and carry on," her dad mused.

"And then move on," Graham said. "They got on with life, went forward, had families, created postwar lives, and thrived. Though I have no doubt they never forgot. Those memories were embedded deep inside."

Bailey stretched on the floor and made a weird, garbled sound, which broke the silence that had descended on the room.

"Comic relief," Lexi told her dog as she dried her eyes. "I can count on you for that every time."

Graham flipped over his phone. "It's getting late. Guess I got carried away. I'm supposed to meet with my dad and sister pretty soon."

"Where did you park?" Lexi asked.

"Not far, behind the square."

He stood up, startling Bailey, who reluctantly moved aside. Lexi stood with Graham, and her parents gave him polite goodbyes before Lexi led him to the front door then joined him outside. She shut the door as they stood on the brick porch together.

On an impulse, Lexi moved forward and leaned up to grasp him in a hug—sincere but fast—then backed away again. "Thank you for today. It meant so much, reading those letters, feeling close to Gigi again. I discovered parts of her I never knew about."

He gave a half grin. "I don't think I can take credit for all that."

"Well, you were a big reason for it. In lots of ways."

"It was my honor to be part of it. I should be thanking you." He touched her arm as they locked eyes, then he turned away to hustle down the brick walkway.

Lexi headed back inside then returned to the letters, careful to place them back in chronological order. With the ribbons tied snugly around them again, Lexi left them on the side table and went to look for her parents. She could smell the strong scent of spicy minestrone wafting through the house. Her parents were in the kitchen, hugging near the sink. It seemed the letters had taken the same emotional toll on all of them. Lexi cleared her throat, and they separated slowly, still clutching each other's waists.

"I really like him," her mother said. "Graham. He's very personable."

"I can't place his accent," her father said. "I didn't want to be rude by asking."

"He grew up in England." Lexi came closer and leaned against the kitchen island. "He's been incredibly helpful with everything—the necklace, the attic, the letters. And he knows so much about that time period, the war. I'm glad he was here for this. It felt... serendipitous." Her thoughts bounced back to James. "Do y'all think anyone else ever knew about James? I mean, besides Blanche. Did Gigi ever tell Paw-Paw about him?"

Her mother shrugged. "It's possible. Maybe they both kept her secret all that time, together. But I've never doubted their love, and even after hearing these letters, I still don't. I think she loved them both."

"I think so too," Lexi said. "Even though I never saw them together, I remember the way she talked about Paw-Paw. Very affectionately."

"She was devastated when he died. The funeral was very hard for her."

Her father chimed in. "Those two built a good life together. A legacy, with their kids, grandkids, great-grandkids."

"I can't stop wondering, though... Why the secrecy?" Lexi asked. "Even all those years later after Paw-Paw died. Didn't she know that her family would understand? That there could be room in her heart for both men?"

"Maybe it was too painful," her father said. "A dream shattered by the war."

"Plus," her mother said, "she'd already had to keep James a secret from her own family all that time."

"Or maybe it was as simple as Gigi wanting to keep him all to herself," Lexi mused. "A treasure she held privately for all of her life." She traced the granite counter's veins with her fingernail. Even with the letters' discovery and reading James's own words then seeing the teardrop necklace around her great-grandmother's neck in the photo, Lexi still had unanswered questions that she would eventually have to let go of. "I guess in the end, we might never know."

Chapter Eight

Need a break? Graham sent the text and chewed the inside of his cheek as he watched for Lexi's reply.

Seconds later, she answered. *Are you in Morgan's Grove?*

Yep. Looking at Greg's horses. Just pulled up to the ranch. Want to join?

Her lengthy response time told Graham she was probably about to send him some completely legitimate excuse about having to mind the store or work on inventory. But instead, she replied, *I'll be there in five.*

Ecstatic, he slipped the phone into his jeans pocket and shut his car door. Graham hadn't seen Lexi since he left her parents' house after reading James's letters a few days before, though they'd exchanged occasional texts. For the most part, he'd decided to leave her alone for a bit, knowing that she was probably as busy catching up with work as he'd been. But today had felt like the right time to reach out again.

Graham scanned the ranch house and surrounding property: lush green grass, thick trees, and rolling hills that led to the edge of the horizon. He had lucked out with beautiful weather—the perfect afternoon for a ride—having made the appointment with Greg a couple of days before. The sky held a few harmless puffy clouds that floated carelessly overhead, casting roaming shadows on the ground.

Graham walked toward Greg, who was leading the horses out of the barn. They whinnied when they saw Graham.

"I have some bad news." Greg winced as he brought the horses to a halt. "I didn't have time to saddle them up. I just got notified about a Zoom meeting that starts in ten minutes. It involves a big new project for my firm. Totally unexpected. I'll have to take the meeting inside the ranch house."

"Oh. Well, we can reschedule, then." Graham was being overly polite to hide his disappointment. Truth be told, he was crushed at the idea of having to text Lexi and cancel. He might have to think of a different excuse to spend the afternoon with her.

"You can still give them a walk if you want." Greg handed him one of the horses' leads; she was a jet-black beauty. "Check out their temperaments, see how you like them. We could always ride another day."

"Okay, sounds good." Graham clasped the lead as he raised the back of his hand to the horse's nose.

"That's Cinder, the mare."

The horse gave Graham's hand a hesitant sniff then nodded twice.

"Hey, girl." He brought his hand flat against her velvety muzzle for a rub.

She blinked long eyelashes at him.

"And this one is Jem." He handed Graham the lead of a chestnut horse with a white streak down his nose. "He's a bit younger, more spirited, but he's gentle with kids." Greg's phone buzzed, and he whipped it out to look at the screen. "Gotta go. Sorry about this!" He was already walking backward toward the ranch house. "Stay as long as you'd like. Take 'em back to the barn and put them in their stalls when you're done. I'll tend to them right after the call."

"No worries!" Graham shouted after him, causing Cinder to jolt her head.

Graham had had riding experience in England as a boy, and he'd taken his sister out on a few equestrian excursions at a horse ranch far north of Austin over the years—though it was quite a drive, so they didn't ride very often.

"Hey, boy. How are you today?" he asked Jem, who snorted out his reply. Graham rubbed Jem's neck while Cinder grazed leisurely beside him. "We're going for a walk. Just waiting on Lexi. I think you'll like her."

Sensing a certain comfort level in Jem, Graham began to examine him—eyes and ears, hair and skin, then the hooves. Finally, running his hand along the overall frame of the horse and feeling the smooth hair and taut muscles underneath, Graham was assured that the horse was in good health.

As he moved on to Cinder, Graham heard a car nearby and twisted his neck to see Lexi pulling up. Straightening up and patting the dust from his hands, he watched as she parked beside his car and got out with a cheery wave. Her silky blouse ruffled in the wind as she came toward the horses. She slowed to a careful stop in front of Cinder, who had raised her head and pricked her ears at the sight of this new stranger.

"Well, hello," Lexi told Cinder, raising her hand slowly for a sniff.

She's done this before, Graham thought.

"This is Cinder, and that one's Jem." He took up Jem's lead again.

"They're beautiful." She had already begun rubbing along Cinder's nose, making the horse drowsy. After a moment, Lexi gave a side-glance to Graham. "And hello to you too."

"I'm glad you were able to get away."

"I probably shouldn't have, but Ruby insisted—practically shoved me out the door. We've been swamped ever since the grand opening. It's a blessing, but it's kept me busy. Plus the electricity went out for a while yesterday. I've hardly had time to breathe since the last time I saw you." She reached for Cinder's lead with her other hand and paused. "Is Greg joining us? I assumed you'd take them out for a ride."

Graham explained about the Zoom call and the postponed ride. "Greg suggested taking them for a walk 'round the property to get a sense of their temperament."

"Good idea. It couldn't be a more perfect day." She leaned her face toward the sky and blinked. Her wavy hair cascaded over her shoulders, while her profile showed a pert nose and straight teeth as her lips parted to take it all in. If Graham were a photographer, he would ask her to freeze, right then and there, to capture the moment. She was a natural beauty.

Together, they maneuvered the horses into a U-turn to face the ranch's wide-open spaces then walked the dirt path while the horses flanked them on either side, ambling along and bobbing their heads. Graham assumed the horses had taken this very route hundreds of times before.

"I'm hoping for something similar to this." Graham gestured outward. "For our future property. Lots of trees, some good-sized hills. This terrain is ideal."

"The countryside around Morgan's Grove all looks pretty similar to this," Lexi said. "I used to go exploring as a kid—sneak onto other ranches, pretend I was alone and lost in the woods. I love it here. This town, this place. I never want to leave."

The path took a bend, putting them closer to a thick crop of trees and offering shade from the bright sun. "I envy that. Having roots—a real sense of home," Graham said.

"You mentioned once that England felt the most like home for you?"

"It did. And even when we moved, my mum was the one who made Texas home for me. But when she passed..." He looked ahead at a lake snaking into view. "I was quite lost. I don't think I've found my bearings since. In the way of feeling 'home' again, I mean."

"It's so hard to lose someone. And it takes a while to find our footing. The world is never really the same again without them in it.

I mean, memories help—thinking of the good times. But when they leave us, they take that feeling of home with them when they go."

Somehow, Lexi had put into words exactly what Graham had been feeling since his mum died but could never formulate or express.

"I think you're spot on," he said softly.

They walked in silence for a few minutes, and Graham paid attention to sights and sounds he was usually too busy to notice in his everyday life—birds chirping, squirrels playing, leaves rustling. In his fantasy, he wished he could abandon his teaching job altogether and spend the rest of his days on a ranch: tending to the land, raising horses—and maybe a family too. Someday...

"How about a pause?" Lexi asked, pointing toward a bench that sat under a stately oak tree. The lake ran behind it, carved into the land.

"Where did this come from? It seems so random—a park bench in such an open space."

"There's an inscription." Lexi walked Cinder over to view the engraved brass plate imbedded in the bench's center plank: "'The calm retreat, the silent shade, with prayer and praise agree.' By John Cowper."

Lexi led Cinder toward the side of the bench then dropped the lead on the ground, waiting to see if the horse might stay in place and graze. She did, so Graham did the same with Jem before joining Lexi on the bench.

"Have you made your decision about the horses?" Lexi crossed her legs.

"I think I made the decision the minute I saw them." Graham stared toward the wide pasture ahead of them. "There's a sweet look in their eyes. Gentle souls."

"I picked up on that too. Perfect for a therapy ranch. Maybe their original sale fell through for a reason."

"You mean fate?"

"Maybe. So, what made you and your dad interested in doing this? Starting a therapy ranch?" Lexi readjusted herself on the bench, which made her jeans lightly touch Graham's.

"My sister, Shelley. She's the inspiration. Here, I have a photo."

He pulled out his phone and scrolled through photos until he came to his favorite one—Shelley, smiling at a butterfly that had landed on the back of her hand. She had brought it up to her face then grinned and blinked her eyes shut just as the butterfly flapped its wings. And Graham had captured the shot.

"She's seven years younger." He passed the phone over to Lexi. At this point in any conversation that involved his sister, he always became hesitant. He felt a vigorous over-protection of her, even if she wasn't in his presence. "She has Down syndrome."

Graham waited for Lexi's reaction as she held the phone and zoomed in closer. "She's beautiful."

"I think so too. Inside and out. She's the purest, most unjaded person I know. I don't deserve her." Graham could feel himself choking up and cleared his throat to mask it.

Lexi passed the phone back. "I can tell how much you love her. Do you get to see her often?"

"Every week. She lives in Austin too."

"And she's the inspiration for the ranch?"

"Right. I want to name it after her, give her a legacy."

"What an amazing gift. Does she know about it yet?"

Graham pocketed his phone. "We're keeping it a surprise. I don't want to get her hopes up too high yet. Her concept of time is somewhat skewed, so if I promise her a ranch, she'll expect it ready by tomorrow."

Lexi giggled. "Cute. How old is she?"

"Nearly twenty-six. She houses at Care Living in north Austin. It's a wonderful place. She's quite independent, lives on her own in one of their apartments, and has a part-time job on the premises."

"That's where you went on Saturday, to see her, with your dad?"

Graham shook his head. "No, I saw her alone. Dad backed out. We were supposed to break the news together, about Beth."

"Your dad's new fiancée."

"Right. And we're not sure how Shelley will take it. Especially since Dad's moved the wedding up to next month."

"Yikes."

Graham crossed his arms over his chest. "I guess I'm no better. In the end, I chickened out. I was all set to tell Shelley that afternoon, but she was working this puzzle and looked totally content. I didn't have the heart to say anything. But she's got to know soon. I'll try again this week... maybe Dad will have the guts to go with me. Strength in numbers."

"I'm sure you'll find the right words."

"I hope so."

A warm breeze suddenly blew Lexi's hair all around her face. She giggled and combed it back into place with her fingers. "It's beautiful here. I could stay all day. But..." She slapped her open palms against her thighs and rose from the bench with a tiny grunt. "Duty calls."

"Back to the store?" Graham asked as they collected the horses, who had to be perked up from their sleepy state and convinced to move back onto the trail.

"Actually, no." She led Cinder beside her as they took up their same relaxed pace toward the ranch house. "I told Jo—my cousin, Jolene—that I would show her a couple of James's letters. Gigi was her great-grandmother, too, so Jo's been dying to see them, but I haven't had time to swing by yet."

"Jo works at the founder's mansion?"

"Yes, and you'd probably love seeing it—a historic site, over a hundred years old. Come along if you have time."

Graham couldn't believe his luck. When he'd texted Lexi to join him with the horses, he hadn't imagined she would say yes, or especially that she would say yes *and* extend their afternoon together. "I actually do. I had carved out a couple of hours for a ride, but without Greg here, it'll have to wait."

Graham watched as Lexi's gaze was suddenly drawn elsewhere, to the patch of land beyond the trees. "Bluebonnets," she said. "Probably the last ones of the season."

"Let's go for a look." He nudged Jem off the beaten path, and the horse obediently followed with a quiet snort.

Lexi and Cinder stepped in line beside them, and in a matter of seconds, they had come upon a stunning field, thick with bluebonnets twitching slightly with the wind.

"I never get tired of seeing them," Lexi whispered, stopping to take them all in. "That blueish-purple hue can't be matched anywhere else. They were such a huge part of my childhood, every spring. I remember my mother dressing me up and plopping me down right in the middle of a patch, exactly like this one, for endless photos."

"How about a grown-up one right now?" Graham brought his phone out.

She waved away the idea with a grin. "It's kinda corny now, taking pics with bluebonnets. Everyone does it these days. It's become a cliché."

"Well, not everyone has a horse with them in the shot."

Her eyes lit up. "That's true!" She maneuvered Cinder to back up along the edge, as close as she could, without trampling a single flower.

Graham dropped his horse's lead and backed away with his phone then steadied it for the perfect shot. He took a few—some with Lexi and the horse to the side in order to showcase the bluebonnets and then a couple of close-ups for good measure.

He lowered his phone as Lexi and Cinder rejoined him. "I'll text them to you."

"Ariel will love them. She's been bugging me to send her some social media content. She always updates our store's account. 'We need to humanize you,' she's always saying. 'People eat that stuff up.'"

"Well, she's right. With that blouse picking up the blue in your eyes, and the bluebonnets behind you..." He realized he might've crossed an invisible line and dipped his head. "Anyway, I think Ariel will be pleased."

They made their way back to the ranch house at an easy pace, and Graham knew that the walk had done him a world of good. The troubles that had plagued him when he first arrived at the ranch—lectures to prepare, his father's insensitivity to Shelley, concerns about how she would take the news—had all evaporated by the time they reached the barn.

Horse therapy, indeed.

JO STUDIED THE PHOTO Lexi had handed her, the black-and-white of Gigi and James standing together. "Okay, this is gonna sound weird. But you know how men in black-and-white photos aren't very... attractive? They look sort of stilted and unsmiling and have slicked-back hair. I guess the standards of what was considered pretty or handsome were different back then." She looked at the photo again. "But James *is* handsome, even by today's standards. And of course, Gigi, well..."

"Always beautiful," Lexi said.

Minutes before, Lexi and Graham had arrived at the mansion while Jolene was finishing up an important call, so while they waited,

Lexi encouraged Graham to take a tour of the mansion on his own and roam around. After Jolene's call ended, she and Lexi had met up in the parlor, where an elongated glass case stood in the far corner, displaying some World War II memorabilia.

Jo handed Lexi the photo back then switched her attention to the letter that accompanied it. While Jo read the letter, Lexi texted Graham, telling him their location so he could find them when he'd finished exploring the house. She put her phone away then watched her cousin's eyes skim across the letter's text, widening every so often as she stopped to reread a passage.

"Amazing, reading an eighty-year-old letter. So, who is this Blanche person?" Jo asked as she folded the letter and placed it back inside the envelope. "I don't remember anyone in the family ever mentioning her. I called to ask my mom last night, but she had no clue."

"My mother doesn't remember either. I've contacted Savannah, to see if maybe she could research Blanche's address and find more information on her."

Jo handed the envelope back to Lexi. "I can't believe you found all those letters, and in such pristine condition. What a piece of history. *Our* history."

"I was stunned when we found them."

"We?" Jo leaned in and whispered, "You mean Graham? I can't wait to meet him, finally!"

"Shh." Lexi chided her, knowing Graham was probably nearby, coming to meet them at any moment. "Can we please stay focused and professional and not be twelve years old?"

Jo cleared her throat and suppressed a grin. "Focused. Professional. Got it."

"You mentioned USO photos? Maybe they'll hold some clues."

A baby's cry pierced the air from the next room as a boisterous family entered the mansion.

"Right. I'm pretty sure Gigi's photo is in this case of mementos since she worked as a volunteer for the USO. I remember seeing it."

"Did our family donate the photo?" Lexi asked. "How did it get to the mansion?"

"There are some records I can look through in the basement. I might have some time this afternoon," Jo said. "Years ago, when I worked here as a teenager, the curator did sort of a town-wide inquiry, asking all Morgan's Grove residents if they'd be willing to donate their World War II memorabilia for these cases. It was advertised in the paper, and we got a ton of responses. I think she even spread the word past the Austin area. So I'm not exactly sure how the photo got here or who delivered it to the mansion." Jo raised the glass hatch then let her eyes roam the photos. After a minute, she squealed. "This is it!"

She bent down and delicately pulled out a black-and-white five-by-seven.

Lexi felt as breathless as she had when she'd discovered the letters under the attic's floorboard. "Is it her?"

Jo raised the photo between them. "Yes!"

Lexi instantly recognized Gigi, side-by-side with another young woman, a blonde. Both of them wore the typical forties fashion—knee-length skirts with tight waists and bobbed, curled-under hair.

"Is that..." Lexi pointed to the woman standing beside Gigi.

"Blanche," Jo said. "Look at the back side!" She flipped the picture around so Lexi could see.

Someone had scrawled "Louise and Blanche, Autumn 1941."

"Right before Pearl Harbor," Lexi said. "Maybe she first met James here, in the mansion—at the USO."

"It's where a lot of soldiers met the young female volunteers. And often fell in love with them."

"I wish we had a photo of James at the mansion too. It would fill in some gaps in the timeline." Lexi clasped the photo and brought it closer. "I don't think that's Gigi's writing—"

"Hey there," a man's voice said, making Lexi jump.

"Sorry!" Graham chuckled as Lexi swiveled to see him. "Didn't mean to startle you."

"We were looking at this photo. Of Gigi." Lexi handed it to him. "And that's Blanche."

Graham studied the photo and smiled. "What a find."

Jo piped up. "I was just telling Lexi that someone donated the photo to the mansion years ago. These are all from the USO—the mansion was one of its headquarters. I'm Jolene, by the way. And you must be the famous Graham."

"Not sure about the 'famous' part, but yes. That's me."

"What do you think of the mansion?" Jo asked.

"Incredible." Graham let his eyes roam around the room. "The architecture and details, the history." His eyes returned to the photo then darted toward Lexi. "What's the next step? I mean, this confirms their friendship and that this is *the* Blanche."

"I called Savannah yesterday and gave her the address on the envelope, Blanche's, to see what she could find out. I'm sure Blanche is deceased by now. But maybe one of her relatives owns the house and could give us more information. A long shot but worth asking."

"Good thinking," Graham said.

"But a search for James is the real challenge." Lexi sighed. "Since he was killed in the war, it means no wife, no children to contact..."

"Maybe there are nieces and nephews? Or cousins?" Graham handed back the photo.

"That's what I was thinking." Lexi hesitated then said, "Y'all, don't laugh, but I'm thinking of hiring a private investigator. Is that crazy? Am I too obsessed with this?" Both Graham and Jo shook their heads, and Lexi was relieved. "It's just... I don't have time to do much more on my own. I'm at an impasse."

"It's worth a try." Jo's phone buzzed in her hand, and she glanced at the screen. "Duty calls. I've gotta take this."

Lexi hastily gave back the photo, and Jo replaced it inside the case then closed the lid with a soft click. As the phone's relentless buzzing continued, Jo backed out of the room—"I'll text you about those basement records"—then turned away to answer the call.

Graham slid his hands into his pockets then sidestepped along the glass case, pausing to lean in and read a document or study another photo. Lexi had already viewed the case before, so she quietly texted Ruby about tomorrow's estate sale while Graham finished his tour of the room.

"I'll recommend this place to my students next week, show them the website. Maybe offer some extra credit for a tour," he said, joining Lexi again.

"Good idea. Jo would love that." She finished reading Ruby's text about the store being suddenly swamped and pocketed her phone. "I'd better get back to work. But today was fun. I'm glad you asked me to see the horses."

"I'll call you again if Greg has time to take them for a ride."

As she walked with him out the door and down the front porch stairs, Lexi brushed away the idea that his invitation nearly sounded like the setup for a date. She was glad Jolene wasn't there to listen in. Lexi would've never heard the end of it.

Chapter Nine

"How's he doing?" Lexi asked Ariel, who had emerged from the store's back room.

"Better. I added another blanket and freshened up his water bowl."

Bailey was notoriously spooked by storms—which occurred frequently during the months of April and May. Thirty minutes earlier, when most of Central Texas had been placed under a tornado watch, Ariel had offered to lead Bailey inside the back room, to the kennel where he preferred to stay during storms. He felt safer inside the cage, with a blanket draped over it and a sleep machine turned on nearby.

"Thanks for looking out for him," Lexi said.

Storms usually meant fewer shoppers, so for much of this morning, the store's traffic had been scarce. Currently, there were two customers, sheltering in place. Lexi peered out a nearby window and watched a jagged streak of lightning touch down far across the field. She braced for the imminent crack of thunder, which hit several seconds later. The lights flickered in the store.

She pivoted toward the desk, where Ruby was busy knitting at a ferocious pace.

"That one seemed farther away than the last one," Lexi said, hoping to reassure her friend.

Ruby nodded, not looking up from her needles, which moved deftly over and under the yarn. "The tornado watch has just ended." Her phone displayed an updated radar page for the Morgan's Grove area.

"Well, that's a relief."

As long as Lexi had known her, Ruby had monitored the weather daily, even if skies were cloudless and blue. When Ruby was nine years old, her family's home was caught in a tornado on the outskirts of Morgan's Grove. While she and her siblings were hunched over in a bathtub for protection, the tornado ripped the entire roof off their house before moving on and causing more damage elsewhere. The family, and even the dog, had remained miraculously untouched. But Ruby's trauma from the experience never truly resolved—and always had her watching the skies, especially when alerts came. Knitting soothed her, gave her hands and mind something to do.

The bell above the door tinkled, and a silver-haired man walked in with a dripping umbrella in one hand and a thick bouquet of multicolored flowers in the other. Lexi had trouble seeing his face until he lowered the bouquet, and then she recognized him.

"Henry?" Lexi hadn't spoken to him since he'd shown up at the grand opening last week. Frankly, she hadn't expected to see him ever again, since his role with Gigi's necklace was essentially over. But here he was in Morgan's Grove for the second time in one week.

"What are you doing out in this weather!" Ruby said it more like an accusation than a question. "How could you drive during a tornado alert?" She had abandoned her knitting and rounded the desk to stand beside Lexi.

"Well, that's not a very friendly greeting," Henry said with a lopsided grin. "Especially for a man who's bringing you flowers."

He extended the bouquet toward Ruby, whose face melted into an appreciative smile. "They're lovely." She accepted them and brought them to her nose for a deep whiff.

"The storm wasn't *so* bad when I left for Morgan's Grove. Just a few drops on the windshield."

"Didn't you look at your weather app?" Ruby asked. "It's always wise to check the radar before you drive anywhere."

"I'll remember that next time," he said with a wink.

Another peal of thunder startled Ruby, and she jumped in place, her eyes opening wide. Lexi was close enough to set a protective hand on Ruby's back.

"I'll put these in water," Ruby said then swiftly disappeared into the back room.

Lexi made cordial chitchat with Henry until Ruby returned. To pass the time, Lexi caught him up on the letters found in the attic and the USO photo from Jo at the mansion, all a direct result of Henry's help with the teardrop necklace.

"How marvelous," he said. "To think that a hidden love story was uncovered eighty years later."

When Ruby emerged, it was obvious to Lexi that she was not only calmer but had also taken time to freshen up. She wore a fresh coat of lipstick and had added a silky scarf to her peach blouse.

Henry rubbed his hands together nervously, and Lexi was suddenly a third wheel. She saw Ariel across the store, keeping busy with some discreet dusting, so Lexi decided to join her. She could hear Henry's voice drifting behind her as she walked away: "Let me take you for brunch. My treat."

It wasn't long before Ruby approached Lexi. "I think I'll take my lunch break earlier than usual." She held her phone and refreshed the weather's radar. "The danger has passed, it seems."

"Of course. Take your time. And have fun!"

"Thank you, sweetie." Ruby drew in a deep breath then walked with Henry out the door. As he opened it for her, Lexi could tell that the rain had lessened to a mere whisper of a sprinkle.

Ariel had moved to the back room and was sitting cross-legged on the floor by Bailey's cage, wiggling her fingers at him through the grate. Lexi found them and bent down to sit beside Ariel. "So, what's up with Ruby and Henry? Are they a thing now?"

"They've been texting a lot."

"Since when?"

"The grand opening. They also play some word game online that I forget the name of."

"How interesting. She didn't tell me."

"She didn't really tell me either. I've been catching her giggling at the screen, and then I accidentally saw Henry's text coming through a couple of times."

"Well, good for her." It had been years since Ruby's husband had died, and she had always waved away the idea of ever getting involved with someone new. But here came Henry into her life, completely unexpected, with flowers in hand. A nice reminder for Lexi that life could still hold surprises around the corner.

Bailey stretched to lick Ariel's fingertips, which made one corner of her mouth turn upward in the first near-smile that Lexi had seen from her in a long while. Ariel's dark hair looked unbrushed today, and she wasn't wearing her usual harsh eyeliner.

"Are you doing okay?" Lexi tiptoed around with her word choices. "You seem a little tired."

Ariel placed both hands in her lap and stared down at them. "Mom's back in rehab. Since yesterday."

"Oh, honey." Lexi placed a hand on Ariel's wrist for comfort. "I'm sorry."

"Twice since last year. And this time, Bobby couldn't take it. So he left the house last night. Cleared out all his stuff."

From what Lexi remembered, Bobby had been her mom's live-in boyfriend for the past two years. Which meant that, at the moment, Ariel was living totally alone, without either of them—or their incomes. The pressure must've been debilitating for her.

Lexi moved her hand back to her own lap and studied Ariel's face, which was still downcast. "And how are *you* doing with all this?"

She received a dismissive shrug in return, and Lexi had her answer.

After a beat, Ariel shuffled to get to her feet then leaned forward to open Bailey's kennel.

Lexi pushed off the floor. "If you need anything, let me know. Okay?" She waited for Ariel to make eye contact, which she finally did in a flicker.

"I will."

GRAHAM STARED AT THE ceiling, studying the moon's bright reflection from the window in his bedroom. He had gone to bed two hours ago, his body exhausted from the workday, but his mind remained frustratingly wide awake.

He grunted and rolled over, smushing his pillow and attempting a new position. But even that didn't help. Giving up, he threw off the covers and got out of bed in defeat. Insomnia had won. He didn't often struggle with it, but some nights, for no particular reason, it plagued him.

His mum had always told him milk would lull him back to sleep, so he gave it a try. He let the moon light the way as he fumbled in the dark toward the kitchen and moved toward the fridge. Before he even cracked open the door, he knew: there was no milk. He hadn't had time for a grocery run after school.

He rumpled his already rumpled hair and made his way to the living room, where he clicked on a lamp and settled onto the couch. He used a nearby blanket to cover his bare legs—he always slept in a T-shirt and boxers—and hoped sleep would find him there. He brought his laptop to rest on the blanket, intending to browse the internet or watch a couple of mindless dog videos.

When he opened the laptop, he saw the document he'd been steadily working on for the last two days—scattered ideas, brainstorming... for what? He wasn't sure yet.

The last three weeks involving Lexi's necklace had sparked something in him he hadn't experienced in years. An excitement, an inspiration that held his attention and kept him curious. Two days ago, he'd typed in some ideas about the home front during World War II—how girlfriends and mothers and war widows, specifically, had to keep the home together *and* replace the soldiers in the workforce in jobs they'd never held before, all while fighting a persistent worry about their loved ones overseas. Lexi's necklace and the letters had brought the home front's plight into a tangible light for Graham. He didn't realize how affected he'd been until he couldn't stop thinking about it.

Ideas came again, and he hastily got them down—living with death as a daily possibility, staying strong for the children's sake, remaining upbeat in letters to the soldiers—and he felt an enthusiasm rise in his chest.

Finished with his brainstorming, finally empty of ideas, Graham closed his laptop and let his mind wander backward, to Theresa. She would have rolled her eyes over his obsession with the necklace or at least gently mocked him. She had never understood his fascination with history. "It's long gone, in the past," she would say with a flippant tone. "Why does it matter? We can't do a single thing to change it." It used to bother him that he couldn't fully be his true self around her and geek out about his excitement over "boring" historical events. And even now, as he observed their relationship from the rearview mirror, little things would still jump out at him—the way her eyes drifted casually down to her phone when he was telling her about his day or how she would sometimes cut him off, mid-sentence, to talk about herself.

Why hadn't he seen it back then? Or more importantly, *why had he put up with it for so long?* They were not a good match and never had been, even in the beginning.

Graham yawned as he stared into the air. He supposed it was the normal course of any breakup, reliving bits and pieces of memories afterward and analyzing them through a different lens. But rather than making him pensive or miss Theresa, the memories did the opposite. He realized, more than ever, that their personalities weren't compatible. Maybe Theresa knew it, too, before Graham did, and was wise to break it off when she did. If so, he was grateful for it.

LEXI POPPED OPEN THE microwave to reveal the perfectly warmed glazed donut she'd inserted ten seconds before. She'd already poured a glass of cold milk, and she reached for it then shut the microwave door with her elbow. Lexi would *not* feel guilty about this early-morning indulgence. Recently, she'd decided it was better to enjoy an occasional donut rather than deprive herself completely. Otherwise, she might be in danger of eating half a box all in one sitting. Better to enjoy her guilty pleasure in moderation.

She carried her plate into the living room, where a lamp cast its warm glow from the corner. Still groggy, she sat on the couch and spread a quilt over her bare legs. Even though the donut was the perfect temperature to devour, Lexi let it sit on her lap, on top of the quilt, as she held the milk and listened to the silence.

She had awakened two hours before her alarm, when it was pitch-dark outside. Bailey had whined to go out, so Lexi had trundled downstairs with him and opened the back door then figured she might as well eat an early breakfast, knowing it would be impossible to go back to sleep.

Staring at the coffee table her mother had helped her decorate a couple of years ago, with baubles and knickknacks and a silk plant, Lexi wondered why the stillness of the morning was bothering her. Usually, her life was filled to the brim with noise and busyness. There was always someplace to be or something to do—tasks to accomplish, lists to make, plans to carry out. Even now, she could easily grab her phone and scroll, stay distracted. But this morning, in the dark pocket of an early dawn, Lexi wanted to sit inside the quiet and figure it out.

It wasn't exactly loneliness, this uncomfortable sensation. Lexi was fulfilled in every area—her work life was satisfying, she had a comfortable home, good friends, loving parents, a sweet companion in Bailey. Every area except love.

And there it was. For the last few years, since her divorce, she had convinced herself that she was happily single and independent. And she *was*. But what if that was shifting or changing for some reason? What if there was a yearning, no matter how slight, that had begun creeping in? A desire for a partner in her life—someone to share the small things with, and the big things too. Someone to seek out whenever she had a bad day—or a good one. She thought about people who had successful and loving relationships: her own parents, Ruby and her former husband, even Gigi and Paw-Paw. They had built their lives together, had shared decades of mutual experiences together, vacationed together, laughed together. And Lexi knew she might want that too. Eventually.

She remembered telling Jolene a couple of weeks ago that this life of hers—busy and bustling and active—was "enough." But here in the silence, staring at her uneaten donut, listening to the sound of her own breathing, she wondered if it really was.

Chapter Ten

Lexi tapped her foot against the bench leg and stared at her phone, impatiently waiting for Jolene's text. She'd just gotten off the phone with her, and Jolene had told her some good news—that not only had she located the records for who submitted the USO photo with Gigi and Blanche, but she had a phone number, too, which she promised to text shortly. Apparently, Heidi Middleton, Blanche's granddaughter, lived in Morgan's Grove fifteen years ago and had donated the photo to the founder's mansion. Jo had no idea if she still lived in town—"It could be an old, out-of-date number, so don't get your hopes too high," Jo had cautioned—but promised to send Lexi the information when they hung up.

As she waited, Lexi pondered over how much detail she should give to Heidi and what she hoped to gain. *Did Heidi know anything about Gigi? Had she ever heard about James and their love story—and his death? Had Blanche ever revealed the secrets to her own family, or had she carried them to her grave?*

The chattering sound of happy quilters drifted on the breeze toward Lexi as she waited. Earlier, she had decided to swing by the warehouse before work and check on Let's Get Crafty to see how things were functioning. "Very smoothly," Pam told her, and what Lexi saw with her own eyes confirmed it. Lexi had walked the space, with Bailey in tow, to see a whole party of senior ladies seated in a circle, being tutored on quilting scarves. And farther down, a class of students on a field trip created paintings for their parents. And at the end of the warehouse, a seventy-something man with his hand deep inside wet clay spun a pottery wheel with strict concentration as the instructor looked on. This was what she had envisioned, even from the first brainstorming idea two years before. *Making learning fun.*

When the pottery instructor had spotted her and waved his clay-covered hand, Lexi received Jo's call and had to step away. She'd whisked back through the building and exited to the bench outside with Bailey.

Just when Lexi had wondered what the hold-up was with Jo's follow-up text, the *ding* came through. Before she could lose her nerve—or overrehearse—Lexi clicked on Heidi's phone number then watched her phone dial it for her.

A female voice floated up to Lexi's ear, but it was only a voicemail greeting. Still, the recording confirmed that it was, indeed, Heidi Middleton, so Lexi left a message. She had only intended to leave her name and number, but she wasn't sure if Heidi would consider it spam—most people didn't return strangers' calls. So Lexi spilled the whole story, as concisely as she possibly could, onto Heidi's voice-mail. Lexi told who she was, mentioned Gigi and the USO photo then brought up the letters with Blanche's address and James Fisher too. It was a complicated story, and Lexi hoped what she was saying made any sense at all.

She finished the message and clicked off. Realizing that was all she could do and hoping she would hear back from Heidi at some point, Lexi pushed off the bench and steered Bailey toward the antiques store. As soon as she grasped the door handle, her cell rang.

It was Graham. She couldn't wait to tell him about Heidi, but he preempted her. "Hey, listen, I don't have much time—I'm running late to a faculty meeting."

Lexi could hear him puffing out the words, and she grinned, picturing him fast-walking on campus in his blazer and tie.

"I wanted to ask you something."

"Sure, what's up?" Lexi had released the door handle and remained outside the store. Bailey looked up at her in confusion.

"Well, I'm meeting my sister this afternoon, and I was thinking... would you want to join me? At her place? My dad flaked again. I don't want to be on my own, telling Shelley about the wedding. I need some moral support, and I thought of you." He took a moment to take a couple of short breaths then went on. "This is a big ask, I know. But you wouldn't have to say anything—I'll do all the explaining about Dad and Beth. I just thought it might be good to have someone else with me."

Lexi, flattered, did a quick mental check of the day's schedule then said, "Sure. I'll be in Austin anyway, meeting with the PI."

"Nice. I wanted to be at her place by two. I'll text you the address, and we can meet there after my faculty meeting ends."

They said goodbye, then Lexi opened the door for Bailey, who sprinted toward Ariel the minute he saw her squatting down, her arms extended.

LEXI TUGGED AT HER paisley blouse then smoothed out her hair again as she stepped out of her car. During a quick break from the store, before driving to Austin, she had dashed home to change clothes and brush her hair into a ponytail then add a little lipstick. She had a strong desire to make a good impression on Shelley—perhaps since she was someone so important to Graham.

She had followed Graham's text instructions to park at Care Living's main entrance and meet him outside. She was early enough to slow her pace and glance over the property—gorgeous landscaping, pristine buildings in matching taupe brick, benches dotted all around, even a man-made lake in the distance. Beyond the lake, she saw two tall apartment buildings. The grounds were similar to a college campus, warm and inviting.

Lexi heard a voice from behind her. "You beat me here."

She swiveled to see Graham approaching, dressed in dark slacks and a light-blue shirt, unbuttoned at the neck.

"I didn't want to be late," she said.

When he stopped in front of her, she noticed light bags underneath his eyes and wondered if he'd been sleeping well. Her first instinct was to reach up and touch his face, but she squashed that impulse and asked, "How did your meeting go?"

"Boring, as usual. And there's always that one professor who asks a thousand pointless questions and keeps us there overtime. Anyway—I'm glad to be here instead. Thanks for coming. It means a lot."

"I'm glad you asked. I've wanted to meet Shelley ever since you mentioned her."

"Speaking of meetings, how did yours go? With the PI?"

"Not much to tell—I'll fill you in later. It was only an initial meeting. But I did get a piece of potentially exciting news this morning, before you called me." She pivoted toward the main building then linked her hand through his arm and guided him forward. "I don't want to be late meeting Shelley. That would be a bad first impression. So I'll talk as we walk." As they took leisurely steps, she recounted that Jolene had unearthed Heidi's contact information and passed it along to Lexi. "I left Heidi a lengthy voicemail, and I'm waiting on her call. Hopefully today!"

"Sounds promising. I hope you get some answers." Graham held the front door open, and Lexi passed through to view a high-ceilinged lobby with a seating area to one side and a desk to the other. The middle-aged woman behind it gave Graham a cheery wave.

"You have a guest today, I see."

"I do. This is Lexi Price."

"Well, let's get you a name tag. Graham, you can sign in for both of you."

Already knowing what to do, he took the pen from its holder and scribbled into a hardcovered book. The woman wrote out Lexi's name in all capital letters with a bright-blue Sharpie, peeled back the sticker, then handed the name tag to her as quiet giggles floated down from the hallway.

"Shelley will be thrilled to see you. Both of you," the woman said with a knowing smile then peered down at some paperwork.

Lexi patted the name tag under her shoulder. "Is it straight?" she whispered to Graham, hoping she wasn't letting her nerves show.

"Perfect," he whispered back as he leaned in closer, creating strong, flirty eye contact, making her nerves grow stronger.

Graham grasped her hand and guided her down the hall, where the jumbled mixture of voices and laughter grew louder. The hallway itself was as exquisitely decorated as the lobby had been—artwork adorned the textured walls, a seating area flanked a cozy table in the corner, and soft piano music piped out of a speaker somewhere. Graham led Lexi toward a set of imposing double doors, one open and one shut, where he paused.

"So, way down there"—Graham released her hand and pointed—"is the dining area." He moved closer to the double doors. "And this is the activities room. It's where they hold most of their events. Concerts, crafts, meetings, game nights, choir rehearsals, parties, movie nights, you name it."

Lexi followed Graham through the open door and saw a spacious area with hardwood floors, high ceilings, and a whole wall of windows that let strong light into the room. At one end was a stage, and at the other was a coffee bar.

Half the space was unoccupied, but the other half held four round tables with about two dozen people of all ages, either standing or sitting together, working intensely on various arts projects. One young man elbowed another one beside him, pointed to the table, and let out a huge belly laugh that echoed throughout the room. Two other girls were hunched together in a whisper, clearly the best of friends. An older man thrust his tongue out of his mouth as he applied glue to a wooden piece he held.

Lexi followed Graham as he waved at someone across the room and picked up his pace. The young woman who had caught his attention jumped up from her seat and met him in the middle. Lexi paused to watch them hug as if they hadn't seen each other for years. She couldn't remember the last time she'd seen—or shared in—such a pure and gleeful embrace.

Graham whispered into the girl's ear, and she peeked around him to look at Lexi.

"This is my sister—" Before Graham could even get the name out, Shelley had bounded around Graham to approach Lexi with a huge grin, arms extended. She leaned upward for a hug. Lexi gladly complied, tightening her embrace to match Shelley's and feeling like she was greeting an old friend.

Backing away, the girl pointed to herself. "I'm Shelley." She had wide-set blue eyes, the same color as Graham's, and a beautiful bow of a mouth. Her light-brown, shoulder-length hair bounced with each syllable.

"It's great to meet you. I'm Lexi."

Graham took the few steps to stand between them and put a gentle hand on both of their backs. "I think we're a couple of minutes late?"

"Nope!" Shelley held up her phone close to his face. "On time." She paused and frowned. "Dad here?"

"He couldn't come." Graham winced. "But he wants to take you out for lunch next week."

"What are y'all working on?" Lexi asked, peeking over to see the table where Shelley had come from, with everyone at work on their tasks.

"See this, see this!" She took Lexi by the wrist and led her to the table. But Lexi's grin disappeared when she recognized the project they were working on.

Shelley released Lexi's wrist and pointed.

Gnomes. The nasty little creatures stood all around the table. They were being painted by the crafting participants. Before anyone could notice her shock, Lexi recovered, shoving her angst down to the pit of her stomach. She cleared her throat and readjusted the purse strap on her shoulder. She could do this.

"You, Graham, share—the gnome. Decorate together!" Shelley was already seated, pushing the paints toward Lexi and Graham's appointed gnome. Lexi zoned in on the mischievous face and recognized it instantly. Then she scanned the rest of the table—eight in all. *The same gnomes from her shop.*

Graham stood behind Lexi, also staring at the gnomes. "Okay, hang on a sec, Shelley." Graham stepped away from the table a few feet and motioned for Lexi to join him. He leaned in for a whispered explanation. "Listen, Ruby told me about your phobia last week. I bought up the gnomes from your store and donated them to Shelley's place, assuming they would be displayed around the gardens—not used as an art project on the very day you're visiting! I promise—this is all some bizarre coincidence."

The concern in his eyes was palpable. Lexi believed him. And before they could move on with the rest of the afternoon, it was her job to reassure him. She mentally took her anxiety by the throat and flung it aside then reciprocated his whisper, turning her face closer to his and away from Shelley's view. "No, it's fine. Totally. It's not even a phobia. More like... an aversion."

Graham studied her face and smiled.

"My aversion is funny?" Lexi asked, faking shock.

"No. It's just... really cute."

Shelley called out Lexi's name then impatiently patted the extra seat beside her.

"We're being summoned," Lexi told Graham.

She stepped forward again and took the seat next to Shelley, forcing herself to stare at the gnome in front of her—eight inches high, beady eyes just visible beneath his cap, and displaying a wicked smile through his long white beard. She pushed down the shiver running along her spine and looked around at the other gnomes, already half painted. One gnome across the table was painted all white, and its expression had been transformed into something rather sweet and jovial. Another one had a yellow top and polka-dotted pants, with a pink face—nearly unrecognizable as a gnome. More of a friendly elf. *This wasn't so bad.*

"You're *sure*?" Graham mouthed as he sat beside Lexi.

"Yes. You were sweet to buy them. Let's paint!" But first, she had to make a quick adjustment. She rotated the gnome so that Graham was the one seeing its icy stare.

They collaborated on how to approach the project and decided to make it as cheerful as possible. "Big happy flowers" was Lexi's suggestion. "Like those big cartoonish flowers they used in the sixties. You know, flower power?"

"Orange and pink. Peace and love?"

"That's it."

Shelley introduced the rest of the table to Lexi—Brad, Amanda, Lois, June, Allison, and Andrew, who all stopped long enough to acknowledge her then returned eagerly to their tasks.

Before long, Lexi and Graham were making progress, catching up to the others. From time to time, Lexi would peek over at Shelley's creation and compliment her bold colors and precision with the brush.

"This is harder than it looks," she said, confiding to Shelley.

Lexi watched Shelley give her own gnome red pants and a bright-red top. "Hey, that almost looks like…"

"Santa Claus Gnome." Shelley nodded. "I love Christmas."

"She really does," Graham said. "She wishes it were Christmas every day."

"Yes!" Shelley finished a stroke that turned the gnome's hat a bright brick red.

"How are we all doing here?" An older woman with a gray shoulder-length bob approached the table and put a hand on Shelley's chair.

"Great!" said a couple of the table's participants in unison.

"Oh, hello," the woman said, seeing Lexi. "You're a new face here."

"This is Lexi," Graham said.

"Very nice to meet you. I'm Margaret Sherman, the events director."

They shook hands, and Lexi realized she had some orange paint on her index finger. "Oops, sorry."

"No worries. It's a messy job, isn't it? Welcome. And I hope to see you again."

"Me too," Shelley said, her eyes focused steadily on her gnome.

Lexi had never met so many strangers in the space of a few minutes who felt more like good friends. The atmosphere teemed with acceptance and warmth. As she returned to her work and made a stroke along the gnome's waistline, she accidentally met Graham's finger with her brush.

"Hey, what's that about?" He smirked, jerking his hand back. "Stay on your side of the gnome, okay?"

"This *is* my side of the gnome. You're the one who's trespassing," she quipped, gesturing with her brush. She dotted it onto his wrist, leaving a pale orange mark.

"Oh, *that's* how this works." He dabbed his brush into his green paint.

"Okay, okay." She made surrender hands. "It was an accident."

"Nope, you don't get out of it that easily." Graham retaliated with a dab of his own, on the back of her hand. It came out as a perfect circle. "Not bad," he said. "Let me finish it off..."

Lexi waited, suppressing a giggle, while he took up his other brush, already dipped in white. The entire table had paused to watch their antics, and Graham finished adding white oval shapes that created flower petals.

"Hand art. Very attractive." She thrust her hand out toward the table, showing it off.

"Ooh, aah, pretty!" some exclaimed. And a couple of them even began to paint their partners too.

"Oh no." Graham grabbed a towel nearby. "Hey, guys, *not* a good idea. It was just a joke. See? Let's keep painting the gnomes, shall we? And not each other." He held Lexi's hand and rubbed it, creating another mini-masterpiece of swirled green and white until it faded into a light stain.

The participants followed suit and cleaned up each other's hands with their rags. Graham blew out a small "whew" that only Lexi could hear. "I can't be a bad example," he whispered. "Margaret would have my hide."

"She doesn't look that dangerous," Lexi said. But when she peeked up and saw Margaret standing in the distance with a raised eyebrow and crossed arms, she knew he might be right.

At one point during the gnome painting, Shelley tapped Lexi's arm. "Do you have boyfriend?" Her voice carried louder than Lexi was comfortable with for the subject involved. It wasn't exactly a conversation she wished to share with the entire table.

"Nope," she said as casually as possible, paying strict attention to the back of her gnome's hat, hoping Shelley might take the hint.

"Ever have boyfriend?" Shelley was persistent, her volume raised even higher to match her curiosity.

"Well, yes. He was actually more than that. He was a husband. *Ex*, now."

Shelley's eyes grew wider. "Why no husband anymore?"

Before Lexi could answer, Graham gently intervened and leaned across her to point at Santa's trousers. "Hey, Shell. Look. You missed a spot."

Shelley sucked in a breath and reached for her paintbrush, dropping the boyfriend subject altogether.

A few minutes later, piano music started up out of nowhere, and Lexi craned her neck to find the source of it.

"Over there." Graham pointed to the corner at an empty piano.

"A player piano?"

"One of the parents donated it a few months ago, for the holidays."

Half the room stopped to watch the keys go up and down, a musical ghost.

"I've never seen one in person before," Lexi said.

"I love piano," Shelley told her dreamily. "I want to play."

"Well, you can," Graham said, standing up and grabbing hold of her hand. "C'mon."

They whisked over to the piano, with all eyes watching, and Graham placed his sister's hands on top of the keys lightly. He set her up at the treble end, while he "played" the bass. Lexi had never seen Graham act this way—hamming it up, bumping hips with his sister, singing along to "Come Fly With Me." Lexi wondered what his college students would think of their refined and polished professor right now.

The brother and sister put on an animated performance, and when it ended, Graham twirled Shelley around to milk the applause. Then, they both took a deep bow.

Lexi was still clapping when they arrived back at the table. "That was amazing!" she told Shelley.

"Hey, I was playing too," Graham said.

"You were *both* amazing."

An hour later, most of the table had finished their gnomes and were ready to present them. Lexi snapped pics of each gnome then sent a couple of them to Ruby and Ariel and Jo. Each of Shelley's friends told why they chose their paint theme. The last to present were Shelley with her "Santa Gnome" and Lexi and Graham with their "Hippie Gnome."

"Hippy?" Shelley asked with a crinkled nose.

"Hippie with an *i* and an *e*. It means... peace and happiness," Graham said.

Lexi liked that definition very much. It seemed to fit the day.

"GOOD TIME," SHELLEY mused as she strolled the outside grounds with Lexi and Graham, ice cream in hand from the snack center in the dining room. Graham had insisted on treating them after their gnome-painting project, for a "job well done."

"A very good time." Lexi walked between Graham and his sister.

"Good *Friday*," Shelley said, emphasizing the holiday.

Lexi stopped in her tracks, her mouth agape. She looked at Graham. "Is that right? This is Easter weekend?"

Graham nodded then took a generous bite of his ice cream cone.

Lexi continued walking with them. "I honestly thought it was next weekend. I can't believe I let time get away from me." She remembered Ariel giving her an egg count total yesterday—three hundred—and wasn't sure why she'd counted them so early. But it wasn't early. Lexi was late!

She let the spoonful of ice cream dissolve on her tongue as she contemplated inviting Shelley to the town's egg hunt on Sunday. But it would involve Graham driving her, crack-of-dawn early, to Morgan's Grove, and Lexi didn't want to put him on the spot. Besides, they might have already made Easter plans with their father and Beth. She could mention it later on when she and Graham were alone again.

"What's that?" Shelley asked Lexi, pointing to Gigi's necklace.

Lexi had decided to wear the teardrop on rare special occasions rather than treat it like an heirloom to be protected and tucked away. It had been hidden for too long already.

"It's a necklace that belonged to a very special person." She extended the piece between them so that Shelley could examine it.

"Who?" Shelley paused on the sidewalk and ran a delicate finger along the teardrop's filigree border.

"My great-grandmother, Gigi."

Shelley removed her hand and gave her cone a generous lick then continued walking. The sidewalk that rounded the man-made lake was dotted with ducks and their babies. "Grandmas are nice."

"Yes, they are."

Lexi watched Graham toss his half-eaten cone into a nearby trash receptacle, dust his hands off, then say, "Hey, Shell, how about we take a break, sit down for a bit?" He gestured to one of the nearby benches. Lexi recognized his nervous mannerisms—he always scratched his jaw and twisted the corner of his mouth.

"Okay!" Shelley took another bite of her cone then plopped down in the center of the bench, patting the seat beside her for Graham.

As Lexi gravitated toward the bench, she remembered back to a week ago, when Graham had been in the middle of her own family situation, opening extremely personal letters that her great-grandmother had hidden. *This is a family matter,* he had told her that day, asking if he should leave. Realizing that Graham was about to talk to Shelley regarding their father's wedding, Lexi wondered if perhaps she should bow out under the same pretense, make an excuse to go. But then she remembered—Graham had asked her here specifically for this purpose, to be his support system when he told his sister the news. And unless he'd changed his mind, Lexi would follow through and be that support for him, no matter how awkward things might become.

Lexi took another spoonful of ice cream from her cup as she perched on the right side of Shelley, while Graham took the other side of the bench.

Shelley pointed at a duck whose colorful head had disappeared under the water, leaving his tail feathers and webbed feet pointed skyward. She giggled at the sight.

Graham cleared his throat then looked past Shelley toward Lexi, his whole face a question mark. Lexi gave him a single "you can do this" nod. He blinked and moved his attention toward his sister.

"Hey, Shell. I've been wanting to talk to you for a while. Dad sort of asked me to do this. I mean, he wanted to *be* here, but he had... some work thing. You know how busy he gets." He rubbed his jaw again. "Anyway..."

It was a bumpy start, and Lexi hoped he could regain his footing. She willed him to gather his courage and continue.

"So, you know that Dad has a girlfriend—"

"Beth," Shelley said definitively, staring at the duck who had emerged from the water, feathers dripping, and was swimming toward the shore.

"That's right. Beth."

"She's nice. *So* pretty... curly hair, white teeth."

"Well, she's come to mean a lot to Dad. He's been spending lots of time with her."

"He love her," Shelley said, quite matter-of-factly.

"Yes. He does love her. And when two people love each other, it's natural that they want to spend even *more* time together. Which means—"

Shelley turned to Graham with a gasp. "Get married?" Her tone suggested hopeful enthusiasm rather than dread.

Graham studied his sister's expression. "That's right. They're getting married."

"Yay!" Shelley slapped her thigh once, a clap of approval, then bobbed her head a couple of times in celebration.

Rather than relieved, Graham seemed positively bumfuzzled at the response. He crinkled his brows and leaned in. "You understand what this means, right? You'll have a new stepmum. We both will."

Shelley cast her gaze back on the water, where a new duck family glided across the surface. "Sure."

"And you're okay with that, right? I mean, she can never replace *our* mum," he assured her.

"I know. Silly brother." She flicked him on the knee with the back of her hand.

Graham put his hand on Shelley's back and rubbed it, staring at her profile, studying her reaction.

"Beth make Dad smile," Shelley mused, peering down at the empty cone she held. "Make him un-lonely."

For the first time since they'd sat down, Graham gave a shadow of a smile. He dipped his head and returned his hand to his knee. "That's the best explanation I think I've ever heard."

Lexi's heart warmed at this exchange. Since Shelley was more than fine with the wedding, maybe it would give Graham permission to be more than fine with it too.

"I have one more thing to tell you," he said after a minute had passed. "The wedding is soon. Like, really soon. A couple of weeks away."

"Me, be flower girl? Or put them in my hair?" Shelley pointed to her temple.

"I'm sure you can do anything you want." Graham chuckled then leaned in for a generous hug, burying his face in his sister's hair as Shelley reciprocated the hug. Because of their tight proximity on the bench, Lexi's face was fairly close to this intimate scene, but she couldn't turn away from the sweet sibling embrace. She blinked back tears then focused again on her ice cream, which had all but melted inside her cup.

BACK INSIDE THE LOBBY, Graham reminded his sister why it was time for him to leave. "You've got choir practice in ten minutes."

Removing her name tag and wadding it up, Lexi suddenly remembered something. She reached deep inside her purse until her fingers found a box. She presented it to Shelley. "This is for you."

"Present? Not my birthday. Or Christmas."

"True. But this feels like a special day, meeting you."

Shelley took the box carefully then struggled with the top, which appeared to be stuck.

"Here." Graham clutched her bottom hand with his own and worked the lid off the box.

Shelley bit her lip in anticipation as she removed the cotton square to reveal the present inside. She drew out a monarch butterfly.

"It's a pin," Lexi said. "From my store. It came in two weeks ago. Your brother showed me the picture of you with the butterfly the other day. This reminded me of you."

Shelley held the butterfly closer to her face as Graham lowered the box. She ran her fingers along the deep amber surface of the wing. "Like real butterfly."

"I agree. Can I pin it to your shirt?"

"Yes!"

Lexi was never good at this sort of thing—tying ties or pinning pins on other people—but for some lucky reason, she managed to snap the pin into place on Shelley's lapel with total ease.

"There." Lexi took a step back and admired how it looked.

"Thanks." Shelley craned her neck downward to see the butterfly. "Selfie?"

Before Lexi could even answer with a hearty "of course," Shelley had already grasped her phone and poised it in front of her. Graham and Lexi joined her, and they all said, "Butterfly!"

"I want a copy of that," Lexi told her.

"Goodbye hug?" Shelley asked Lexi, with the first bit of shyness Lexi had seen from her that entire day.

"Of course! If you didn't ask me, I was going to ask you." Lexi leaned down for a warm, strong embrace.

As Graham signed them out, Shelley exclaimed, "You forgot—the hippie! Gnome!" She pointed to it, perched on the corner of the welcome desk. "Yours."

The eagerness on her face melted Lexi, so she accepted the gnome and hugged it close.

Outside, after the door had closed behind them, Graham paused and extended his palms to Lexi. "You don't have to take him. I could find a place somewhere for him in my apartment. I'll tell Shelley we're sharing joint custody."

Lexi tightened her grip. "He's growing on me. And now that we've made him all colorful and cheery, I want to keep him. If that's okay."

"He's all yours." As they ambled toward their cars, Graham bumped his arm against Lexi's, in rhythm with their steps. "That was thoughtful of you. The butterfly."

"It had her name on it." Lexi squinted in the sun's glare bouncing off the cars. "It's funny. Sometimes, a piece will come into the store, and—it sounds crazy—but it's for a reason. It's waiting for a specific person to come and claim it. It happens over and over again. I'll hear a customer say, 'This is it! The one! Exactly what I've been looking for!' I mean, what made that person come into my store, on that specific day, to find 'the one' they'd been searching for? Or even a piece they didn't know they needed? Meant to be. It felt that way with Shelley—you had just shown me the photo, and a day later, I remembered the butterfly that had come into the store recently. Right time, right place."

"Sounds a bit like magic."

"It does, doesn't it?"

Chapter Eleven

Graham followed Lexi through the doors of The Pizzeria and was immediately hit with a mixture of delicious scents—garlic, tomato sauce, and yeast. The idea to grab a bite after visiting Shelley's place had been his, but the restaurant choice had been Lexi's, a mile up the road. She claimed it was the "best pizza in Texas."

The idea of having a meal was spur-of-the-moment—they hadn't planned on anything else after seeing Shelley. But as he had walked Lexi to her car, Graham suggested a meal, and Lexi agreed. They left the hippie gnome in her car then got into his for the restaurant. Graham had a strong urge to stay in Lexi's presence a little longer. He wasn't ready to say goodbye yet. The more he got to know her, the more he wanted to keep getting to know her. And for the first time since they'd met, their conversations hadn't centered around what had brought them together in the first place—the necklace. They seemed to be developing something else, on its own.

"I can't believe I haven't been here before," Graham said as they entered the foyer. "I notice it every time I visit Shelley, but I'm always busy coming or going, I guess."

A woman carrying menus greeted them from the dining room. "Hey, it's been a while!" she told Lexi.

"It has. Too long."

"I'll have your table ready in a moment," the woman said then rounded the corner into the restaurant.

"VIP treatment, eh?" Graham looked around and paused on a series of framed photos on the wall. He stepped closer to one of them. "Is that your dad?" He pointed at the bearded man wearing an apron, kneading a lump of dough. "This must be..."

"His restaurant, yep. Well, one of them. My favorite, actually."

"How long has it been open?"

"Nearly two years. I'd been telling him for ages that he needed to open a pizza joint. Of course, his idea of a 'joint' is this." She gestured around at the terracotta walls, tiled floors, and white fairy lights near the ceiling. Every table was decked out with white tablecloths and candles.

"Ritzy."

"Yeah, my mom decorated everything. It's got her stamp all over it."

"Ready for you," the woman told them, crooking her finger for them to follow.

Graham walked behind Lexi into the main dining area with stucco walls, more fairy lights, and a twelve-foot-long tapestry of the Italian countryside hanging on the opposite wall—a Tuscan scene realistic enough to walk into. The woman seated them in the corner, and Lexi sat in what Graham presumed was her usual chair at her usual table. He took the other chair and was handed a menu.

"Everything is good here," Lexi said. "And I'm not saying that because my dad designed the menu. It really *is* all good."

"Well, in that case..." Graham shut his menu and placed it on the table. "I'm in your capable hands. Order for me."

"That could be dangerous. Are you allergic to fish? Or saffron? Or beets?"

"Beets? On a pizza?"

Lexi laughed. "I'm teasing. It's all pretty standard fare. I usually get the pizza margherita." She closed her menu too. "Simple but delicious. Tomato sauce, fresh mozzarella, basil."

"Colors of the Italian flag."

After they ordered, Graham settled back in the cushioned chair and adjusted his napkin.

"Thanks for asking me along today," Lexi said. "I loved meeting your sister."

"You're the one who did me a favor."

"Well, she handled it like a champ. About the wedding."

"Yeah, that was a relief. She can be kind of unpredictable sometimes."

"She almost seemed ready for the news—in a weird way, she knew it before you even told her."

"Yes! Spooky. She has an intuition that surprises me."

"She's got this... light inside. A sweetness that's infectious. You can't help but feel happy around her."

Graham peered at Lexi through the candlelight. For someone he'd known a handful of weeks and who had only met his sister once during a brief afternoon, Lexi "got" his sister—saw how unique she was. He remembered the single time that Theresa had met Shelley. His ex had been completely awkward and standoffish, like she had no idea how to interact—never relaxed and natural, as Lexi had been. He let out a soft chuckle.

"What?"

"Nothing. I was thinking of the look on Shell's face when you gave her the butterfly. I guarantee she'll wear it on every outfit. She'll never be without it. She might even sleep with it under her pillow."

"I hope she does! It'll bring her good luck."

The server brought a basket of bread and placed it between them. Graham waited for Lexi to take the first piece. "Mm," she said after popping one of the small bites into her mouth. "Cheesy bites. They're sooo good."

"Your dad's idea?" Graham took one, unable to resist, and tossed it into his mouth, producing an explosion of flavors and textures. The dough was crispy and chewy at the same time. *Delicious.*

"Mine, actually. He was asking my opinion about breadsticks versus rolls, and I came out with 'cheesy bites.' They're simple. Pizza dough dressed in garlic butter and parmesan." She took another one from the basket. "I could eat a hundred of these in one sitting."

"I can see why." After swallowing another bite, he said, "So, when Shelley asked you that question—"

"Here we are!" The server approached the table with two pizzas, one in each hand. The gourmet pies had succulent-looking bubbles of carefully placed cheese on top of herb-infused sauce with a border of perfectly charred crust from a wood-fired oven. Usually, for Graham, Domino's would do fine. But he had a feeling what he was about to eat would spoil him for life.

When the server disappeared, Lexi waited. Graham gave her a puzzled look. He'd expected her to dive straight in.

She explained as she touched the crust with the tips of her fingers, separating the slices. "As hard as it is to wait, and as hungry as I am, I've had too many experiences where hunger outweighed my rational side and I ended up burning the roof of my mouth." She looked up at Graham. "Dad's pizzas always come straight to the table after leaving the oven. Waiting a minute or two makes a world of difference. And it's worth it." She put her hands in her lap, presumably to avoid temptation. "Anyway, what were you saying a minute ago? About Shelley?"

"Oh yeah." Graham took his hands off the slice he was separating from the others and rubbed his fingers on his cloth napkin. "That question she asked you, about a boyfriend? I'm sure it was pretty intrusive. It's just... Shelley has a way of surprising some people—even strangers—with bold personal questions. Sometimes, her filter disappears. But you handled it well."

Lexi reached for a slice, lifting it carefully from the plate as the cheese stretched into thin strings. "I didn't mind." She blew on the slice. "She was being curious."

"I admit, I'm curious too. I didn't know you had an ex-husband." Graham tried to act casual, biting into his first slice. "Mm." His eyebrows crinkled. "That's incredible. And hot!"

Lexi grinned. "Told ya." She held her slice poised, the picture of patience. She stared at the table thoughtfully. "His name is Neil, my ex. We met in college, at UT, then got married afterward. It lasted nearly four years…" Her voice trailed off as she brought the pizza to her lips for her first bite, and Graham instantly regretted pressing her.

"I'm sorry. About the divorce and about my rude intrusion. Apparently, I don't have a filter either. Runs in the family, I guess."

Lexi finished chewing and shook her head. "No, don't be sorry. You can ask me anything. The divorce isn't a secret or anything I'm ashamed of. It happened five years ago. I don't think about it very often anymore." She made eye contact for the first time since she'd mentioned her ex. "I found out he was cheating on me when one of his friends accidentally let it slip. Neil was caught, so he didn't bother lying about it, and I had a decision to make. Forgive him and trust him again, somehow—or leave. I chose the latter."

Lexi dabbed her mouth with a napkin. "The thing nobody tells you is how disorienting a divorce is. Your entire future—the one you'd built up in your head, of kids, a family, a whole life together, old age together—completely goes up in smoke, and you're left to try and reconstruct it somehow. It's almost like driving on a highway, focused on your destination, when somebody comes along and blindsides you, totals your car—and your whole day suddenly changes. Everything feels out of whack, and there are pieces to pick up and try to repair." She shrugged. "That's probably a silly analogy. It's hard to explain."

"I think you explained it very well. I can't imagine the upheaval involved. I've had mates of mine who've divorced, and they're devastated by it. I'm sure your family were supportive, though?"

"They were the best. They circled the wagons and did everything they could to make the process easier. But as much as all that helped, nobody really knew how to comfort me. They didn't understand how it felt. They couldn't. In my family, divorces are incredibly rare. My parents, grandparents, great-grandparents—there's maybe one divorce among all of those generations. So I became isolated, navigating through it. I was on a desert island by myself, experiencing all these raw emotions that I didn't know how to handle." Lexi took a sip of water. "I didn't mean to get all deep and serious. This is supposed to be a light lunch."

"I don't mind. Your past is yours. And it informs who you are today."

"True. For good and for bad, I suppose."

"And there's no mood requirement for this lunch. Frankly, I'll take an authentic, deep conversation over shallow chitchat any day. So. How about another question, but in a totally different direction?"

"Sure." Lexi took another bite.

"It's nearing the semester's end, and my students are already in summer mode. So I'm struggling to hold their attention and push through the final unit. I've been wracking my brain to think of projects to keep them interested, to show them how history matters, to leave them with something that makes an impression before they leave my class. And then it dawned on me. Gigi's letters, the necklace—they're so personal. A tangible way the students could see and hear about the war experiences. Not reading from a history book or listening to me drone on about it. Knowing about the necklace and letters might put things in perspective for them, something they can relate to."

"The human side of the war. The separation and anxiety."

"Exactly. And I guess I was hoping..." Graham twirled his straw's paper cover between his thumb and index finger. "Well, that maybe you'd come and be our guest speaker for a day? Talk about the letters, maybe show the students a photo of the necklace?"

He couldn't read her expression—*was she leaning toward no?*

But then, she smiled and said, "I'll do better than that. I'll bring the necklace and a few of the letters along with me. I could read from them, too, if you want."

"They would be gobsmacked. It's what I was hoping for."

"We can figure out a good day. Next week?"

"Whatever you want. You choose the day."

A HALF HOUR LATER, when the server carried away their empty plates, Graham reached for his wallet.

"No, you don't," a voice said from behind him. Lexi's father rounded the corner and paused at the table. "Your money is no good here."

"Daddy! I didn't know you were here."

"Walked in a few minutes ago. Parked in the back." He gave her shoulder a squeeze. "You know I can't stay away from my restaurants too long. I didn't know you were coming in today, sweetheart."

"It was a last-minute decision. Graham and I went to visit his sister, and then, we got hungry. I had to suggest my favorite restaurant."

Her father placed a hand on his heart. "I'm flattered." He offered Graham a hearty handshake then lifted an index finger. "Before y'all leave, let me get some donuts started."

As quickly as he'd arrived, Lexi's father was gone again, back to the kitchen.

"Donuts?" Graham asked. "At an Italian restaurant?"

"When they opened this place, Dad insisted on putting them on the menu, knowing how much I love them. They're actually Italian donuts, called zeppole."

Graham leaned in. "Are you sure I can't pay? I feel funny walking away on a full stomach for free."

"Don't even try. It's on the house. My dad won't let me pay. Like, ever. It's standard policy, for me and any guests. But I always pay the tip."

"I can manage that." Graham pulled out some bills and closed his wallet again.

When the dessert arrived, Lexi's father nodded toward the plate. "I added some extras for the road. And here's a bag for the overflow." He placed the dish and folded bag down in the center of the table.

"Thank you, sir," Graham said.

"You're more than welcome." He craned his neck toward the kitchen. "I've got to get back in there. All good here? Need any-thing?"

"I think this is *plenty*." Lexi's eyes widened at the sight before her.

After her father said goodbye, Lexi reached for the first pow-dered-sugar treat on top of the stack.

"Wait," Graham said, and Lexi froze with her donut in midair. "A toast." He selected a donut and held it between them. "To me—for not scarring my sister for life today with my shocking news."

Lexi grinned. "And to me, for facing my weird fear of gnomes and coming out the other side."

"Cheers!"

AS GRAHAM PULLED OUT of the parking lot on his way back to Shelley's place, Lexi reflected on something—aside from the quick mention of his class, they hadn't discussed the necklace or the letters during the entire afternoon. The past few weeks, that had been the primary connection between them, the main topic of conversation headlining every phone call, every text.

But since it was on her mind anyway, she gave him an update. "You asked earlier about the PI."

"Oh yeah." Graham rested one hand on the wheel and the other on his thigh. "How'd it go?"

"Pretty well. His name is Ed Minor. I told him the whole story, showed him the necklace, then the letters, then the black-and-white photos. Offered to email him copies of everything I'd documented. I also told him what Savannah discovered—she verified in a text this morning that Blanche did live at that address from 1937 to 1949, but then, the trail went cold. Her family moved away. Or she might've moved out before then if she got married. Who knows."

"Did he give you any hope about hunting down more details?" Graham pulled into Shelley's parking lot, straight into the empty slot beside Lexi's car. He shifted in his seat to rest his elbow on the middle console.

"He was hard to read, sort of stoic. But he said he'd do some research and—" Lexi's phone vibrated in her hand. She saw the screen and sucked in a breath. "This is the call. It's Heidi!"

"Want me out?" he gestured over his shoulder.

"No, no." She tugged on his sleeve. "I want you here." She clicked the speaker phone. "Is this Heidi?"

"It is. I'm returning your call. Lexi?"

"Yes. I apologize about the rambling voicemail. It must've caught you off guard."

"Wasn't rambling at all." Heidi's voice held a thick Southern accent—bordering on a drawl. "I appreciated the detail. I hate it when people leave a name and number, and then I've got no idea why they called. But yep, you caught me totally off guard. In a good way. It's pretty incredible to hear about a connection between our two relations. Especially eighty years back."

"Before we begin—I've got a friend sitting here, Graham. Is it okay if he listens in? He knows all about the situation."

"Fine by me." The woman rustled papers on the other end. "I have an appointment in a few minutes, but I had to call you back. If we don't say all we need to say, we can try another call tomorrow, maybe?"

"Sure! Anytime."

"So—I jotted down the people you mentioned in the voicemail. Your great-grandmother... Louise. And somebody named James."

"Fisher, that's right."

"Well, my grandmother—Blanche—passed away a decade ago, and I inherited a lot of her things. Photos, vintage clothing, and a couple of journals."

Lexi didn't realize that her hand was still placed lightly on Graham's arm, and she squeezed it in excitement. "Journals?"

"Right. After your call, I dug them up out of a box—it was under my bed—and sorta flipped through the pages, searching for any references to those names."

Lexi heard more rustling of papers.

"Anyway, it was just a quick look-through—I can do a more careful one tonight—and I found several pages that mention Louise. It appears they were best friends. And a few entries mention this James person. Mind if I read a couple of paragraphs to you? I bookmarked them."

"Mind? Not one bit!" Lexi continued gripping Graham's sleeve. She needed a physical place to channel her anticipation. He returned her hopeful smile.

"Here's the first one where James and Louise are mentioned. This entry is from... June 14, 1941. I believe my grandmother was eighteen or thereabouts? This is what she wrote: 'Louise and I met our soulmates tonight. Or, at least, I think we did. A group of us went to a graduation party in Austin, and there they were. Tony and James, friends of friends, standing in the corner of the room. They caught our eyes and approached us, and we spent the rest of the night on the porch, talking, the four of us. Tony has chocolate-brown eyes and a devilish grin. And Louise finds James feverishly attractive, says he looks like a movie star, right off the screen. They're both older boys, though. Maybe even mid-twenties. I wonder if our parents will approve.' And that's where the entry ends."

Lexi had barely taken a breath since Heidi began reading. "Tony—was that your grandfather?"

"Sure was. Guess they were soulmates after all." After a pause, Heidi said, "Oh, shoot. Listen, sorry—I need to get going. I can't miss this appointment. But I can snap some photos of the rest of these pages and text them to you, maybe later tonight or in the morning. Would that be okay?"

"That would be more than okay. I can't thank you enough for this." She and Graham exchanged a happy nod. "Oh, I wanted to mention... I've hired a PI who's trying to track down James's family so that I can find out more about him. May I let the PI know about your grandmother's journal?"

"Of course. You can share the entries with him too."

"Thanks for all your help. You don't know what this means to me and my family."

They hung up, and Lexi took her first significant breath since the call began. "How amazing," she whispered to Graham.

"Incredible, to fill in some of those gaps. The pieces are coming together."

"I can't wait to see what the journal says about James. Maybe it'll explain why Blanche had to be the one receiving his letters. And tell more about Gigi's father disapproving." Lexi looked down and blushed. "Oh. Sorry. You can have your sleeve back."

"I didn't mind," he whispered.

To break the tension, she said, "I nearly forgot—I have your blazer hanging in my car."

"Blazer?"

"The beige one you were wearing when we found the letters. You left it up in the attic that day. I'll get it."

She had expected to dip into her car then place the blazer in Graham's backseat while he remained in the driver's seat. But Graham had already gotten out to join her, engine still humming. She held the blazer between them.

"I enjoyed today," she said. "Shelley, the pizza..."

"Even the gnomes?"

"Even them. Speaking of..." She had abandoned Mr. Hippie in the backseat, and Graham seemed to read her mind. He took the blazer from her, hung it inside his car, then grasped the gnome.

Shutting the door, he came closer to Lexi in the tight space between their cars and passed the gnome over to her. "You made today easier for me. I was having a pretty crap day, actually, but watching you with Shelley, and then your excitement over the journals..." He peered down at his empty hands.

"What?" she asked.

"It's just... Being around you is easy."

She recognized the warm flutter in the center of her stomach and let it fuel her courage. "I feel the same way." When their gaze lingered for a second longer than it usually did, Lexi blinked and took a step backward. "I'd better get going. I should check on the store. Ruby will wonder where I've been all day."

Graham guided the top of her car door as she opened the driver's side. "And I'd better get back to my essay grading."

"I'll call you tomorrow." To clarify, she said, "To let you know if I hear from Heidi."

She transferred the gnome to her passenger seat then started the engine while Graham shut her door gently. He backed away with a wave while she pulled out of the space.

Re. Bound.

Chapter Twelve

"Well, this is ironic timing." Lexi clicked open the photo Shelley had sent of herself, Lexi, and Graham. Lexi tilted the photo so Ruby could see the butterfly sparkling on Shelley's shirt.

Lexi had spent the last few moments, after closing the store, telling Ruby all about the afternoon's visit with Shelley, including the exciting call with Heidi afterward.

"Precious photo. Isn't she sweet? You had a lovely day all around, didn't you. And—a big bonus—you seem to have conquered your gnome phobia!" Ruby gestured toward Hippie Gnome, who now held a permanent place on the counter near the register, a cheerful greeter to all. Ruby had dubbed him the store's mascot.

"Well, I wouldn't go that far. 'Conquered' is a strong word. Let's just say that a coat of paint helped me get over my phobia of this *particular* gnome. You'll notice that I still don't want him in my house. But I'm fine with him here."

"Fair enough."

"Anyway, the place where Shelley lives is amazing—the people are so kind and happy."

"Sounds like you want to visit again."

"I think I do." Before Ruby could ask a follow-up question—likely about Graham—Lexi shifted the subject. "We haven't talked about Henry yet." She had waited and waited for Ruby to bring it up, but since she hadn't, Lexi couldn't resist. Her patience had run out. "How was your brunch yesterday?"

The corners of Ruby's mouth lifted in a wistful smile, and when she didn't return the eye contact, it told Lexi everything she needed to know.

"It was fine. He took me to Christine's." Ruby fidgeted with the business card holder on the counter then rearranged a nearby cup of pens.

"A lovely choice," Lexi said. "Did he pay?"

"He did indeed."

"Ruby—was this... a date?"

"We didn't label it." She smoothed out her blouse and faced Lexi. "Let's call the brunch... exploratory. We learned quite a lot about each other. Did you know he's a fully licensed pilot? And that he used to volunteer as a Round Rock firefighter?"

Lexi pictured Henry in the cockpit of a plane or donning a heavy fireman's suit. "That's amazing. I had no idea."

"He has four grandchildren and two great-grandchildren."

"Just like you."

"Isn't that an incredible coincidence? The conversation flowed so easily. And then he texted me last night, just to say goodnight. Wasn't that thoughtful?"

Lexi couldn't remember the last time she'd seen Ruby light up this way. She had always been a positive person, a contented soul. But her demeanor today was borderline giddy.

"I'm happy for y'all," Lexi said. "*Whatever* this is."

"Well, it's surprised me, that's for sure." Ruby stared at the countertop and drew an infinity symbol with her fingertip. "I mean, at my age... I never expected a Henry to walk into my life. There's something about him. I can't explain it." Her eyes met Lexi's. "Don't laugh, but in some ways, I'm a teenager again."

"I would never laugh at you. It's written all over your face. I'm thrilled for you." Lexi leaned in for a hug. "I want you to be happy."

As they backed away, Ruby held onto both of Lexi's arms. "I want *you* to be happy too."

Lexi received the message loud and clear—*it's time for you to accept love in your life*—reminiscent of Jolene's continuous prodding and encouragement. "I am. Busy. But happy."

"Any plans for tonight?" Ruby thankfully shifted into small-talk mode.

"Nope. Jo's got a date, so I'm on my own." Before Lexi could receive a pity look, she quickly said, "Which is fine by me. I need a night to wind down—I'm looking forward to it."

"I hear ya. Those new quilting classes for seniors are bringing customers into the shop in droves. I don't think Ariel and I took a break all afternoon!"

"What are your plans tonight?"

"I'm meeting Henry for a movie in Austin, a reshowing of *Singin' in the Rain*. It's playing at this new classic theater."

"I love that movie."

"So do I." Ruby patted the counter. "Well, I'd better finish up the inventory."

"Do it tomorrow." Lexi closed her laptop. "In fact, why don't we both leave now? Everything else can wait. It'll give you time to prepare for your... date?"

"My outing." Ruby corrected her with a smirk. "I've got a couple more quick things to do around here before I go, but then I'll be off." She turned toward the back room then paused. "Ariel wanted me to tell you—she already filled up the tote bags with the eggs. For Sunday's hunt."

"I'm glad you reminded me! I completely forgot to tell Graham about it. I wanted to invite Shelley along."

"I think she would love it."

Lexi leaned down to hitch up Bailey's leash as she and Ruby said their goodbyes. Bailey blinked up at Lexi then followed her out the door, which she locked behind her. After a pause to fish out her phone and dial Graham's number, she and Bailey took off toward home. She noticed another gorgeous spring evening, with the comforting coo of a dove floating from a nearby tree branch.

No answer. Rather than leave a voicemail, Lexi clicked off, deciding to try him again later. She slowed her pace and thought about Ruby. *Why hadn't Lexi considered Henry as a potential partner for Ruby early on?* It made perfect sense—similar ages, the loss of a spouse around the same time, an active work life with retirement on the horizon. But Ruby had seemed content, so it hadn't even dawned on Lexi that there could be a void in her life. Perhaps Ruby hadn't even known it until romance presented itself to her unexpectedly. Ruby had been the opposite of Jo—no dating apps, no seeking and searching, no high expectations about a future soulmate, no longing and talking about love. But it had found her anyway.

Bailey approached the house and hopped up the two porch steps as Lexi's phone rang. She saw Graham's name on the screen.

"Hey." She answered the call while jiggling the key into the lock. Bailey's tail thumped impatiently against her calf.

"Sorry I missed the call. I was lugging groceries in from the car."

She heard the rustling of bags. "No problem. I was calling to ask a question. The visit with Shelley reminded me of something today, and I wanted to run it past you."

"Sure."

Lexi shut the front door behind her. "Hang on a sec." She released Bailey from his leash and let him roam free, nails clicking on the wood floor. He stopped at his bowl in the kitchen and whimpered. "I just got home too. Bailey's hungry." She set the phone on the breakfast table and clicked the speaker. "Okay. My hands are freed up."

"Mine too. I'll put away the groceries while you feed him. Carry on when you're ready."

She heard the suction of a refrigerator door opening and closing on Graham's end as she scooped Bailey's food into his bowl. When he was contentedly chomping away, she sat at the table and took up the phone again. "So, back to Shelley. She reminded me that today is Good Friday, which means our town's Easter egg hunt is coming up! I was going to invite Shelley—and you—to come to Morgan's Grove. But I didn't want to mess with any Easter plans you already have, so that's why I didn't bring it up earlier."

The ruckus on Graham's end came to an abrupt halt. "We don't have specific plans this year. Usually, we either meet at Shelley's place—they have a special Easter service—or go to the Methodist church downtown with my dad. Tell me more about this hunt."

Lexi heard her stomach growl and hoped Graham couldn't hear it through the phone. She got up and set her phone on the kitchen island. "Is it rude if I make a salad while we talk?" Although the meal at the pizzeria had been gut-busting, it had been several hours ago. The cold, crisp salad she'd bought the other day would hit the spot for a light supper.

"Not if I can do the same. I was about to break open this bag of crisps."

"Chips?"

"Ha, yeah. Chips. Cheetos, to be precise."

"Be my guest. Anyway..." Her voice grew in volume as she opened the fridge and brought out a bag of lettuce, ranch dressing, and some cheese. "The egg hunt is this massive community event—we've done it for fifty years." She placed her items near the phone and brought out a bowl and fork from the cabinets. "All the townspeople participate, especially the stores in the square. The goal is to fill up ten thousand plastic eggs with treats—"

"Ten thousand?"

"Yeah, but it's more feasible than it sounds. Each business strives for a few hundred eggs each. And then the schools participate, too, and the churches. Pretty much everyone."

"That's a lot of eggs."

"Kids from other towns come and join us, too, so we always want to have plenty. We usually find unrecovered eggs hidden in corners and shrubs for months to come." Lexi opened the salad bag as quietly as she could and dumped a third of it into the bowl. "But since they're not real eggs, it doesn't matter—no rotting, no stench. The eggs are filled with candy and plastic toys and sometimes even Bible verses or encouraging messages. Sorta like a fortune cookie." She doused her salad with the dressing and jabbed at it with her fork, trying to disperse the globs evenly onto the crisp leaves. For a final touch, she sprinkled some shredded cheddar cheese on top. Grabbing both the phone and the bowl, she made her way to the breakfast table. Bailey was lying beneath it, so she carefully slipped the chair out and sat down, then she placed her bare foot gently on his back and petted him with her toes. His tail gave a couple of wags in response. "Anyway, I thought Shelley might want to come and help us hide the eggs on Sunday morning. It begins early, though—at eight o'clock sharp. Then, the kids all come at ten and search for the eggs. Then, the church services are at eleven. Shelley's welcome to come to some of it, all of it, whatever she wants. And you, too, of course." She took a bite of salad—crisp and delicious, with a perfect dollop of zesty ranch on top.

"To hide the eggs?"

She swallowed before answering. "Sure. That's the fun part for the adults." She speared another leaf of lettuce and paused before going on. "It's neat to see the community come together. And to watch the kids' faces during the hunt. Even people who don't have kids get a big kick out of it. It's one of my favorite events in Morgan's Grove."

"I'll tell Shelley. I'm sure she'll want to go. Thanks for the invite."

Lexi took another bite, trying not to crunch too loudly.

"Shell already texted me about the butterfly pin you gave her. She loves it. I got a series of selfies from her about a half hour ago, with all her friends, showing it off."

"She texted me the selfie of us a few minutes ago. So cute."

As Lexi finished her salad, the conversation shifted to Graham's dad and how relieved he was to hear about Shelley's reaction to his wedding news. He had thanked Graham profusely and even apologized for backing out twice. "My dad *never* apologizes. For anything."

Lexi got up to place her bowl in the sink. She took her phone with her. "It's weird, how some people genuinely can't face hard talks." Lexi made her way into the den, where she clicked on the fireplace with a remote then tucked her legs underneath her as she sat on the sofa. Bailey jumped up out of nowhere to join her. "My mother is like that. She lets my dad handle the emotional stuff in the family. And she rarely apologizes."

"I'm kinda hard on my dad," Graham said. "But his dad was the same way. Didn't show much emotion. My mum was the one who handled the hard stuff. I guess I'm more like her in that way."

"I can see that about you." Lexi pulled an afghan over her legs and shifted the phone. A peaceful drowsiness descended on her as she stared into the mesmerizing fire.

"How so?"

"Well, watching you with Shelley, I noticed your sensitivity to her. You were always aware of her needs, making her comfortable. Like, hovering without being annoying, if that makes sense. It came naturally to you. It's obvious how much she loves you."

"I've always been protective of her. The world is sometimes not so nice. And I want her to experience the best of it, not the worst. I can't protect her from everything. But I can try."

"She's lucky to have you." Lexi patted Bailey's sleepy head. "I just thought of another example of your sensitivity to people. The gnomes."

"What do you mean?"

"Well, the fact that you knew how much they bothered me, and so you bought them all up, just to alleviate my anxiety. Honestly, that might be one of the most considerate things anyone's done for me."

"For all the good it did." Graham laughed. "There they were, right in front of you today. The exact opposite of what I was trying for."

"I admit—at first, I thought it was some cruel joke. But the look on your face... You went sheet white. You were horrified."

"I was! That day, of all days, for them to be used in a craft project."

"I'm almost glad it happened, though. I think it cured me. Or, at least, half cured me. Now, when I give Jolene her gift, I won't cringe."

"What gift?"

"She loves gnomes. I had Ruby set a couple of them aside for her birthday—it's a few weeks away. And our hippie gnome has found his permanent home at the store, on top of the counter."

"Well. That *is* progress."

Lexi rested her elbow on the back of the sofa. "You know, it's not fair that you know this deep, dark secret about me, but I don't have anything on you. Tell me something weird or quirky about yourself. Make me feel better about the gnomes."

"Hmm."

Graham's lengthy pause told her he was thinking long and hard about it—or maybe weighing whether to reveal too much. She twirled a piece of hair between her fingers while she waited, imagining him relaxing on his sofa the way she was.

"Okay, here goes," he finally said. "Whenever I crack open a new novel—always a physical book; no e-books for me—I have to remove the jacket. Like, put it away and not look at it until I'm done with the book."

"Why?"

"I don't want to be influenced by the cover when I read. I like to formulate my own ideas about characters or settings. And if there's someone's face on the cover or a specific scene, then that's all I can see. Same for the author's photo. I never look at it until the end, or else I sort of imagine that person writing the story. I want my authors to be faceless."

"What about paperbacks? Ones without a jacket to remove?"

Another pause. "I rarely buy paperbacks, but when I do, I've been known to create a blank book jacket."

"Like the way we did with textbook covers in grade school?"

"Sort of. There are some exceptions. *Band of Brothers*—that cover shows the backs of a group of soldiers. It doesn't interfere with my reading. But most of them? I have to cover them up. Did that help, making things even with your gnomes?"

"Actually, it did."

"I don't think I've ever told that to anyone."

"Not even your ex?"

"Not even her."

Lexi swiveled on the sofa to lie down so that her head rested on the soft, generous cushion and her feet lay lightly atop Bailey's back. He didn't even stir.

The conversation deftly shifted from childhood experiences (Graham was bullied for his British accent, Lexi for her clumsiness) to sports (he played tennis, she played volleyball) to taste in music (he loved British pop and Beethoven, she loved jazz and eighties rock). Only when Lexi let out a silent yawn and noticed her phone icon—battery down to five percent—did she realize an entire evening had flown by.

"It's nearly midnight?" She sat up.

"I can't remember the last time I've been on the phone with anyone this long."

"I think phone conversations have become a lost art. Like writing a letter by hand."

"It's all texting's fault. Quicker, easier," Graham said.

"True. But this was fun tonight. Unexpected."

"It was. I'll see you on Sunday, then? For the egg hunt?"

"Definitely."

Lexi clicked off and let her groggy mind go over the conversation. She patted Bailey's back as he gave a deep and satisfied sigh. Lexi usually hated talking on the phone—even to Jo or to her own parents—for much longer than a couple of minutes, tops. The main goal was always to give or accept information. Otherwise, she could become quickly bored or distracted, thinking of the million things she had to do other than be on the phone. But maybe because of the late hour or the empty evening, the call with Graham hadn't bothered her one bit. In fact, she was in happier spirits hanging up than when she had first dialed his number. He was having that effect on her more and more.

LEXI PUSHED THE DOORBELL for a second time then stood back on the ragged Welcome mat, which actually said "elcome" due to a worn *W*. She hadn't thought this far ahead—*what if no one was home*? She supposed she could walk the sandwich platter back to her own house and pop it into the fridge, maybe try again later. The burn in her forearms after carrying it the couple of blocks from Christine's Bistro increased with every moment that the doorbell wasn't answered.

Her phone vibrated for the second time in her pocket, so she balanced the platter against her hip to free up one hand and see who was contacting her. Pam—again—asking what to do about the low stock in paints, since a huge party had just reserved a spot for later in the evening. An important question in need of a fast answer. But what Lexi was doing was important too.

She slid her phone back into her shorts pocket and raised her free hand once more to the doorbell. But a split second before her finger tapped the button, the faded blue door squeaked open, revealing Ariel—hair scooped up in a messy bun, eyeliner smudged beneath both eyes, Paramore T-shirt half tucked in.

When she saw her boss standing on the doorstep, Ariel froze. "Oh. Hi. I didn't expect... what are you...?"

Relieved Ariel was home, Lexi offered a warm smile. The last thing she wanted to do was give off an intimidating air. "I've got something for you. May I come inside?"

Ariel widened the door for Lexi. "Of course. Sure. Yes." Her eyes darted toward the living room as she let Lexi in.

Lexi entered and discreetly surveyed the scene: a compact living room with a loveseat and recliner, both of which had seen better days; a paused TV video game softly emitting some anime music; and a coffee table stacked high with pizza boxes, wadded-up napkins, and plastic cups. When Ariel followed Lexi's gaze toward the table, she rushed to collect the trash, snatching up several cups and napkins at once.

"No, please don't go to the trouble. You don't have to clean up for me. Really."

Hesitantly, Ariel tossed the trash she'd already gathered into a nearby can and crossed her arms. "Is everything okay? With the store? I mean... Did I do anything wrong, or—"

"Heavens, no." Lexi stepped closer to the sofa and sat down, placing the sandwich tray on her lap. "I came to see how you're doing. I hope you don't mind. I've been thinking about you and your mom. And I wanted to check on you."

Ariel's brows rose slightly as her expression softened. She brushed away a strand of hair that had grazed her cheek and joined

Lexi on the sofa. "I haven't heard anything from my mom yet. But that's typical." She gestured with her hands. "They want the patients to be absorbed into the program at first. No distractions. But they might let me visit in a few days—"

"That would be nice. I'm sure she's in good hands."

"Yeah." Suddenly, Ariel moved her attention to the TV and used the remote to silence the background music.

"I brought you some food." Lexi held up the platter between them. "Sandwiches. And the bag has some chips and snickerdoodle cookies too. I figured you might not have time to think about fixing meals."

Ariel smirked toward the table. "Yeah. I was getting tired of pizza and frozen dinners. Thank you." She accepted the platter and bag, transferring them to her own lap.

"I have something else for you too." Lexi reached inside her purse for an envelope. She extended it to Ariel. "It's two weeks' worth of extra pay. I assumed... without your mom or her boyfriend living here, things might be getting tight for you, and so—"

Without warning, Ariel closed the gap between them and leaned across for one of the tightest hugs Lexi had ever received. She could feel Ariel's shoulders shaking with quiet sobs, so she wrapped her arms around her, patting her back in a soothing rhythm.

"Thank you." Ariel's whisper quivered near Lexi's ear.

"You're very welcome."

With a sniff, Ariel let loose of the hug and wiped her cheeks. "I don't know what to say."

"You don't have to say anything." Lexi snatched the only clean napkin on the table and handed it over to Ariel. "You're someone I can always count on, and I don't tell you that often enough. The money isn't a handout—or an advance. It's a bonus. And it's long overdue, to show you how valued you are."

"But you probably can't afford this." She raised the envelope.

"The store is doing double its business! You've seen the huge surge in customers the past two weeks. So I can *totally* afford this. Besides, you've earned it. I never have to ask you twice for anything, and you're at the store morning and night. Plus you're great with the customers—never too pushy or neglectful. You're valued, Ariel."

Ariel dipped her head and turned the envelope over. Lexi wondered if more tears were forming or if she was even planning to hand the money back to her.

But instead, she whispered, "Okay. Thank you. I accept."

"That's the answer I was looking for!" Lexi's phone vibrated again, and it was Pam. Again. "Listen, I'd better go. Minor emergency at Let's Get Crafty."

"Can I help?"

"No, it's okay. I have some ideas to help put out the fires. It'll be fine. But thanks for offering." Lexi rose from the couch, and Ariel followed after leaving the platter and envelope on the couch.

As they approached the front door together, Lexi said, "Thanks for doing all the eggs this year. It was quite an undertaking."

"That sort of mindless activity is good for me." Ariel pushed her fingertips into her jeans pockets. She looked more relaxed, more peaceful than when she first opened the door to Lexi.

"I'll see you tomorrow? For the egg hunt?" Lexi asked.

"I wouldn't miss it."

Chapter Thirteen

Graham buttoned up his lavender Oxford shirt, leaving two holes open at the top. He'd already decided to store a dark-plum blazer and matching tie in his backseat for the later church service, assuming they would get in the way during the egg hunt.

Suppressing a yawn, he blew on the surface of his just-made coffee and rubbed his eyes. He wasn't used to waking before the sun came up, even on school days. He was *not* a morning person despite the façade he put on during his morning classes.

He cast a glance over to the corner table, where he had spent most of yesterday wading through research papers. He still had a final exam to prepare, but he could do that later in the evening. He didn't usually spend all day Saturdays grading—he reserved that day for some down time, to relax his brain and gather the strength for the week ahead. But he didn't want his work nagging at him on Easter Sunday, so he'd purposely cleared the day for Shelley—and for Morgan's Grove.

When Lexi had asked them to be part of the egg hunt, he was glad she couldn't see his smile broaden through the phone—he didn't want to let her know yet how much he enjoyed her company. Timing was important, and he was trying not to scare her off. Through their recent interactions and then her admissions about her cheating ex-husband, Graham could sense that she was understandably resistant to forming a serious relationship. She'd made it clear that she didn't have time or room for anything new. But somehow, over the weeks, they had made time for each other, inch by inch. Even so, he knew his own limitations too—that he was a bit raw over Theresa. No matter how much progress he'd made since their text breakup, she was still part of his thoughts, though the space she took up in them dwindled every day. Whenever he did venture into another relationship, he wanted to be able to give all of himself to someone else. And he wasn't there. Not quite yet, anyway.

A slice of unexpected sunlight pierced through the crack in the curtains. Graham pulled them open so he could appreciate the brilliant sunrise of wispy blurred golds and pinks. *Easter morning.* Graham held particularly fond memories of Easter celebrations with his mum in their Cotswold village when he was growing up. It was her favorite holiday, as she surprised Graham and Shelley with a special Easter basket in the living room when they awoke. Shelley would eagerly sort through each chocolate egg, stuffed rabbit, and plastic toy. Then, as a family, they would walk to the church service together, where they'd sing beautiful hymns about redemption and grace and mercy that echoed inside the three-hundred-year-old stone structure. Afterward, they would share a sumptuous roast dinner back at the cottage, which his mother had lovingly prepared in the early-morning hours. Even his father seemed more relaxed during that holiday—more engaged with his family than other days of the year.

Last night, Graham had actually rung his father to let him know about today's egg hunt, but he had no real expectations that he and Beth would make an appearance. Still, he anticipated the joy Shelley would get from their arrival, so he held out a smidgen of hope—but not enough to have told her about the invitation.

Noticing the time, Graham dropped the curtain and downed his coffee, knowing he couldn't be late. When he'd told Shelley yesterday about the egg hunt over their video chat, her excited giggles and thousand questions about the event showed how eager she was to attend.

WHEN GRAHAM PULLED up at Shelley's place, he saw his sister clutching her tote bag, the one Mrs. Anderson always packed for any outing. It usually contained a bottle of water, Shelley's fidget toys, a notepad and pen for doodling, and a packet of cherry sours, her favorite.

"Happy Easter!" Graham called out as he emerged from the car with the palm-sized chocolate egg he'd bought for her yesterday. She was already galloping toward him, her pretty sundress fluttering, her arms flung wide open for a hug. After he squeezed her tight, Graham handed her the chocolate egg then waved to Mrs. Anderson, who had gotten up extra early to make this happen. Normally, no one was supposed to leave the premises before the building opened at nine—when check-out could occur—but he had called Mrs. Anderson yesterday to ask for a special exception. She had happily complied when she discovered the circumstances.

With a yawn, Mrs. Anderson waved them off and went back in the direction of her apartment, likely to return to her warm bed.

"Are you ready for this egg hunt?" Graham asked, relieving his sister of her tote bag and placing it in the backseat.

"*So* ready." She plopped into his front seat and immediately adjusted the air conditioner vents.

He shut her door, rounded the car to get in, then put on her favorite playlist—an eclectic mix of the Beatles, Carrie Underwood, and Pink—and turned it low for background music.

"Just remember," he said as he backed out of his spot, "we're there to help instead of hunt."

Shelley tsked and rolled her eyes. "I know. Not a kid. Too old to hunt!"

Graham gave a satisfied nod as he pulled out onto the empty street, heading for the nearly empty freeway. "That's the spirit."

AN ELECTRIC EXCITEMENT filled the square as townspeople gathered on the library's lawn, awaiting instructions. Doris Johnson—the head of the Festivities Committee and founder of the Sassy Ladies Book Club—frowned at the defective microphone in her hand. She shook it and tapped it with her open palm then consulted someone nearby. Lexi stood patiently between Ariel and Ruby, who stood next to Darius and his brother, all of whom carried egg-filled tote bags they'd hauled to the square minutes ago from the antiques store.

The buzz was palpable as participants quietly exchanged strategies for how and where to hide their eggs and anticipated the looks on the children's faces. The sky brightened with a newly risen sun, and Lexi breathed deeply of the chilly morning air—which had required a sweater to cover her Easter dress—and recalled her own first memories of the egg hunt. She was around five or six years old, joined by her mother and Gigi, and was allowed to run off on her own, within reason, to explore and fill up her basket with the treasured eggs. Since the event had a decades-long history, even her own mother held many of the same memories of herself as a little girl, hunting eggs around the town square.

A shrill squeal emanated from the speaker, causing a collective wince from the crowd. Mrs. Johnson cleared her throat. "We'll begin in about five minutes. I'll be back to give instructions. Happy Easter, y'all!"

By Lexi's estimates, the growing crowd included more than a hundred people—grandparents, aunts and uncles, shopkeepers, teachers, clergy. She had already said cheery "good mornings" to Lucille and her corgis, Jill and Rick, Chaynie and Greg, and her own parents, who stood a few feet away with filled-up tote bags of their own. Even Jolene had secured a place in front of Lexi and tapped her heel in eager anticipation.

But someone important was missing. Two someones. Lexi tried to be subtle as she let her eyes roam the crowd, looking for a hint of either Graham or Shelley. She had texted Graham late last night about the idea of parking at her house—knowing the spaces behind the square would all be taken on this busy morning—but he hadn't texted back. It was possible he was running late. Or maybe he'd changed his mind or even forgotten...

"Lexi!"

She spun around to see Shelley rushing toward her, her smile stretching wide, her arms already opened up. Over Shelley's shoulder during their hug, Lexi saw Graham walking at a slower pace.

"We late?" Shelley asked as she backed away.

Lexi noticed the butterfly pin on Shelley's flowery sundress, a perfect match. "Right on time." Lexi stooped to reach for two tote bags. "One for you and... one for you?" She wasn't sure if Graham would want to participate or whether his primary role was as chaperone, to bring Shelley along for the event.

"Of course! Gimme that." With a quick wink, he grabbed the handles.

Lexi introduced Shelley to her surrounding family and employees, then Graham stepped in beside Lexi. He opened his palm to reveal a miniature chocolate Easter egg wrapped in foil. "Happy Easter. Where's Bailey?"

"At home, sleeping." She took the egg, grinning at his thoughtfulness. "I thought the event might be too intense for him. Plus I didn't want him underfoot today. Did y'all park at my house?" She unwrapped the foil and popped the chocolate into her mouth.

"We did. Thanks for the tip."

Lexi realized that Graham was holding a dark-plum blazer. "Here, I can take that. We'll drape it over the back of my chair."

"It's for the service later. Didn't want to ruin it during the egg-hiding. Oh, did you ever hear from Heidi? I'm curious about those journals."

"Not a word. I'm dying to reach out, but I don't want to bother her. Hopefully, she'll text me today. But since it's Easter, probably not."

The irritating screech of the microphone's feedback filled the square once again as Mrs. Johnson pushed it away from her then brought it back sheepishly. "Sorry about that, folks. Welcome, y'all, to the yearly Morgan's Grove Easter Egg Hunt! This year, if our calculations are correct, we have close to eleven thousand eggs ready to hide. For those who didn't bring any eggs of your own, that's okay. We've got tons of extras for you, already filled."

This drew thunderous applause from the crowd. When it faded, Mrs. Johnson explained the basics. Three large kiddie pools had been inflated and stuffed with the extra eggs on the side lawn of the library. The participants would hide eggs within the perimeter of the square, balanced on top of low tree branches, under shrubs and benches, atop staircases, or near shop doors—anywhere was fair game, as long as it wasn't beyond the square. During the actual event, traffic around the square would be blocked completely for the children's safety and parents' peace of mind.

"And don't forget to put yourself in the children's shoes," Mrs. Johnson said. "Make it a challenge but not an impossible one. Some eggs should be very easy for the youngest children to find, and others, a challenge for the older kids. When your tote bag gets depleted, come to the kiddie pools and fill up again. As many times as you need. The goal is to empty the kiddie pools and fill up the square."

After reminding the crowd about the time limit—"We *must* finish by nine fifteen on the dot!"—she looked at her watch, waited an anticipatory few seconds, then simply shouted, "Go!"

It wasn't a race or a competition—everyone's goal was exactly the same, to hide the eggs for children to find. But somehow, the buildup of anticipation, as well as the strict time limit, always made the hunt seem more like a race. Participants thrust their hands into tote bags while moving at swift speeds, eyes keenly on the lookout for the perfect spot for each egg, careful not to steal someone else's. "Excuse me, sorry" was whispered often as people eyed the same hiding place but then quickly retreated to let someone else have it.

For the first leg of the egg-hiding, Shelley stayed close to Lexi, observing her strategy and mimicking it. Lexi would often place an egg then point to a nearby spot that Shelley could use as her own. Shelley quickly got the hang of things and would find a hiding place, peeking back at Lexi to see if it was viable.

By the time they had filled up their totes a second time at the kiddie pool, Shelley was completely on her own, tucking her eggs around corners, up trees, and behind benches.

"Shell's really good at this," Graham said, coming up to surprise Lexi as she spied an empty spot on a window ledge at The Pit's restaurant front. Lexi hadn't seen him since the egg-hiding first began.

"She's a natural."

"Hope you didn't mind her shadowing you," he said. "I wanted her to go with me, but she insisted on sticking with you."

"Didn't mind at all. She picked it up quick. And egg-hiding isn't as easy as it looks."

"That's the truth. I'm running out of creative places to leave them."

It was nice to take a small break from the mad dash of the event. Lexi tilted her head, noticing Graham's lingering stare. *Did she have a leaf in her hair? Or a smudge of mascara under her eye?* She reached up to check. "What?" she asked, curious.

Graham blinked. "Sorry. It's just... I always thought your eyes were blue. But here in the sunlight, they look..."

"Green?" She finished for him and laughed, peering down at her teal sweater. "Yeah, my birth certificate says blue eyes, but if I wear *any*thing green, they always change to match the outfit. Kinda spooky."

"Not spooky. Beautiful." He said it matter-of-factly, as though it wasn't up for debate, then took out an egg. "Down to my last one. I'd better go fill up again." He placed the egg behind a potted plant then darted across the street toward the library.

"Always hard to find spots, isn't it? The longer this goes on."

Lexi spun around to see who was speaking and saw a middle-aged woman fishing an egg out of her tote bag. It took a moment, but it finally dawned on Lexi who the woman was—Tessa, co-owner of The Pit. Lexi was used to seeing her behind the counter, without makeup and with her hair smoothed back into a tight bun. But this morning, she wore a long dress, and her lightly graying hair was tousled around her shoulders.

"So true," Lexi said, seeing Tessa's sister, Darlene, approaching from the courthouse, her bag filled to the brim.

Darlene wore her hair in a similar fashion as her sister. In fact, they were often mistaken for twins. The sisters co-owned The Pit, which served the best barbecue in the surrounding area.

"Happy Easter," Lexi said with a friendly nod, and they returned the sentiment.

"We'd best be on our way," Darlene told her sister. "We got a late start," she said, explaining to Lexi.

"Not my fault." Tessa's tone had turned sassy.

"Did I *say* it was your fault?" Darlene asked. "C'mon. We've got a lot to make up for."

Lexi hid a snicker as the always-bickering sisters made their way past her, toward the opposite row of storefronts. As Lexi determined where next to set her eggs, she marveled at how an activity that was meant exclusively for children could bring together anyone and everyone, no matter their circumstances. The Pit sisters were both single and childfree, like Lexi, yet they could all be completely comfortable participating in this "family" event. But that was the beauty of Morgan's Grove and the activities offered. Even the Valentine's Day movie event, hosted by Chaynie on the library's lawn a few weeks ago, purposely didn't highlight couples and lovers. *All* were welcome in Morgan's Grove, and every single person was a vital and cherished member of the community, no matter their status. And Lexi was proud to be part of it.

BY TEN THIRTY, WELL into the Easter egg hunt, a dazzling sun had warmed up the square significantly. Lexi wriggled out of her sweater and hung it on the back of the lawn chair she was sitting in—one of a few that her dad had thoughtfully brought from his car. People in Morgan's Grove often treated town celebrations and festivities as sporting events—bringing refreshments, gathering in clusters to watch, sitting in portable chairs to gossip and chat and snap photos.

Most adults were mere spectators of the yearly egg hunt, but some would take turns going to comfort a crying child or help the littlest ones grab a hard-to-reach egg. And it wasn't always the parents getting involved. Retired grandmothers or couples without children would often participate as well.

As she inhaled a deliberate breath, still tired from waking so early, Lexi became aware of various noises and sounds all blending together around her—squeals of joy from the children, encouraging words of guidance from the adults, happy dogs barking in the distance, enthusiastic chatter nearby as neighbors caught up with each other, and instrumental gospel music piping in from the library's outside speakers.

Lexi shielded her eyes and searched for Shelley. Minutes ago, Shelley had spotted a distressed child—another boy had snatched an egg right out of a little girl's hand—and Shelley had rushed to the crying child's side for support. Lexi had watched as she'd shadowed the little girl, pointing out eggs and helping add them to her basket.

At the opposite end of the square, Graham was lifting a boy on top of his own shoulders. Lexi watched with amusement as Graham held fast to a tree trunk to allow the boy to grab an egg perched on a high branch. When he clutched it, Graham raised the boy above his shoulders then placed him gently back on his feet, giving the boy a high five.

"How adorable was that?" Jolene asked from the seat beside Lexi. She had obviously been watching the same scene. "He's a keeper," she muttered from the side of her mouth.

Lexi elbowed her cousin then moved her attention to her parents, sitting in lawn chairs to her left. Her mother was chatting to someone on the other side, and her father was staring straight ahead, not focused on any particular activity or person. He seemed zoned out.

"Dad? Are you all right?" She touched his arm.

After a beat, he blinked. "Oh. Sure. A bit tired. Woke up extra early to prep the Easter ham." He patted her hand with his own. "Are you coming to the house for lunch after church? You and your young man?"

Lexi's eyes widened, praying that Jolene hadn't overheard. "Dad! He's not 'my' anything. We're only friends."

"Well, that's what I meant."

His eyes shifted behind Lexi, and she turned to see Graham, jogging up toward the chairs. *Impeccable timing.*

"I was just asking Lexi," her father said to Graham as he stopped by their chairs, "whether you're coming to Easter lunch at our house after church? And your sister is welcome too."

Graham gave a quick glance toward Lexi, probably seeking approval, so she nodded as though she were in on it too—even though she and her dad hadn't even discussed Easter lunch until that moment. But since they shared *every* Easter lunch together, it was always a natural assumption, going to her parents' house after the service.

"Well, sure. We'd love that, thanks," Graham said. He was slightly out of breath as he told Lexi, "You didn't say how much fun this could be for the adults too. I feel like a kid again."

"Son?"

Graham pivoted on his heel to greet a couple coming toward him. "Dad. Beth. Glad you could make it." He shook his father's hand then leaned in to hug the blonde by his side.

Lexi felt the urge to stand—she didn't want to greet Graham's father for the first time while looking lazily up from a lawn chair—so she awkwardly pushed up to her feet. Not easy to do in a sundress.

Graham saw her struggle and grasped her hand, giving her support as she regained her balance. "Lexi, this is my dad," he said. "And Beth Foster."

"So nice to meet you." Lexi introduced her parents and Jolene to them as Shelley came bounding up.

"You came!" She squeezed in between her father and Beth, putting her arms around them both.

"Sorry we're late," said Mr. Faulkner. "We took a wrong turn. Meant to be here at ten sharp."

Lexi watched him gesturing and realized how much he resembled Graham. Same stature, same thick hair, even the same almond-shaped eyes. But he lacked a particular warmth she was accustomed to seeing from Graham—a light in his expression, a gentleness in his gaze.

"Were you participating?" Graham's father asked Shelley, nodding toward the library's lawn.

"I was *help*ing."

"She's been wonderful," Lexi said. "She was guiding some children who were having trouble finding eggs."

A few minutes later, the sudden bleat of an air horn pierced the air, and Mrs. Johnson took up the microphone again. She waited patiently until the adults rounded up the children, leading them back toward the lawn. Earlier, when she'd given instructions, Mrs. Johnson had informed the children of the strict rule they must follow: the egg hunt ended when they heard the air horn—otherwise, the children would want to hunt for missing eggs all day long and would skip church in the process. They could return to the square *after* church and hunt for leftover eggs all they wanted.

Chairs were folded and trash discarded as the spectators readied themselves for the procession to their individual houses of worship. Lexi locked her eyes on a little girl across the square with crossed arms and a scowl on her face, unwilling to budge from her spot and abandon the hunt. An elderly woman that Lexi assumed was her grandmother approached the girl, her arms open wide, trying to reason with her, likely explaining what her granddaughter couldn't understand—that she had to leave this incredibly fun and exciting activity, even with eggs still to be found.

Something about the way the elderly woman tenderly treated the little girl, with a soft expression and outstretched arms, reminded Lexi of Gigi. She had been present at every Easter egg hunt when Lexi was young and would often follow along, stooping and bending over to point out eggs or help her reach for them—even when, at Gigi's age, it was probably a particular challenge to do so.

One year, when Lexi was about seven years old, she had made a secret bet with Jolene to see who could snag the most eggs. The challenge of this filled Lexi with delight and added a particular edge to the otherwise harmless, fun activity. Lexi had insisted on finishing alone, with no help from Gigi. The entire hunt, Lexi had raced around the square, snatching eggs and counting them up, trying to hold a running tally in her mind. When she caught sight of the town square's clock and noticed that she had barely two minutes until the air horn would sound, Lexi sneaked around to the back of the square, hoping she could continue on past the signal... a couple of extra minutes... and that no one would notice her absence. When the air horn bleated and the call was made to stop, Lexi continued on even faster, spotting a cluster of eggs underneath a shrub. Thrilled, she headed toward it and began filling her basket. *Surely* this *would push her egg count over the top, and she would beat Jolene!*

"Lexi?" Gigi had called out after her, rounding the courthouse. "Honey, did you hear the horn?"

Lexi stopped and swirled around as her great-grandmother came closer.

"Lexi. The hunt is over now." Gigi stood in her Easter finest—a pale-pink suit with matching painted nails—her hands clasped at her waist. Her tone was gentle, but her eyebrow was slightly cocked, which told Lexi one thing. She'd been caught.

Lexi gripped the handles of her basket tighter and watched an egg roll off the top of the heaping pile. She contemplated how to answer.

"Well, I saw this pile over here. And so I raced over, right in time."

"Before or after the air horn went off?"

That was when Lexi knew for sure that Gigi knew. About the bet. Jolene had probably spilled it earlier. She never could keep a secret.

"Well, I..." It would've been easy to shrug and say that she hadn't heard the horn—that she was simply too busy finding eggs. Gigi could never prove otherwise. But she couldn't lie to Gigi. Her face would always give her away. "I heard it." Her voice had dissolved into a whisper as her eyes lowered to the ground.

Gigi didn't scold or yell or even cross her arms or frown disapprovingly. She simply asked, "What shall we do about it?"

Lexi was aware of the right answer but didn't wish to say it aloud. She grumbled through clenched teeth, "Put these eggs back? The ones I found after the air horn?"

"Well, I'll leave that up to you. If you choose to keep them, I'll never tell a soul. But if you win your contest with Jolene, I wonder if you will feel like you won at all."

That did it. Lexi understood what she must do. She set down her basket on the freshly cut grass and mentally subtracted from her grand total of eggs. She grasped each one she'd retrieved after the horn and put them all back where they belonged, tucked underneath the shrub. When she finally got up from her squatting position, Gigi placed a hand on Lexi's braided head then brushed her bangs gently before they walked together back around the courthouse.

"I'm very proud of you," Gigi said softly.

Lexi lost her bet with Jolene by one egg that day. The result of losing was letting Jo wear her favorite bracelet for a whole week—but later, as an adult, Lexi knew she had actually won. With a patient tone, kind expression, and wise words, Gigi had taught her a life lesson that would stick with her the rest of her life.

"Lex? You okay?"

Graham stood at her side, wearing his plum blazer and a matching tie. He was holding two lawn chairs with one arm. When he noticed her staring at them, he explained. "Your mom is leading my dad and Beth and Shelley to the church. And I'm going to help your dad with the chairs, take them back to his trunk."

Lexi blinked away tears. "Okay. I'll help too."

"You were lost in thought."

"It was a memory about Gigi. And some Easter eggs."

"Sad memory?"

"Actually, no. The opposite."

Graham nodded as though he understood. Lexi folded the remaining lawn chair and clutched it comfortably under her arm. As they followed her father to the car, she asked Graham, "Does that ever happen to you? A memory of your mom hits you, out of the blue, completely unexpected?"

"All the time. Even after all these years. I can be driving to work or changing clothes or pouring a glass of milk, and there it is. Something Mum once said or the way she laughed with this high-pitched giggle. Or even realizing I have something to say but will never have the chance to tell her. Out of the blue. Wham."

"Same for me. Wham." They rounded the corner of the B&B at the edge of the square, still following her father, who was several steps ahead. Graham seemed in no hurry to catch up. Lexi said, "I find those sudden memories sort of cruel."

"How do you mean?"

"Like, they spring up on you when you're not ready, when you haven't braced yourself enough for their impact. Because when I'm doing it on purpose—thinking about Gigi or conjuring up a memory—it's easier. I'm the one in control of them. But when it hits me, a vivid memory when I least expect it—"

"It's jarring."

"Yes. And it takes a minute to right myself again. What's weird is, it's only been a handful of years since Gigi passed, but I have a hard time recalling her face. She's become this distant shadow, and I have to force my brain to remember all those details—her button nose, her sparkling eyes, her rose-lipstick smile and slightly crooked bottom teeth."

"Yep. My mum's ash-blond hair, her nail polish, even the scent of her floral perfume. But if I work hard enough to remember, it's all there."

"And thank God for that. I mean, they're right here with us, aren't they?" Lexi pointed to her temple.

"And in here." Graham patted his chest.

They spent the rest of the walk in companionable silence as Lexi processed everything—the busy morning, the exciting hunt, the strong memory of Gigi, the comforting solidarity from Graham—and decided that she would rather endure the brief prick of pain than not have the memories come at all. Because remembering Gigi in the past meant that she was a part of her present. She *was* still here.

Chapter Fourteen

Most people, when asked, would easily claim Christmas as their all-time favorite holiday. But Lexi had always loved Easter the most. In her younger years, it was likely due to a mixture of the balmy spring weather, the anticipation of the Easter bunny, the hunting for eggs, and the chance to buy a pretty new pastel dress—and matching shoes!—for church. But as she grew older, Lexi let those superficial things melt away, and she grew to cherish the deeper meaning of the holiday. Christ's somber crucifixion and joyous resurrection became tangible to her in a personal way—He died and rose not only for the whole world but for her, individually. It made her appreciate the special day even more.

Lexi particularly enjoyed the yearly Easter church service, where the congregation would join together and celebrate—sing songs, read scripture, say prayers, and hear a rousing sermon. The happy, beaming faces created a Sunday experience unlike all the others, and that included Christmas. There was a spark of joy in people's expressions and in their voices as they gathered for the same purpose.

It was true of the service she had attended after the egg hunt with her parents, Jolene, Graham, and his family, all sitting side by side on a row near the front of the carpeted sanctuary. On the way to the church, walking with Graham, Lexi had experienced a pinch of awkwardness, realizing that they hadn't had any deep conversations yet about religion. She wondered if he felt the same way she did about the holiday or whether he and his family were merely being polite by attending. But during the service, she noticed Shelley clapping along with each song, and it was clear that Graham knew all the words to the hymns. When it came time for the sermon—about how Jesus approached the women first after His resurrection—Shelley was glued to the message, barely blinking as she hung on the pastor's every word.

Lexi's one disappointment, when they filtered out of the church and into the sunshiny day, was when Shelley had to leave with her father and Beth, unable to make it to the house for Easter lunch. She had a special Easter party to attend at her place and was in charge of pouring the sweet tea.

AT HER PARENTS' HOUSE after the service, Lexi had insisted on helping her father with his gourmet mac 'n' cheese, merely so that she could sneak a quick "test" bite as she stirred the creamy concoction before topping it with even *more* cheese then baking it off for a final few minutes in the oven, all at her father's careful instruction. Graham had stayed busy helping her mother in the dining room, folding cloth napkins for each place setting, while Jolene filled the glasses with tea.

The meal was soon set out on the table—honey-glazed ham studded with cloves, creamed corn, new potatoes with fresh dill, green beans coated in olive oil, grill-roasted carrots, gouda mac 'n' cheese, and homemade biscuits. After Lexi issued a prayer of thanks, platters clanked as they were passed around the table, with everyone filling up their plates with more than they could possibly eat.

"I'm sure you've heard this more than once," Graham said, topping his full plate with a scoop of fresh green beans. "You're lucky to have a chef in the family."

"We are." Lexi broke open a flaky biscuit and watched the steam unfurl in smoky ribbons. She never took it for granted that her father had taken the time to craft homemade and delicious meals all her life. "To Dad!" She set down the biscuit and raised her glass.

The table joined in as they toasted the chef, while he bent his head and waved away the praise, clearly embarrassed. "Y'all know I enjoy doing it. No need for thanks."

As they chattered about the morning's activities, the early-afternoon sun cast angled shadows into the room. Graham looked amused by Lexi's mother's observations about the fashions worn at church and her father's elation that they sang his favorite Easter hymn and Jolene's insistence that the idea of a traditional parade should be reintroduced into next year's festivities. Lexi listened intently as she savored her meal—every bite more scrumptious than the last—and occasionally inserted her opinion into the conversation, whenever she dared get a word in edgewise. She assumed Graham wasn't used to so much overlapping of animated conversation in his family. His father seemed a more formal sort of man and probably frowned upon such conversational interruptions. But Graham didn't seem to mind, chuckling or nodding in between generous bites.

When the dinner had run its course and the plates were practically empty, Lexi insisted on clearing them away, and Graham insisted on helping her.

"Dad, you've done enough," Lexi told her father, remembering his weary face earlier that morning. "It's our turn. We'll clear away and clean."

"While you collect the plates," her mother said, "I'll get the dessert!" She disappeared into the kitchen.

Lexi leaned in toward Graham. "The one and only thing my mother ever bakes is an Easter cake. The recipe has been passed down through generations."

Her mother appeared in the doorway again, holding her pièce de résistance—a white-iced cake, lightly sprinkled with coconut shavings.

"Ta-dah!" she exclaimed, prompting a smattering of claps from around the table.

"I'll get the dessert plates," her father said.

"No. You stay put." Her mother gave his shoulder a squeeze after she'd set down the cake on the table with a flourish. "Your daughter is right. It's our turn to serve you."

The cake was as delicious as Lexi remembered, and she wasn't ashamed to ask for a second slice, knowing that the next time she would taste it was a whole year away, next Easter.

As dessert wound down, Lexi heard her phone chime for the second time during the meal. The pull was strong to check her phone, but her mother had a hard-and-fast rule: *No* cell phone usage at the table. Especially not during a holiday meal.

Lexi gave Graham a side-glance, wondering if he'd read her mind. She considered excusing herself from the table.

"Okay, you two, what's going on?" her mother asked. "You're sharing a secret over there."

Lexi cleared her throat before explaining. "We're expecting a text. Maybe. From Blanche's granddaughter, Heidi. I told y'all about her. Anyway, Heidi was supposed to send me the snapshots of Blanche's journal yesterday but never did. We've been on pins and needles all day. But since it's Easter Sunday, I figured I probably wouldn't hear from her until tomorrow."

"Well, what are you waiting for? Let's see if she texted," her dad said.

Her mother sighed and shook her head. "It seems I'm outnumbered. Go on. I'm curious too."

Lexi set down her fork then reached into her purse for her phone. She felt a tangible rush of excitement as she scrolled. "I was right. Heidi sent pictures of the diary entries." She zoomed in. "This first one is the same entry she read to me and Graham over the phone."

"Where she and James initially met at that party?" Jolene asked.

"That's the one." Lexi scrolled farther down. "She's sent six entries. I'll post them to a group chat so you can all see too." After a moment, she heard various dings around the table.

"The next entry comes from July 18th, 1941," her dad said, reading from his phone. "About a month later?"

"That sounds right. Read it for us, Dad."

"'We shared a double-date tonight: me and Tony, James and Louise. We went to the pictures first (*Dance Hall*, with Carole Landis and Cesar Romero). I wish they wouldn't show those depressing newsreels beforehand. Hitler's angry German voice and all those Nazis. *Very* disturbing. They look positively menacing, all marching in a row, arms held high. After the movie, James and Tony kept talking about it, debating whether America should become involved in the war. I'm aware such discussions are important, but I don't like thinking about it.

"'Then we went to Giuseppe's near downtown Austin and had the most delicious spaghetti I've ever eaten. And gelato afterward. Pure heaven! When the boys dropped us off at my house, Louise and I sat on the porch swing, chatting away and discussing our feelings. Louise says she's "in love" already. After three and a half weeks, imagine that! She says she can see a future with James—filled with kids and dogs and a two-story house on Sycamore Drive. Her voice changed when she talked about him. It got all dreamy and high-pitched. Louise is the most practical, level-headed woman I know. I've never seen her this way before. It *must* be love. I told her I wanted to be her maid of honor, and she agreed. I hope she asks for my input on the dress. Yellow is *not* my color!'"

Lexi's dad ended the journal entry with a chuckle and looked toward his wife, who had donned her reading glasses and glanced at the next entry in the series. "Graham, I think you'd better take this one. Dated December 7th."

Graham read from his phone. "'*A dark day for us all.* That's what Daddy said before he retired to his bedroom with a deep frown. Earlier, Louise was at our house, having lunch with the family, when Daddy clicked on the radio. There was news of a bombing by the Japanese at some place called Pearl Harbor. Daddy says it's located in Hawaii. After he clicked off the radio broadcast, he whispered to Mama—"Everything has changed." I wasn't sure what that meant, but Louise understood. She grabbed my sleeve and pulled me into the parlor. Her voice was composed, but her face showed utter panic as she told me she was worried about Tony and James. I always tune them out whenever they have their "war talk," but Louise has been paying close attention for all these past months. And tonight, she mentioned the draft and America entering the war. Surely not. I think she's overreacting. How can something that's happening thousands of miles away be of any real concern to us, here at home? But that's not true anymore, is it? The war is on our own soil now. Louise repeated Daddy's words, that Pearl Harbor had "changed everything." Then she grabbed her sweater and purse and rushed out, saying she had to find James.'"

Jolene read the next entry. "Dated the next day, December 8th. 'What a day. Emotions are up and down and sideways. Louise came to my house this afternoon, breathless, face tear-stained, to tell me the news. That James has signed up for the military. He told her it was his "duty," and that if he didn't sign up, he'd get drafted anyway. He explained his obligation, that he was committed to fighting for our country. Selfishly, I asked if that meant Tony would also be sent away? Drafted? She said yes, she thought he would be, unless he failed the physical exam. Is it wrong for me to hope he does? And James too? I don't *want* things to change. This has been the best few months of our entire lives. Blissful and happy and wonderful. But now, everything feels ruined. And scary and unknown. Topsy-turvy. I said some of this to Louise, and she shook her head at me with a chuckle under her breath. She seems so much braver than I am. She said she understands James's decision and even respects him for it. She said he wouldn't be the man she loved if he didn't sign up for the service. I can't agree with this, as I want Tony all to myself. Maybe I'll feel differently soon, but I don't think I will.

"'A few hours later, Louise telephoned our house to tell me the amazing news, that James asked her to *marry* him tonight! He got down on one knee and everything! He took her to their favorite spot at the gazebo, where they usually have picnics, and explained that he wants to marry her when the war is over. He said it will give him the hope of a future. She said yes, *of course*, and will tell her parents at some point. But she wants to savor the news, keep it all to herself for a bit. So, all in all, a hard day, but a good one for Louise. I am truly, genuinely happy for my best friend in the whole world.'"

Lexi's mother, as though realizing it was her turn, adjusted her reading glasses, then scrolled her phone with one hand while she gripped her husband's hand with the other. "February 18th, 1942. I don't think it's a melodramatic statement to say that this was the saddest day of my life. Louise and I put on our finest Sunday dresses, checked our makeup and hair three times each, and headed over to Tony's house. He and James were leaving at twelve noon, sharp, to drive together to Camp Bowie near Brownwood, headed for basic training. They will train for several weeks, maybe longer, and might be sent to Oklahoma for even more training! Goodness. Then, after that, they'll get their orders to go overseas. Tony says he and James might not be assigned to the same company and they probably won't be able to reveal their exact locations when they're in actual combat, but he absolutely promises to write. Louise and I made a pact before we arrived at Tony's. *No tears.* We needed to appear brave and strong for our boys. But I broke the pact almost immediately and, like a blubbering fool, cried all over Tony's shoulder as he hugged me tight. I wondered secretly if it was for the very last time. Louise and I locked arms together as we waved goodbye. Louise ribbed me and whispered 'Smile!' through clenched teeth, so I obeyed as their car turned the corner until we couldn't see it anymore.

"'I have to pause my writing. I hear pebbles against the window.'" Lexi's mother raised her eyebrows then continued. "'I'm back again. Louise had to escape her house for a while. She told me she was about to run away from home tonight, but I convinced her otherwise (she has no job, no real money of her own). I asked what happened, and she said she and her parents had the most awful fight tonight. She revealed to them about her engagement to James, and instead of being glad and supportive, her father was "horrified," in Louise's words. He said that James was too old for her (only by four years!) and that he was going off to war and might not make it back. Her father said he was merely thinking of her best interests, her future happiness, trying to protect her heart. When Louise stood firm and said she was marrying James "with or without" her parents' approval, her father shouted at her and forbade Louise ever to see or speak to "that young man" ever again! I don't know what I'd do if my daddy ever talked to *me* that way! When Louise finished telling me, she was calmer. She wiped away her falling tears and asked me to do the biggest favor in the world. She said she will defy her parents in secret. She wants me to be an intermediary for James's letters to her. She's already sent him a letter at boot camp, telling him the plan and giving him *my* home address. Even before asking me! But she's my very best friend in the world, and so I agreed wholeheartedly. Truth be told, this is all quite exciting. A fight with her parents, a forbidden love, secret letters. It sounds like some sort of Brontë novel. I'm happy to be part of it!'"

Lexi scrolled through Heidi's final text to read the last entry, a somber one confirming the worst. "'September 10th, 1943. Whenever a letter from James comes, I call Louise and let her know, and we drop everything we're doing and meet at the gazebo. That's what we did today. But I knew, the moment I saw the envelope, that something wasn't right. The handwriting wasn't James's. It was someone else's. And the letter wasn't nearly as thick as it usually is. Louise was already at the gazebo when I showed up, and she could tell from the look on my face what was wrong. We sat together and I held the letter between us without a single word.

"'Usually, we chat for a bit and catch up on our day, then she tucks the letter into her purse, to savor the words alone in her bedroom. But today, she stayed on the gazebo's bench with me. She slid her finger under the envelope's flap until it tipped open then untucked the letter and found a photo inside, of her and James. When she began to read the letter, only a single page long, I watched her eyes dart back and forth, line to line, as they brimmed over with tears. "Oh, James," she whispered, staring at the photo trembling in her hand. Then she held it close to her chest. I thought she might scream or yell, or faint or hyperventilate. But instead, she gave one firm nod and then slipped the letter and photo back inside the envelope.

"'She told me in a whisper, 'He's gone.' I leaned in and grasped her as tightly as a human being could, waiting for her shoulders to shake in a sob. But it never came. When I released her, I saw a vacancy in her eyes, an almost soullessness that made me shiver inside. She squeezed my hand and thanked me for all my support and friendship then walked down the gazebo steps alone. It had begun to rain, but she didn't even notice. I wondered if I should go after her, but I knew the answer. She had to be alone, to sort this out. I can't help her with this. No one can. She has to deal with the pain on her own, figure out how to overcome it. Or maybe how to live with it for the rest of her days. I had gone to the gazebo with news of my own—that Tony had asked me to marry him and I had written back, "Yes!" I want Louise to be my maid of honor. But all I can think about is my friend and her grief. Nothing else matters today. Nothing.'"

As Lexi lowered her phone, the only sound in her parents' house was the soft tick of the grandfather clock in the hallway. She stared at the cream tablecloth to process Gigi's reaction to the tragic news—her first love, killed in action, and their entire future killed along with it. Even though Lexi was already aware of James's death, experiencing the scene through Blanche's eyes, firsthand, was particularly unbearable. Lexi saw her great-grandmother's strength, pictured her familiarly rigid spine as she walked down those gazebo steps, proving her refusal to crumble over life's challenges. That core strength was always there, but never more so than in this journal entry. Her world, forever changed.

"I wish I could reach out through time and hug her," Lexi heard herself say. She blinked and looked around at the table. Everyone seemed equally affected by the journal entry. "That sounded weird," she whispered.

"No, it didn't." Graham reached over with his warm hand to cover hers and squeezed gently.

"Gigi's strength was admirable." Lexi's mother wiped a tear before it could fall. "I wish she had confided in us at some point about all this. Let us know what she endured. But I suppose it was too painful."

"Sorry I brought the mood down," Lexi said, feeling Graham stroke her hand with his thumb. "This was supposed to be a celebration."

"I'm glad we were all here for this, honey," her dad said, reassuring her. "Together."

AFTER STOOPING TO PLACE the final plate in the dishwasher, Lexi straightened up with a grunt and stretched out her back. She noticed her father in the corner of the kitchen, popping a pill into his mouth then capping an antacid bottle. She had never known him to take an antacid in his whole life—he often bragged about having an "iron stomach." Maybe all those spices over the years had caught up to him.

His eyes met hers, and he slid the bottle away then stepped toward Lexi. "So, what happens next with the journal? Didn't you hire a private eye for the case?"

Lexi closed the dishwasher with a satisfying click then leaned against the counter. "I did. And Heidi gave me permission to share the new journal entries with him. I'm not sure what good they'll do or what clues they might hold. But the next goal is to see if we can find James's family. I would love to get my hands on Gigi's letters to him if they still exist. It's a slim chance, but—"

"Anything is possible." Graham had come to stand behind Lexi at the sink. "I mean, look at what we've uncovered so far. The mystery of the necklace."

"And letters tucked under the attic floorboards," Lexi said. "And now, Blanche's journal entries. One thing leading to another. You're right—there's reason to stay optimistic."

"That's my girl." Her father leaned in for a hug, and she felt the warmth of his chest against her cheek.

"Thank you again for the meal," she said, squeezing his waist.

"You're welcome, my love." He kissed the top of her head then released her. "Happy Easter to both of you."

A few minutes later, after Jolene had left for the founder's mansion to pick up some paperwork before heading home, Lexi stood in the front entryway with Graham at her side. She faced her parents then unclasped Gigi's necklace, dangling it toward her mother. "I want you to have this."

"Why? I thought you enjoyed wearing it."

"I do, but I'm afraid of losing it someday. I wouldn't forgive myself. Plus, I only ever took the necklace so that we could research it.

But I think it belongs here, at Gigi's house. Like an artifact. It feels right somehow." She spooled the chain into her mother's open palm.

"Well, it'll be safe here," her mother said while leaning in for a hug. "I'll take good care of it." As Lexi accepted the unusual gesture—her dad was usually the hugger in the family—she wondered if perhaps the necklace and the letters were starting to create a fresh, stronger bond between mother and daughter. As though Gigi had reached forward through time to help nudge along their fragile relationship.

Chapter Fifteen

After an early morning of egg-hunting, followed by church, then the scrumptious meal at Lexi's parents' house, Graham had assumed the day had come to its natural conclusion—that Lexi would walk him to his car and that he would leave for Austin to brace for another Monday. But Lexi's leisurely pace as her father shut the door made Graham hopeful that she was reluctant to let the day end.

"That's Lucille's house." She pointed to the home on the corner as they strolled along the sidewalk.

"The baker? The one with the corgis?"

"You've been paying attention."

"She specializes in gingerbread cookies." Graham remembered seeing the sign in the window last time he was in Morgan's Grove. He loosened his tie with his index finger.

"It sounds weird—gingerbread, year-round. But it's the most delicious you'll ever taste. Goes beyond a seasonal dessert."

"I'll have to try some. Next time."

The square was eerily silent as they came upon it, with every business on the block respectfully shuttered for the Easter holiday. Graham pictured weary families in their homes, napping in the late afternoon after a filling Easter meal and a busy morning of activities.

He felt a prick of envy, realizing that Easters were like this every year for the residents of Morgan's Grove. Not a novelty for them, as it was for him. In the past few years, each Easter, he had picked up Shelley and taken her to a formal Methodist service downtown. Perhaps their father would join them, perhaps not. Afterward, they would find a restaurant, usually cafeteria-style—overly crowded and noisy—then Graham would drop Shelley off again and return to his apartment to grade or plan for the upcoming workweek. The day never seemed particularly special, not the way his mum had always made it when he was growing up. But today, he'd been welcomed with open arms by the small-town community—and by Lexi's entire family—which had warmed him from the inside out.

Sensing that Lexi was in no particular hurry during their walk to her house, Graham sucked in a quick breath and took a chance. "So. How about you show me your favorite place in Morgan's Grove? Somewhere I haven't been yet."

Lexi paused at the curb, right outside the library, and placed a hand on her hip as she raised her teal eyes to him. The sun had caught her hair at the perfect angle, and it glowed from behind. "You mean like a hidden treasure?"

"Right. That only residents would know about."

"I've got just the place."

She guided him to the bed-and-breakfast beyond the edge of the square. Puzzled, he watched her walk around the building's side then into the backyard. And there he spotted it, in the middle of an enormous, manicured lawn.

"The gazebo," he said under his breath.

"The one in Blanche's journal," she said as they moved toward it. "But that's not actually the hidden treasure. We're passing through."

Lexi climbed the steps to the gazebo—roomy and sturdily built, with bright-white paint that Graham assumed was freshened up every couple of years or so to keep the structure looking new. He noticed clear lights wrapped around the roof and sides and imagined it lit up at night.

"Mrs. Haversham rents it out." Lexi paused in the gazebo's center and did a quick spin in place, arms extended, her dress fanning out. "Weddings, parties, engagements. Big life moments."

"Including the reading of certain important letters from a great love during World War II."

"That too."

As she paused, Graham imagined her revisiting Blanche's entry about Gigi, reading the letter that told her James had been killed, in the very spot where they stood. He wished he could read Lexi's thoughts, but before he could even try, she had blinked and walked toward another set of steps to exit the gazebo. With the tour clearly over, Graham followed, crinkling his brow as she walked farther and farther toward the back of the property, past a wall thick with ivy.

"Where are you taking us?"

"Patience." She paused at a tall iron gate.

Graham watched her punch in a code. "You weren't kidding. Hidden *and* prohibited. Is this illegal?"

Lexi snickered. "Hardly." She swiveled to face him. "My mother redecorated the entire B&B, room by room, about a decade ago. And so, as a special thank-you, Mrs. Haversham gave her—and our entire family—access to this secret space on her property. I haven't seen it in a couple of years. I forget that it's even here. But with spring in full bloom, I'm assuming it's as breathtaking as I remember."

With that, she opened the creaky iron door and stepped inside. Graham pushed the door wider for both of them and peered out at one of the most lush, magnificent gardens he'd ever laid eyes on. "Whoa," he whispered, hardly realizing that Lexi had already stepped in behind him and clicked the gate closed.

"Amazing, isn't it?" She took him gently by the hand, leading him inside.

The colors and sounds hit Graham's senses all at once. Bees buzzing quietly near bright-pink azalea bushes, hummingbirds hovering to retrieve the nectar from hollyhocks, squirrels hopping from delicate tree limb to tree limb. Someone had lovingly, painstakingly designed the garden, with its neatly clipped shrubbery leading to a focal point at the center, a serene pool with a fountain trickling water into it. Beyond that, there were slate-stone paths with brightly colored perennials lining the way. As they moved deeper inside, Graham inhaled the fresh, perfumed scents coming from everywhere at once.

"Stunning," he said as Lexi released his hand and paused with him near the fountain's edge. "It's an English garden, transported."

He almost added "Like my mum's" but couldn't quite get the words out. He was experiencing a vivid flashback to their garden in the Cotswolds—on a much smaller scale and less grand. But every bit as carefully and lovingly maintained, with the same capacity for producing sensory overload in any observer. As a little boy, Graham would often explore hide-and-seek passages with his sister or sit alone beneath a tree and read books through the dappled sunlight or play soldiers with his beagle around the hardy shrubbery. Over the years, it became his solace from an uninvolved father and school bullies.

Lexi had moved to sit at the edge of the fountain, so Graham joined her, the concrete gritty and solid under his fingers. A yellow butterfly fluttered near Lexi's face, and she raised a dainty hand to see if it might perch. Instead, it drifted toward Graham then flew away, past a tall oak tree.

"What do you think?" Lexi asked in a reverent whisper.

"Breathtaking. It really does remind me of England."

"That's what I was hoping. Did you have a garden like this back home?"

"Similar but smaller. I spent much of my childhood there, exploring. Escaping." He gestured outward. "This makes me realize..."

"What?"

He could feel the weight of her stare. "Well, how much I miss it. Room to roam, to look at nature." He turned to meet her gaze. "I love Austin, don't get me wrong. It's energizing, being in the heart of an active city. But there's hardly any place to breathe, stretch your legs, have some real space to call your own."

"I'm ashamed to admit that I take living in a small town for granted." Lexi crossed her legs at the ankles. "I'm so busy with the store that I hardly look up sometimes. Especially when it comes to my own backyard. Literally." She smirked. "It's awful. I've done nothing with it. You're making me want to revisit it—maybe have my mom help me with some gardening. She's got a green thumb that I didn't inherit."

As she spoke, Graham's mind formed an idea. He had made steady strides into Morgan's Grove, with the potential of owning property for a horse ranch someday. *But why not a house of his own at some point?* A real home in a slow-paced small town instead of a cramped, one-bedroom apartment with no balcony and a view of the parking lot. *What was stopping him from exploring moving as an option, from becoming a full-time Morgan's Grove resident?* He didn't have to give up his job. He could ask for more online classes and then commute to campus when needed. The best of both worlds.

"I think this garden is a few decades old." Lexi broke into his thoughts. "I wonder if Gigi ever visited it with James. It was a public garden until the seventies, I think, when it was vandalized."

"And then out came the padlock."

"Exactly. And the wall of ivy to hide it from the public." She shifted to look at Graham. "Speaking of Gigi, I was thinking… maybe I could include the new Blanche journals. When I talk to your class."

"The students would love that."

"Although, you might have to read out the entries for me. I'm not sure I could make it through them a second time without getting emotional."

An easy silence settled on them as a mockingbird called out for its mate in a nearby tree.

Lexi spoke in a quiet voice as she stared at a nearby squirrel. "I think what amazes me about the journals—about all of it, the necklace, the letters—is that kind of bold love. Gigi only knew James a few months before she took a risk and went all in. She committed to him in the middle of a war, when the world was on fire and everything was so bleak and unpredictable. In the letters and the journal, I didn't sense a hint of reservation or fear. She even defied her own parents to be with him. I don't understand that kind of courage. Or that sort of big, overpowering love. It didn't happen to me, not with my ex-husband. I never felt the urgency that Gigi did—head-over-heels, all-consuming love. I thought it only happened in movies."

Graham nodded. "It's rare. I haven't experienced it yet either. My own parents had a... polite love. Almost formal and even cold. My grandparents died when I was young, so I never saw a warm marriage modeled for me growing up. But—I'm prone to believe it can happen, that big love. Maybe I'm waiting for it to prove me wrong."

Lexi shifted her gaze to the pink azaleas. "I like that. Letting it prove me wrong—keeping the door of hope cracked open, giving love the benefit of the doubt. But from a healthy distance." She shook her head. "Jolene seems to chase down love. She's never afraid of it. I'm amazed at how wide-open she is, using all those dating apps, looking for love around every possible corner. I guess I'm more..."

"Jaded?"

"Realistic."

"Well, we *are* in a magical garden, sitting at a fountain, which I assume is partly here to make wishes come true." Graham stood and reached inside his pocket for loose change. He found two pennies and handed one over to Lexi. When she took it, he clicked his penny against hers. "To the hope of finding that big 'Gigi and James' sort of love—maybe, someday."

"Someday, maybe... I can commit to that." Lexi shut her eyes for a second then tossed the penny behind her into the fountain with a *kerplop*.

Graham followed suit as Lexi covered her mouth for a sneeze. And then another.

"It's the pollen." She sniffled. "I've been noticing it everywhere the past few days—that evil yellow dust on top of every mailbox, garbage can, car. Probably doesn't help, us being dead center in the middle of a lush garden."

"Likely not. Wanna head for your house?" he asked, knowing he could've easily remained in the garden for hours—with her—until the dwindling sun dimmed their eyesight.

"Yeah, it's time." She walked with him toward the entrance. "Poor Bailey. He's never alone for this long. Probably wondering if I abandoned him."

"Let's go reassure him you didn't."

WHEN THEY ARRIVED HOME, Lexi assumed Graham would pause at his car, exchange polite goodbyes with her, and then be on his way. But before he could even think of leaving, the question had already exited her lips. "Coffee? I can make us a quick cup. And Bailey would love to see you."

Graham halted at the curb, considering her offer. "Sure. But only half a cup—I've got some ungraded tests to finish, so I can't stay long."

Even as she walked up the path, Lexi recalled the unkempt state of her house—an entryway with scattered dog toys, a blanket flopped casually over the back of the living room sofa, three pairs of shoes kicked onto the rug nearby, and the kitchen table with its crooked placemat and a half-finished novel splayed out on top. *Is there a pile of dishes in the sink?* She couldn't remember.

She cringed as she walked up the three steps to her porch and noticed the swing—covered in a thick layer of golden dust. She had intended to clean off the pollen yesterday, but other priorities had crept in, as they always did.

It was too late to back out. She had already issued Graham the invitation, and even considering the embarrassingly haphazard state of her dwelling, it would be rude to rescind it. Her Southern upbringing wouldn't allow it.

So she sucked in a breath and whirled around as Graham paused on the second porch step. They were eye-to-eye. "Promise not to judge the state of my house? Honestly, I wasn't planning on company, so I didn't have the chance to tidy up."

"That doesn't matter. I promise."

"But you're used to seeing my mother's ultra-pristine home, without a cushion out of place. My house is nearly the opposite. It's... livable."

"Well, that's the best kind," Graham assured her.

Feeling marginally better, she pushed the screen door aside then unlocked the front door. Graham followed her inside and proclaimed the space charming even as he accidentally kicked one of Bailey's toys with the tip of his shoe, sending the stuffed dinosaur flying across the room.

She led Graham past the den and into the kitchen—only one tumbler occupied the sink, thankfully. When she opened the back door, she saw Bailey pushing his head through, eager to get inside. Panting, nose in the air, Bailey completely sidestepped his owner in favor of the new guest in the house. Graham squatted down and caught Bailey's face in both hands, and they greeted each other nose-to-nose. Lexi was fast enough to catch part of the reunion on her phone—Bailey's high-pitched whimpers and wagging tail, Graham's closed eyes and grins as he tried to contain the face-licks coming his way.

"Sweet," Lexi whispered, stopping the recording.

Graham stood and dusted off his hands while Bailey switched his attention to Lexi, bumping his head against her shin, his usual greeting.

"Silly boy." She bent down to rub his neck and scratch his head. "Did you miss me too?"

"Hey, listen, there's something I forgot," Graham said. "I'll be right back."

Intrigued, Lexi stood up again. *What could he have remembered so suddenly? Or maybe it was a polite excuse to grab some privacy and send a text to someone?* "Okay. I'll make the coffee."

"Perfect."

Graham headed back out the front door while Lexi poured Bailey's dry food into his bowl, refreshed his water, then made the coffee. As the strong, bitter aroma filled the room, various movie-like reels, specific images of the day, flashed through Lexi's mind: brightly colored eggs, Shelley's infectious smile, Graham's handsomely tailored suit, the organ playing rousing Easter hymns, her father's scrumptious food, her mother's coconut cake, Blanche's journal entries, roses in bloom at the secret garden, Graham's hearty chuckle as Bailey play-attacked him.

Moving one coffee cup to replace the other, Lexi realized it was the first day in a long while that she hadn't even *thought* about the store or planned for the following day, the following week, and so on. She had simply... lived. Inside each moment as it came, as it occurred. She wished she could live more days like this one—savoring the nows instead of planning the thens.

The coffeemaker told her the task was done, and she took both steaming mugs by their handles, curiosity getting the best of her. She decided to stop waiting and instead take Graham's coffee out to him and find out what he was up to. Bailey was munching contentedly at his bowl, so she walked toward the entryway. Graham had conveniently left the front door open, so she nudged the screen door with her foot and stepped through. Letting the door bang shut again, Lexi glanced up to see Graham, bent over the porch swing, scrubbing the wooden slats. His jacket was draped over the porch rail behind him.

"What's happening here?" she asked, amused.

"Blimey, I'm caught. Thought I had another minute," he said, slightly out of breath, then swung around with a slight ta-dah motion toward the swing. He was holding a dirty rag in one hand and a palm-sized bottle in the other.

The swing wasn't yellow with pollen anymore. It sparkled the original bright white that her dad had painted it last year.

"It's pristine!" She marveled at the swing, stepping closer.

Graham set down the rag and bottle on the porch railing. "I remembered I had this window cleaner in my car. Hoped it would do the job."

"It certainly did." She met his gaze. "Thank you."

Graham gave an aww-shucks shrug like a little boy who was caught doing a good deed. "A small gesture for such a huge day."

She came closer and handed him the coffee mug. "What do you mean?"

"This whole Easter. It was special, as corny as that sounds. The meal, your parents, Blanche's journal, the garden. And especially Shelley at the hunt. She had more fun than I've ever seen her have." He produced his phone. "She sent me these."

Lexi moved in, shoulder to shoulder with Graham, to watch him scroll through a series of selfies Shelley had taken with various townspeople during the morning's hunt—with Lucille, Chaynie and Greg, the Pit sisters, and even Lexi. All smiling, bent over head to head with Shelley.

"Precious," Lexi whispered as Graham shut off his phone and slid it back into his pocket.

"Wiping down the swing was the least I could do."

"You didn't owe me anything. I enjoyed it too." She switched her cup to her other hand then asked, "Are you sure you can't stay longer? Try out the swing, watch the sunset?"

Graham winced. "As tempting as that is, I'd better get back to those tests. The students are expecting them first thing tomorrow. And I've still got a drive in front of me." He took a generous sip then set the mug on the railing before wriggling into his jacket, pushing his arms through the sleeves.

Lexi admired his work ethic and didn't want to tempt him further. Besides, the long day was catching up with her, too, and she sensed a yawn forming at the back of her throat. She stifled it and said, "At least we both had a break from the grind."

"Today was exactly what I needed. Beginning to end."

A wisp of Lexi's hair, caught by a light breeze, caressed her chin. She watched Graham raise his hand to tuck the wisp back into place at the nape of her neck. A light chill ran through her as his eyes remained on her, steadfast and intense. Normally, intimate situations brought a swift shyness that made Lexi look away—her first instinct was to blink and fill the pause with awkward conversation. But she couldn't stop matching his gaze, mesmerized. She felt a gentle grazing of his fingers against her cheek and wondered if he might lean in to kiss her. But he remained at a careful distance, and his light stroke of her cheek was fleeting. When it was over, she wasn't sure it had even happened.

"It should be dry by now."

Lexi frowned. "Dry?"

"The swing. Ready to sit on."

"Oh. Right."

Graham took up his rag and cleaner again.

"Drive safe," she told him as he jogged down the stairs.

"Will do."

As she watched him pull away, Lexi took up her neglected coffee and tipped the cup to her lips. She took a deep, satisfying swallow, letting it warm her whole body, then moved toward the swing. She lowered all of her weight onto the slats, easing the swing into a hypnotic rocking motion, then looked outward, past her house, to see the row of other houses. Beyond them were brilliant-white clouds reflecting a sun almost ready to set.

Her mind drifted back to Graham, to his soft fingers, his warm expression, his sweet gesture of cleaning the swing. Then much farther back, to his constant support of her necklace research, his involvement with her family, his loving devotion to Shelley. She could hardly believe he was the same inattentive Graham she had met on that first day inside his classroom. The cliché was true—you should never judge a book by its cover alone.

Lexi wasn't certain when it happened or at what point over the past several days, but things with Graham had begun to shift. Early on, he was an occasional part of her week, an outsourced professional helping her with the necklace. But lately, she'd begun to anticipate his near-daily texts—and look forward to them. He was becoming a habit, a steady part of her life. *Had he sensed it too?*

Lexi reached into her sweater pocket for her phone and opened a text to Jolene. She wanted to talk this over with someone else—get out of her own head and make sense of things. But her thumb hovered over the keyboard and paused. *How could she put into words what she didn't yet understand? How could she explain to Jolene her confusion about her emerging feelings for Graham? That push and pull she couldn't wrap her mind around?*

"He's a rebound" was becoming a terribly thin excuse for continuing to hold Graham at arm's length and for keeping up the invisible wall between them.

Deciding not to tread yet in murky waters—and wanting to keep the afterglow of this serene porch moment all to herself—Lexi replaced her phone in her pocket to finish her coffee and savor the sunset from her lovely clean swing. Jolene could wait.

Chapter Sixteen

Above the shuffle and drone of students zipping up bookbags and gathering water bottles, Graham shouted, "And don't forget to read Chapter Twenty-One! It'll be on your final exam next week."

Graham ran a hand through his wavy hair, wishing he'd gotten it trimmed, and checked the time. Lexi would be walking in any minute. He had texted her last night, suggesting that she arrive shortly before the appointed class, so that they could set up anything she needed—PowerPoints, props, etc. They hadn't rehearsed how this would go, because he'd wanted her to have complete freedom to present Gigi's information to his students in whatever format she wished. But he had prepped his laptop with some media in case Lexi needed it.

As the next batch of students filtered into the classroom, Graham pretended to be busy on his phone—when, really, his mind was on one thing: seeing Lexi again for the first time since Easter Sunday, since that significant pause on her front porch.

He had been captivated by her surprised expression as she'd thanked him for cleaning the swing. Her mouth was irresistible. He'd wanted to kiss her. But when his hand grazed her cheek, he recalled what she'd said mere moments before, in the secret garden, expressing her doubts about love. *Something that happens mostly in movies... someday, maybe.*

She wasn't ready yet. And so his hand had respectfully dropped away as he resisted his initial impulse. He couldn't risk spooking her. Besides, he enjoyed what they had—an easy friendship with the potential for more. *Why rush it?* He was happy to wait.

"Dr. Faulkner? I have a question about my essay."

A student had been standing politely beside him, waiting for his attention. Graham placed his phone on the desk and shifted his focus toward the student.

"Sure. How can I help?"

WHY HAD SHE COMMITTED to this? It had sounded good in the moment—sharing James's letters and the story of Gigi's necklace with a room full of college students. But the closer Lexi came to the actual class visit, the more nervous she was.

She checked the time on her phone again—twelve minutes until Graham's class began—and climbed the stairs, relieved she wouldn't be late. Traffic had not been kind to her as she left an estate sale that went longer than expected then got stuck in a sea of unmoving cars on a busy Austin highway. But the seas finally parted, and Lexi entered the college grounds and located a parking space in the nick of time. She'd spent the last few minutes rush-walking to Graham's building, hoping she wasn't too out of breath and harried-looking when she arrived. And also hoping that the windy day hadn't mussed up her hair to ridiculous proportions. She'd decided to wear it down, with loose waves grazing her shoulders.

Last night, while rehearsing what to say to the class, she became queasy at the thought of public speaking. *Wasn't it the most common fear for many people? Even above death?* She could see why. In fact, it was probably what had stopped her from considering a career in teaching. It wasn't natural, being in front of a whole group of students, day after day, having them staring at her the entire time, waiting for her to speak and lead the discussion. *How did Graham manage it? Or even Jolene, who gave tours to new groups of complete strangers at the manor on a weekly basis?*

While Lexi had been practicing her opening comments in front of the mirror, she remembered a horrifying moment in college when she'd had a panic attack in front of her entire speech class. It didn't even matter that she'd been confident in her topic—free daycare offered for college students. The moment she cleared her throat and looked out at all the eyes staring back at her, she froze. She tried to swallow but couldn't, and her mind turned fuzzy, her thoughts dissolving into thick cotton. Her breathing increased, and she started to sweat. After a moment, when her teacher gently whispered, "Take your time," Lexi was plucked out of her own head, and her mind became clear again. Thankfully, presenters were allowed to read straight from their papers—for a grade reduction—so Lexi read off her first paragraph, and her body relaxed as the words finally came, one after another. By the end, she hadn't needed the aid of her notes. Still, it was the last time she'd spoken in front of a large audience.

She didn't wish for a repeat of that awful day, so last night, Lexi had decided to treat it more like a conversation than a presentation. If she could approach the talk as simply feeding the students information, the same way she'd already done it several times over to various people—her parents, Jo, Ruby—maybe the pressure would be lessened. And perhaps Graham could even step in and help explain things with her. She'd chosen four of James's letters, as well as two of Blanche's diary entries, to read to the students.

Lexi's other concern was that she would somehow bore the class. She pictured the students shifting in their seats, checking their phones, counting down the minutes. Surely, they would never find journals and entries and a necklace from eighty-plus years ago as thrilling as she and Graham had. The students were a whole generation apart from Lexi—their interests were different than her own. And they had no idea who Gigi was. *Why should they care? Gigi wasn't anyone special to them.*

Lexi swatted away all the insecurities from her mind as she entered the hallway near Graham's classroom. She saw a glass case that housed some university announcements and checked her hair in the reflection, tousling her side-swept bangs and straightening her jacket. She'd gone with a professional business-look—a tan blazer and black slacks.

"Deep breath," she told her reflection then moved toward Graham's classroom.

He stood in the same position where she'd first met him, weeks ago, but this time, when he saw her, his expression was warm and welcoming. "Hey," he whispered as she approached.

"Sorry I'm late."

"You're not. Right on time. I've got your documents ready for the big screen. If you want to use it." He pointed toward the laptop and scrolled through the entries and letters she'd chosen to share.

Seeing how well prepared he was gave Lexi an extra shot of confidence. She could do this. "Thanks. This makes things much easier."

"I can be your assistant." His grin created tiny crinkles at the edges of his eyes. "Here, scroll through them yourself, to organize them. However you want."

He changed places with her so that she was behind the laptop. Students continued to file in, chattering with each other or tapping on phones. Lexi turned toward the laptop to see that Graham had even added photos of the necklace, blown up for the students to see. She felt utterly prepared and suddenly confident. If the students hadn't been there, watching, she might have given Graham a quick and grateful hug for his unexpected help.

When class began—filled nearly to capacity, with close to a hundred students in the lecture hall—Lexi stepped aside and allowed Graham to give the students some routine class announcements, including reminders about when final exams would begin next week, a quick recap of the study material, and the items they would need to bring (two blue books, a pen or pencil, and "a sharp and ready mind").

"We have a special guest today," he said next, pivoting toward Lexi. "This is Lexi Price. She's a colleague and friend of mine. She's also a businesswoman who owns Antiquated, an antiques shop located in Morgan's Grove."

"I've been there before!" a student exclaimed from the second row. "With my grandmother last year."

"Wonderful," Graham said. "Well, Lexi has an incredible story to share with us today, about her great-grandmother's experience during World War II. I'm hoping that her story will put a human face to the history you've been studying this semester. I know you'll find it as riveting as I have. Please give her your full and respectful attention. That means all cell phones off." He pointed to a couple of students, who sheepishly obeyed, shutting down their phones and setting them aside. "Ms. Lexi Price." Graham led the applause, and the students dutifully followed as Graham exchanged places with her and stepped behind the laptop, ready to help out.

As Lexi approached the podium and the students watched her movements, she remembered Jolene's one piece of advice—*Relax your face and smile, even if you're scared to pieces.*

Lexi thanked the students for having her and realized her voice was too quiet and shy to reach them all in the huge space of the lecture hall. So she forced herself to project and speak louder, even though it felt completely weird and unnatural. Graham gave her a warm nod from where he stood. *You can do this,* his expression read.

She treated her presentation like a story. She started at the beginning, with the discovery of the necklace. As though reading her mind, Graham had already placed the image on the screen behind her, and she heard a couple of students gasp lightly. She remembered her own first reaction to the necklace and its inscription.

As the minutes ticked by, Lexi relaxed, realizing that the students *were* interested. She could tell by their body language—forward-leaning, eyes glued to the screen and to her. She wasn't wasting their time with some old, boring information about an old, boring event. They had already studied the time period, and as Graham had hoped, Lexi was putting a human face onto those events.

She explained to the students Graham's role in the hunt along the way and encouraged Graham to give his input too. His retelling of events added a richer layering to Lexi's story. They were in synch, almost as though they'd rehearsed it, with a back-and-forth approach that took the students on the journey with them. Graham clicked onto image after image—first, of the letters they'd discovered together in the attic and then, of Blanche's handwritten diary entries, sent by Heidi.

When Lexi came to the final entry, she expected the lecture to come to a graceful, natural conclusion. But when Graham asked if there were questions, more than a dozen students raised their hands high. Graham called on the students one by one:

"Did Gigi's parents ever come around and approve of the engagement?"

"What happened to Gigi's letters to James?"

"How big is the teardrop necklace?"

To answer that last one, Lexi said, "I'll let you see for yourself. I actually brought the necklace with me." She drew the case out of her purse and set the piece onto the desk. This morning before the estate sale, she had dropped by her parents' house and asked for the necklace—temporarily—for Graham's class. She would return it to the house later in the afternoon.

"Very generous of Ms. Price to bring it along. As we end today's class, anyone who wants to see the necklace up close can make a single-file line," Graham said. "And don't pick up the necklace—let her do it for you if you want to view the inscription. Remember that this is a historical artifact. And for those who have questions, we've got a bit more time here after class, if Ms. Price is willing."

Graham's instructions worked, and the students lined up to view the necklace and pepper her with more questions. Whenever she couldn't answer the historical ones, she deferred to Graham, who was happy to respond. He stood near her, protective, as though making certain his students would remain respectful. Lexi held the necklace in her palm and flipped it gently for each student to see both sides. A couple of times, female students leaned forward to see it as close as possible and even asked if they could take a photo. Lexi said yes. *What harm would it do to have it circulate on social media for a day or two and then vanish into oblivion?* She didn't think Gigi would've minded.

In fact, Lexi had already grappled with that issue a couple of days before, in preparation for her talk. Gigi had tucked her necklace away for decades into a dark corner of an attic and hidden James's letters from view, even from her own family. Obviously, she wanted to keep them private. But as Lexi watched student after student eye the necklace with reverence and awe, and as they asked more specific questions about the letters and journal, Lexi knew, beyond doubt, that if her great-grandmother could've witnessed the excitement of these students, she would've been honored to have these young people—the next generation—show such unabashed interest in her life, in her love story, in the wartime pain she endured.

A sudden knock pulled her and Graham's attention to the open classroom door. Apparently, they had run overtime, and the next class was waiting—along with the professor—impatiently outside.

"Guess that's our cue to leave." Graham waved the awaiting students inside and rushed to log off his laptop.

"Sorry," Lexi told him, showing the necklace to the final student in line.

"Don't be sorry. That's the best class I've ever held. In seven years!"

"That can't be true. The students love your lectures."

Graham closed his laptop and nodded his apology to the incoming professor as he and Lexi swiftly gathered all their belongings and headed out the door.

"Thanks for saying that, but nothing can beat this hands-on history lesson you just gave them. Gigi would be amazed."

Lexi fought the sensation of tears. "I was thinking that earlier—hoping she wouldn't mind my sharing her story with a whole classroom of students."

"I think she would've been humbled by it. In the best possible way."

Lexi and Graham descended the stairs toward his office, and Lexi felt the weight of all her earlier anxiety lift away. She was relieved the presentation was over but also sad it had ended. She couldn't wait to tell her parents and Jolene how it went. And Ruby too.

"Can I take you to lunch?" Graham asked as he unlocked his office door and stepped inside to flick on the lights. "As a thank you."

"I should be thanking you. That was an incredible experience. But yeah, lunch sounds good. I only had coffee this morning. I'm hungry."

As Graham set down his laptop, Lexi drew out her phone, planning to text her parents about the presentation. But she stopped short when she saw her notifications.

"What's wrong?"

"Five calls. All from my mom." She looked into Graham's face. "That can't be good." She fumbled with the phone, and it fell from her fingers, bouncing onto the hard tile floor. As Graham retrieved it for her, Lexi prayed that the screen hadn't shattered. It hadn't, so she sucked in a breath and slowed down, not wanting to drop it again.

"Want some privacy?" he asked, moving toward the door.

"No. Stay."

He shut the door and hovered nearby as she clicked on the three voicemails from her mother, putting them on speaker for Graham.

Message one, from nearly two hours before: "Honey, I don't want to alarm you, but your father has had an... incident. Shortness of breath, discomfort in his left arm. At first, I thought it was an injury—you know how he likes to overdo—but he's in pain. I called an ambulance, and they're on their way to the house. I'll call you again as we know more."

Message two, sixteen minutes later: "I'm following the ambulance in my car. The EMTs think your father has had a heart attack." Her voice cracked. "Try not to worry. I'm sure he's in good hands. I'll call again soon. I remembered that you had your class presentation with Graham..."

The third message produced a lump in Lexi's throat: "They've taken your father back for some tests. Please come. I need you. We're at St. David's on 32nd Street."

"Daddy," Lexi whispered, feeling numb all over.

"I'll take you there," Graham said. "It's close."

"Okay." Better for Graham to drive, clearheaded, than for her to scramble with her GPS system.

AFTER GRAHAM DROVE Lexi right up to the ER's entrance and let her off, she stepped through the sliding doors, calling her mother's phone for the fourth time in a row, wondering where in the building her parents might be.

"Mother, turn on your phone," she muttered aloud as she approached the front desk and was greeted by a flustered receptionist.

"I'm Lexi Price. My father, Benjamin Price, was brought here by ambulance."

"Okay, hon. Let me see what I can find out."

Lexi tapped her fingernail on the countertop and felt a hand at her arm. She twirled around to see her mother, her face tight and emotionless.

"*There* you are," her mother said. "I was hoping you got my messages."

Lexi ignored her almost-accusatory tone—surely, it was from all the built-up stress. "I tried calling you back. But your phone must've been off."

"I was in with the doctor. They're seeing him now, doing some tests."

"Is he awake?"

"Yes, but groggy. He seems to know what's happening. He never lost consciousness."

"Well, that's good."

Lexi had wanted to reach out and give her mother a quick hug, at least, but her body language was so clenched and closed off that Lexi thought better of it. Instead, she followed her mother through a back hallway to a series of thick gray curtains hanging from the ceiling by stainless-steel hoops. Along the way, her mother finally filled in the details Lexi was anxious to know.

"Your father was lifting a carton of milk—I was at the kitchen table, oblivious, scrolling through the news on my tablet. Anyway, he dropped the carton, and I went to help him clean it up. But then I realized he was having pain in his arm, clutching it as he sank down to his knees beside the milk."

"That's awful," Lexi whispered, picturing the entire scene and wishing she could've been there to help somehow.

"The paramedics came swiftly. Your father protested, of course, said he was 'fine' and didn't need an ambulance. But his face was full of panic. I've never seen him that way before."

Just as they reached the third gray curtain, a doctor emerged, chatting with a nurse. When he saw Lexi and her mother, he paused and crossed his arms over his tablet.

"What can you tell us?" her mother asked.

Lexi felt her mother's hand clutch her own at their sides.

The doctor adjusted his glasses. "The tests confirm that your husband has experienced a myocardial infarction."

"Heart attack?" Lexi asked.

"Mild, but yes. A heart attack."

At that, her mother gasped softly and squeezed Lexi's hand.

"We'll keep him overnight," the doctor said. "I'd like to perform a PCI first thing in the morning."

"PCI?" Lexi asked.

"Percutaneous coronary intervention. It's a common, minimally invasive stent procedure, used to help treat narrowed arteries and let the blood flow more steadily. I can have the nurse give you some material on it."

"Common," her mother said. "Common is good?"

"It is. Your husband is fortunate that he got medical care in time. He can follow up with his internist for further bloodwork and guidance about diet and medication in the weeks to come. But the stent should solve this current issue."

Her mother released her grasp on Lexi's hand. "Thank you. May we see him?"

"Yes. He'll be moved to a room shortly, but you can talk to him. He's groggy but awake."

Lexi's mother slid back the curtain to reveal him. His eyes were closed, and his hand, lying on his abdomen, revealed an IV emerging from the top of his wrist, the lines leading to a bag dripping in the corner. A beeping monitor in the other corner echoed his heartbeat—it sounded steady and strong to Lexi's untrained ears.

"Daddy?" she whispered, and he opened his eyes into slits.

"My Lexi." His free hand extended toward her.

"No, no, don't move," she said. "Rest. Mom and I are right here."

"Always," her mother whispered from the other side of the bed. "Both my girls."

Lexi watched him close his eyes again as he patted her hand with gentle fingers. She recalled four days ago, Easter Sunday, when he had seemed overly tired during the egg hunt. Then, hours later after lunch, chewing a couple of antacids, thinking no one was looking. Maybe he'd been experiencing concerning symptoms but had hidden them from Lexi and her mother so they wouldn't worry.

Lexi rarely ruminated on the fact that her father was mortal and that someday, she wouldn't have him with her anymore. But now, seeing him lying motionless in a bed while she and her mother looked helplessly on, Lexi experienced a surreal moment, viewing the scene from outside herself. He had always been bigger than life, always strong and capable, the backbone of their family, a dependable and steady constant. Had she taken him for granted all this time, selfishly assumed he would always be there for her? Why did it take an emergency to be shaken out of life's commonplace moments to recognize what really mattered? Lexi squeezed her father's hand and willed him to be okay.

During the next two hours, nurses came and went, checking vitals, tapping results into a nearby computer, and asking whether her father was comfortable or whether Lexi and her mother needed anything. Soon, a young male nurse told them a room upstairs was ready and that the orderlies would transport her father there. It was suggested that in the meantime, Lexi's mother should fill out some necessary insurance paperwork waiting at the front desk.

Lexi joined her, not knowing what else to do. Without any windows nearby, she had no real sense of time—she assumed maybe it was late at night. Her tired body told her it was. But when they reached the lobby, she could see the glint of a sunset through the front glass doors, telling her it was early evening.

"I'll stay with him tonight," her mother said, pausing with Lexi at the desk. "You should go home and get some rest. There's really nothing more that can be done. He's in good hands."

Since Lexi had arrived at the hospital, she hadn't seen her mother show much vulnerability or fear—she was a rock. Almost too much of one. Frankly, Lexi would've welcomed some honesty, a confession that she, too, had been shaken up, seeing her own husband hooked up to wires and lying flat in a hospital bed. Lexi would've appreciated a half smile, a furrowed brow, a warm hug—anything that indicated her mother was experiencing even a small portion of what Lexi was feeling.

"I don't mind staying." But even as Lexi spoke the words, she knew the hospital room might not have enough space for the three of them—her father could even have a roommate, making things more cramped.

"You don't have to. I promise—I'll let you know how he's doing. You can come in the morning for the procedure."

Lexi searched her mother's face for even a shadow of emotion but still found none. To the outside world, all was well, nothing was a disaster. Everything was manageable. This was how her mother functioned, especially in crisis situations. A defense mechanism.

"I'll bring you some fresh clothes tomorrow," Lexi said.

"That would be nice. Choose anything from my closet. I won't be picky." She patted Lexi's arm twice then curled a stray hair behind her ear and began speaking with the receptionist, who was poised to answer her questions.

Feeling suddenly useless, not certain how she might occupy her time in the empty hours between now and her father's procedure, Lexi took a couple of steps into the waiting room and remembered that she'd gotten a ride from Graham after her presentation—and that her car was sitting in a visitor space on his campus, miles away. She was stranded.

This knowledge, more than anything else that had happened in the last few hours, brought a sting of tears to Lexi's eyes. Not having her car readily available somehow amplified her own helplessness, reminding her starkly of the strange and sudden situation she'd been swept up in. She felt oddly alone, abandoned. Even with her mother standing a few feet away.

Lexi was about to make a U-turn and ask to borrow her mother's car for the night when she spotted a familiar profile on the other side of the waiting room. He was sitting in a chair, tapping on his keyboard.

"Graham?" She approached him, and he looked up at the sound of his name. "You're here. I assumed you'd dropped me off and left."

He slid the laptop to the seat beside him and stood up. "I knew you didn't have a ride. Plus I wanted to know how your dad was doing." Graham's warm hand was at her elbow, and that gesture was the very one she had been craving all along from her own mother. When her eyes filled with tears, Graham pulled her close in a warm hug. His hand cradled her neck as she melted into his shoulder and let the tears come. She had been acting bravely for her parents' sake all this time. But she could relax with Graham. He made it okay.

After a moment, she backed out of his embrace and wiped her cheeks. The worry in his eyes made her realize that her tears were probably misinterpreted. She hadn't answered his still-lingering question about her father's condition.

"He's going to be okay. They're transporting him to a new room. Sorry if my reaction said otherwise."

"I admit, I was thinking the worst."

"Sorry," she said again, smiling through tears. "I've been holding back all this time, and my emotions came out in a rush. Daddy had a minor heart attack and is having a stent put in, first thing in the morning. Mother wants to stay with him tonight, so she told me to come back tomorrow. But then I remembered my car, still at the college…"

"I'll take you there." He shut the laptop and slipped it inside the case.

"I can't believe you waited here this long, not knowing when—or if—I would show up."

He shrugged. "I could grade here as easily as anywhere else. In fact, I got quite a lot done."

"Didn't you have a faculty meeting to go to? I heard you mention it before—"

"It wasn't important."

"You missed it because of me. Will you get in trouble?"

"No, I texted my department chair. He understood."

It was immensely comforting that someone was sacrificing time and meetings for her, looking out for her best interests, even when she hadn't been aware of it. She wasn't alone after all.

Chapter Seventeen

Let me know when you get there, Graham had texted Lexi minutes after picking up food (a quick drive-through stop at Whataburger) then dropping her off at the college, waiting for her to climb safely inside her car before pulling away.

Lexi typed her reply. *Just walked in the door.*

Slipping her phone into her purse while clutching the Whataburger bag, she stepped inside her parents' home—eerily quiet without either of them there—and noticed the remnants of their sudden and unexpected departure earlier that afternoon. All the shades in the living room were still up even though it was pitch-dark outside, and none of the lamps her mother used each evening had been turned on. The cat's litter box was dirty as well, and his water bowl was empty.

Lexi's stomach growled for the hamburger she held, but she resisted, wanting first to move swiftly through the tasks at hand. Within minutes, she had taken care of the cat's needs and lowered all the shades. Then, she scurried upstairs to fill a tote bag. She grabbed the half-read Grisham novel from her father's nightstand and a stack of home-and-garden magazines from her mother's side. Then, Lexi went in search of her mother's favorite silk pajamas, a change of clothes, and her makeup and toiletries. *What else could bring them comfort?*

She assumed there were snacks or treats in the kitchen that might qualify, so she headed back downstairs. A crystal bowl filled with wrapped Easter chocolates sat on the dining table. She grabbed a handful and dropped them into the tote before opening the kitchen door.

Lexi set down her tote, purse, and burger bag on the island but stopped short to stare at the mess in front of her. The refrigerator door remained open, the light on. The floor was splashed with milk, and Lexi could smell the sourness of it as she moved closer to investigate. A couple of footprints remained in the milk, evidence that a traumatic event had occurred exactly the harrowing way her mother had described.

Her hamburger forgotten, Lexi got to work on hands and knees, disregarding the slacks she wore—they could be dry-cleaned later. Paper towels sopped up the mess in moments, and she disinfected the tile floor twice for good measure. Next, she tossed out all the refrigerated items one by one, knowing they were well past the safe point to consume after all those hours had rolled by with the door wide open. She created a list of the items and brands so she would know exactly what to shop for the next day and accurately restock them.

It was a big job, lengthier and more tiring than she'd anticipated, and by the time she was finished, she had filled six trash bags of spoiled products and hauled them out to the trash bin outside the garage. Back inside the kitchen and out of breath, she saw the cat wander in, likely feeling the unusual absence of his owners.

"They'll be back soon." Lexi stroked his back to the end of his curlicue tail.

Noticing her burger bag slumped sadly at the end of the island, she doubted the contents inside were even salvageable. She would try anyway. Waiting for the food to heat in the microwave, Lexi let her thoughts tumble backward to the morning, when her only concern had been speaking in front of a room full of college students without stuttering or bumbling. *How quickly a day could change.*

She opened the beeping microwave's door and brought her plate to the edge of the island, where she remained standing to eat a few limp fries and the mushy burger.

Questions about her father swirled in her mind—*What other symptoms had he hidden and brushed aside as nothing to worry about? Had the heart attack weakened or damaged his heart? Could it happen again?*

Lexi wondered if the heart attack would change the way she and her mother saw him moving forward—whether they might coddle him too much, fret over his eating habits, even see him as weaker, older. Of course, her mother would never say those things out loud or confide in Lexi. It wasn't her way. So Lexi would keep her thoughts private.

Deciding the half of the burger and six fries she'd eaten were enough, Lexi tossed her food into the new lining she'd put in the wastebasket and wished for another job to keep her occupied. There *was* one more task to fulfill, she recalled as she approached her purse, which sat on the opposite side of the island. The necklace. She needed to return it to its proper place in her parents' home. Her fingers found the box immediately, but when she pried it open, the interior was empty. Lexi stared agape at the black velvet. *It should be here.*

Refusing to panic, she emptied her purse onto the speckled granite countertop, sorting swiftly through the items: wallet, keys, roll of mints, handful of change, packet of disposable wipes, lip gloss. But no necklace.

Back to the purse, she unzipped every single pocket then turned the entire bag inside out, praying the necklace would magically clink down onto the island and this growing sense of dread could be eradicated.

But after all that searching, twice through, Lexi knew it was true. The eighty-year-old necklace, her great-grandmother's heirloom, had gone missing. And it was all her fault.

Her mind went into overdrive, going over the day moment by moment, rolling backward in time—pulling up to her parents' house, the UT parking lot with Graham, the emergency room. Before that,

Graham's office, and before that, the classroom, where she'd last seen the necklace, showing it to the students before she and Graham were rushed out by the next class entering.

It could be anywhere.

Lexi grabbed her keys and headed for her car to make sure the necklace hadn't somehow fallen out of her bag. She used her phone's flashlight to illuminate the brick path along the way then rummaged around both driver's seat and passenger's, where she'd laid her purse for the journey. She even shined her flashlight underneath the car on both sides—perhaps the necklace had fallen onto the street.

Nothing.

Feeling a new rush of panic, she called the ER, told a receptionist the situation, and received an earnest but unhelpful response. "No, hon. Nobody's turned in a necklace."

Lexi's hopes dropped as she thanked the woman then dialed Graham's number. When he answered, she pounced. "The necklace. I can't find it. Anywhere!"

Graham was silent for a moment, as though processing the news, then said, "Okay, let's think. Last we both saw it was—"

"Your classroom. I've already checked my purse, the walkway, my car. Twice over. I called the hospital, and nobody's reported it. It must've fallen out somewhere." Her words tumbled out faster and faster. "I can't *believe* I wasn't more careful. All I keep thinking is that some lucky person found it and kept it."

"I don't want to go there yet. So, you were in my car twice. Let me check it now. Maybe it's there. I'll go look and call you right back. Okay?"

"Okay. Thank you." She was saying that a lot lately.

Giving her car one last check, she locked it up then headed back indoors, scanning the walkway and even the surrounding lawn, praying as she went. She opened the front door clutching the phone, waiting for Graham's call. Winston meowed at her as she reentered the kitchen. Halting at the island, Lexi closed her eyes and tried to picture the necklace in Graham's classroom. She could see the students lining up to view the necklace—*why* hadn't she kept it safely in its case?—then she had followed Graham to his office, where she'd heard her mother's voicemails. When she'd gotten the news of her father, nothing else had mattered. Had she clutched the necklace in her palm and somehow left it on Graham's desk? Or maybe earlier, it had slipped out of her hand and onto the classroom desk or floor. Perhaps a student had noticed and, rather than be a good citizen and return the piece to her, had snatched it and slunk out the door with everyone else, with grand plans to sell it? *Surely not.* But anything was possible.

Lexi rubbed her eyes, wishing all the speculation away. It was maddening.

Her phone rang, startling her. "Any news?" she asked Graham.

"I'm sorry. It's not there. I looked all over the car—between the seats, on the floorboards, then the pavement. Nothing."

"I feel so stupid. I didn't protect the necklace well enough. I should never have taken it from my parents' home in the first place. Where could it be?"

Graham's tone remained calm, his voice reassuring. "It could still be on campus. Maybe in my building or even my office."

"Or even the parking lot." Her hopes sank deeper.

"Maybe. All the buildings are locked up tight at this hour, but I've got access to mine, so I'll go and have a look 'round."

Lexi realized the late hour and that Graham was probably already settled in his apartment, relaxed and preparing for bed, and she was sending him on yet another mission. She had asked enough of him today.

"Oh, you don't have to do that tonight—"

"I want to. It won't take me long. If the necklace isn't there, I can call campus safety in the morning and get them on the case. We also have a lost and found—"

"Do you think someone would be honest enough to turn it in?" She couldn't hide her skepticism.

"Actually, I've seen it happen before. Last semester, a student found a hundred-dollar bill in the hall and took it to the dean's office. So don't lose hope. We'll find it."

She wished she could believe him, but Lexi's exhausted brain couldn't muster the same positivity. "Thanks for looking. Sorry to bother you this late."

"You're never a bother. Are you still at your parents'?"

Lexi shifted her focus from the necklace long enough to tell Graham all about the spilled milk and the open fridge and the spoiled food. It felt good to tell someone else about her stressful evening.

They ended the call with Graham promising to ring as soon as he had any news about the necklace. As she hung up, Lexi's head pounded with the beginnings of a migraine. She returned all the items spread out on the island to her purse then took the bulging tote bag by the handles and exited the kitchen, clicking off lights as she went.

At the front door, she gave a backward glance to make sure there wasn't anything else to do then shut and locked it.

Starting her engine, Lexi planned on going home, taking care of Bailey, brushing her teeth, crawling into bed, and staying by the phone in case Graham called—the manageable things that *were* in the realm of her control.

Chapter Eighteen

"Too tight in the shoulders?" Mr. Prescott, the tailor, stepped backward, his index finger poised at his lips.

Graham twisted so he could see himself in the mirror, paying special attention to his chest inside the tuxedo jacket. "Feels fine to me."

Graham's father had set up this spur-of-the-moment fitting in downtown Austin, promising breakfast afterward. Graham had said yes, hoping they would finally have time to talk. He couldn't recall the last time his father had asked him about his students, his job, his life. Maybe over breakfast, his father might surprise him.

"Good." Mr. Prescott broke into Graham's thoughts. "We'll make these alterations and call when they're ready." He helped Graham gingerly shrug out of the jacket filled with carefully positioned straight pins.

Seeing an opportunity to check his phone, Graham scrolled through his texts, hoping to spot one from Lexi, a response to his text from minutes ago about his search for the necklace. Last night, he'd phoned her with the update that he had scoured the faculty parking lot—no luck. Then he'd gone straight to his office then up to his classroom, praying the necklace had dropped to the floor and he would miraculously find it. Since that search had proved futile, this morning, he'd driven to the campus security office and filled out a missing-item report. He was assured that the security officers would be on the lookout for the necklace. Graham impressed upon them the importance of the piece—an heirloom, a rare treasure from World War II—but that didn't seem to make a significant difference to the officer, who finished filling out the report with a nod then a grunt and a "We'll be in touch if we find anything." Graham was not impressed. Or hopeful.

Even so, he had sent a brief text to Lexi before arriving at the tailor's, letting her know about all his efforts. Perhaps it might assuage some of his irrational guilt over the missing necklace. *If he hadn't asked Lexi to speak at his class, she wouldn't have lost it in the first place.*

Graham pushed against his impulse to text her once more, since her father's procedure was already underway. He also fought his even stronger impulse to skip breakfast altogether and go be with Lexi in the waiting room. But that was a family situation, and he didn't want to overstep.

"Well, that's not good enough." His father pushed the curtain open with an angry *swish* and continued his phone call as he handed his suit, perfectly hung, to Mr. Prescott then halted in the middle of the room with a frown. "It was supposed to be done last night... That's not good enough. Tell him to file it ASAP. I want to see him in my office at noon." Clicking off, he looked around the room.

Mr. Prescott stared at him with wide eyes, still clutching the suit.

"Sorry. Incompetent people. They're everywhere. My new paralegal didn't make the filing date, which is causing us big headaches. Anyway..." He sucked in a breath and blinked. "Are we all done here?"

"Yes, sir. I'll have these ready by the end of the week."

"Excellent."

Graham was used to his father's occasional work-related tirades. As a child, Graham often saw his father bring legal work home—burying himself in his study until all hours of the night or sometimes spreading paperwork out on the dining room table, making call after call, sometimes calm, sometimes angry.

"Ready to eat?" he asked his son.

"Sure. How about—" Graham was about to suggest Marco's down the street when his father's cell rang again.

He held up an index finger as he answered. "Yes? I already spoke to him. He knows the stakes..."

Graham tuned him out and returned to his own phone.

"I'll be there shortly." His father finally rang off. "Sorry, son. I'll need a rain check. We're short-staffed this morning, and I've got some unexpected fires to put out. No one else can handle it."

"I understand." That was the standard, expected lie that Graham always gave, even as a teenager, whenever his father's work responsibilities conflicted with promised family time. *How many tennis matches had he skipped? How many band concerts? How many birthday parties were a near-miss because of work?*

"Good man." Graham's father took a step toward the front door of the shop then stopped and whirled around. "Nearly forgot. I want you to be my best man. For the wedding."

It wasn't exactly a question, more of a statement. And the blasé tone matched someone who was requesting extra tartar sauce for his cod as an afterthought.

"Um, sure. I'd like that," Graham said, not knowing what else to say.

"Terrific." His father leaned in and double-slapped Graham's shoulder. "I'll text you with the details."

He was out the door and back on the phone before Graham could even respond. Beside him, Mr. Prescott quietly cleared his throat. Over the years, he had probably witnessed an immeasurably wide range of awkward father–son moments during fittings. Mr. Prescott gave an understanding nod toward Graham then turned to walk both suits into the back room, where Graham imagined the alterations took place.

Alone on the main floor of the shop, surrounded by racks of suits and ties and soulless mannequins, Graham settled onto the tufted cushion nearby and stared out the window. It was a stunning late-April day, and he could hear a lone bird, somewhere in the distance, whistling his heart out. He tried not to be disappointed in his father's behavior. At least he had wanted to meet for breakfast. The intent was there. And at least he wanted Graham to be his best man, however crudely he went about asking. Shouldn't he be grateful for that much unexpected effort?

Graham remembered his mother making constant excuses. "Your father is tired, that's all. He wanted so badly to be at your tennis match, but work pulled him away. He does his best for the family—he has a hard time showing it, emotionally." As an adult looking back, Graham sometimes wondered if those excuses enabled his father to continue distancing himself from his family. He was never held accountable by anyone. Whatever the case, Graham was old enough to know that his father would never change. He might make occasional and miniscule strides, but he could never be the father that Graham genuinely desired to have, especially since his mum died. And Graham had to be okay with that—to accept his father for who he was, not who he wished he would someday become. That was advice his mum would have given had she been sitting on the tufted cushion beside him.

Graham peered down at his phone and thought about what to do with the empty hour ahead. He might as well go to Marco's alone and have breakfast before his office hour. Before heading out, Graham gave in to his earlier impulse. He clicked on his phone, typed out a brief text, then sent it to Lexi.

LEXI'S PHONE BUZZED, and she saw a new text from Graham: *Thinking of you. Hope all goes well with your dad.*

She'd forgotten to respond to his other text, about all his efforts looking for the necklace. She had started to read that message when the orderlies had come into her father's room to wheel him back for the stent procedure. Nothing else had mattered in that moment, so she'd stuffed her phone into her pocket—the text neglected—and followed her mother and Jolene to the waiting room, where they'd sat for the past sixty minutes, listening to the soft drone of the local news showing on a TV mounted near the ceiling.

Lexi reread Graham's previous text then responded to both messages. *Thank you for all the necklace searching. I'm waiting with Jo and my mother. Daddy's procedure still ongoing. I'll keep you posted.*

She realized she needed a new distraction to keep her from imagining her father a few rooms away, surrounded by medical equipment and IV bags, and enduring local anesthesia during the stent procedure, all at the mercy of perfect strangers. Hopefully, perfectly capable strangers.

Rising from the grape-patterned upholstered chair, she made her way to the corner of the room, where a coffeemaker stood beneath the TV. Her mother and Jolene, both reading magazines—or at least pretending to read them—already had coffees of their own, so she decided not to break the silence and offer them more. She heard the weatherman jabbering away on the screen above her head, talking about the unseasonably warm temperatures that Central Texas would experience that day. Lexi noted the irony as she pulled her sweater tighter—it seemed every room in the hospital was a frigid sixty degrees.

Just as she had separated one Styrofoam cup from the top of the stack, she heard footsteps and saw a man in blue scrubs enter the waiting room. When he pulled down his mask, she recognized him as her father's doctor. Abandoning the cups, Lexi joined her mother, who had already stood to approach him.

"The procedure went beautifully" was his first sentence. The stress drained out of Lexi's body. "The stent went in as planned, no problems, no complications. He's being wheeled to recovery. You can see him within the hour. A nurse will be by soon to take you there."

"Thank you, Doctor."

Lexi could hear the quiver in her mother's voice as she shook his hand. When he left, her mother brought Lexi in for a tight hug. She felt her mother's breathing, ragged and disjointed, and assumed she might be crying. When they parted, her mother's eyes were glossy.

"He's okay," her mother managed to say.

"He *is*," Lexi said, squeezing her mother's arms.

AFTER ANOTHER WAIT, not nearly as agonizing as the first, Lexi and her mother were tiptoeing into the patient's room, eager to see for themselves how he was. Jolene had slipped out minutes earlier, headed for a late-morning meeting at the mansion.

Lexi followed her mother, who hunched over her husband's bedside, stroking the top of his arm. "We're both here," she told him.

Lexi remained distant, standing at the foot of her father's bed. She would never admit it to anyone, but in that moment, she felt like her little-girl self: timid, uncertain, hesitant. Her father, a healthy man his entire life, had never spent a single night in a hospital room. Seeing her father in a gown and hooked up to tubes and wires and surrounded by bags and beeping machines was still unnerving. He blinked several times, groggy from the sedatives, then smiled toward Lexi.

Her mother stroked his temple delicately. Lexi watched them and finally let herself realize—her father was safe. He had survived a heart attack, gotten help in time, come out of his procedure successfully, and by all accounts (she had googled it the night before), his heart would be stronger than ever, as though none of this had ever occurred. All was well.

Her mother whispered something to her father out of Lexi's earshot. It was such an intimate moment that she wanted to back away and let her parents share this reunion alone. As she watched them interact, Lexi felt a specific surge inside—a realization that she wanted that too. A big love. A companion. Someone to care deeply about, someone to worry and fret over, someone to build a whole life with. She wanted what her parents had—in real, living color. Not the fake movie romances with perfect, happy, sappy endings. She wanted a partnership where, even in a cold hospital room, they could be caught up in a world all their own.

But as unexpectedly as that strong impression came, it fizzled away, and another sensation took over. Lexi had been independent of a relationship for so long that she barely knew how to navigate one anymore. She'd become too settled over the past five years, content with being on her own. *Or was that her fear talking?*

"Honey, join us." Lexi's mother was gesturing toward the bed and patting it.

Lexi did as she was told and approached her parents. "I'm so glad you're okay." She found her father's hand and squeezed it gently.

"Thank you, sweetie." He licked his dry lips.

Lexi's mother noticed this immediately and clicked the button for the nurse. "We need some water in here. With a straw. A bending one," she told the intercom.

It was obvious Lexi's father would be in the best possible hands, with his wife at his side, meeting his every need, being his primary advocate. But Lexi was suddenly sorry for the nursing staff, being ordered around by her mother from this point on.

A voice responded through the speaker. "Be there soon."

"You should shut your eyes again," her mother told her father, "and rest. You've just had a challenging procedure done, and it went very well. Your one job is to heal up and come home. The doctor said it might be another day or two."

Lexi heard her stomach rumble. "Sorry." She gripped her abdomen and chuckled. "I forgot to eat this morning." She had taken some aspirin on an empty stomach two hours before, and the hunger had shifted into mild nausea.

"Honey, go get some breakfast," her mother said. "I'll stay with your father."

"Are you sure?"

"Positive."

Her father closed his eyes again. It was clear he wouldn't be very chatty over the next hour.

"Okay. Mom, do you want something?"

"No, I'm fine." She had already pulled up the nearby chair and settled in, clasping her husband's hand with both of hers. "You take your time."

Lexi's stomach growled again. She patted her dad's leg through the thin hospital blanket and gave a silent prayer of thanks that he was, indeed, fine then backed away from the bed. Her parents, still in tune with each other, barely noticed she was leaving.

LEXI TAPPED ON HER playlist—classical music, soft and soothing—and reached inside the donut bag to let her fingers find the pillowy dough.

She hadn't wanted to go out for breakfast, didn't wish to make small talk or chitchat with a server. She needed to be alone with her thoughts, process the past twenty-four hectic hours. So when she'd spotted Rusty's, a donut shop on the outskirts of downtown Austin that she'd always wanted to try, she'd pulled into the parking lot. Usually, she ordered the same thing every time she got donuts, but this morning, she wanted a change. She parked, went inside, and picked out three donuts she'd never tried before: blueberry cruller, chocolate éclair, and cinnamon twist.

Eating her feelings—that was what Jolene would've called it. *Well, so be it.*

Lexi returned to her car and drove back toward the hospital. When Graham had driven her there the evening before, she remembered seeing a park across the street. She stopped in a spot under a shady tree, cracked her windows, and pulled out the cinnamon twist. She would save the other donuts for later in the week.

Lexi was surprised even to have an appetite, but as she took the first delicious, sugary bite, she remembered she hadn't eaten a thing since the pathetic microwave-warmed burger the night before, standing at her parents' kitchen island.

The donut was scrumptious—her new favorite. The hint of cinnamon gave the dough a lovely warmth. She made a mental note to order a cinnamon twist next time—and every other time after that.

A concerto by Mozart played next, and she watched the shadows dancing off her windshield from beneath the tree branches. Another gorgeous spring day. She let her mind wander to the call she'd made on the way to the donut shop—she had forgotten to phone Ruby and give an update about her father. Once she'd reassured Ruby he was fine, they'd moved on to store business: the upcoming auction, the broken chair arm that Darius had repaired that morning, and a big sale of an armoire the day before. Lexi also received a report about Bailey—she had dropped him off early at the store. He was sound asleep in his bed, contented.

Finishing her final bite then sipping the cold milk she'd also bought, Lexi found her phone and dialed Graham's number. She couldn't remember if he had class at this hour—what time was it, anyway? She had lost all track—but he had reassured her once that she could call anytime. If he was in class, his phone would be on silent, and she could leave a message. She was preparing to do so, after the fourth ring, when he answered.

"Lex, hey. How's your dad doing?"

Graham sounded winded, and she wondered where he was. Probably climbing stairs to his next class.

"Very well. The doctor was pleased and said Daddy should make a full recovery. Sorry I didn't call earlier."

"No worries—I'm glad it went well."

"My mother kicked me out of the room, made me go get some breakfast. I just got through talking to Ruby, checking in on the store." Lexi watched a bird flit through the air, doing a carefree dance, then land on a branch of a nearby tree.

"How are *you* doing?" Graham asked.

"Better. It's been one giant blur. From last night until now. I don't think I've processed anything yet. Not fully."

"Understandable."

She could hear other voices on the line, probably students in the background.

"Listen, I'd better let you go. You've got a class starting."

"Not yet. In a couple of minutes. So, you got my text about the necklace?"

She could practically hear the wince in his voice. "Yeah. It was a long shot. But thanks for trying." She wasn't ready to face that the necklace was permanently gone. They had to keep searching. "Should I file a police report?"

"I think you should. It wouldn't hurt. Where are you?"

"At a park close to the hospital. I stopped off to get donuts and then came here. It's peaceful." The ruckus on Graham's end suddenly grew louder, and she could hear the distinct voice of a student trying to ask him a question. "You need to go," she said. "I'll text you later. I promise."

They ended the call, and Lexi folded the top of her donut bag and set it aside. Ruby had insisted that Lexi take the whole day off from the store, but Lexi was already behind on some paperwork and phone calls—plus she needed to check in with Pam and her staff at

Let's Get Crafty—so she planned to revisit the shop sometime in the afternoon. But for now, she wanted to see her father again, linger a bit, check on him once more. She reversed her car out of the parking space and headed back to the hospital.

THE GRANDFATHER CLOCK chimed deeply from the back of the store, reminding Lexi of the late hour and nudging her to finish and leave. It was already dark out, and Ruby and Ariel were long gone while Lexi remained at the front desk buried in overdue paperwork. Tomorrow's to-do list had grown to gigantic proportions, including making a call to the same contractors who had finished the Let's Get Crafty warehouse for her. Based on the success and strong numbers of that venture, a more serious look at the glassblowing center inside the second warehouse space was warranted. Earlier in the evening, Lexi had set up a second meeting with Mike in a couple of weeks to work on some further details about the project, including a budget proposal. The groundwork was being laid, at least.

"Okay, that's it," she told Bailey as she tore the lengthy list from its notepad and folded it into her purse. "Time to go home!"

She suppressed a yawn and scratched Bailey's head, receiving a lick in return. "If I had any energy for it, you'd be getting a bath tonight. But that can wait too."

Bailey's nails clicked along the hard floor as they ambled toward the store's exit, with Lexi turning off the few remaining lamps as they went. Unexpectedly, Bailey tugged hard on the leash, dragging her in another direction, toward a specific corner of the store. His nose was leading the way.

"Please tell me that's not a mouse you're smelling. I don't think I could handle it."

Bailey would not be deterred and yanked harder, straining his neck toward the far corner. Lexi flicked on a light and gathered her courage to stoop down past Bailey's nose and investigate the culprit.

"Bailey, no!" Lexi caught a swift glimpse of two colorful candies on the floor but couldn't scoop them up fast enough. They had already gone into Bailey's mouth and down his throat by the time her hand reached the floor. Usually, Ariel's end-of-day sweeping was thorough enough to catch every stray candy or toy that a child might have accidentally left behind. But not this time.

"You're too fast for me." She gave Bailey's head a gentle pat, watching him lick his lips in proud defiance. At least the candies hadn't contained any harmful chocolate. Lexi had recognized the brand.

As Bailey maneuvered his way back out of the tight corner, he nudged an end table with his shoulder, and Lexi watched a Lladró weave and wobble precariously. She steadied it with her hand before it was in real danger of falling.

"A *beagle* in a china shop. That would be a more accurate cliché," she told him with a wry grin.

A sharp memory came to her, of another Lladró, a couple of decades before, that hadn't been quite so fortunate. As Lexi led Bailey out the door and locked it up tight, she let her mind wander to that day inside the shop. She'd been eight or nine years old, and Gigi had given her the very important job of dusting the antique figurines on a bookcase shelf. Lexi had come to her last one—a tiny girl playing with her dog—and hummed a tune as she clutched it with one hand and began to dust every crevice with the rag Gigi had given her. Lexi's work would be assessed, and she wanted an A+ from her great-grandmother. But halfway through her task, she became distracted by a wailing baby a few feet away. The mother was scrambling to find a pacifier to soothe the red-faced infant. Rather than focus on the figurine, Lexi kept her eyes on the baby. Next thing she knew, the Lladró—already slippery to begin with—had slid out of her hand and onto the floor, shattering into four pieces at her feet. With a gasp, she abandoned the rag and squatted down to see if anything could be salvaged. But the moment she tried to fit two of the broken pieces together, she saw that it was futile. Beyond repair.

A minute later, Gigi had spotted her, crumpled in the corner, shoulders heaving in silent sobs as she held two of the broken pieces. Lexi had no intention of lying or covering up her crime. She wondered how much money she had cost the store with her stupid mistake—*hundreds? Thousands?* At nine, she had no real concept of what anything cost and assumed everything in the store was what Gigi called "invaluable." Which sounded like a *lot* of money to Lexi.

"Honey, what's happened?" Gigi bypassed the other broken shards and came to sit near Lexi in the corner with a quiet grunt, her knees cracking and popping.

Lexi's sobs had calmed slightly, but she couldn't speak except between breaths. "Lladró… broken." She handed the pieces over.

Gigi inspected them with a nod then set them down. Brushing her palms together, she scooted closer to face her great-granddaughter, knees to knees.

"Look at me." Her voice was soft and kind as she wiped Lexi's falling tears then took Lexi's hands in her own. "Honey, you've done nothing wrong. It was an accident."

"But it's invaluable. You said so."

Gigi frowned and searched the air. "When did I ever say that?"

Lexi found the words as her tears slowed. It was important to explain. "I watched you whisper to this figurine. You called it a treasure. It's important to the store. To customers. To you. And I broke it—"

"Not as important as you are." Gigi brought her hand to Lexi's wet cheek and cupped it, making eye contact. "I have a very important 'P.S.' to add to my earlier statement." Whenever Gigi lowered her voice to a gentle whisper, Lexi knew that what was coming next would be almost sacred in its wisdom. "*You*, my darling, are the real treasure. Not a piece of porcelain. That figurine is replaceable. My precious great-granddaughter, however, is not." Gigi patted Lexi's knee then gave the rest of her store a casual wave. "These are just things. And things are never as important as human beings. Don't ever forget that. Some people place a high value on money, on objects. I've witnessed families break apart because of it—adult children turning viciously on each other when a parent dies, bickering over wills, salivating over property, even resorting to stealing from each other. Shameless. And shame*ful*. They've lost all sight of what matters." Gigi scooted around to sit beside Lexi once more and wrapped a loving arm around her shoulders with a tight squeeze. "It's people that matter in this life. Not the things surrounding us, whether they're whole or lost or broken. Understand?"

Little Lexi could only respond with a nod, since the tears were reemerging—but this time, they were tears of pure relief rather than fear or sorrow.

Bailey tugged hard on his leash again, and Lexi realized she had been standing in the middle of the parking lot behind her store during her vivid Lladró memory. Incredible how Gigi's words from decades past still held powerful lessons for Lexi's situation today.

She thought of the teardrop necklace—the panic, the shame associated with losing it. A thousand times greater significance than a shattered Lladró. But if Gigi had known about the necklace's loss—especially with all of her great-granddaughter's efforts to find it—Lexi would've received the very same response: "It's people that matter... Not things... *You* are the treasure."

Chapter Nineteen

"Two, please." Graham paused at the hostess table, amused at the fact that Chad had selected Tuscano's for their late lunch together. It seemed like fate, since Tuscano's happened to be another one of Lexi's father's establishments, one that Graham hadn't visited yet. He saw the group photo on the wall—and easily recognized him standing in the middle of a few smiling patrons.

"Follow me." The hostess carried two hard-covered menus to a table in the corner. The space was as expertly decorated as the pizza restaurant had been, and Graham suspected Lexi's mother had been the designer of both. He noticed the terracotta-painted walls, the framed photos of Tuscan countryside and villas, the clusters of ivy draped near the ceiling—those special touches gave the restaurant an exquisitely Italian feel.

"I'm starved." Chad sat and took the menu, giving the hostess an appreciative nod.

Graham cracked open his menu and perused the items, settling on the veal. He waited politely for Chad to make his selection and wondered how Lexi's father was doing. Today was the day she'd expected him home from the hospital. While he'd waited outside Tuscano's for Chad, Graham had sent her a "Hope all goes well today" text that hadn't required a response. He knew it would be a busy day, with all her attention geared toward the homecoming.

When the server introduced himself, both Graham and Chad were ready to place their orders.

Afterward, Chad rearranged the napkin in his nap and settled back in his chair. "I'm glad you were free for lunch. It's been too long."

"It has. I think we skipped a month. Or two."

Years ago, Chad Ingram was Graham's college roommate at UT, and they'd managed to keep in touch regularly over the past decade, while other college friendships had fallen away. They met for lunch at least once a month, taking turns choosing the restaurant—and paying. Chad lived about an hour from downtown Austin, in a cozy suburb with his wife, Donna, and their two daughters. Graham had been the best man at their wedding eight years before. Every time he saw Chad, Graham had to swat away the annoying flit of envy at the seemingly ideal family life his friend had constructed. Graham wanted all those things, too, but could never seem to manage even getting close.

They spent the appetizer portion of the meal catching up on work then shifted to politics and economics—Chad was employed as a political consultant for various independent candidates in and around Austin—and then finally to family.

"Here's the most recent one of the twins." Chad tapped on his phone then showed Graham.

"Beautiful," Graham said and meant it. Two blond-haired, ringleted girls, smiling at each other, looking very much like carbon copies of their mother. Mini-Donnas.

"Your turn. Catch me up on things." Chad put his phone away and returned to his plate. He was already halfway through his chicken scampi and pierced another tenderloin with his fork.

Graham had been dreading this part of the conversation since they'd arrived.

"You know, the usual. Busy with work."

"We've already covered work." Chad tilted his head. "I'm not-so-subtly asking about Theresa. Things still going well with y'all?"

Theresa had been Chad's favorite of Graham's girlfriends over the years—she was stable, successful, and gregarious.

"We broke up a few weeks ago."

"And you're just now telling me?"

Graham shrugged. "Guess I knew you'd be disappointed."

"Not if you aren't. What happened?"

"Well, we..." Graham flipped his extra fork over on its tines. "Outgrew each other. Or more accurately, she outgrew me. She was the one who wanted to break up."

"Sorry, man."

Graham abandoned the fork and smoothed out a wrinkle in the heavy white tablecloth. "It's fine. In hindsight, I could see all the signs. We weren't compatible."

"That's rough. Well, I admit, you don't seem too broken up about it."

"That's probably because I've... sort of met someone else."

"That fast?"

Graham chuckled. "Yeah, well. I wasn't looking for it, trust me. It happened the same day Theresa split up with me. Her name is Lexi Price." Graham could feel the edge of a smile rise to his lips and was powerless to stop it. "She's pretty wonderful."

"You're smitten."

"I am. I'm considering asking her to be my plus-one at Dad's wedding. But..."

"What 'but'? If she makes you this happy, I'd say it's a no-brainer. Don't 'consider.' Do it. Ask her."

"It's not that simple. It would be a big step for her. Lexi is super independent. She was divorced in her twenties, and so she's extremely cautious about relationships. Skittish is more accurate. We've taken things slowly, developed an easy friendship—which is great, don't get me wrong. Theresa and I were never truly friends."

"Friendship is important. It's a foundation to build on. Donna and I were best friends for two years before we fell in love."

"I remember it well. And I want that for myself too. But with Lexi, I'm not sure we'll ever get beyond this point. I think she's scared."

"So help her be unscared."

Graham smirked. "That's not a word."

"Show her what a good relationship looks like. What a good man looks like. It should be easy for you."

Graham dipped his head at the unexpected compliment he hadn't realized he needed. The one that, frankly, he had been hoping to receive from his father one day.

"Thanks for that."

LEXI HUNCHED HER SHOULDERS inside the passenger seat to reach for the box of cookies she'd purchased from Lucille's bakery—sugar-free macaroons for her father. Practically the first minute he'd come home from the hospital yesterday afternoon, her mother had given them both a stern speech about "from this moment on, changes will be made," and the primary one involved a new low-sugar, low-fat, low-carb, heavy-vegetable-and-chicken diet. Her father had balked and muttered from his side of their master bed about pasta surely being an exception. Her mother further explained that the hospital's blood tests revealed he was prediabetic—yet another reason that his diet *must* be changed.

The bakery had recently added a few sugar-free items to its menu, and Lexi hoped they tasted as scrumptious as they looked. To be sure, Lexi paused midway down her parents' brick walkway, cracked open the glossy white box, and chose the smallest macaroon. She took half a bite, assessed the flavor, and was relieved her father wouldn't be able to tell the difference between it and its sugary counterpart. Satisfied, she closed the box, popped the other half of the treat into her mouth, and proceeded toward the house.

She had talked to her father on the phone a couple of hours before—his voice sounded raspy but strong—and had promised to stop by after work if he wasn't too tired. "I'm never too tired to see you, honey" was the response. She couldn't wait.

A vase bursting with an enormous stately bouquet of spring flowers in every color of the rainbow stood in the middle of the welcome mat, so Lexi juggled her purse and the bakery box in order to lean forward and grasp the glass vase carefully with her free hand. She had hoped to use her key and not bother her parents with her entrance, even though they were expecting her, but having her hands full forced her to ring the doorbell with her elbow. Thankfully, her mother was already on the first floor and opened the door immediately.

"What's all this?" she asked, relieving Lexi of the vase.

"These were on the porch. For Dad, I assume. I didn't read the card. And these are from me." She shut the door behind her and opened the box. Before her mother could complain, Lexi said, "They're sugar-free."

"Nicely done." Her mother paused, placing an ice-cold hand on Lexi's wrist. "Listen, I know what you did."

Lexi wondered what she could be in trouble for, racing backward in her mind for any misdeed her mother could be thinking of.

Her mother relaxed her expression. "Don't look so scared. I'm talking about the kitchen. I forgot to mention it yesterday—I noticed that you'd cleaned up all that milk. And replaced the items in the fridge. You even bought the special mustard that I love."

"I didn't want y'all returning home to the mess. Or to the reminder of what happened with Daddy. Plus I knew you wouldn't have time to go shopping. Your priority needed to be his homecoming."

Her mother released her grasp and readjusted the vase in her hands. "Well, it was more appreciated than you know. I didn't have the energy to face it yesterday, and it was incredible, having that taken care of. Thank you, Lexi." She cleared her throat and seemed to push down any further bubbling-up of emotion. *Back to business.* "Just let me know what I owe you, and I'll write you a check."

"Mother—you don't owe me a thing. It was my way of helping."

"It couldn't have been cheap. You probably bought hundreds of dollars' worth of replacement items. I had some gourmet cheese and some filets..."

It was a losing battle, but Lexi dug in anyway. She could be every bit as stubborn as her mother. "I would be offended if you handed me money. I took care of it and was happy to. Let's leave it at that. I did it for Daddy. And for you. Okay?"

Her mother finally relented, possibly too weary to argue. "Well, then. Thank you."

"Why don't we swap? I'll find a place for the flowers, and you can take the macaroons up to Dad. I'll be there in a minute to see him." As they made the exchange, Lexi glanced around for a place that wasn't currently occupied by other vases of fresh flowers from well-meaning employees, friends, and relatives. Her dad was a popular guy. "Where can I put these?"

"The breakfast table has more room." Her mother placed a hand on the smooth, polished banister before heading up. "I'll let your father know you're here."

Lexi carried the vase—growing heavier by the moment—through the immaculate kitchen and into the breakfast nook. The space was lit up by bright sunshine streaming through the wall-to-wall windows. Lexi set down the flowers in the center of the table then took a long whiff of a deep-red rose as she rubbed its velvet petal with light fingertips. Her phone buzzed in her pocket at the same time. Tilting the screen to see the caller, she recognized the PI's name, Ed, and answered swiftly. She hadn't heard from him in several days. Perhaps he had some good news.

"Ms. Price, hello. I have a name for you." She appreciated that about him—no chitchat, just the facts. He was old-school in another way too. An older gentleman in his early seventies, he rarely used email and preferred to communicate in person or by phone. "It's the brother of James Fisher."

Lexi's heart rate accelerated as she picked up the pencil on the breakfast table—the one her mother always used to jot down important to-do notes for the day. "James's brother?" Lexi did the math in her head. "He must be in his... nineties?"

"Ninety, exactly. He was a younger brother. Ten years old when James died in the war."

"Oh, wow."

As Edward rattled off some details, Lexi captured them on the blank notepad then read them back out to the PI, making certain she got them correct.

"Vincent Fisher, lives in Round Rock at 422 Winding Way."

"That's correct. And he's a widower." Ed smacked on something, possibly his lunch, then continued. "I'll send you an email shortly with all the details. I've verified them online and through some other connections, but I have not made contact with Mr. Fisher. I'll leave that up to you."

"This is amazing. Thank you so much. What do I... tell him? Once I contact him?"

"That's entirely up to you. My job here is done. Unless there's anything else?"

"No, this is perfect. Exactly what I was hoping for. Please be sure to bill me for everything."

He wished her a good day then rang off as Lexi tore the paper from its pad and stared at the name again. *James Fisher's brother, ninety years old.* Her first impulse was to phone him right away, but she needed a minute to collect her thoughts, to rehearse what to say. Funny how she'd never moved past this moment in her mind—past the time when she would actually have tangible information about James's close relative in her hand. *What now?*

Knowing her father was probably waiting on her upstairs, she toyed with postponing a call to Mr. Fisher, but she couldn't wait. Her mind would be wandering instead of committed to seeing how her dad was doing. She would make the call first then devote her full attention to her father. One thing at a time.

Stepping out into her mother's pristine garden, with the afternoon sun slanting diagonal shadows across the clipped lawn, Lexi made her way to the shade of a huge oak tree and considered what to say. She looked at things from the brother's perspective—not having a clue who Lexi was or why she was calling or that anyone had been seeking him out in the first place. As well, the topic she was going to bring up—his deceased brother—was a sensitive one, sure to conjure sad memories for Mr. Fisher. Lexi had to choose all the right words and slow down her speech. She had a bad habit of speeding up when she was anxious.

Blowing out a purposeful sigh, she tapped in the phone number and double-checked it then clicked the button to make the call. As the phone rang three times, four times, five, Lexi contemplated leaving a voicemail, much like the one she had given Heidi a couple of weeks before. But for some reason, this was a call she wanted to experience live. She was just about to hang up and try again later in the evening when she heard a gravelly voice answer.

"Yes? Hello?"

"Mr. Fisher? Is this Vincent Fisher?"

"That's me." His tone sounded warm and jovial, which put Lexi at ease.

"Hi there. My name is Lexi Price, and I—"

"Let me stop you right there, hon. Is this a sales call? I've been told by my daughter not to accept any sales calls of any kind." His voice was not irritable, just matter-of-fact, like he'd rehearsed the line many times.

"No, sir. I'm not selling anything. I have some information for you. And I'm hoping you have some information for me as well."

The pause told her he was contemplating it. "Okay. Go on, then."

She explained who she was and who her great-grandmother was and the connection to James Fisher. She went backward in time, all the way to when she found the letters in the attic—she left out the necklace for the sake of not dragging out an already lengthy tale. As she rounded out her story, Lexi realized it was possible that the man had no idea what she was talking about—that Gigi's letters to James had *not* been kept safely beneath the floorboards of some attic for decades. It was possible that the letters had, instead, been lost to time, to the decades between the war and today's call. It could be that the call would result in the biggest dead end of all—that Gigi's letters would never be found.

But toward the end of Lexi's account, Mr. Fisher interrupted her. "Oh yes, yes, yes. I think I know what you're talking about." She could almost picture his elderly hands waving in recognition, his eyes bright with understanding. Her pulse accelerated. "James was my elder brother, you know. I was ten years old when he was killed overseas. During the war. Nowadays, my memories are pretty sketchy—can't even remember what I had for lunch. But those child-hood years, during the war. I can remember them like they were yes-terday."

She prodded gently. "Those letters I mentioned, sent from my great-grandmother to your brother, James, during the war. Do you know if they still exist?"

"Let's see. When my brother died, there *were* letters from some girl... Oh, I forget her name."

"Louise?"

"That sounds about right. Louise. And when my family received my brother's effects from the war office, there were bundles of letters included."

Lexi held her breath then asked, "Do you have those letters?" She waited patiently through the lengthy pause.

"I believe so. I haven't laid my eyes on them in quite a long while. But this would be the business of my daughter, Frankie Jo. She keeps all that stuff—old postcards, photographs, family mementos. She's always been that way, holding on to clutter and such. Borderline hoarder, if you ask me. I could see if she knows about those letters."

Lexi heard a muffling of the phone and assumed Mr. Fisher was holding a landline rather than a cell phone. She could hear him calling "Frankie Jo! Frankie!" and soon, there was more muffled back-and-forth chatter. Finally, a female voice got on the line with Lexi. "Hello? I'm Frankie Jo Spears. My father tells me you're looking for some letters, written during the war?"

"That's right." She explained again, briefly, who she was and why she was calling—to make sure that the woman knew Lexi wasn't trying to take advantage of an elderly man.

"I do have a box of old memorabilia from the war," Frankie Jo said. "And if we have those letters, that would be the place for them. I'm going to my house in a bit—I live right next door—and I'll have a look 'round. Can I call you if I find something?" Her thick Southern accent was warm and charming.

"Please do! I would be thrilled."

After their exchange of contact information, Lexi ended the call and clutched her phone to her chest, looking at the roses bobbing in the wind but not really seeing them. She pushed down the rising hope, praying she wouldn't be disappointed. She was one huge step closer to completing the circle and finalizing the questions floating around.

Remembering why she was at her parents' house in the first place, Lexi sprang to her feet, eager to tell them the news.

LEXI PLOPPED INTO HER driver's seat, willing her phone to ring. She wasn't about to call Mr. Fisher and bother him and his daughter again, not when it had barely been an hour since she first phoned him.

"Patience," she told herself, pulling away from her parents' curb and onto the streets speckled with shadow and light from the towering trees' branches draping overhead. Her favorite time of day, especially in spring, was the late afternoon into evening. People closing up shops, heading home, barbecuing in backyards, putting feet up, spending precious moments with family or winding down from a chaotic day. Time always ran a little slower in the evenings, particularly in Morgan's Grove.

She thought back to the visit with her father. He had looked well—some color had returned to his cheeks, and his energy increased each day. He had already eaten two macaroons by the time Lexi entered the bedroom, and when her mother had noticed, she'd removed the box from his bedstand. "Don't eat them all at once," she'd scolded playfully. "They should be savored."

When Lexi told her parents about Mr. Fisher's call, they had been as hopeful as she had. Speculating about whether they would ever lay eyes on Gigi's letters to James had also given Lexi's father a welcome distraction from talk of medicine and dosages and diets and follow-up appointments. Lexi's mother was a magnificent caretaker and showed her love and care through staying busy in that role, even becoming rather obsessed by it. But such ardent care could be exhausting for the recipient, and Lexi was glad to offer her father a brief respite.

As Lexi turned the corner toward her house, her thoughts drifted farther back to her father's hospital bedside, only days ago, with strong images of IV lines and bags and beeping monitors and hospital gowns. Another world. But this afternoon had been different. Her father had seemed back to his old self for the most part. Lexi sometimes wished a special camera existed, where people could click a button and view a still shot of the future. If that worried-at-the-hospital Lexi could've seen the Lexi today in his bedroom, listening to her father chat as though nothing dire had ever happened, she would've been better able to cope in the moments of crisis. But that wasn't how life worked. Nobody was allowed to see even one second into the future, to know how an event would turn out, for good or for bad. *We're at time's mercy,* Lexi thought. *Locked in the present moment.* But maybe that wasn't such a bad thing. The not-knowing made life exciting and fascinating too.

As Lexi entered her driveway, her phone rang too loudly through the Bluetooth connection to her car, startling her. She rolled to a stop and accepted the call.

It was Frankie Jo on the other end, and her first statement was "I found them. The letters! They were right where I thought they'd be."

Lexi gasped and covered her mouth.

"There must be about fifty or sixty of them, all written on fancy pink stationery," Frankie Jo said. "I vaguely remember my momma pulling these down from the attic, ages ago, forcing the entire family to read them together. She was on this big genealogy kick back then. I was a teenager, so I was bored out of my skull and probably yawned all the way through them, shame on me. But now—"

Lexi heard shuffling through the intercom.

"They seem like such treasures. Maybe they belong in a museum or somethin'."

"Could I... see them?" Lexi asked in a near-whisper.

"Yes, of course! They're yours, quite frankly. They belong to your family, not ours."

"I feel the same way about James's letters. That they weren't mine to read. I admit, I thought I was doing something wrong, looking over a total stranger's intimate thoughts."

"Oh, I understand, hon. Well, I think some sort of exchange ought to take place, don't you?"

Lexi wanted nothing more than to get her hands on her great-grandmother's letters. It couldn't be soon enough.

They wrapped up the call by agreeing on when and how to meet. "After church tomorrow?" Frankie Jo had asked, and Lexi gave an emphatic "I'll be there!"

Lexi's next call wasn't her mother or father or even Jolene. It was Graham. She had to tell him first. And when she did, he was even more elated than she'd hoped he would be.

"I can't believe this. The brother is still alive. And they kept the letters all these decades?" His voice lifted half an octave higher than it usually did. "You said he's ninety years old? And remembers the war? This is amazing, Lex. Were they trying all those years to find James's letters too?"

Lexi chuckled. "Slow down a sec. I can barely catch up. You're where I was a few minutes ago, when I first found out."

Graham laughed. "Gobsmacked, as we Brits would say."

"Exactly. Would you... go with me?" Lexi hadn't planned on asking him but didn't want to face this delicate and emotional situation alone. It was brand-new territory. She couldn't think of anyone else she would rather experience it with.

"They live in Round Rock?"

"Yep, twenty-something miles from Morgan's Grove."

"Hm. I'm actually inundated with final exam prep this week."

"Oh, that's right. I totally forgot—"

"But I'll make the time. I can handle a few hours away from work." He was silent for a long moment, and Lexi assumed he was already changing his mind. "But... don't you want to take someone else? Jolene or even your mother? Someone from your own fami-ly—"

"My mother? Are you kidding? We're oil and water. We'd probably argue the entire way—fuss over the best way to get there, what time to arrive, what to say, what not to say. No thanks. Too stressful. Besides, she's on nursing duty with Dad. She won't leave his side."

"Good point."

"And Jolene probably has a few mansion tours to give. One of her tour guides is out sick, and Sunday is always their busiest day. Any-way, you were my first call for a reason. I'd love for you to join me."

"Well then, the answer is emphatic. Yes!"

Chapter Twenty

Nothing about the upcoming outing with Lexi held any characteristics of a date. There was no planned meal involved, no movie to watch, no garden to stroll through, no couples' party to attend. Merely a brief car ride to a stranger's house in Round Rock to discuss some eighty-year-old letters then an equally brief drive back to Lexi's house in Morgan's Grove.

Still, as Graham parked beside her mailbox, he glanced at his hair in the rearview mirror then made sure all the buttons on his shirt aligned properly. He switched off the engine and mulled it over. Perhaps there was one component of the outing that made it seem slightly date-like—the intimacy factor. Lexi was trusting him and him alone to be with her during the potentially emotional or exciting visit ahead with Mr. Fisher. Graham wasn't her consolation prize or an afterthought. When Lexi had been faced with a significant moment in her family's life, learning new information about her beloved great-grandmother, she had chosen him first.

Shaking off the pressure of trying to be everything for Lexi today that she needed him to be, Graham exited the car and heard Bailey's mournful howl from inside the house. Graham paused when he saw Lexi lock the front door and skip down the stairs while tapping on her phone. She wore tan slacks with a powder-blue blazer, and her hair had been swept up in some sort of twist, with purposeful wisps of hair framing her face. A thick tote bag was slung over her right shoulder. She looked quite professional for a Sunday afternoon, as though she were headed off to a business meeting. Perhaps, in her mind, she was.

"Mind if I drive?" she asked, hardly registering Graham's presence except to glance in his direction as she led the way to her car, parked in the driveway.

"Not at all." He had to trot to catch up with her.

"I'm just antsy," Lexi said after they'd both climbed inside her car and shut the doors. She maneuvered the tote bag carefully between them and onto the backseat's floorboard. "Driving helps me keep my hands occupied." She started the engine then paused, finally looking at him. "Hi."

"Hi."

"Sorry if I'm being abrupt. I'm a bundle of nerves."

"It's okay. You don't seem flustered. You seem… focused."

"Ha, that's probably a nicer way to say obsessive. That's what Ruby calls me when I get into 'focused' mode." She took in a breath and released it, shaking her head. "Why am I so nervous about meeting Mr. Fisher?"

"I think a lot's riding on it, maybe? Weeks' worth of questions and speculation and trickles of clues adding to the mystery?"

"Well, when you put it that way…"

"You don't want to be disappointed."

"I think that's what it boils down to. I won't believe Gigi's letters actually exist until I lay eyes on them. Part of me believes this is all some weird hoax or mix-up, and they've got the wrong Louise. Or I've got the wrong Fishers. I mean, after the disappointment of losing the necklace—"

"I checked with campus safety again on Friday." Graham tsked. "Still nothing."

"I think it's a lost cause. I haven't had the courage to tell my folks yet. That's one conversation I'm not looking forward to. I can't even find the words. 'Mother, Dad, I just so happened to lose our family's priceless, decades-old heirloom.'"

"They'll understand."

"I hope you're right."

"WANT ME TO KNOCK?" Graham stood shoulder to shoulder with Lexi at Vincent Fisher's front door. They had already been standing on the welcome mat for more than a few awkward seconds.

"Oh. Yeah." Lexi shook her head. "That might help."

Graham squeezed her hand, which dangled near his, then with his other hand, he gave four precise knocks. Lexi adjusted her tote bag, the one with the antiques store's logo on it. Tucked carefully inside were the all-important James letters. The night before, she'd spent time making sure each of the envelopes and letters matched up and they were placed in consecutive order, with the ribbons tied neatly around them exactly as they'd been when she'd discovered them underneath the attic's floorboards.

Mr. Fisher's house was a modest home on a leafy street behind the main square. The small town of Round Rock reminded Lexi of Morgan's Grove.

The doorknob turned, and a tall woman in her late sixties smiled brightly.

"Hi, I'm Lexi. And you're Frankie Jo?"

"That's me. Come on in, y'all!" She waved them inside.

Lexi and Graham were ushered into a cozy living space with dark-brown carpet, wood wall paneling, and a brick fireplace. A patchwork quilt lay neatly on the back of an empty sofa, and an elderly man with thinning silver hair sat in the adjacent recliner. He stretched out his hand toward Lexi, who accepted it before he could try to rise to his feet.

"Vincent Fisher."

"I'm Lexi Price. And this is Graham Faulkner."

"A friend," Graham said.

"A well-trusted friend. I hope you don't mind that I brought someone along."

"Course not."

Lexi and Graham were offered seats on the sofa as well as plastic cups of sweet tea, which were already laid out on a tray in front of them, making them hard to refuse. Lexi remembered Graham telling her once that sweet tea disgusted him, always had. It was the one thing that his British side could never fully embrace, even as a Texan of two decades. He'd tried hard, convinced himself that the sweetness wouldn't be too much, but was always overwhelmed by it. "Give me a cuppa strong English tea, with a splash of milk, and that's all I'll ever need," he'd told her.

Lexi watched him receive the cup from Frankie Jo, the ice cubs clicking against the plastic. He proceeded to take a sip then swallowed, smacked his lips, and forced a nod. "Good."

Mr. Fisher winced as he shifted in his chair, and Lexi's eyes drifted to the walker beside him and then to the brass-framed photograph on the table nearby, showing a couple with their heads leaning together, clearly in love. She assumed the woman was Mrs. Fisher in her earlier years. Lexi wondered how long he had been widowed.

After a few moments spent on the typical Southern niceties—general information about each other, like how long they'd lived in their respective cities, what their occupations or former occupations were, and even the Texas weather—Lexi gathered her courage and steered them toward her main purpose in visiting. The tote bag leaned against her leg, practically begging to be opened.

During a pause in conversation, Lexi reached inside the bag and pulled out a manila envelope, the one she'd filled the night before. "I have something for you, Mr. Fisher. Included with the letters from James to my great-grandmother were two photographs." She opened the envelope to produce the photos then stretched out her hand.

"These are yours to keep. I made copies for my own family too—hope you don't mind."

"Not at all. Smart thinking." Vincent adjusted his glasses and squinted through them to stare at the first photograph as Lexi explained about the dog that the troops had adopted. "This is exactly how I remember him, my brother. Look at him, in that uniform." He smiled, lingering on the photo, then moved to the next one. "And this must be your great-grandmother."

"Louise," Lexi said. "We called her Gigi."

"And they were in love..."

"Engaged to be married. Secretly. That's what James's letters indicated." Lexi handed the envelope over to Frankie Jo. "And these are copies of a few journal entries, written by Blanche."

"The journal that you'd mentioned on the phone? So, let me get this straight. Blanche was your great-grandmother's best friend and was the go-between during the war for my Uncle James and your great-grandmother."

"You've got it."

"Which is why the letters from James are all addressed to Blanche instead. How amazing," Frankie Jo whispered, taking a peek inside. "And where did you get ahold of these journal entries?"

"Oh, it's been quite the adventure." Lexi gestured toward Graham. "We've been following the trail of Gigi and James's love story for the past several weeks. And it finally led us here. The journal pages came from Heidi, Blanche's granddaughter. Those entries also mention James. The copies are yours to keep."

"Thank you," Vincent said, clutching the photos.

Frankie Jo clasped the envelope on her lap. "Tell me again why they needed a go-between? James and Gigi?"

"Gigi's father didn't approve. He thought James was too old for her. And with the war going on—"

"They wanted to protect her," Vincent said, finishing for her.

Frankie Jo nodded. "That makes sense. Well, I got curious and skimmed some of Louise's letters last night. James didn't keep any of the envelopes. So our family had the letters but with no address and no last name. We were at a dead end from the beginning." She set Lexi's envelope aside and produced an oversized shoebox, one made for roller blades or boots.

"She was a mystery to you too?" Graham asked. "So James never told his family about Louise?"

"Not that I recall," Vincent said.

"I guess they were both keeping secrets." Frankie Jo handed over the box. "Sorry they're in a shoebox. Doesn't seem worthy of what's inside. But at least the letters were protected. They're yours. Back where they belong."

Lexi sensed the unique reverence of the moment as she gathered the straps of the tote bag containing James's letters. "These too. Back where they belong."

She rose from the sofa and crossed the room to meet Frankie Jo halfway, and they traded treasures. A shoebox for a tote bag, finally finding their proper homes.

"Look, Dad." Frankie Jo brought the tote bag to her father and knelt beside his recliner. She pulled out one of the bundles of letters, and he touched it with a withered hand.

"You'll never know what this means." Vincent's voice was shaky. "I didn't think I'd live long enough to lay my eyes on them. You've brought my brother back to me, in a way."

Lexi couldn't bring herself to speak—the words wouldn't come through the tears forming. Graham's warm, supportive hand sweetly stroked her back. She swallowed then found her voice again. "I think they wanted us to find the letters, all these years later. A special connection between our two families."

"Meant to be," Graham whispered beside her.

AT THE RED LIGHT ON Main Street, Graham snuck a glance at his phone to remind him of the correct address. When he and Lexi had left Mr. Fisher's house, she had asked Graham to drive, which gave him the perfect opportunity to take his quick detour. It might not be the appropriate time for a frivolous surprise, but he wanted to give Lexi a diversion from the intense exchange of heirlooms they'd been part of. He hoped this classic Round Rock institution might do the trick.

From his peripheral vision, he could see Lexi balancing the shoebox on her lap, still unwilling to look inside. Graham wondered if she worried about getting emotional seeing Gigi's letters, or maybe she wanted to view them privately, at home. Or both.

As he turned onto West Liberty Avenue and saw what he was looking for, Graham grunted under his breath.

"What's wrong?"

He pulled into the empty lot and parked. "I wanted to surprise you."

Lexi peered out the windshield. "With donuts?"

"But not just *any* donuts..."

"Round Rock Donuts." She beamed, peering up at the sign.

The sugary concoctions were famous, and not only inside the Austin area. The donuts had gained fame all over the country for being made with ultra-fresh eggs, which gave the donuts a yellowy tinge and delectable flavor. They were also famous for their "Texas-sized" donut, a gargantuan glazed treat that required two hands—or more—to hold and eat.

"I haven't had a Round Rock donut in ages," she said.

"But it looks like they're closed."

Lexi shifted toward him. "It's the thought that counts. Thank you, Graham. And for coming with me today. It helped, having you there. More than you know."

"I was honored to be part of it... but I didn't help much. You had the whole thing under control."

"But I needed you. Having you sitting there was... comforting. It gave me strength."

She clasped her fingers on top of the box then stared out the window. She was lost to him again, her thoughts elsewhere. Graham knew she might not say another word all the way home. He shifted into drive and moved the car back toward the road.

He'd meant it when he said he didn't think he had helped much at the Fishers'. On the way there, he didn't know what his expected role would be—maybe answering some historical questions, perhaps adding unique details to the conversation (since he'd been involved from the start). But Lexi was right. His role wasn't to *do* anything. It was to be something. For her. A column of support, an anchor, a silent advocate.

He had hoped that the ride home would be filled with animated conversation led by Lexi, recapping the meeting and speculating about the letters, the same way all the other discoveries had been handled—the necklace, James's letters, the journals. But today was decidedly different. Lexi had turned inward, perhaps processing the treasures she held and knowing that they contained the last remaining words from her great-grandmother. A somber and unexpected goodbye, somehow. A finality. The mystery was over, and maybe it was cause for contemplation rather than celebration.

Twenty minutes later, they arrived at Lexi's home, and Graham parked her car in the driveway. As he exited, he noticed the distinct wisps of an orange-and-lilac sunset above the roofs across the street.

"Beautiful," Lexi said, reading his mind as she shut her door. "Wanna come in?" she asked as they met together near the car's trunk. "Coke or tea? *Un*sweet, of course." She shifted the shoebox against her right hip.

But Graham read it in her eyes—she was only being cordial. Her invitation lacked the usual energy and easy authenticity, instead smacking mostly of the obligatory Southern hospitality of someone who had just been done a favor and needed to return it. Graham knew she was eager to get inside the house, settle in, and open the shoebox to read the letters privately. She didn't need several minutes of small talk intervening.

"No, thanks," he said, even though he wanted to accept. "I'd better get back. Lots of work ahead, getting ready for finals."

"When will you be free for the summer?"

"Thursday. The online finals will come in tomorrow, so I'll grade those first. Then in-class finals after that."

"Sounds exhausting."

"It is. But I've got a pretty good system. It's not unbearable."

"Well, I'll try not to annoy you this week, let you concentrate on work."

"You never annoy me. Call or text anytime. I would welcome the break." He took two steps down the driveway in the direction of his car then paused. Pivoting toward Lexi, who had already made her way toward the front porch, he called out, "Hey, wanna go to a wedding with me?" He had no idea where it had come from—the timing of the question. He'd had every opportunity this afternoon to ask it and hadn't planned on tacking it on, so haphazardly, at the end of the day as a mere afterthought. But something had compelled him, and he'd seized the moment. "My dad's wedding," he said, clarifying.

Lexi swiveled on the lawn, looked above his head at the sunset, then gave a shrug and a small smile. "Sure."

His heart gave a tangible leap inside his chest as he struggled to keep his expression neutral.

"When is it?" she asked.

"Saturday." He grimaced. "Short notice." He hoped she wouldn't back out.

But after a couple of seconds of mulling it over, she said again, "Sure."

"Yeah? Okay, great. I'll text you the details."

Lexi gave a nod then moved toward her porch with the shoebox. Graham opened his car door and climbed inside, starting the engine and watching Lexi shut the screen door behind her.

Before putting the car into gear, he found his phone and grinned at the screen as he typed out a text to Chad. *She said yes.*

LEXI, WEARING HER FLANNEL doggie pajamas, shifted her crossed legs and reached for the final sheets of perfectly folded stationery. She had spent the last two hours poring over Gigi's wartime letters to James, reading portions softly aloud, chuckling over certain sections and tearing up over others.

As eager as she'd been to rush through them, she'd taken her time. She'd wanted to be fully composed and relaxed, with no burdens or chores to pull her attention away. First, she'd gotten Bailey settled and fed; then, she'd munched on a quick salad, grabbed a bottled water, and headed upstairs to change into her pajamas.

Bailey had curled up in his corner pillow and was snoring softly within minutes. By the time Lexi had lifted the lid of the shoebox, it was dark outside. Crickets chirped and bullfrogs bellowed through the cracked-open window.

Removing the letters, Lexi had been able to tell that they were in chronological order. She'd spread out all the letters onto the quilt in order, creating a patchwork of pink stationery on her bed. She'd kept the letters in their original shape—folded half-wise to fit inside the now-missing envelopes. Before opening the first letter, Lexi had looked across the room to the petite desk in the corner—the one her mother had brought over when she'd helped decorate Lexi's bedroom on the day she'd moved into the rental house a few years back. The desk had belonged to Gigi, she'd been told, and Lexi had wondered if it was the very place where she'd written all her letters to James. She'd imagined her great-grandmother pausing to find the words, pen hovering above paper. Or perhaps the words had come swiftly, eagerly, and she couldn't write fast enough to catch them on the page.

Lexi had read each letter slowly, savoring the words, along with her great-grandmother's familiar flowery handwriting with strong loops on her *g*'s and *d*'s. It was clear she'd been taught proper cursive as a child. Much of the content was similar to James's letters—a young person, clearly starry-eyed and completely smitten with the recipient. And some of it was downright racy: "I can taste the sweetness of your lips... I want to feel your arms on my face, my neck, my waist..."

Lexi had never known Gigi to be sentimental or overly romantic when it came to love. Gigi never read romantic novels or watched movies about love and would tease those who did. "Soppy," she would call them. Gigi had always seemed entirely practical about family and marriage. Levelheaded. She loved her family deeply but sometimes had trouble expressing it in words. But the letters Lexi held were so different, filled with palpable longing and aching, a young woman's heart displayed vulnerably on the page. Lexi assumed the war had something to do with it—the life-and-death mentality they had all lived with every day, the heightened emotions, the drama, and even the excitement of it all. But Gigi's words didn't seem to be drummed up or overly sentimental. They were genuine and real. Real enough for her to have kept James's letters—and his necklace—for eight decades.

Some portions of each letter were filled with newsy chatter about ordinary family occurrences: the bland meals Gigi's mother would create while making the most of the rationed butter and sugar; the radio shows her father insisted they listen to in the evenings, like Perry Mason, Agatha Christie, Abbott and Costello; and the model airplanes her younger brother worked diligently on each evening. Maybe the specific detail was Gigi's attempt at normalizing her letters, helping James to imagine everyday humdrum happenings as he sat under a tree or inside a tent, hearing bombs explode nearby. She was giving him a taste of home, no matter how mundane.

Gigi also mentioned bits of her own daily life: her tedious clerical job at a law office in Austin three days a week; the regular meetings to help organize parties at the USO for the soldiers on leave; the Sunday-morning church services where the congregation would pray for their boys in the fight and comfort those families in mourning.

Near the end of one letter, Lexi giggled when she read the foreshadowing in one particular paragraph, regarding the years-later, postwar creation of the antiques shop: "Mother busied herself today with clearing out a closet. But she ended up not throwing *a single thing* out! Old lace tablecloths (Daddy calls them ancient), figurines handed down by her mother, a clock that's stopped working. Daddy says she's 'hoarding,' not saving, and that she should open up a shop of her own someday, to sell her 'antiquities.' He meant it as a joke, but Mother wasn't laughing."

The closer Lexi came to the final batch of letters, the more often Gigi's topics centered around wedding details, perhaps to give James (and herself) a happy event to look forward to beyond the horrors of war.

Lexi held the final letter, wishing there were more, and unfolded it carefully. The greeting was the same as in every other letter: "My Dearest James."

But the penmanship was slightly different than in the other letters. Narrower, slightly angled, perhaps more hurried? It wasn't as loopy or flowery as her previous cursive. And the letter was shorter than the others, by an entire page. The beginning of it mentioned the usual daily activities and goings-on, but midway through, the letter became serious. It was a strong and fervent proclamation of her love, as though James must be told precisely how she felt—as though he didn't know already. "I will love you for the rest of my life... so glad we met that wonderful day... can't wait to call you 'husband'... please, please be careful wherever you are... come back to me, my love."

The passage contained a hint of desperation. *Was she concerned that James's love was fading? Or was there something darker at work? Had Gigi experienced a sort of sixth sense or premonition about his upcoming death?* The very next letter she would receive, according to the dates, was the one from his soldier friend, telling about James's tragic death.

It was as if Gigi knew somehow. Which would explain her reaction from Blanche's journals when they met at the gazebo that fateful day, with Gigi's calm demeanor and a quick acceptance, almost as though she was already prepared to hear the worst news.

The letter ended with a quote from Charlotte Bronte: "'I offer you my hand, my heart, and a share of all my possessions... I ask you to pass through life at my side—to be my second self, and best earthly companion.'" And the closing was: "You will always keep my heart. Forever, Louise."

As Lexi leaned back onto the pillow, the open letter clutched to her chest, she stared at the ceiling and wondered if James had read it and understood it too—the uneasy premonition between the lines.

A tear slid down her cheek. She wasn't crying for Gigi and James. She was crying for all the soldiers and their loved ones who experienced the unspeakable horrors and turmoil and uncertainty they did at such a young age. Eighteen, nineteen, twenty. Just babies, beginning their lives. Millions of them, never to experience a wedding, a career, children, a real home back in the States. Many soldiers' lives ended there, in trenches or camps in Europe and the Pacific, sacrificing their lives for the world's freedom.

No textbook or documentary could ever fill Lexi with the same level of appreciation and understanding that reading Gigi's and James's letters had produced. She would be forever grateful.

Chapter Twenty-one

"Knock, knock?" Lexi tapped on her parents' front door. When she found it unlocked, she stepped inside.

"Come in, honey." Her father's voice carried from the living room.

Lexi found him relaxed in a recliner, glasses on, staring at the tablet in his lap.

"You look comfortable." She set the shoebox down on the sofa. "The crosswords, I see."

"I'm having trouble with the last word, seven letters. 'A dishonest schemer.' Begins with an *s*."

Lexi considered it then said, "Scammer?" as she sat down next to the shoebox.

"That's it!"

"Where's Mother?"

"I'm here." She entered through the French doors wearing a broad-brimmed hat as she peeled off a glove. "Doing a bit of weeding. I've been neglecting my garden." She gave Lexi's shoulder a gentle squeeze as she passed behind the sofa then removed her hat and sat down in the empty straight-backed chair across the room from her husband. "I was coming in for a break. Did you bring us something?"

"Yes. They're—" Lexi's cell interrupted her. "Sorry, I'm expecting a call." She shifted the phone inside her purse and saw the name. "I have to get this. It's work. Be right back."

Lexi took the call and headed for the dining room. After a minute, she returned to the couch.

"Everything all right?" her father asked. He had set his tablet aside.

"Great, actually. That was Lenny, the contractor who worked on the Let's Get Crafty warehouse. I'm in negotiations for him to convert the second warehouse into the glassblowing space."

"That's fantastic, honey. Congrats," her father said.

"So soon?" her mother asked. "I had hoped you might postpone, at least until next year. It's a lot to take on."

"It is. But the store is doing better than ever—thanks in part to the success of Let's Get Crafty. It's a good time to piggyback on that momentum and move forward. I'm meeting with the bank in a couple of weeks to discuss financing. And Mike, the professor at UT, wants to involve his students—let them work at the furnace, give them assignments or extra credit for it, even let them sell their art in the warehouse. Lots of good ideas. It's the right time for this."

"Well, we trust your business acumen," her mother said. "Still, I can't help but worry about the risk."

"But I've considered everything. Trust me, Mother. Please."

Her mother nodded and plucked a slender blade of grass from her khaki shorts.

"So, what's in the box?" her father asked, pointing to it.

Happy about the shift in topic—and strongly suspecting that her father asked the question to accomplish just that—Lexi moved the box to her lap and placed her hands on top. "Gigi's letters."

She heard a soft gasp from her mother. "You went to see Mr. Fisher?"

"Yesterday. With Graham."

Her mother pursed her lips slightly. Lexi wasn't sure if it was a reaction to the fact that she went with Graham or the fact that she went without her mother.

"Sorry I didn't let you know about the trip. Everything happened so fast, and Graham was willing to go to Round Rock with me. Daddy wasn't up for the drive, and you needed to stay with him. And so we went."

As she detailed yesterday's events, Lexi remembered the hugs she'd received from both Mr. Fisher and Frankie Jo at the end. She and Graham had entered the house as strangers but exited as something more significant. They had all shared a moment in that living room that was impossible for Lexi to put into words for her parents. The past met the present in the exchange of those letters, in the shared emotions. The presence of beloved relatives, long gone, seemed near and vivid in that moment.

"One of Gigi's letters mentions her father complaining about all the 'clutter' in their house. He suggests she should have a yard sale—or better yet, open an antiques store and make some real money off of them."

"You're kidding!" Her mother lifted her hand to her mouth to stave off a giggle. "So that was the origin of the store."

"Anyway, I want you to have the letters." Lexi placed them on the coffee table. "Keep them here. I have some ideas about how we can preserve them—one idea is to create some sort of framed collage with some of the letters."

"Interesting idea," her mother said. "I have a lady in Austin I can contact about that."

"Or we could buy a special treasure box to put them in, or maybe put them in a safe..."

"Lots of possibilities," her dad said.

"I'll make copies of them for you," her mother said. "That way, you can keep them at your house too."

"I would love that." Lexi had considered making copies before bringing the letters over, but the busy morning had gotten away from her, and she was eager to deliver the letters to her folks. "There's something else I've been keeping from you." Lexi cleared her throat and stared at her hands, threading her fingers together. "It's about the necklace. Remember how I took it to Graham's students last week? The day that Daddy was taken to the hospital? Well... I sort of... lost it. The necklace." She gathered enough courage to glance at her mother's expression, which displayed the expected level of shock. "I thought the necklace was in my purse, inside its case." She explained how she'd looked everywhere for it then detailed all of Graham's efforts to search the campus. "I even filed a police report. I've tried everything to find it. Truly."

"And maybe they will, honey," her father said, reassuring her. "We can't give up hope."

"I've felt so guilty ever since. I'm sorry for losing it."

"Lex, don't apologize." Her mother reached out to touch her daughter's knee. "It was an accident. You were worried about your father that day."

Lexi remembered back to that horrible afternoon and all the chaotic events that followed. "I didn't even realize I'd lost the necklace until I came over to your house that night to get your clothes for the hospital."

"It's a piece of jewelry. An object," her mother said. "It's not important in the scheme of things."

"That's what Gigi told me once."

"Well, your Gigi was never wrong. Don't give it another thought." She gave Lexi's knee a reassuring squeeze. "I'm parched. Anyone else in the mood for a nice glass of tea with lemon?"

Lexi shook her head, unable to process her mother's incredibly kind and tempered reaction. She had expected the opposite.

"I'll take one." Her father lifted an index finger. "Thanks, love."

When her mother left the room, her father crossed his legs and leaned in Lexi's direction. She scooted to the edge of the couch to get closer to him.

"How was it, reading the letters?" he asked.

"Incredible. Even more special than reading James's. And more heartbreaking, knowing how things ended, with his death. It was like reading a novel where I already knew the tragic outcome. One particular thing struck me, looking back. That the letters—all of them, both Gigi's and James's—are romantic and hopeful. They had no hesitation sharing their feelings, putting them in print. Do you think it was mostly because of the war? How everything was magnified somehow?"

"Mm, could be. Those were pressurized, unique times they were living through. I'm sure it played a role."

Lexi hoped she could accurately put her thoughts into words. She could always show her philosophical self with her dad, without judgment. "Honestly, reading those letters made me look at myself and reflect on my own life—what I would do in those situations, how I might feel. Mostly, it made me realize something. I'm not even sure I know what real love feels like. I don't think I've ever experienced it before. Gigi's love for James was so much deeper, more alive, than what I ever had with Neil."

Her father folded his hands and placed his index fingers to his lips. Lexi always called it his "thinking pose"—when he gave his full attention to a dilemma or issue. He lowered his hands to his lap and looked at Lexi. "Love is complicated. And it's different for each person. Some couples run hot and cold, but they don't last very long. And some go over the top to convince everyone else—and maybe themselves—that their love is authentic, but maybe it isn't. And others may seem lukewarm toward each other, but they might have a solid friendship, a good foundation. Look at the relationship between Gigi and Paw-Paw. It might not've had the same level of drama or emotion as she had with James. But they built a family around it, a legacy. That's real."

"I'm still amazed that Gigi was able to move on after James, say vows to someone else, have kids with him. But I think she was brave, trying again. Opening up that way."

"I suppose any relationship is a risk—that the other person might not stay faithful or might break your heart or even pass away. It's corny to say, but how will you experience the rewards unless you jump in and take the chance?"

Somehow, they weren't talking about Gigi and James anymore. Or Gigi and Paw-Paw. Just as the letters had served as an unexpected mirror into Lexi's own life, so had the conversation about the letters with her father. He patted Lexi's wrist then gave it a knowing squeeze.

"Like Gigi did," Lexi whispered.

GRAHAM RUBBED HIS EYES and tried again. He'd read the same paragraph twice already, but his mind couldn't hold the words. Wedging his red ballpoint into the bluebook and slapping it shut, he set it aside and grabbed his phone. *Was it too late to call?*

Lexi was, after all, the reason he couldn't concentrate on the students' exams. Every time he read about a WWII battle or struggled through a mediocre analysis of the war's origins, Graham could only see one thing: Lexi's face. The flush of her pink cheeks in the warm sun, the smile that spread across her lips when she teased him, the chestnut hair that blew lightly in a gentle wind. They hadn't spent much time together the day before—only a couple of hours on their journey to and from Round Rock—but it had been significant time, and he hadn't wanted to pull away from her curb.

Before he could tap the button to call her, a text popped onto the screen from Theresa. It was the second time she'd texted since Friday, and both texts hinted strongly at the same thing: she wanted to get back together. He had politely responded to the first one, making it crystal clear he wanted nothing to do with a reunion, hoping she would get the hint and never contact him again. But there she was, on his screen once more, being persistent:

I really want to talk. I'll meet anywhere you want.

Graham knew he was officially over her when seeing her name on his screen did nothing but fill him with dread. He wasn't excited to hear from her, wasn't secretly pining for her, wasn't glad that she'd texted. In fact, the opposite—he wished she would leave him alone, move on with her life. The life that she had envisioned without him when she broke up with him. Because he had already done the same, with Lexi.

He texted her again—a polite but firm no. When he sent the text, he promised himself that if she reached out a third time, he would ignore her altogether. As far as he was concerned, there was nothing else to say.

He set the phone down but then picked it up again and rang Lexi's number. After two rings, her face appeared on the screen—Graham had tapped a video call by accident—and she seemed content and relaxed as she waved into the camera. She wore a red tank top, and her hair was pulled back into a casual style. From what he could tell of the background, she was sitting in her kitchen.

"Hey there," she said.

"Too late to call?"

She took a bite of something, swallowed, and shook her head. "Not for me. I'm always up late. I assume you're buried under work?"

"Bingo." Graham did a quick mental check of his own disheveled appearance—gray T-shirt, shadow-beard, tufted hair. *Oh well.*

"So. You're basically using me as a distraction from all that tedious final-exam grading you should be doing."

"Basically. Does that bother you?"

"Not in the slightest. I've been working, too, so you can be my distraction." She held up a piece of paper for the camera then set it down. "It's the contractor's bid for the glassblowing warehouse."

"That happened fast."

"Yeah, it seems like it, but I've actually been thinking about doing this for two years. It's a long time coming. I'm excited to get some details on paper. Hopefully, we'll get the project finished by the end of this year." She looked down. "Can you hear that through the phone?"

She moved the camera to show Bailey, his head propped up on Lexi's bare foot. "Snoring, as usual." She set the phone back onto the table and adjusted it so she was hands-free.

"Lucky him. Not a care in the world."

"I'm always jealous of him. Two meals a day, no bills to pay, daily walks, and a big fat pillow to sleep on wherever he goes—the store, my bedroom, the living room. And of course, head scratches from about a dozen people a day who move through the store."

"A dog's life."

"Oh, did you see my text earlier, about Gigi's letter?"

"I did but never got the chance to respond. School was crazy today."

"It was a screenshot of the final letter she wrote to James. Mother will make copies of all the letters for me to keep. When she does, I can show them to you. Or I'll make you copies—and maybe you can share some with your classes next semester."

"I'd love that."

She took a swig from a pink tumbler then tapped the screen. "Something just came through... A new message from Chaynie in a group text. It's about the barn dance." She squinted to read it. "Says, 'Confirmed date—one week from today. The Peterson Ranch. Would love to have some help with the decorating. I'll provide everything, including snacks. Drop by anytime between ten and ten this

Thursday or Friday. Pass the invite along to anyone you want.' So what do you think? Wanna help out with the barn dance?"

"I'm free on Friday. Well, at least in the daytime. That night is my father's rehearsal dinner. I'll see if Shelley wants to come and help too. She's got a new boyfriend, by the way."

"Is it Andrew? I noticed they were pretty friendly when we were painting gnomes."

"Good memory. Yeah, that's him. They're having their first official 'date' this week. A picnic on the grounds, with Mrs. Anderson chaperoning."

"So adorable. Tell Shelley she's welcome to bring him to the dance too."

Graham settled back into the sofa cushion and thought about what a good idea it had been to call Lexi. His whole body relaxed talking to her, letting the chat veer into various topics with ease. The perfect break from tedious grading.

LEXI HEARD THE CLOCK chime in the hallway and could barely believe an hour had passed so swiftly. She never had to carry the weight of a conversation with Graham, which was probably why she enjoyed talking to him on the phone in the first place. It was similar to the balance of a good tennis match, lobbing the conversational ball over the net to each other with ease, back and forth.

At the moment, they were talking about Lexi's mother. "I got a call from Lenny yesterday, about the bid, and told my folks about the glassblowing center. Predictably, my mother warned me that I was moving too fast. She's being protective, but it feels like a criticism every time she says it. She's doubting me."

"My father does that too. Nothing I do pleases him. I think he wanted me to be a solicitor too."

"Solicitor?"

"Sorry. Brit-speak. A lawyer."

"I can't see you as a lawyer. No offense to your dad, but... that profession wouldn't fit your personality. You're perfect right where you are, in the classroom. Anyway, the weird thing is—my mother sometimes shocks me by being super attentive or affectionate right after she's semi-insulted me. It's emotional whiplash."

"Maybe her way of giving a nonverbal apology?"

Lexi smirked. "It doesn't seem like much of an apology. Do you think they're aware of what they're doing—your dad, my mom? Making us feel we're not totally measuring up? As though there's this super-high invisible bar we'll never be able to reach."

Graham shifted in his seat. "I hope it's not calculated on their part. And that my father doesn't realize that he knows exactly what it takes to deflate me—one word, one look. I don't think he understands how deep it goes. Ever since childhood."

"Same here. Mother's jabs aren't intentional, surely. But to play devil's advocate, I never really show her how much they bother me. I've never vocalized it. So I guess that's on me."

"I never thought about it that way. I'm too uneasy to stand up to my dad. And I don't see that changing in the near future. We're both stuck in these same roles we've played, forever."

"Families are weird that way. We don't give ourselves room to grow or change. I think we *want* to see each other the same way, always, because it's predictable. But maybe we're the ones who should keep trying to reach them, make some progress. Even if they won't."

"It's worth a try, I guess."

When Graham stifled a yawn with his fist, Lexi knew it was time for them both to get back to work.

"I'd better sign off and finish looking this over." She showed Graham the paper again. "Plus, I have an unusually early start. Ruby's got tomorrow off, so I have to open the store bright and early. She and Henry are taking a day trip to Fredericksburg."

"Henry? Are they getting serious?"

"I think so. She's walking around on cloud nine these days. It's pretty annoying. But I'm happy for her."

"Henry's a good guy. So, then, guess I'll see you on Friday, at the barn?"

"See you then."

As the screen went dark, Lexi saw a fresh text pop up from Jo. They always had one long, never-ending string of texts throughout the day. Jo was a night owl, too, so it wasn't unusual to receive a late message.

Lexi scrolled backward to scan their last two texts—Lexi telling Jo about the Round Rock trip with Graham then the reading of Gigi's letters that evening.

Jo's newest text was on a different topic entirely: *Did you get Chaynie's ask for help to decorate the barn? I can send it to you.*

Lexi texted back: *Got it. I'll be there. I forgot to tell you I have plans on Saturday night. Graham asked me to his dad's wedding.*

Lexi watched the three floating dots telling her Jo was typing and waited for Jo's predictably explosive response. She didn't disappoint. Except that the answer didn't come in as a text but as an animated gif: an actor with his mouth dropping open and the caption "Whaaa?" underneath.

Lexi chuckled and started to type out "It's not a date" when she was interrupted by a new text from Jo.

It's totally a date!

Lexi didn't have the energy to try and explain why it probably wasn't a date, so she clicked on the ha-ha response then set down her phone.

But there was another reason Lexi didn't attempt to push back against Jo's assumption. Because the minute Lexi had had time to process the wedding invitation, she'd asked herself that very thing too—whether Graham had intended it as a date. And what surprised her even more was that she didn't mind if he had.

Chapter Twenty-two

"Is your side straight?" Lexi asked.

"I think so." Jolene, hands on hips, shifted toward the center of the chunky hay bale. "Looks fine to me."

Ever since they'd arrived at the Petersons' big red barn a half hour ago, they'd been tasked with a variety of jobs. Chaynie was the one delegating, walking around with her tablet like the organized librarian she was, making sure everything was in order and everyone was on task. Jo and Lexi's current job was to cover the enormous rectangular hay bales with thick, sturdy blankets for comfortable seating. The bales, four in all, had been placed on one side of the high-ceilinged barn, presumably for those guests who wished to rest or chat in between dancing and eating.

"I need a water! Can I get you one?" Jo asked her cousin.

"Sure." Lexi tested the bale by sitting down on the blanket and watched Jo proceed to the other side of the barn, where an ample snacks table had been established for those who were volunteering to help decorate the barn for the big night a few evenings away. A warm breeze from the nearby open doors brushed Lexi's face, and she was glad she'd chosen to wear shorts and a T-shirt, with her hair pulled into a loose braid. The first week of May had seen characteristically hot afternoons, with temperatures already soaring into the mid-eighties.

Lexi crossed one leg over the other and surveyed the buzz of activity—Jill and Rick helping string fairy lights from the second-floor loft, Lucille and Ruby pouring sweet tea at the drinks table, Greg sweeping the barn floor with an industrial-sized broom, and the Pit sisters squabbling about the best strategy to fill up the empty barrels with bags of peanuts. Eighties music piped in from somewhere, and Lexi hummed along to Bryan Adams's "Summer of '69."

Seeing Jo get caught up at the snacks table, chatting away with Mrs. Haversham, Lexi checked her phone again. She hadn't heard from Graham since their video chat earlier in the week, understandably. But she'd assumed he was free today, having finished with his finals yesterday and submitted grades early this morning. She also assumed he would've remembered about Chaynie's invitation to decorate the barn.

She saw an older text from Lenny and one from her dad. Nothing else. Swatting away her disappointment, Lexi popped up from the hay bale when she saw Jo walking across the barn.

"Thanks." Lexi accepted the cold, sweating water bottle and uncapped it. "So, continue your story."

"Which one?" Jo crinkled her brows while taking a long drink of water. She had dressed in shorts, too, and her hair was pulled back in a ponytail.

"About Matthew. Your upcoming date?"

"Oh! That." Jo sat on the hay bale, and Lexi joined her. "Well, we've been talking for almost two weeks, every day. He's not my usual type—which, as you know, is rugged cowboy, rough-around-the-edges, sorta dark and mysterious. Matthew is... polished. Sturdy. He just finished med school, summa cum laude. And he's wearing a suit in his profile pic on the app. I guess I would describe him as nerdy-cute." She curled a stray strand of hair around her ear. "But maybe that's what I need. Someone different from the rest."

"Different can be good."

Jo's eyes darted behind Lexi, then she whispered, "Turn around."

Curious, Lexi craned her neck and saw a figure entering the barn. Because the sun was so bright at the entrance, she had trouble making out who it was. She squinted and raised a hand above her eyes.

It was Graham, approaching the hay bale.

Lexi smiled and stood. "You came."

He looked sheepish. "Sorry I'm late. I hoped you might forgive me when you saw the reason."

Lexi realized what he was holding—three colorful boxes with the Round Rock Donuts logo. "You didn't!"

"I absolutely did. Since it's a weekday, I thought there wouldn't be much of a line, but I was wrong. It was out the door. I stayed patient and was lucky enough to grab one of these." His gaze drifted toward the top box. "Open it."

Jolene had come to stand at Lexi's side and watched her open the box. The smell hit Lexi's senses first—that delectable mingling of sugar, butter, eggs, and yeast. Then, she saw the Texas-sized donut filling the entire box.

"It's all yours," Graham said. "And I got these regular-sized donuts for everyone else." He tapped on the bottom boxes.

"I'll take 'em to the snack table," Jo said, probably in an attempt to give Lexi and Graham some privacy.

Lexi removed the top box while Jo relieved Graham of the other two then darted away. "Look, everyone! Donuts!"

Lexi set down the king-sized donut box on the hay bale while Graham handed her some squished-up napkins he'd also been carrying.

"I can't possibly eat this all by myself." She dusted off her fingers with a napkin then lifted the donut out of its box. "C'mon, you have to help me."

She extended the donut toward him, afraid it might break in half but remembering from past experience that the donut was dense enough to handle almost anything.

Graham shifted to stand apart from her by a couple of feet and grasped the donut's sides while Lexi held onto her end.

"Okay, huge bite. Don't be shy. It's all in with a donut like this." Lexi performed the countdown. "Three... two... one..."

They took a bite together, noses a few inches apart, and chewed, barely containing their laughter. Lexi saw the glazed crumbles on Graham's chin and could feel them on her own. There was no polite way to eat a Texas-sized donut.

"Oh my gosh," Lexi said with her mouth still full. "*So* good!"

Graham nodded, still chewing, and helped her guide the rest of the donut safely back into its box. He grabbed the napkins and handed one to Lexi, who wiped her chin then paused. "Did I get all the crumbs?"

"You did. Me?"

"You're good." Lexi had been so mesmerized by the donut boxes that she hadn't taken in Graham's full appearance—boots peeking out beneath faded denim jeans and a gray T-shirt. "You fit right in. Shelley didn't come?"

"She wanted to but has the sniffles. She didn't want to get anyone sick."

"Sweet of her. Hopefully she and Andrew can make it to the dance."

"Lexi, would you—" Chaynie had approached, staring down at her tablet, then looked up to see Graham. "Oh, sorry. I'm interrupting."

"This is Graham."

"Oh, hi. Greg has mentioned you. Thanks for coming to help out. And for the donuts." She gestured backward toward the snacks table. "I think they're already gone."

"Glad to be here. Put me to work." Graham rubbed his palms together while Lexi stole another pinch off her own donut before closing the lid.

Chaynie consulted her tablet. "How about the stalls? It's not a very glamorous job—we've got them sectioned off for the kids to play games and such. They need some serious sweeping out. Then you'd set up the crates and games too—they're sitting outside each stall."

"Sure, no problem," Lexi said then realized she'd spoken for Graham.

"We can handle that," he said.

"What about me?" Jo asked, joining them once again, holding a half-eaten chocolate donut wedged inside a napkin.

"How about the DJ booth?" Chaynie asked. "It needs to be decorated. There should be some fairy lights sitting in a roll to the side." She pointed toward the back of the barn.

With all the tasks assigned, the group quickly dispersed. Lexi took her donut box along with her then paused to place it discreetly on top of a water cooler hidden underneath the snacks table, where it would hopefully remain until she was ready to leave. "Watch this for me?" she mouthed to Lucille, who gave her a thumbs-up.

Lexi and Graham found the three stalls, along with two of those same dense brooms Greg had been using earlier, and got to work. It was an easy job, almost cathartic and hypnotic, as they swept in long strokes, in opposite directions, meeting in the middle with their thick piles of dust. When they had finished sweeping, collecting, and dumping the dust into a nearby waste can, they set up a crate in the middle, with two smaller ones on each side, then pulled out all the games Chaynie had mentioned. People had donated card games, dice games, and board games for each stall, and all Lexi and Graham had to do was set them up near the crate for the kids to choose from.

By the time they'd swept out the second stall, Lexi's arms were getting tired. After they'd disposed of the dust pile and set out the crates, Graham suggested a break.

"We deserve one. How about some Go Fish?" He picked up a pack of cards.

"You're on."

They sat across from each other as Lexi shuffled the cards.

"How's your dad been doing? I've meant to ask."

"Better than expected." Lexi had visited him just yesterday, in fact, and he'd been in the kitchen, experimenting with a new recipe. "He's even back to work. Only 'light' work, my mom insisted."

Lexi dealt the cards then put the rest of the deck in between them on the crate, trying to recall how to play. She had played a few rounds at the store a couple of years ago with Ruby's granddaughter.

Graham studied his cards and asked Lexi if she had any eights.

"Go fish."

As Graham reached for the center pile, Lexi asked how his finals had gone.

"Good." He studied his cards as Lexi asked for his queens. Graham winced then handed over two of them. "It's always a blur. The last week, I mean. I work intensely for several days in a row—grading, answering panicky student questions, triple-checking my gradebook, entering grades. Hardly a minute to breathe. But then when it's over..." He flipped his wrist slightly. "It's all over. Feels weird, being this free from work."

"How summer used to feel as a kid," Lexi said. "Any sixes?"

"Nope, go fish. Yeah, but it's like a phantom limb. I keep thinking I need to grade something. Or print off tests. Or attend a faculty meeting. It's still there, that pressure. On both shoulders."

Lexi slipped a card from the center deck as Graham's phone rang.

He studied the screen. "Better take this." He clicked the button and held the phone to his ear. "Hey, Dad."

Lexi pretended to study her hand, trying to give Graham some measure of privacy.

"Great. Yeah. I'll sign as soon as she sends them." He rang off and beamed. "I think we just bought ourselves a ranch."

"Already?"

"Yeah, I gave Dad three addresses a couple of weeks ago, properties that Savannah's been showing me. He finally got around to looking at them this morning. He made an offer. About three and a half miles from here. It's got twenty acres with two barns and a ranch house—they need some fixing up, but nothing too dire. Dad thinks we can be up and running early next year."

"I'm so happy for y'all."

"Thanks. Me too. And for the kids the ranch will be helping out. This could become a real legacy for our family." He paused. "Doesn't it seem that things are really happening lately? I mean, your new glassblowing center, now the ranch. Who knows what's next?"

BY THE FINAL STALL, they had the sweeping down to a science. After Graham emptied the dust into the can, Lexi reached for the crates.

"Wait," Graham said. She paused to see his eyes searching the air. "Is that... George Strait?"

Lexi heard the familiar opening chords of "Amarillo by Morning" piping through the speakers.

He extended his hand to her. "Dance with me. I need the practice for Dad's wedding."

"Here? In the middle of a dusty stall?"

He took two steps toward her. "It's not dusty anymore. Spic-and-span. We did our job well."

She abandoned the crates and placed her right hand in his. He pulled her in tight, his arm wrapped around her waist, guiding her around the cramped space in time with the music.

"The professor can dance!" she said, following his lead. They were gliding. "Where'd you learn how to do this?"

Graham spoke softly near her ear without missing a beat. "Mum enrolled me in some two-step dance classes when we came to Texas. I guess she was trying to assimilate me."

As the song continued, Graham would occasionally twirl her in a tight circle then bring her back into his arms. It left Lexi breathless. She could hear him humming along to the melody, and she closed her eyes, carried away.

At the end of the song, Graham tilted her into the crook of his arm in a smooth dip and held her there. She opened her eyes to see him staring at her. He brought her smoothly out of the dip and twirled her once more to the center of the floor, releasing her hand by the tips of his fingers.

Lexi tried to stay cool, to act like she wasn't completely dumbfounded by Graham's flawless confidence on the makeshift dance floor. Up to this point, she had seen him as a somewhat shy, self-effacing guy—qualities she admired. But give him a just-dusted dance floor in the middle of a horse stall with a George Strait song in the background, and any hesitation or shyness in him evaporated.

The next song, an old hit by The Cure, wasn't one you could dance to, so Graham shifted once more into work mode as though he hadn't just blown Lexi's mind. "I'll grab the crates if you'll get those games."

As she moved toward the pile, still feeling the ghost of Graham's confident hand around her waist, all she could think was: *Yes, things are definitely happening...*

Chapter Twenty-three

Graham craned his neck to peer at his reflection in the window of the hundred-year-old downtown Methodist church. He had decided on his navy-blue suit for the rehearsal and the dinner to follow, with a burgundy tie his mum had given to him on his first day of teaching. He adjusted it, wishing she were here. But that would be weird. His father was getting remarried to another woman tomorrow—which was also, truthfully, weird.

Even as much as Graham had come to terms with the remarriage over the past several weeks, and even as well as he genuinely liked Beth, there remained an uneasiness inside, from that little-boy part of Graham who felt a tangible missing piece every time his mum's image grazed his thoughts.

But today is for Dad, he reminded himself, shaking off the maudlin thoughts. He had to be mature and brave, especially for Shelley. This was a happy occasion, a day for new beginnings, the creation of a new family unit. Of sorts.

Opening the heavy wooden door, Graham remembered he was a few minutes early and slowed his pace as he walked along the slate stone foyer and toward the elegant double doors that led inside the sanctuary. He'd been here for worship services but never a wedding or rehearsal. His footsteps echoed in the nearly empty space as he entered the grand sanctuary, its walls lined in rich wood, with matching beams overhead, and a pulpit area overshadowed by a tall wooden cross hanging from above. He heard some chatter, and his eyes landed on his sister, standing up front, speaking animatedly with the minister and Beth.

Graham noticed his father sitting three rows from the front, staring at his phone. As he got closer, Graham realized his father was wearing earbuds and listening to an NBA game. Usually, Graham would have bypassed him, not wishing to interrupt. But today, emboldened by his chat with Lexi a few nights ago, Graham slid into the pew beside his father. It took a moment for his father to notice anyone else in his presence, and when he did, he looked up from the phone.

"Hey, son."

"What's the score?" Graham pointed toward the screen, not caring who was winning but knowing it was the smoothest way to enter into conversation.

"77, 79. Chicago."

Graham watched his father's eyes return to the screen. "Dad, I have something for you."

"Huh?" His father's gaze remained on the phone, and after the shot was made, he pulled away again. Graham wondered if Beth already knew about his father's affinity for all things sports and the life she was *really* getting into with him.

"This. It's for you," Graham said, holding out a package. Earlier this morning, an idea had occurred to him, and he'd driven to Henry's jewelry store in search of the perfect item. "A wedding gift."

"You didn't have to—"

"I wanted to. I thought it might look good in your new place. Maybe the mantel?"

His father set the phone to his side—screen facing up—and accepted the gift, raising the lid to see the engraved clock inside.

"Very nice. Beth will love it." He closed the lid. "Thank you."

"I'm happy for you both. Glad to be a part of this day." Graham's heart beat faster. He wasn't used to showing any level of true vulnerability with his dad.

His father peered down at the closed box and grazed it with his thumbs. "You know, I wasn't sure how you—or your sister—would handle all this." He gestured outward toward the altar, his eyes firmly set on the gift box. "It happened so fast. And even though your mother's been gone for many years..." He removed his earbud and raised his clear brown eyes toward Graham. "I assumed you were okay with the wedding. But I never really asked, did I?"

Graham placed a hand on his father's arm. "No. But I am. Okay with it. I want you to be happy."

His father nodded. "We never talked about her, your mum. I sort of left you and your sister on your own. To sort things out. I... didn't know how to help. Or what to say."

"I know." Graham squeezed his father's arm, remembering all the times his father had buried himself in work or stayed late at the office. Even back then, Graham knew his father was doing his own version of grieving.

"I'm sorry."

Graham swallowed hard. He didn't know if he'd ever heard those words come from his father's lips. "Thanks," he whispered.

His father placed his free hand on Graham's knee and firmly patted it twice. He breathed in, discreetly wiped his eyes, then cleared his throat. "So, tell me about things. You're finished with the semester?"

"Yep." Graham moved his hand back to his own lap. "Grades are in the bank, sealed up tight. Summer has officially started."

"How will you fill the days?" In the past, the comment would've been more like a couched insult—*You need to work; it's lazy for you, a grown man, to be off during the summer*. But after his father's rare apology and open demeanor, Graham chose to give him the benefit of the doubt.

"I'll probably teach a session of summer school." Graham shifted in the pew, marveling that his father had resisted the temptation to glance at his phone to see the most recent score. "But I've also got this... project." He hadn't intended on sharing it with his dad—or anyone else, other than Lexi—but since it was out there, he had to follow through. "I might be writing a new book."

His father's eyes widened. "What about?"

Graham told him about his original idea from a few months before, then the more recent inspiration of Lexi's great-grandmother's wartime experiences. As he explained, his defensive wall evaporated. He wasn't certain whether this easy level of communication with his father would become permanent or if it was merely due to the intense emotion that arose with almost any wedding. Or maybe Beth had had an incredibly unexpected and positive influence over his father during the past few months. Whatever the case, Graham hoped it was a promising start toward something lasting.

HOW MANY TIMES IN YOUR life can you describe an evening as "magical"?

It looked like a scene from a movie, where everything was carefully planned and selected down to the final detail. The venue for the wedding reception emanated charm and elegance, invoking a feast for the senses. Beth had chosen The Tavern, an upscale Irish pub on the outskirts of downtown Austin, to celebrate her brand-new marriage to Graham's father. Lexi had eaten there many times over the years, especially since her father had become an investor a decade ago. But she hadn't visited since the recent makeover, which included an elegant overhaul of the outdoor patio—which used to house a lush, spacious lawn with wooden benches and umbrellas. In the past few months, the space had been completely transformed into a massive deck with room enough for a live band, dance floor, and tables, all covered by a white tent. The venue had a new reputation as the perfect setting for graduation parties, special birthdays, and wedding receptions.

Lexi sat at one of the white cloth-covered tables, sandwiched between Graham and Shelley and across from the bride and groom, who were whispering to each other. Easy jazz floated from the band across the dance floor, and miniature white lights dotted the manicured topiaries in every corner. A bright chandelier lit the entire space from above. *Magical.*

Lexi focused again on her plate and selected another delicious crab cake. She noticed Shelley's empty plate. "Do you want this one?"

Shelley was dressed in a lovely blue taffeta that matched her eyes. "Please!" She held out her cupped hand. "*So* yummy!"

"They definitely are." After passing it to her, Lexi selected another cake and brought it to her lips, trying not to get any crumbs on her peach dress, the one she'd bought yesterday for tonight's occasion. She ate the cake in two bites.

"Did you try the steak skewers?" Graham asked. "They're my favorite." He held one up and moved it to Lexi's plate. "Take it. I have plenty."

She removed a piece of steak with her fingers and took a bite. "So good!"

As the song changed over, Lexi twisted her head around to view the scene—guests eating and drinking, laughing, chatting, and bobbing their heads along to Sinatra's classic "Under My Skin."

Lexi's phone buzzed. It was the alarm she had set half an hour before. She leaned toward Graham and whispered, "It's time." He had asked her to nudge him thirty minutes into the meal so he could stand up and give his best-man speech.

"Already?" He patted his chin with his napkin. "Okay. Here goes nothing."

He rose with his champagne glass and walked over to his father. After waiting out the last several seconds of the song, Graham tapped a fork against the glass and watched the guests speak in hushed tones as they turned in his direction.

"Hey, everyone. Thank you for coming out tonight to celebrate this evening with a very special couple."

It sounded to Lexi like Graham had done this a million times before—even though he'd confessed earlier that he was incredibly nervous about the speech. His words flowed effortlessly, and he even managed a couple of jokes that received a few chuckles from the audience. *Short and sweet.* That had been Lexi's recommendation to him.

After the toast, while Graham made his way back to Lexi, the singer approached the stage and launched into a relaxed, airy rendition of "The Way You Look Tonight."

"I love this song," Lexi whispered.

Graham must've heard, because instead of sitting back down, he extended a hand. "Shall we?"

The bride and groom had already done their first dance, so the floor was open to all the guests.

Lexi joined Graham on the outskirts of the dance floor with the other couples—including Shelley and her boyfriend. Graham wasn't as technically precise as he'd been inside the barn's stall, dancing to George Strait. Instead, he held Lexi tight and swayed to the music, careful not to bump into other dancers.

At some point during the song, Lexi rested her head on Graham's shoulder. She was comfortable. Safe and happy. She couldn't recall the last time she'd danced to Sinatra under a white tent with twinkly lights everywhere. Maybe never. Most of the weddings she'd attended after college—as well as her own—had been more rustic affairs, with beer, barbecue dinners, and line dances.

A night like this was a rare treat for Lexi. Since taking over Gigi's store, she'd spent most all her days and nights worrying over the business or brainstorming about future profits or finishing endless paperwork. She'd never known that running a business could be so all-consuming and often wondered if that had been Gigi's experience as well.

But Lexi's mind wasn't anywhere else but on the dance floor tonight, in Graham's arms. She released any distractions or worries and let herself *be*. In the moment. With him.

As the song shifted to the more upbeat "You Make Me Feel So Young," Lexi lifted her head and watched as Graham's father and Beth twirled nearby. Their wedding, an hour before at the Methodist church, had been subtle and understated but beautiful. Graham had worried about Lexi being on her own. "I'm standing up front with my dad," he'd told her with a wince, minutes before the ceremony began. "And Shelley too. I mean, here I invite you to a wedding and then leave you to sit with strangers..." He'd been eyeing the rows of guests to see where she might feel the most comfortable.

"I don't mind," Lexi had said. "I'll find a spot somewhere."

That had seemed to ease Graham's conscience, and after giving her a quick kiss on the cheek—along with a "Did I tell you how gorgeous you look?"—Graham had disappeared to perform his prewedding best-man duties.

Lexi had scanned the guests on the groom's side and discovered Shelley's boyfriend, Andrew, sitting beside Mrs. Sherman, the events director at Shelley's place. When they spotted her, they waved her over enthusiastically.

During the ceremony, Lexi's eyes had drifted toward Graham, dashing in his black formal suit. More than once, his gaze had caught hers too. The first time it had happened, she'd looked shyly away, down at her lap. But when it happened again, her eyes had stayed locked on him. He'd given her a half grin then moved his attention back to the bride and groom exchanging their vows.

Lexi was snapped out of her memory by the crowd's applause as the singer finished the song and moved on to the next. Expecting a third dance, Lexi placed her hand on Graham's arm, but he took her hand in his, squeezed it, and said, "I want to show you something."

Intrigued, she let him guide her through the dancers, past the tables, and outside the tent to a stone pathway that opened up into a dense forest lit up by fairy lights on tall branches. Looking above, she could see the night sky, punctuated with stars and the hint of an almost-full moon.

"What is this?" She took in a breath and absorbed her surroundings, still grasping Graham's hand.

"The tavern owners bought the vacant lot next door and carved a path through it. A sort of enchanted garden."

They strolled farther into the forest, and Lexi noticed wrought-iron benches spaced out on either side of the slate-rock footpath lined with an array of colorful flowers and illuminated by comforting ground lighting. Some quirky lawn ornaments and figurines, resembling fairies and other woodland creatures, completed the effect.

"It's a fairy tale," she whispered, swinging his hand gently with hers, feeling the cool night air on her flushed cheeks.

"I'm glad you said yes to tonight. The wedding, I mean." Graham paused on the footpath and turned to face her. He rubbed his hands softly on her bare arms while the fading chords from the band floated out of the tent.

"It's been a special night."

Graham lifted one hand to stroke her cheek, and in that moment, she knew he was going to kiss her. And she wanted him to, more than anything she'd wanted in a long time. As he leaned in, Lexi closed her eyes and tipped her mouth to meet his. His lips were soft and warm, and a rush of adrenaline coursed through her body, intoxicating her every pore. As the kiss deepened, she raised a hand to touch his neck then his clean-shaven jaw. She felt his arm move around her waist, bringing her even closer.

Somewhere inside her heightened senses, she heard the echo of shrieks and giggles coming from nearby. Two little girls whizzed past them, nearly knocking them over and ending the kiss prematurely. Graham had to hang on to Lexi's waist to prevent her from toppling over.

The little girls hadn't noticed the kissing couple until after they'd pulled apart, and out of breath, they told the couple in unison, "Cake cutting! Cake cutting! It's time!" Lexi recognized one of them as the flower girl from the wedding ceremony.

As quickly as they'd entered the garden, the girls swirled around and whisked past Graham and Lexi again, one of them shouting, "Tag! You're it!"

Graham ran a hand through his thick hair with a sly grin. "Well, that was quite the interruption."

Lexi bit her lower lip, still tasting Graham's kiss. "To be continued?"

"Definitely."

AFTER THE CAKE CUTTING, Graham offered to grab slices for Lexi and Shelley.

"Dance again!" Shelley said to Lexi while they waited at the table.

"I think the singer is taking a break, resting her voice."

Lexi heard a buzz and shifted to see her phone, face down, beside her discarded napkin. She didn't remember leaving her phone out—she'd assumed it was tucked away safely in her purse.

She flipped it over and realized it wasn't her phone after all. It was Graham's—they both had the same slender black case. But before she could discreetly flip the phone back over, she caught a glimpse of the screen—and the name of the person buzzing Graham. *Theresa.*

Lexi froze, unable to look away from the first few words of the message that showed through on the Welcome screen. *Let's meet at that coffee place on Vine and Front. I've been wanting to...* and then the text cut off. It would require a password to see the rest.

Lexi placed the phone face down, exactly where it had originally lain, and set both of her hands in her lap. The room went quiet as her thoughts piled on top of each other, a train wreck she was powerless to stop. She couldn't help but jump to the worst-case scenario: *Theresa and Graham are seeing each other again.* Maybe they never really stopped.

Her brain played devil's advocate with itself, tried to slow down and examine the other possibilities in a rational manner. But the other, more salacious conclusions won out.

The text clearly wasn't a first text, where Theresa, after weeks of zero contact, had approached Graham cold tonight. The wording seemed a continuation of an ongoing chain, a back-and-forth conversation, as though a meeting had already been discussed between them at an earlier point.

Lexi studied her hands in her lap. Her initial gut instinct, weeks ago, had been to avoid any romance with Graham, to protect herself from falling for him. *He was a rebound.* And apparently, she had been right. He wasn't over his ex, so how could he realistically begin anything new with Lexi? He wasn't free, not yet. Or else Theresa wouldn't be asking for a meeting. There was still something between them.

Lexi should never have let down her guard. She'd worked hard to prevent this very scenario, but it had happened anyway. She knew how it would end. Whenever someone's heart was divided between two people, one of them was bound to get hurt. And in the past, that one had always been Lexi.

"So stupid," she muttered under her breath.

"What?" Shelley asked beside her.

"Oh, nothing. I'm only talking to myself."

"I do that lots!"

Lexi was jarred back into reality, back to the beautiful lights and the flowing champagne and the sound of the mellow saxophone. It was a fantasy, all of it. Including the kiss in the garden.

Clutching her purse and scooting back her chair, Lexi eyed Graham walking up to the table, balancing four slices of cake.

"Ladies' room?" he asked. "I think it's to the right, inside."

"No. Um, I have to..." Lexi hadn't thought this far ahead, to what would happen next. She couldn't stay at the table, making casual chitchat with Graham, or spend another song in his arms. It would be rude to leave too abruptly—but, she reasoned, the meal had been eaten, the dances had been danced, and the cake had been cut. The evening was coming to an end anyway. An idea came to her. "I have a headache. I need to get going." It wasn't a total lie—she could sense the throbbing at her temples intensify.

Graham frowned and set down the slices. He gently grasped one of her arms and bent down a few inches, eye to eye, and searched her face. "Can I do anything? You want me to find some aspirin?"

"No, no." Even in her fog of frustration, she could admire his caring side, and it made the pain even sharper. "I need to go home. Close my eyes, sleep it off. Nothing else works."

"Let me take you," he said, insistent.

"No. You stay here with your family. I'll be fine. I brought my own car." It was oddly fortuitous that when Graham had offered to pick her up in Morgan's Grove, Lexi had insisted on taking her own car. Graham was already tasked with carting Shelley and Andrew from place to place, and Lexi hadn't wanted to add more complications to his overly busy agenda.

"I promise. I'll be fine," she said again. She squeezed his hand and looked away, unable to continue seeing the confusion behind his eyes.

"Leaving, Lexi?" Shelley's eyebrows crinkled as she stood.

"Yes, hon. I'm sorry. But this was an enchanting night, wasn't it?" Lexi reached down for a tight squeeze. "You take care, okay?" she whispered into Shelley's ear, then she threaded her way through the tables, toward the pub's interior, craving the comforting escape of her car and of Morgan's Grove.

Chapter Twenty-four

Lexi had assumed the fifty-minute drive from the restaurant to her house would center her, calm her emotions, offer some room for rational thought. But all it did was intensify the doubts and second-guessing about Theresa's message. Through the bright head-lights, Lexi could envision the text, the wording. In spite of herself, she imagined their conversation, pre-text. *How far had it gone? How far would it continue to go?* And then she asked the bigger question: *Why, if he was still hung up on another person, did he kiss me tonight?*

Reaching her house with its familiar gables, she saw Jolene's car parked in the driveway. "She came," Lexi whispered, turning off the ignition.

The minute before leaving the restaurant, Lexi had called Jo, not knowing whether she was on a date or had made other plans. She'd gotten Jo's voicemail and spilled everything on it. She wondered if she was even making sense, remembering that her cousin's voicemail account was set to cut messages off after two minutes. Lexi man-aged to let her story tumble out, including the kiss, the text, and the headache excuse, right before the beep sounded and rudely cut her off.

Opening the screen door, Lexi was greeted by Bailey, baying ex-citedly, front paws bouncing off the floor with each new howl.

"Hey, boy!" Lexi emptied her hands of her purse and keys then stooped over to take his head in both her hands. "You're a sight for sore eyes!" She nuzzled his face with her own, wishing she had his capacity for joy in any and all situations and remembering Graham's comment from the other night. "A dog's life."

That, more than anything, struck her—although they hadn't been romantically involved until tonight, she and Graham had grown steadily closer every day, through visits and late-night video calls and chatty texts. She had invested time in him—in them—and had felt the relationship tangibly expanding, day by day. She knew his favorite fruit was tangerines and that his guilty pleasure was dancing to ABBA songs (his mum was a huge fan) and that he sometimes got nervous speaking in front of his colleagues. He knew that her least favorite song in the world was "All the Single Ladies" and that she hated the smell of boiled eggs and that she secretly loved binge-watching corny eighties movies.

But during all those moments, all those weeks of learning more about each other, had he been equally invested in Theresa too? Had he been torn between them the entire time, vacillating back and forth between his feelings for two women—intrigued by a new possible relationship with Lexi but also pulled backward by his history with Theresa? Had he ever fully closed his heart to his ex? *So many questions...*

Jo called out from the kitchen, "I'm almost ready. Meet you at the couches!"

When Lexi entered the living room, with Bailey tagging along behind, a familiar scent hit her—chocolate chip cookies. She kicked off her too-tight low heels and took in the comforting room in front of her: a blazing fire, the glow of lamps lighting up the corners, a velvety throw blanket crumpled over one half of the sofa, and a wide array of snacks scattered on the coffee table, including all of Lexi's favorites: tortilla chips, Milk Duds, Cheez-Its, powdered donuts, and fresh popcorn.

"All this and cookies too," Jo said, reading Lexi's mind. She entered the room with a plate piled high as Lexi sank into the sofa cushions and gathered the blanket around her bare legs. She didn't have the energy to traipse upstairs and change into pajamas, as much as she wanted to. So the fancy peach wedding dress would have to remain.

"I can't believe you did all this." Lexi set her purse on the table and selected a cookie off the top of Jo's plate. The first bite told her it was Gigi's recipe, the one she'd made so often in Jo's and Lexi's childhoods. "When you didn't respond, I thought maybe you hadn't heard my message. Or maybe you had a date."

Jo waved a dismissive hand, grabbed a cookie, then set down the plate. "I'm completely dateless tonight. I heard your message. Time was ticking—I only had a few minutes to head over and mix up the dough."

"Thank you." Lexi finished the cookie then dusted her fingers.

Jo placed her free hand on Lexi's knee, on top of the blanket. "Talk to me."

Lexi shook her head, fighting off tears. "I'm numb, honestly. I had the whole trip home to process everything, but I'm back to square one, so confused. I don't know what to make of it."

"Which part?"

"Any of it. The dancing, the kiss, the text. Everything's blurring together."

Bailey's head popped up between Jo's and Lexi's knees out of nowhere.

"Where did you come from?" Jo asked, patting him.

"I think he can sense my anxiety," Lexi said.

"And my cookie." Jo diverted it away from his nose.

"You wanna come up?" Lexi patted the cushion between them. Bailey lunged upward, and Lexi caught him to help his hind legs finish the leap. He made a circle between them then settled into the cushion, placing his head on Lexi's knee as Jolene finished her cookie. Lexi scratched his ears and continued. "It was emotional whiplash. I mean, one minute, we're dancing and kissing, and I'm feeling free and happy and excited about what it all means. And I'm even sort of proud of myself, because my guard, at this point, is lowered *way* down—which is hard for me. Let go, lose some control, don't over-think. And the next minute... there's Theresa's name, right on his screen."

"So, you never told him you saw the text?"

"It didn't even cross my mind to. I sort of... froze. My brain couldn't function. And my main instinct was to get out of there."

"Fight or flight."

"Yeah, exactly." Lexi heard a vibration from deep within her purse on the table. She peered at Jo for guidance. "Should I look?"

"Up to you."

It would nag at Lexi all evening if she didn't peek. She saw a text from Graham, kind and caring but confused: *Hey, Lex. Hoping you're okay. You left so suddenly. Text me back and let me know you made it safe.*

Lexi read it aloud then lowered the phone. "I don't want to re-spond. But if I ignore this..."

"He'll text again. And keep worrying."

Lexi nodded then typed her reply: *Made it home. Thanks for checking. I'll be okay.*

She slipped the phone back into her purse.

"What's bugging you the most?" Jo shifted her feet underneath her.

Lexi leaned her shoulder against the cushion. "That Theresa's message wasn't brand-new to him. That they'd been talking before tonight."

"What did it say, exactly?"

"*Meet me at that coffee place. Vine and something.* Which tells me she's been texting him recently. Or all along? It wasn't a 'Hey, I haven't seen or talked to you in six weeks, so let me awkwardly tip-toe into a fresh conversation.' It was an in-the-middle-of-a-conversa-tion text. Maybe they never really got over each other. I thought she was part of his past. He *told* me she was—he said that they hadn't talked since the breakup. But there she was tonight, asking him to meet." She looked across at Jo, the hurt bubbling up through her voice. "Was he lying to me all this time?"

"Maybe it was more of a 'failed to mention it.' Have you thought about this—what if it's all her? That it's all happening on Theresa's end, and he's rejected her advances?"

"Even so, why wouldn't he have mentioned it to me? I thought we were closer than that. We've both talked about our exes before."

"Well, you weren't romantically linked until tonight—the dancing, the kissing. It's not like you were a couple and he was blatantly cheating on you."

"I considered that in the car. He didn't owe me anything about Theresa. But I would've still liked a heads-up. I just can't shake the feeling that he was keeping it from me deliberately. It feels sneaky." Lexi stroked Bailey's fur. "Sorry, I'm going in complete circles here."

"Will you ever tell him? That you saw the text?"

"I guess I'll have to, eventually."

"Don't hate me for saying this"—Jo held up a hand—"but I think he deserves to explain. You rushed out of there tonight based on a whole lot of presumptions. You didn't even see the whole text string. Just a few words of hers. You need more information before coming to a solid conclusion."

"My head agrees with you. But the disappointed part of my heart is still bugged that they're even talking, especially when he told me they weren't. I've never been that friendly with my own exes, that we'd meet after we're broken up. It means Theresa wants to get back together. What else could it mean? The bottom line is—if he's not over her, then how can he possibly have room enough for a new start with me? I don't want to be anyone's second choice."

"I know. But maybe he's too nice to ignore her, and she can't take the hint?"

"All these 'maybes.'" Lexi smirked. "Sounds like you're on his side."

"I'm on yours. Always. But... I've seen the way you talk about him. You light up from the inside. He makes you happy."

"An hour ago, I would've agreed with you." She felt his kiss on her lips again. "I'm mad at myself for getting carried away tonight. But there was something about the atmosphere—the wedding, the music, the twinkly lights, the pretty outfits, the secluded garden. Jo, it was perfect. Until that stupid text. I'm being overly dramatic—leaving the reception early, not explaining why. But tonight was this weird betrayal from someone I really trusted. And it hit right at my weak spot. I've been cheated on before, lied to before—"

"Neil."

"Exactly. And I promised myself I would never be put in that position again. But tonight, I was sideswiped and surprised. I let my guard down too soon. And I shouldn't have. Not yet."

Jo's voice softened. "It's hard to control the heart, Lex. No matter how we try. Promise me that you won't lock it all the way up where Graham's concerned."

"I'll try. But that's the best I can do." She placed a hand on her forehead. "The irony is that I actually do have a full-blown headache now. I'm not used to all this drama."

"I've got a cure for that too!" Jo hopped up and scrambled back into the kitchen, returning with an aspirin bottle and glass of water. "You'll be right as rain in no time." She unscrewed the cap, tapped two pills into Lexi's open palm, then joined her again on the couch and leaned forward to scoop up a bowl of overflowing popcorn while Lexi swallowed the aspirin.

"No, you don't, Bailey." Jo chided him playfully, watching his head rise and his beagle nose sniff strongly at her popcorn bowl. "This is not for dogs."

Bailey gave up and sank his head back down on the blanket.

"Well, nothing is going to be solved tonight. And besides, I'm sick of talking about me." Lexi grabbed a bowl of her own. The popcorn smelled delicious. "Distract me. We didn't get to talk about last night. You never told me what happened with Mr. Blind Date."

"That's because there's nothing *to* tell. He was the total opposite of his profile picture—balding, shorter than me, with this explosive laugh. You know that guy in *Back to the Future*? Michael J. Fox's dad, in the flashback parts?"

"Yeah, the nerdy guy?"

"Blind Date's laugh was worse than that. I nearly died of embarrassment every time he found something funny. He did this weird snort-grunt thing." She imitated it and nearly spit out her popcorn.

Lexi giggled, imagining the scene. "That's horrible."

"I rushed the waiter and even rejected dessert and another drink. Couldn't get out of there fast enough." Jo raised an index finger. "In fact, I went home and promptly canceled my online dating apps."

"All four?"

"All *five*! I've had enough. You're looking at an officially single, off-the-market, on-my-own, not-looking, independent gal."

Lexi knew it wasn't true—that the loss of the dopamine hit of having *five* dating apps would soon gnaw away at her cousin, and she would give in and sign up again. But for tonight, they were two completely single girls, attempting to enjoy that status in spite of what their hearts were telling them.

At least if Lexi had to nurture her own bruised heart, she could do so with chocolate chip cookies, buttery popcorn, a crackling fire, and the best company a girl could ask for.

GRAHAM ALWAYS LOVED the idea of summer break—of finally having time to keep dentist appointments or deep-clean his entire apartment or binge-watch a series he'd been waiting to see. But the reality was different. He quickly missed having a schedule, a routine, somewhere to be every day, classes to prepare for. And each summer break, inevitably, he would email his department chair to see if there were any second-session summer classes he could teach. In fact, he had clicked "send" on that email an hour ago.

At least he'd had the barn decorating and his father's wedding to distract him last week. But two days later, he found himself sitting in his half-dark apartment with his laptop, hearing the annoying tick of a wall clock, struggling to work on his new book. Even that—an exciting and productive activity to occupy his time during summer—had proved to be a challenge.

He shut his laptop, set it aside, and drew out his phone. *No new messages.* He knew the primary reason for his restlessness. It wasn't the blank summer days or the writer's block. It was Lexi. Ever since Saturday night, when she'd abruptly darted away from the reception, Graham hadn't been able to force her from his mind. His last two texts to her had received no response. At first, he had believed her headache excuse—that perhaps the loud music or the tent full of people or the bustling activities had been the cause. But as the days dragged on, he wondered if he was being purposely ignored. Lexi's last text to him, Sunday afternoon, mentioned having "a busy week ahead." Possible code for "I'm distancing myself." She was politely preparing Graham for her future nonresponses to his texts under the guise of being "busy." It felt predesigned.

Since the reception, Graham had run over the events of that evening in his mind more than once and decided that it was the kiss that had triggered the possibly fake headache. He had taken a risk when he'd pulled her into the forest, when he'd paused on the walkway and leaned in toward her. But he hadn't been able to resist. He'd wanted to kiss her since he first saw her arrive at the church in that beautiful dress, with her hair pulled back and a few strands framing her face. She looked like a dream. Everything he ever wanted. And when the moment was right, when he could sense Lexi's openness and acceptance, he went for it. Leaned in, kissed her gently—and she had reciprocated. It wasn't his imagination. She had participated, lingered inside the kiss with him, until they were interrupted by the little girls' ruckus.

It wasn't until later, when he'd disappeared to fetch some cake, that Lexi's entire demeanor had changed, one moment to the next. When he came to her side, she'd seemed distracted, even agitated, and had stood immediately. She wouldn't even make steady eye contact with him.

When she left, the cheer and festivity went out of the tent with her, a brilliant sunset that turned dark too quickly. Graham spent the rest of the evening concerned about her health—*Was it a migraine? Should she be driving in that condition?*—and the next day wondering if it wasn't something else. He had even texted Shelley to see if maybe anything might've been said or done during those spare few minutes he was absent from the table, or whether Shelley had observed any odd changes in Lexi. But Shelley couldn't think of anything. She said Lexi was fine.

Which meant that the headache was an excuse to escape. Which also meant Graham had pushed too hard with the kiss. He knew that she was leery of a new relationship. She'd had a rough marriage and divorce not that long ago and was admittedly overly cautious with her heart. Graham didn't know what a divorce was like—an ordinary breakup was hard enough, grueling enough. But one that took place after vows were exchanged and a future was planned, maybe with a family in mind? *Unthinkable.* He knew friends who waited years in between marriages, vowing that "divorce will never happen to me again." They couldn't go through the pain a second time.

So perhaps Lexi *had* wanted the kiss in the moment it happened but then regretted it immediately afterward. It was the only logical explanation.

Graham had spent yesterday chiding himself about it, wishing he'd let Lexi be the one to initiate whenever she was ready. But he'd gotten caught up in the romance of the evening and followed his instincts to kiss her. And it might've cost him everything.

Against his better judgment, he typed out a new text to her: *Hope your Monday is going well. Is the barn dance still on for tonight? Shelley's looking forward to it.*

He read it then deleted it, letter by letter, watching the text disappear. No. He would let Lexi make the next move, give her space, respect her boundaries. It wasn't what he wanted, backing away from her when he felt like doing the opposite, but at this point, it might be the one thing he could do to salvage the remains of their friendship. Hopefully, they still had that.

A SHAFT OF ORANGE LIGHT pierced through the slats of a nearby window blind and onto Lexi's pad as she scribbled a note in her "pro" column. The jangle of the store's front bell startled her, and she swiveled on the vinyl-covered stool to crane her neck and see Ruby entering the building.

"What are you doing here?" they said in unison then chuckled.

Ruby came closer, leaning against the empty stool beside Lexi at the candy bar. "I'm here to borrow a hat. For tonight's dance." Lexi allowed her workers to borrow vintage hats from the store as long as they returned them the next morning.

Lexi studied Ruby. Something was different—and not just tonight. Lately, Ruby had been fluffing up her gray hair and tucking the sides behind her ears, as well as wearing darker lipstick along with subtle eye makeup. She looked fantastic. This evening, she wore a long, silky scarf that hung effortlessly down both sides of her blouse, touching the denim skirt she wore.

"And you?" Ruby asked.

"Oh, I'm just... brainstorming." Lexi raised her notepad a couple of inches to show her.

"For the store?"

"Nope, something... different." She hadn't told anyone about the ideas rolling around her head ever since she'd left Mr. Fisher's house last week, clutching Gigi's letters. But once the ideas had taken hold, they'd refused to leave. "Ruby, what would you think if I... tried to get some of Gigi's letters published?" She chewed at her lip and watched Ruby's expression for a hint of disapproval.

Instead, Ruby raised both eyebrows in consideration then said, "I think it's a *very* interesting idea." She peeked at Lexi's notepad. "Pros and cons. So what are your cons?"

Lexi hadn't gotten to that column yet, but she already knew the cons by heart—which was why she hadn't told anyone about the idea. She turned to face Ruby fully, placing her hands in her lap and tapping her pen against her thigh. "Well, there's the whole privacy issue. The fact that Gigi carefully hid away James's letters. So—I assume she would've done the same with her own letters if she'd had possession of them. Also, she never told *any*one in the family about them. Not even Mother. Or me. Or you!"

"True."

"Would she want the world to see? Wouldn't this be a betrayal of some kind on my part?"

"Honey, you could never purposely betray your Gigi. Your heart is too pure. She knew that about you, and I have no doubt she would trust your judgment if she were here with us. These letters are precious to you, and frankly, they belong to you now—yours to decide what to do with. This might sound sort of out there"—Ruby made a loopy gesture with her hand—"but I think those letters are in your possession for a reason. It's like your Gigi wanted you to find them. Maybe even helped you find them."

"I've thought the same thing."

"Well, then. If those letters can benefit the world in some way, I think you should seriously consider it."

"They're so raw and heartfelt. You should've seen the students when I introduced James's letters a couple of weeks ago. Those young people were captivated. And I keep thinking of what Gigi said to me, years ago. About this store, these treasures she spent most of her life collecting and selling. She said that antiques and artifacts are 'nature's way of documenting that we were alive,' that our time on earth was meaningful to someone else. And that we won't be forgotten."

Ruby smiled a pretty, lipsticked smile and squeezed Lexi's free hand. "Honey, I think that's as lovely a reason as any to consider publication. With her stamp of approval. She said it herself." She adjusted her scarf with a side glance. "Now. I think you're here, in this dark, closed store of yours, in order to avoid something."

"What do you mean?"

"I've noticed it the past two days. You're antsy. More than usual. Let's see... You stayed here late last night to do inventory when Ariel had already volunteered. And you were here this morning an hour early—before me!—clearing out a closet that could easily wait. You even brewed a pot of coffee and brought donuts."

"I had insomnia. Figured I'd make the most out of it. A spurt of energy."

"You also went to *two* estate sales yesterday—back to back—even though you mentioned the store didn't have room to add to its inventory."

"But I got those two vintage dresses. And they didn't take up much space. Got them at a great price."

"Honey." Ruby drew her face closer to Lexi's. "I've known you since you were born. What's eating away at you?" Her voice softened. "Is it your father? Has he had a relapse? Or is the store in some sort of trouble that you're not telling me about? Time to spill."

Lexi's first instinct was to brush off Ruby's worries and make up an excuse on the spot. But she knew Ruby wouldn't buy it, and besides, she wouldn't stop pushing until she wriggled the truth out of Lexi.

So Lexi caved. "No, on both counts. Daddy's getting stronger every day, and you've seen the accounts. The store is thriving. It's... personal."

"It's Graham." Ruby nodded. "I suspected as much. But—you told me you had a lovely time at the wedding."

"I did. It was a wonderful evening. But I left something out." Lexi shifted on the stool and blew out a sigh before recounting—as succinctly as possible—the Theresa text, the fake headache, the talk with Jolene afterward. "I'm not proud of this, but I've been sort of... ghosting Graham. You know, ignoring his texts—"

"Honey, I know what ghosting is. I'm not *that* ancient." Ruby smirked.

"It's immature, and I hate myself for it. But I don't know what to say to him."

"You could tell him the truth. Everything you've just told me. After all this time you've spent building up a friendship between the two of you, doesn't he deserve at least that? A chance to explain?"

"Jo told me the same thing."

"Wise woman."

"It's just... All these years since Neil, I've been playing it safe, protecting myself. And it's worked so far—my heart hasn't been trampled on."

"Maybe. But it also hasn't soared. I've learned an important lesson throughout my years—not only in my own life but watching other people live theirs too. And I've discovered that if you walk through life in defensive mode, afraid of risks, you'll never get wounded. But then you'll also never experience love—the kind that surprises you, the kind that leaves you breathless. If you leap into life instead of shying away from it, the most amazing things can happen. Aren't you wondering what you might be missing out on? But the bigger question is... Do you think your Gigi lived life that way? Guarded, timid? Afraid of getting hurt?"

Lexi knew the answer in a heartbeat. *Absolutely not.* Gigi took huge risks with her heart twice—once through a wartime romance, defying her father, knowing that James could die and she could end up heartbroken. But she loved him anyway. And when her heart was broken by his death, she didn't cut herself off from another love, didn't use James as an excuse to step out of life and stop trying. Painful as it was, Gigi opened up her heart again and built a life with someone new—had children, created a future.

Allowing tears to sting her eyes, Lexi shook her head. "No, she didn't. She lived her life boldly." Lexi recalled something very specific her great-grandmother had once told her that she hadn't thought about in years. "When I was at her bedside, the day before she passed on, Gigi squeezed my hand, looked me straight in the eye without blinking, and whispered, 'No regrets.' Those were her final words to me. She didn't elaborate, and I could see she was too tired to be pressed. I've always wondered what, exactly, she had in mind when she said it. Was she talking about herself—that she had lived her life without any regrets? Or was the message meant for me? Advice about how I should live my own life?"

"And what do you think now?"

"That maybe it was both. Back then, I didn't know about the existence of James. But now, I think it's possible she was remembering him at the end. That she had no regrets about risking her heart for love, even though it ended too soon. And I think she was telling me that too. Not to have stacked up any regrets when I reached my own end."

Ruby lifted her hand to stroke Lexi's sideswept bangs. "Another message from beyond?"

"That's what it feels like."

Ruby's phone jangled a tune. "Ooh! That's my timer." She patted down both her skirt pockets in search of the phone. "I set it to remind myself to get my tush into gear. I can't be late. Henry's picking me up at seven." She clicked off the timer to make the jangling stop. "Aren't you going to the barn dance? It should be fun! Everyone in Morgan's Grove will be there."

Lexi had toyed with skipping the dance—not feeling up to a couple-filled danceathon at the moment. But Jo would be there, and they'd promised to keep each other company. At the very least, Lexi needed to make an appearance at the event. Maybe she and Jo could sneak out halfway through and go catch a movie.

"And weren't you supposed to pick up those sugar cookies?" Ruby asked, heading across the aisle. She picked up a velvety hat with a purple flower attached and situated it on her head. "I think Lucille's closes at six. You'd better hop to it!" She selected another hat.

"Oh my gosh, you're right. I forgot about the cookies!" Lexi scrambled to tuck her notepad and pen into her tote bag then gathered her purse from the bar. "That one!" She saw Ruby sampling a lilac hat with a turned-up brim. "It matches your scarf."

"So it does. Sold!"

Lexi headed toward the store's front counter to collect Bailey from his pillow disc and stopped short when she saw the hippie gnome smiling at her from its place near the register.

"C'mon, boy," she told Bailey, reaching for his leash. "Time to get out of here. We've got some living to do."

They escorted Ruby out the back door. "I'll see you there!" Lexi called out to Ruby after locking up. "And thanks for the chat. I needed it."

"Anytime!" Ruby blew a kiss before trotting down the pathway.

THE TALK WITH RUBY had rolled around in Lexi's head as she dashed off to Lucille's bakery, apologizing profusely for being later than expected; then as she rushed home to take Bailey outside, remembering to feed him at the last minute; then as she darted upstairs to decide on an outfit for the dance. She landed on a turquoise sundress and, at the last minute, added a short jean jacket, since the unspoken theme of the dance was apparently "western." Chaynie had sent an email yesterday, asking for the donation of any old hats and boots people wanted to get rid of so she could display them around the barn for decoration.

It wasn't until Lexi headed out the door and paused on her porch that she let Ruby's—and Gigi's—words take firm root. She still wasn't ready to leap. But she was ready to listen.

She perched on the swing to type out a quick text to Graham but paused when she saw a new voicemail from him, from a few minutes before. She clicked and heard his voice in small bursts mingled with strong static, then the message cut off entirely. She couldn't make out a single word he'd said.

She could've called him back, but she needed to have this talk in person if at all possible. She'd typed her text quickly, before she could change her mind and take it all back: *Will you be at the dance tonight? If you are, I'd like to talk.*

Send.

EXITING HER CAR, COOKIE box in hand, Lexi couldn't help but scan the vehicles parked in the Petersons' field for a certain white Honda. But in the dusky shadows of a setting sun, it was hard to see the specific makes of the dozen or so other white cars, so she gave up.

She approached the wide-open double doors of the red barn and heard the pulsating country music coming from inside. A cheerful celebration on a perfect Texas night.

"There you are! I was worried you wouldn't come." Jolene met Lexi at the entrance, arms extended for a hug and looking breezy and beautiful in her denim miniskirt, cowgirl hat, and braids.

"I almost didn't. But Ruby convinced me otherwise."

"I hope that means what I think it means. That you'll finally hear Graham out." Jo placed a firm hand on her hip. "Don't get mad at me for saying this, but... I've been thinking about this, Lex, ever since the wedding. That there's a difference between protecting yourself and being stubborn. And frankly? You're moving dangerously close to stubborn."

Instead of being offended, Lexi laughed. She'd heard enough advice the last couple of days to last her a lifetime. She hadn't expected even more at the dance. "You're right. I *was* being stubborn. But now, the door is... cautiously cracked open. See?" She lifted her phone to show Jo the text she'd sent Graham—the one that still had no response.

"I'm proud of you."

"Have you seen him?" Lexi whispered, scanning the crowd of partygoers inside. She recognized practically everyone in the room. Ruby was right—the entire town had turned out for the big event.

"Not yet."

Lexi was grateful that not everyone seemed coupled up. Jo was dateless, and Lucille had come alone too. But Morgan's Grove was inclusive that way. Lexi recalled that several weeks ago, at the *Movie Under the Stars* Valentine's Day event, she and Jo had sat on a quilt together, munching on popcorn, and watching *The Music Man*, singing along with everyone else. It had been one of the best dateless Valentine's Days Lexi had ever had.

"Let's go drop these off at the snack table." Jo tapped the box in Lexi's hand. "But let me sneak one first." She opened the lid and whipped out a cookie and took a huge bite. "Mm. So good."

She handed the other half to Lexi, who took it and let it dissolve in her mouth.

As more people arrived and the party got into full swing, Lexi managed not to check her texts every five minutes and even put her phone away to enjoy the festivities, taking a stroll past the swept-out stalls where kids were playing games, then volunteering to man the snacks table for a bit, and then standing with Jo at the edge of the dance floor to watch the boot-scooting line dances form.

Lexi instantly recognized the DJ's playful song selections as all being nineties pop-country hits: Shania Twain, Winona, Clint Black, Travis Tritt, Faith Hill, Jo Dee Messina, and on and on.

"C'mon, I love this song!" Jolene grabbed Lexi's wrist and jerked her toward the dance floor. Lexi was willing but worried that she'd forgotten how to line dance—it had been well over a decade. The tongue-in-cheek "Achy Breaky Heart" started up with its utterly contagious hook that would stick in her brain for the rest of the night.

She followed Jo's lead as she stepped, clapped, and spun her way through the song, laughing when she would mess up and go the wrong way or forget a step. A wide variety of people had joined them on the dance floor—from kids to seniors—all smiling until their cheeks ached.

By the time the song was over and another, slower song began, Lexi was overheated, and she headed for the double doors, needing a taste of crisp evening air. Jo told her she'd join her in a minute after grabbing some punch.

As Lexi headed for the barn's entrance, past the hay bales lined with cowboy boots and the walls dotted with old cowboy hats, she heard her name being called. It was coming from outside.

She saw Shelley approaching, followed close behind by Andrew.

"I'm glad you came!" Lexi told them, hugging Shelley. Her eyes darted over Shelley's shoulder to see if maybe Graham was close behind, but no one was there. *Maybe he was parking the car.*

"You leaving?" Shelley asked, her expression confused.

"No, I got overheated. They had a line dance going, so I joined in."

"Food inside?" Shelley asked.

"Tons of it."

"There sure is!" Jolene, holding a red cup in one hand and a barbecue slider in the other, approached them. "Hi, Shelley. It's nice to see you again. And this is..."

"Andrew." The young man pointed to his own chest.

As Deana Carter's "Count Me In" floated outside from the barn, Jolene nodded sharply toward Lexi's shoulder, indicating someone was behind her. Lexi knew instantly who it was and pivoted to see Graham. He came to a hesitant stop a couple of feet away.

"Um, Shelley?" Jo's voice held an urgency. "I can show y'all where the punch is. And these sandwiches are great! Let's go inside and get some."

"Okay!" Shelley grasped Andrew's hand as they followed Jo inside the barn, leaving Lexi to focus all her attention on Graham. He wore boots and jeans along with a plaid shirt that brought out his eyes.

"I didn't think you were coming."

Graham shrugged. "I wasn't going to, but I didn't want to disappoint Shelley and Andrew. They were looking forward to the dance. I was planning to make myself scarce inside the barn, in case you might not want me here. But then, getting out of the car, I saw your message." He gestured with his phone.

Lexi pushed away her nerves. "I'm sorry I ignored your texts. It was immature of me."

Graham took a step closer. "I was worried about you. And then I was worried about us. I'm sorry, too, about the reception. I'm not apologizing for the kiss. I enjoyed that. But I'm sorry for... pushing you. Before you were ready. It was a stupid move. You were cautious about a new relationship. But I guess I got caught up in the moment."

For the first time, Lexi realized she'd mainly been thinking of herself the past two days—what *she* thought, what *she* was feeling. She had barely registered what the last couple of days had been like for him. What had Graham been going through, trying to interpret her silence, going over and over the wedding and reception in his own mind, wondering what he did wrong, blaming himself? He had been as agonized as she had been.

Lexi closed the gap between them and put a hand on his arm as the barn's light glowed on Graham's profile. "I enjoyed the kiss too."

He frowned. "Then... I don't understand."

She removed her hand and hugged her elbows. "I saw the text."

"What text?"

"When you went to get us some cake, I heard a phone buzz on the table. I thought it was mine, so I flipped it over and saw the message. From Theresa."

"She texted me about meeting up."

"I promise I wasn't spying. Like I said, I thought it was my phone. Anyway, I set it back down, and you came to the table, and—"

"That's why you left." Graham's frown turned into a relieved acknowledgment. "And avoided me after."

"My mind went into overdrive. I couldn't help it. After that kiss, I thought we were building toward something special."

"We were. We *are*."

"But then..."

"You saw my ex's name." Graham placed his hands on her arms, still crossed. "I should've told you. That was the third time she'd texted me, trying to meet. I had already sent her two firm rejections. But she didn't seem to get the message." Graham removed his hands and tapped on his phone. "Here. It's important for you to see them." He angled the screen between them and scrolled so that Lexi could read the messages.

She saw Theresa's "meet me" requests, followed by Graham's responses: *I can't do this... You ended the relationship, and it was the right thing... I wish you well. Please don't text again.*

The final text was Theresa's—the same desperate one Lexi recalled from the reception. And Graham had never responded.

He replaced his phone in his pocket. "I didn't even see her last text until after I got home from the reception. And this time, I called her."

"You did?"

"The texts obviously weren't making a dent. I told her that we were over, that she'd made her choice weeks ago. I said that I'd moved on with someone else. That I was falling for someone else. I haven't heard from her since."

Lexi swallowed hard. It was exactly what she'd wanted to hear—the confidence in his voice, the certainty in his eye contact.

"Lex, I should've told you about her texts. But... frankly, I didn't want to scare you away. We were building something special. But it felt really delicate. You let it be known from the start that you were skittish, and so I wanted to respect that. I didn't want anything—or anyone—to get in the way. Theresa's texts weren't worth mentioning because she wasn't important enough to me. You're what's important to me."

Graham rubbed her arms, creating shivers down to her finger-tips. She studied his face as his voice softened. "I'm just going to say it—caution to the wind. That I'm crazy about you. Everything good that's happened these past several weeks has been because of you. It's only been two days since we've talked, but it felt like forever. I missed you. I've been wanting to tell you stuff... that my dad and I had a moment at the rehearsal where we really connected. And that one of my students was in an accident this morning, and I went to see him at the hospital. And that I've made some real progress on my book. I've wanted to text you a million times—ask how the store is doing, how your father is. But I had to hold off, give you your space. Well, I don't want any more space, Lexi. I want you. I want us."

That was all Lexi needed. She reached up to hold his face and draw it closer to her own in a kiss—magnetic, passionate, real. He smiled through the kiss then pulled her in tighter, grabbing onto her waist, moving his hand up to her neck. He pulled away, by a few inches, and whispered, "Does this mean...?"

"I'm all in too. Caution to the wind. Head over heels for you."

Graham moved in for another kiss, this time more gently as he swayed her to the music coming from inside the barn. Lexi knew this was different from every other relationship she'd had. *She* was different. The fear had dissolved, and what was leftover might be... love.

"Oh—" Graham ended the kiss and backed away a step to reach deep into his pocket. "There's one more thing I've been dying to tell you. Well, to show you." He lifted up a small plastic pouch that caught the barn's light. "I called you earlier—"

"I heard the voicemail, but it was mostly static."

"Well, the housekeeping department on campus rang me. They found this." He reached inside the pouch to lift out a teardrop shape and dangle it between them.

"The necklace!" Lexi caught it with her fingers. "I was sure I'd never see it again."

He stepped behind her and lifted the teardrop over her head. "Apparently, it had been hiding underneath one of the bookshelves in my office all this time, sneaky little bugger." He secured the clasp as she touched the necklace with tender fingers. "Housekeeping is cleaning all the office carpets this summer, and mine was the first one." He stepped back around to face her. "They had to move all the furniture, and there it was."

"Incredible. We both looked so carefully, under everything."

"One of us must've somehow kicked it far enough for it to hide."

Lexi stroked the necklace and gazed up at him. "I'm glad you're back in my life."

"Are you talking about me or the necklace?"

"Both." Lexi pulled him closer for a slow dance, snuggling into his shoulder.

In a sense, she did owe a measure of thanks to the necklace. It had become a sort of time machine, opening up a portal to the past, teaching Lexi lessons about love and risk and courage she wouldn't have otherwise learned. And the necklace had done the most precious thing of all: It had brought Graham into her life, introduced her to a kind, quirky, smart man who accepted Lexi for who she was. She wondered if Gigi had somehow unconsciously meant for the necklace to be hidden away until just the right moment to emerge and work its magic. This moment right here.

"Thank you, Gigi," she whispered into the night.

Acknowledgments

To my mother, who has always been my greatest cheerleader and strongest support system.

To my entire extended family, whose encouragement means everything.

To beloved family members who are no longer with me and have made their exit to heaven: Daddy, Maw, Pa-Paw, Grammy, Pappy, and Mark. They would have been so supportive of this new book. I miss them every day.

To all those friends who have been my cheerleaders along the way: Augusta Malvagno, Linda Bratcher, Becky Bray, Karen Peterson, Michelle Cotter, Sue Willis, Sheree Webb, Deanna Markham, Stephen and Laurie Stine, Carla Krae, Rebecca Sanders, Rae Champagne, Brittni Tracy, Leigh Ann Olejnik, Carmen Northrup, and my beloved Commando sisters.

To Anne Hernandez for her guidance with the Shelley scenes—her input was so helpful. Also thanks to Lauren Siggelow for her wisdom about jewelry appraisals and diamonds.

Special thanks to my publisher, Lynn McNamee, whose professionalism, knowledge, and ambition have helped create an amazing publishing company that produces high-quality books. I'm honored to be on board with Red Adept.

Also special thanks to my line editor, Laura Koons. Her careful input and guidance have heightened the quality of this book without changing my writing style. She made the editing experience informative and enjoyable.

To the entire Red Adept team, but especially Erica Lucke Dean, Streetlight Graphics (particularly Glendon Haddix), and all the proofreaders and formatters. This novel is what it is because of your diligence and dedication and talents. I'm so grateful to you. And I *love* my cover.

To Clint Jones at Motophoto for my author photo.

Finally, all thanks to God, who makes everything in this life worthwhile. He is the Source.

Gigi's Chocolate Chip Cookie Recipe (Pat Borum's Original Recipe)

Preheat oven to 375 degrees.

Add these ingredients, in order, to mixing bowl and keep mixer on:

1 stick softened butter

1 stick softened margarine

1 cup sugar

2 cups brown sugar (not packed)

2 eggs

1 tablespoon vanilla

1 teaspoon salt

1 teaspoon baking soda

3 1/2 cups flour

After all ingredients have been mixed, add 1 large package chocolate chips. (Could also add one cup chopped pecans or raisins if desired.)

Drop batter onto ungreased cookie sheet in tablespoon-sized balls. Bake at 375 for 10 minutes until lightly browned. Do not over-cook if a chewy cookie is desired. Cook longer for a crispy cookie.

About the Author

Traci Borum is an insatiable bookworm whose first love is fiction. As a little girl, she became mesmerized with books—with the textures, the smells, and most especially, the worlds created between the pages. Years later, she discovered she could create her *own* worlds by writing. She's been scribbling away ever since, writing bits of poetry, articles, and especially fiction.

Traci has been a Creative Writing teacher at a community college for the past ten years. She's a native Texan and an Anglophile at heart. She owns two "British" dogs—a Corgi and a Sheltie—and she's completely addicted to Masterpiece Theater (must be those dreamy British accents!). More than anything, she treasures the friendships in her life and adores her supportive family.

Read more at writerscorner-traci.blogspot.com.

About the Publisher

Dear Reader,

We hope you enjoyed this book. Please consider leaving a review on your favorite book site.

Visit our site to find more quality books!

Read more at https://RedAdeptPublishing.com.

www.ingramcontent.com/pod-product-compliance
Lightning Source LLC
Chambersburg PA
CBHW021244190726
48289CB00005B/1473